USA Today bestselling author **Naima Simone** writes romance with heart, humour, and heat. Her books have been featured in *The Washington Post* and *Entertainment Weekly*, and described as balancing 'crackling, electric love scenes with exquisitely rendered characters caught in emotional turmoil.' She is wife to Superman, and mum to the most awesome kids ever. They live in perfect, domestically challenged bliss in the southern US.

Award-winning author **Jennifer Hayward** emerged on the publishing scene as the winner of the So You Think You Can Write global writing competition. The recipient of a *RT* Reviewer's Choice Award, Jennifer's careers in journalism and PR, including years of working alongside powerful, charismatic CEOs and travelling the world, have provided perfect fodder for the fast-paced, sexy stories she likes to write.

Mills & Boon novels were **Julia James**' first 'grown up' books she read as a teenager, and she's been reading them ever since. She adores the Mediterranean and the English countryside in all its seasons, and is fascinated by all things historical, from castles to cottages. In between writing she enjoys walking, gardening, needlework, baking 'extremely gooey chocolate cakes' and trying to stay fit! Julia lives in England with her family.

Fake Dating

Fake Dating:
A Convenient Deal

NAIMA SIMONE

JENNIFER HAYWARD

JULIA JAMES

MILLS & BOON

First Published in Great Britain 2024
by Mills & Boon, an imprint of HarperCollins*Publishers* Ltd,
1 London Bridge Street, London, SE1 9GF

www.harpercollins.co.uk

HarperCollins*Publishers*
Macken House, 39/40 Mayor Street Upper,
Dublin 1, D01 C9W8, Ireland

Fake Dating: A Convenient Deal © 2024 Harlequin Enterprises ULC.

Trust Fund Fiancé © 2020 Harlequin Enterprises ULC
The Italian's Deal for I Do © 2015 Harlequin Enterprises ULC
Securing the Greek's Legacy © 2014 Julia James

Special thanks and acknowledgment are given to Naima Simone for her contribution to the *Texas Cattleman's Club: Rags to Riches* series.

Special thanks and acknowledgement are given to Jennifer Hayward for her contribution to the *Society Weddings* series.

ISBN: 978-0-263-32266-8

MIX
Paper | Supporting
responsible forestry
FSC
www.fsc.org
FSC™ C007454

This book is produced from independently certified FSC™ paper
to ensure responsible forest management.

For more information visit: www.harpercollins.co.uk/green

Printed and Bound in the UK using 100% Renewable Electricity
at CPI Group (UK) Ltd, Croydon, CR0 4YY

TRUST FUND FIANCÉ

NAIMA SIMONE

To Gary. 143.

One

A man had a few pleasures in life.

For Ezekiel "Zeke" Holloway, they included kicking back on the black leather couch in the den of the three-bedroom guesthouse that he and his older brother, Luke, shared on the Wingate family estate. He had an ice-cold beer in one hand, a slice of meat lovers pizza in the other and Pittsburgh playing on the mounted eighty-five-inch flat-screen television. Granted, he might've been born and bred in Texas, but his heart belonged to the Steelers.

And then there was this. He lifted the dark brown cigar with its iconic black-and-red label and studied the smoldering red tip before bringing it to his lips and inhaling. A hint of pepper and chocolate, toasted macadamia nuts and, of course, the dark flavor of cognac. It could be addictive...if he allowed it to be. These cigars cost fifteen thousand dollars a box. Which was why he only permitted himself to enjoy one per month. Not because he couldn't afford to buy more. It was about discipline; he mastered his urges, not vice versa.

And in a world that had suddenly become unfamiliar, cold and uncertain, he needed to believe he could control something in his life. Even if it was when he smoked a cigar.

He sighed, bracing a hand on the balcony column and slowly exhaling into the night air. Behind him, the muted hum of chatter filtered through the closed glass doors. Guests gathered in the cavernous parlor behind him. James

Harris, current president of the Texas Cattleman's Club—of which Ezekiel was a member—hosted the "small" dinner party. As a highly successful horse breeder in Royal, Texas, and a businessman, James commanded attention without trying. And when he invited a person to his elegant, palatial home, he or she attended.

Even if they would be rubbing elbows with the newly infamous Wingates.

Bringing the cigar to his lips again, Ezekiel stared out into the darkness. Beneath the blanket of the black, star-studded night, he could barely make out the stables, corrals and long stretch of land that made up James's property. He rolled his shoulders, as if the motion could readjust and shift the cumbersome burden of worry, anger and, yes, fear that seemed to hang around his neck like an albatross. It was ludicrous, but he could practically feel the hushed murmurs crawl over his skin through his black dinner jacket and white shirt like the many legs of a centipede. He could massage his chest and still nothing would alleviate the weight of the censure—the press of the guilty verdicts already cast his and his family's way.

Not even the influence and support of James Harris could lessen that.

Lucky for Ezekiel and his family that the denizens of Royal high society hungered for a party invitation from James more than they wanted to outright ostracize the Wingates.

Ezekiel snorted, his lips twisting around the cigar. Thank God for small favors.

"And here I thought I'd found the perfect escape hatch."

Ezekiel jerked his head to the side at the husky, yet very feminine drawl. His mouth curved into a smile. And not the polite, charming and utterly fake one he'd worn all evening. Instead, true affection wound through him like a slowly unfurling ribbon.

Reagan Sinclair glided forward out of the shadows and into the dim glow radiating from the beveled glass balcony doors. It was enough to glimpse her slender but curvaceous body. The high thrust of her small but firm breasts. The fingertip-itching dip of her waist and intriguing swell of her hips. As she drew nearer to him and a scent that reminded him of honeysuckle and cream teased his nostrils, he castigated himself.

At twenty-six, Reagan was only four years his junior, but she was good friends with his cousin Harley, and he'd known her most of her life. She was as "good girl" as they came, with her flawless pedigree and traditional upbringing. Which meant she had no business being out here with him in his current frame of mind.

Not when the dark, hungry beast he usually hid behind carefree, wide grins and wry jokes clawed closer to the surface.

Not when the only thing that usually satisfied that animal was a willing woman and hot, dirty sex. No...*fucking*.

Ezekiel blew out a frustrated breath. Yes, he'd had sex, but made love to a woman? No, he hadn't done that in eight long years.

If he had any sense or the morals that most believed he didn't possess, he would put out his cigar, gently grasp her by the elbow and escort her back to her parents. Away from him. He should—

Reagan touched him.

Just the feel of her slim, delicate hand on his biceps was like a cooling, healing balm. It calmed the anger, the fear. Leashed the hunger. At least so he could meet her thickly lashed, entirely too-innocent eyes and not imagine seeing them darken with a greedy lust that he placed there.

"I know why I'm hiding," he drawled, injecting a playfulness he was far from feeling into his voice. "What's your excuse?"

Those eyes, the color of the delicious chicory coffee his mother used to have shipped from New Orleans, softened, understanding somehow making them more beautiful. And horrible.

He glanced away.

On the pretense of finishing his smoke, he shifted to the side, inserting space between them. Not that he could escape that damn scent that seemed even headier with her so close. Or the sharp-as-a-razor's-edge cheekbones. Or the lush, downright impropriety of her mouth. The smooth bronze of her skin that damn near gleamed...

You've known her since she was a girl. You have no business thinking of her naked, sweating and straining beneath you.

Dammit. He narrowed his gaze on the moon-bleached vista of James's ranch. His dick wasn't having any of that reasoning though. Too bad. He had enough of a shit storm brewing in his life, in his family, in Wingate Enterprises. He refused to add screwing Reagan Sinclair to it.

In a life full of selfish decisions, that might be the cherry on top of his asshole sundae.

And regardless of what some people might think, he possessed lines he didn't cross. A sense of honor that had been drilled into him by his family before he'd even been old enough to understand what the word meant. And as a little dented and battered as the Wingate name might be right now, they were still Wingates.

That meant something here in Royal.

It meant something to him.

"Let's see." She pursed her lips and tapped a fingernail against the full bottom curve. "Should I start alphabetically? A, avoiding my parents introducing me to every single man here between the ages of twenty-two and eighty-two. B, boring small talk about the unseasonably hot summer—it's Texas, mind you—gel versus acrylic nails and, my personal favorite, whether MTV really did need a reboot of *The Hills*. Which, the only answer to that is no. And C, karma—I avoided every one of Tracy Drake's calls last week because the woman is a terrible gossip. And now I find out that I'm seated next to her at dinner."

He snorted. "I'm pretty sure karma starts with a *K*," he said, arching an eyebrow.

"I know." She shrugged a slim shoulder, a smile riding one corner of her mouth. "I couldn't think of anything for *C*."

Their soft laughter rippled on the night air, and for the first time since arriving this evening, the barbed tension inside him loosened.

"And I just needed air that didn't contain politics, innuendo or cigar smoke," she continued. The velvet tone called to mind tangled, sweaty sheets at odds with her perfectly styled hair and immaculately tailored, strapless cocktail dress that spoke of unruffled poise. Even as Ezekiel's rebellious brain conjured up images of just how much he *could* ruffle her poise, she slid him a sidelong glance. "One out of three isn't bad."

Again, the miraculous happened, and he chuckled. *Enjoying* her. "I know it would be the gentlemanly thing to put this out..." he lifted the offending item between them "...but it's one of my few vices—"

"Just a few?" she interrupted, a dimple denting one of her cheeks.

"And I'm going to savor it," he finished, shooting her a mock frown for her cheekiness. Cute cheekiness. "Besides, no one in there would accuse me of being a gentleman."

Dammit. He hadn't meant to let that slip. Not the words and definitely not the bitterness. He was the carefree jokester of the Holloway brothers. He laughed and teased; he *didn't* brood. But these last few months had affected them all. Turned them into people they sometimes didn't recognize.

Talk and accusations of corruption and fraud did that to a person.

So did a headlong tumble from a pedestal, only to discover those you'd known for years were only wearing the masks of friends, hiding their true faces underneath. Vultures. Sharks.

Predators.

He forced a smile, and from the flash of sadness that flickered across her lovely features, the twist of his lips must've appeared as fake as it felt. For a moment, anger that wasn't directed at himself for fucking caring about the opinions of others blazed within him. Now it was presently aimed at her. At her pity that he hated. That he probably deserved.

And he resented that more.

"Gentlemen are highly overrated," she murmured, before he could open his mouth and let something mean and regrettable pour out. Her quiet humor snuffed out the flame of his fury. Once more the utter *calm* of her presence washed over him, and part of him wanted to soak in it until the grime of the past few months disappeared from his skin, his mind, his heart. "Besides, I want to hear more about some of these vices."

"No, you don't," he contradicted.

Unable to resist, he snagged a long, loose wave resting on her shoulder. He pinched it, testing the thickness, the silkiness of it between his thumb and forefinger. It didn't require much imagination to guess how it would feel whispering across his bare chest, his abdomen. His thighs. Soft. Ticklish. And so damn erotic, his cock already hardened in anticipation. As if scalded by both the sensation and the too-hot mental image, he released his grip, tucking the rebellious hand in his pants pocket.

Giving himself time to banish his impure thoughts toward his cousin's friend, he brought the cigar to his mouth. Savoring the flavor of chocolate and cognac. Letting it obscure the illusory taste of honeysuckle, vanilla and female flesh.

"You're too young for that discussion," he added, silently cursing the roughness of his tone.

"Oh really?" She tilted her head to the side. "You do know I'm only four years younger than you, right? Or are you having trouble with remembering things at your advanced old age of thirty?"

He narrowed his eyes on her. "Brat," he rumbled.

"Not the first time I've heard that," she said, something murkier than the shadows they stood in shifting in her eyes. But then she smiled, and the warmth of it almost convinced him that the emotion had been a trick of the dark. "So don't hold back. And start with the good stuff. And by good, I mean very, very bad."

He exhaled, studying her through the plume of fragrant smoke he blew through slightly parted lips. "You think you can handle my bad, Ray?" he taunted, deliberately using the masculine nickname that used to make her roll her eyes in annoyance.

Anything to remind him that he'd once caught her and Harley practicing kissing on his cousin's pillows. That she used to crush on boy bands with more synthesizers than talent. That he'd wiped her tears and offered to pound on the little shit that had bullied her on the playground over something she couldn't change—her skin color.

Anything to reinforce that she wasn't one of the women whose front doors would witness his walks of shame.

With an arch of a brow, she leaned forward so she couldn't help but inhale the evaporating puff. "Try me," she whispered.

A low, insistent throb pulsed low in his gut, and his abs

clenched, as if grasping for that familiar but somehow different grip of desire.

Desire. For Reagan? Wrong. So damn wrong.

Coward, a sibilant voice hissed at him. And he mentally flipped it off, shifting backward and leaning a shoulder against a stone column.

"Let's see," he said, valiantly injecting a lazy note of humor into his voice. "I can put away an entire meat lovers pizza by myself *and* not use a coaster for my beer. I'm unreasonably grouchy if I'm awake before the god-awful hour of seven o'clock. Especially if there's no coffee to chase away my pain. And—this one I'm kind of embarrassed to admit—I buy at least five pairs of socks every month. Apparently, my dryer is a portal to a world where mismatched socks are some kind of special currency. And since I can't abide not matching, I'm constantly a spendthrift on new pairs. There. You now know all of my immoralities."

A beat of silence, and then, "Really?"

He smirked. "Really," he replied, then jerked his chin up. "Your turn. Regale me with all of your sins, little Ray."

As he'd expected, irritation glinted in her chocolate eyes. "I have no idea how I can follow that, but here goes." He huffed out a low chuckle at the thick sarcasm coating her words. "Every night, I slip downstairs after everyone has gone to bed and have a scotch by myself. No one to judge me, you see? Since my nightly ritual could be early signs of me becoming an alcoholic like my uncle James. What else?"

She hummed, trailing her fingertips over her collarbone, her lashes lowering in a pretense of deep thought. But Ezekiel knew better. She'd already given this a lot of consideration. Had already catalogued her perceived faults long before this conversation.

Acid swirled in his stomach, creeping a path up his chest. He straightened from his lounge against the pillar, prepared to nip this in the bud, but she forestalled him by speaking again. And though a part of him yearned to tell her to stop, to warn her not to say another word, the other part… Yeah, that section wanted to hear how imperfect she was. Craved it. Because it made him feel less alone.

More human.

God, he was such a selfish prick.

And yet, he listened.

"I hate roses. I mean, *loathe* them. Which is important because my mother loves them. And every morning there are fresh bouquets of them delivered to the house for every room, including the kitchen. And every day I fight the urge to knock one down just to watch them scatter across the floor in a mess of water, petals and thorns. Because I'm petty like that. And finally…"

She inhaled, turning to look at him, those eyes, stark and utterly beautiful in their intensity, pinning him to his spot against the railing. "Once a month, I drive over to Joplin and visit the bars and restaurants to find a man to take to a hotel for a night. We have hot, filthy sex and then I leave and return home to be Royal socialite darling Reagan Sinclair again."

Heat—blistering hot and scalding—blasted through him, punching him in the chest and searing him to the bone. Jesus, did she just…? *Holy fuck.* Lust ate at him. Lust… and horror. Not because she took charge of her own sexuality. It was a twisted and unfair double standard, how men like him could escort woman after woman on his arm, and screw many more, with only an elbow nudge or knowing wink from society. But a woman doing the same thing? Especially one of Reagan's status? Hell no. So for her to take her pleasure into her own hands? He didn't fault her for it.

But the thought of her trolling those establishments filled with drunk men? Some man who wouldn't have an issue with not taking the utmost care with her? Of potentially hurting her? That sent fear spiking through him, slaying him.

And then underneath the horror swirled something else. Something murkier. Edgier. And better off not being unearthed or examined too closely.

"Reagan..." he whispered.

"Relax," she scoffed, flicking a hand toward his face. "I made the last one up. But turnabout is fair play since I'm almost eighty-two percent sure you were lying to me about at least one of yours. Maybe two."

He froze. Stared at her. Stunned...and speechless. Mirror emotions—hilarity and anger—battled it out within him. He didn't know whether to strangle her for taking twenty years off his life... Or double over with laughter loud enough to bring people rushing through those balcony doors.

"That wasn't very nice," he finally muttered, his fingers in danger of snapping his prized cigar in half. "And payback is not only a bitch but a vengeful one."

"I'm shaking in my Jimmy Choos," she purred.

And this time, he couldn't hold back the bark of laughter. Or the *goodness* of it. Surrendering to the need to touch her, even if in a platonic manner, he moved forward and slipped an arm around her shoulders, hugging Reagan into his side like he used to do when she'd worn braces and friendship bracelets.

There was nothing girlish about the body that aligned with his. Nothing pure about the stirrings in his chest and gut...then *lower*. A new strain took up residence in his body. One that had nothing to do with the whispers and gossiping awaiting him inside. This tension had everything to do with her light, teasing scent, the slender hand branding his chest, the firm, beautiful breasts that pressed against him.

Still, he squeezed her close before releasing her.

"Thank you, Reagan," he murmured.

She studied him, nothing coy in that straightforward gaze. "You're welcome," she said, not pretending to misunderstand him. Another thing he'd always liked about her. Reagan Sinclair didn't play games. At least not with him. "That's what friends are for. And regardless how it appears right now, you have friends, Zeke," she said softly, using his nickname.

He stared down at her. At the kindness radiating from her eyes. An admonishment to hide that gentle heart of hers from people—from *him*—hovered on his tongue. The need to contradict her skulked right behind it.

Instead, he set his cigar down on an ashtray some enterprising soul had left outside on a wrought iron table. He wasn't an animal, so he didn't stub it out like a cigarette, but left it there to burn out on its own. In a while, he'd come back to dispose of it.

Turning to Reagan, he crooked his arm and waited. Without hesitation, she slid hers through his, but as they turned, the balcony door swung open and Douglas Sinclair stepped out.

Ezekiel knew the older man, as he was a member of the TCC. Tall, lanky and usually wearing his signature giant Stetson, he could've been an African-American version of the Marlboro Man. He shared the same brown eyes as his daughter, and right now those eyes were trained on them— or rather on Reagan's arm tucked into his.

A moment later, Douglas lifted his gaze and met Ezekiel's. Her father didn't voice his displeasure, but Ezekiel didn't miss the slight narrowing of his eyes or the barely-there flattening of his mouth. No, Douglas Sinclair was too polite to tell Ezekiel to get his hands off his daughter. But he stated it loud and clear just the same. Ezekiel might be a TCC member as well, but that didn't mean the traditional, reserved gentleman would want his precious daughter anywhere near him.

Not when Ezekiel's family had been accused of falsifying inspections on the jets that WinJet, a subsidiary of Wingate Enterprises, manufactured. Not when three of their workers had been injured on the job because of a fire in one of the manufacturing plants due to a faulty sprinkler system. Not when they'd been sued for those injuries because those inspections hadn't been up-to-date as the reports had stated.

Even as VP of marketing for Wingate Enterprises, Ezekiel had found it damn near impossible to spin this smear on their name. No one wanted to do business with a company so corrupt it would place profit above their employees' welfare. Not that his family was guilty of this sin. But public perception was *everything*.

And while most of the club members had stood behind the Wingates, Douglas hadn't been vocal in his belief in their innocence.

So it was no wonder the man didn't look pleased to find his daughter hiding in the dark with Ezekiel.

Not that Ezekiel could blame him. Reagan shouldn't be out here with him. But not for the reasons her father harbored.

"Reagan," Douglas said, one hand remaining on the door and holding it open. "Your mother has been looking for you. It's almost time for dinner, and Devon Granger is eager to escort you into the dining room since you'll be sitting next to him."

Ezekiel caught the soft sigh that escaped her, and felt the tension invade her slender frame. But when she spoke, her tone remained as soft and respectful as any dutiful daughter to a father she loved and revered.

"Thanks, Dad. I'll be there in a moment," she murmured.

"I'll wait for you," came his implacable reply.

If possible, she stiffened even more, but her lovely features didn't reflect her irritation. Still, anger for the other man's high-handedness kindled in Ezekiel's chest. She was a grown woman, for God's sake, not a wayward toddler. His arm tautened, trapping hers in the crook of his elbow. Next to him, Reagan tipped her head up, glancing at him.

What the hell are you doing?

Deliberately, he relaxed his body, releasing her and stepping to the side.

"It was nice seeing you again, Reagan," Ezekiel said. Switching his attention to Douglas, he gave the man an abrupt nod. "You, too, Douglas."

"Ezekiel." Then, extending his hand to his daughter, he added, "Reagan."

She glided forward, sliding her hand into her father's. She didn't shoot one last look over her shoulder at him. Didn't toss him another of her gentle, teasing smiles or a final farewell. Instead, she disappeared through the door, leaving him in darkness once more.

And yeah, it was for the best.

No matter her father's reasons for not wanting to leave her alone with Ezekiel, his concerns were valid. If anyone else had noticed that she stood alone with him in the shadows, the rumors would've burned like a brushfire.

And the longer they remained enclosed in the dark, the harder it would've become for him to remember that she was off-limits to him. Because of their history. Because she was too good for him. Because her parents were seeking out a suitable man for her.

And Ezekiel—a man with a slowly crumbling business empire and more emotional baggage than the airplanes WinJet manufactured—wasn't a good bet.

Not a good bet at all.

Two

Reagan jogged up the four shallow stone steps to her family's Pine Valley mansion. Once she reached the portico that stretched from one end of the front of the house to the other, she stopped, her chest rising and falling on deep, heavy breaths. Turning, she flattened a palm against one of the columns and, reaching for her foot, pulled it toward her butt in a stretch.

God, she detested running. Not even the beautiful scenery of the well-manicured streets and gorgeous multimillion-dollar homes of their upscale, gated community could distract her from the burn in her thighs, the hitch in her chest or the numbing boredom of it. But regardless, she exited her house every morning at 7:00 a.m. to jog past the mansions where Royal high society slept, the clubhouse larger than most people's homes, the Olympic-size pool that called her to take a refreshing dip, and the eighteen-hole golf course. The chore wasn't about pleasure or even staying healthy or retaining a particular dress size.

It was about discipline.

Everyone in this world had to do things they disliked. But likes and dislikes didn't compare to loyalty, sacrifice, love… And though whether or not she jogged every morning had nothing to do with those ideals, the exercise served as a reminder of what happened when a person lost control.

When they allowed their selfish wants to supersede everything else that mattered.

Her reminder.

Her *penance*.

Didn't matter. She would continue to do it. Even if running never became easier. Never ceased to make her feel like she wanted to collapse and call on the Lord to end her suffering.

Moments later, as she finished her stretching, the door behind her opened. Her father stepped out, and once again that familiar and so complicated flood of emotion poured through her as it did whenever she was in Douglas Sinclair's presence.

Awe. Reverence. Guilt. Shame. Anger. Resentment.

Love.

She was a murky, tangled hodgepodge of feelings when it came to her father.

"Good morning, Dad," she greeted, straightening from a deep lunge.

"Reagan." He peered down at her, his customary Stetson not hiding the frown wrinkling his brow. "Out running again, I see." He tsked, shaking his head. "We have a perfectly good gym downstairs with top-of-the-line equipment, and yet you insist on gallivanting around the neighborhood."

Gallivanting. If his obvious disapproval didn't grate on her nerves like a cheese grinder, she would've snorted at the old-fashioned word. But that was her father. Old-fashioned. Traditional. Conservative. All nice words to say he liked things done a certain way. Including not having his daughter jog around their posh neighborhood in athletic leggings and a sports tank top. Modest women didn't show their bodies in that fashion.

Unfortunately for him, she couldn't run in a high-waisted gown with a starched collar.

Forcing a smile to her lips, she said, "I'm hardly parading around, Dad. I'm exercising." Before he could respond to that, she pressed on. "Headed into the office?" she asked, already knowing the answer.

She could set her watch by him. Breakfast at 7:00 a.m. Leave for the law office at 7:45. To Douglas Sinclair, integrity was a religion. And that included being accountable to his time and his clients.

"Yes." He glanced down at his watch. "I left a message with your mother, but now that I'm seeing you, please don't forget that we have dinner plans tonight. The Grangers are coming over, and you need to be here. On time," he emphasized. More like commanded. "I understand your committee work is important, but not more so than honoring your commitments. I expect you to be here and dressed at six sharp."

He doesn't mean to be condescending. Or controlling. Or patronizing. He loves you.

Silently, she ran the refrain through her head. Over and over until the words melded together. He didn't know about her work at the girls' home in Colonial County. It wasn't his fault he saw her through the lens of another era—outdated traditions, unobtainable expectations...

A disappointed father.

"Devon is attending with his parents. So you need to be at your best tonight," he continued. "You seemed to show interest in him at James Harris's get-together last week. You two talked quite a bit at dinner. With his family, his position in his father's real estate development company and business connections, he would make an ideal husband."

Jesus. This again. Reagan just managed not to pinch the bridge of her nose and utter profanity that would have her father gasping.

He just didn't stop. Didn't give her a chance to breathe. To make a single decision for herself.

Since she'd turned twenty-six five months ago, he'd been on this relentless campaign to see her married. Just as her brother had. As her sister had only a year ago.

It was all so ridiculous. So damn antiquated. And stifling. She could find her own goddamn husband, *if* she wanted one.

Which she didn't.

She loved her parents; they'd always provided a more-than-comfortable home, the best schools, a good, solid family life. But her father was definitely the head of the household, and Henrietta Sinclair, though the mediator and often the voice of reason, very rarely went against him. While the relationship might work well for them, Reagan couldn't imagine allowing a man to have that much control over her.

Besides, she'd done that once. Let a man consume her world—*be* her world. And that had ended in a spectacularly disastrous display.

No, she didn't want a husband who'd give her a home and his shadow to live in.

"Dad, I appreciate your concern, but I wish you and Mom would stop...with the matchmaking attempts. I've told both of you that marriage isn't a priority for me right now." If ever. "I'll show up for dinner tonight, but don't expect a love match. While Devon Granger may be nice and husband material, he's not *my* husband material."

Poor Devon. His most interesting quality had been providing a distraction from Tracy Drake, seated on her other side. And since the notorious gossip had spotted Ezekiel Holloway following Reagan and her father back into the house within moments, she'd been chock-full of questions and assumptions. The woman had missed her calling as a CIA agent.

Her father scoffed. "A love match." He shook his head, exasperation clearly etched into his expression. "Don't be ridiculous. I'm not anticipating a proposal at the end of the evening. I just want you to at least give him a chance." He glanced at his watch again, impatience vibrating off him. "As your father, I want to see you happy, settled. With a husband who can provide for you." He flicked the hand not holding his briefcase. "Don't be naive, Reagan. Do you think people aren't talking about the fact that your sister, who is three years younger than you, is already married? That maybe there's something—"

"I'm not Christina," she interrupted him, voice quiet and steady in spite of how *hurt* trembled through her like a wind-battered leaf. She knew what lay on the other side of that *something*. And she didn't need to hear him state how their friends and associates whispered if she was faulty in some way. Or to hear the unspoken concern in her father's voice that he wondered the same thing. Except swap out *faulty* for *broken*.

"I'm not Doug either," she added, mentioning her older brother. "I have my own aspirations, and marriage isn't even at the top of that list."

"God, not that again—"

"And if you would just release the money Gran left me, I could further those goals. And a life of my choosing. Filled with *my* decisions," she finished, tracing the faint childhood scar on her collarbone. Trying—and failing—not to let his annoyed dismissal of her wants puncture her pride and self-esteem. By now, both resembled a barroom corkboard, riddled with holes from so many well-meaning but painful darts.

"We've been over this, and the answer is still no," he ground out. "Your grandmother loved you so much she left that inheritance to you, but she also added the stipulation for a reason. And we both know why, Reagan."

We both know why... We both know why...

The words rang between them in the already warm morning air.

A warning.

An indictment.

Oh yes, how could she forget why her beloved grandmother, who had left her enough money to make her an instant millionaire, had added one provision in her will? Reagan couldn't access the inheritance until she either married a suitable man or turned thirty years old.

In order to be fully independent, to manage her own life, she had to chain herself to a man and hand over that independence or wait four more years before she could... *live.*

It was her punishment, her penance. For rebelling. For not following the Sinclair script. For daring to be less than perfect.

At sixteen, she'd done what most teenage girls did—she'd fallen in love. But she'd fallen hard. Had been consumed by the blaze of first love with this nineteen-year-old boy that her parents hadn't approved of. So when they'd forbidden her to see him, she'd sneaked around behind their backs. She'd offered everything to him—her loyalty, her heart, her virginity.

And had ended up pregnant.

Understandably, her parents had been horrified and disappointed. They'd wanted to send her away, have the baby and give it up for adoption. And Reagan had been determined to keep her unborn daughter or son. But neither of them had their wish. She'd miscarried. And the boy she'd been so certain she'd spend the rest of her life with had disappeared.

The price for her stubborn foolishness had been her utter devastation and her family's trust.

And sometimes...when she couldn't sleep, when her guard was down and she was unable to stop the buffeting of her thoughts and memories, she believed she'd lost some of their love, too.

Over the years, she'd tried to make up for that time by being the obedient, loyal, *perfect* daughter they deserved. It was why she still remained in her childhood home even though, at her age, she should have her own place.

But ten years later, she still caught her mother studying her a little too close when Reagan decided to do something as small as not attend one of her father's events for his law firm. Still glimpsed the concern in Henrietta's eyes when Reagan disagreed with them. At one time Reagan had made her mother physically ill from the worry she'd caused, the pain she'd inflicted with her bad decisions. So to remain under the same roof where Henrietta could keep tabs on her, could assure herself that her daughter wasn't once again self-destructing... It was a small cost. She owed her parents that much.

Because in her family's eyes, she would never be more than that misguided, impetuous teen. She was her family's well-kept, dirty little secret, a cautionary tale for her sister.

The weight of the knowledge bore down on her so hard, her shoulders momentarily bowed. But she'd become the poster child for *fake it until you make it*. Sucking in an inaudible deep breath, she tilted her chin up and met her father's dark scrutiny.

"I guess we're at an impasse, then. Again," she tacked on. "Have a great day, Dad."

Turning on her heel, she headed inside the house before he could say something that would unknowingly tear another strip from her heart. She quietly shut the door behind her, leaning against it. Taking a moment to recover from another verbal and emotional battle with her father.

Sighing, she straightened and strode toward the rear of the house and the kitchen for a cold bottle of water. The thickly sweet scent of flowers hit her seconds before she spied the vase of lush flowers with their dark red petals.

I hate roses. I mean, loathe them... Every morning there are fresh bouquets of them delivered to the house... And every day I fight the urge to knock one down just to watch them scatter across the floor in a mess of water, petals and thorns. Because I'm petty like that.

The murmured admission whispered through her mind, dragging her from the here-and-now back to that shadowed balcony a little over a week ago.

Back to Ezekiel Holloway.

She drew to a halt in the middle of the hallway, her eyes drifting shut. The memories slammed into her. Not that they had a great distance to travel. He and their interlude hadn't been far from her mind since that night.

Zeke.

She'd once called him that before she'd fallen in love, then fallen out of favor with her family. Before her childhood had ended in a crash-and-burn that she still bore the scars from.

Before she'd erected this imaginary wall of plexiglass between her and people that protected her. But she'd slipped up at the dinner party. The pseudo-intimacy of the dark coaxing her into falling into old, familiar patterns.

An image of Zeke wavered, then solidified on the black screen of her eyelids.

Lovely.

Such an odd word to describe a man. Especially one who stood nearly a foot taller than her and possessed a lean but powerful, wide-shouldered body that stirred both desire and envy. Regardless, her description was still accurate. He'd been beautiful as a teen, but the years had honed that masculine beauty, experience had added an edge to it. The dark hair cut close to his head only emphasized the stunning bone structure that reminded her of cliffs sculpted to razor sharpness by wind and rain. A formidable face prettied by a firm mouth almost indecent in its fullness and a silken, neatly cropped beard framing his sinful lips.

Then there were those eyes.

The color of new spring grass warmed by the sun. Light green and striking against skin the color of brown sugar.

Yes, he was a lovely man. An intimidating man. A powerful, *desirable* man.

Zeke was a temptation that lured her to step closer. To stroke her fingers over that dark facial hair that would abrade her skin like rug burn. To pet him like the sleek but lethal panther he reminded her of. To taste that brown sugar skin and see if it was as sweet as it looked.

But he was also a warning sign that blinked *Danger!* in neon red. Not since Gavin, her teenage love who'd abandoned her and broken her young heart, had she been the least bit tempted to lose control again. None had poked that curious shifting inside her, stirred the dormant need to be… wild. To act without thought of consequence. To throw herself into an ocean of feeling and willingly go under.

Ten minutes with Ezekiel and that tingle deep inside her crackled, already singeing the tight ropes tying down that part of her. The last time she'd loosened those bindings, she'd hurt her family terribly.

No, she couldn't allow that to happen again.

So, though part of her had railed at her father's autocratic behavior that night, the other half had been relieved as she'd walked back into the house and away from him. Okay, maybe Zeke had infiltrated her dreams since then. And in those dreams, she'd remained on the shadowed balcony. He also hadn't stopped with touching her hair. And maybe when she woke, her body trembled from unfulfilled pleasure. A pleasure that left her empty and aching.

It was okay. Because they were only dreams relegated to the darkest part of night where secret desires resided.

Didn't matter. Not when her mind and heart agreed on one indelible truth.

Ezekiel Holloway spelled trouble with a capital *T*.

Best she remembered that.

And the possible consequences if she dared to forget.

Three

Ezekiel hunkered down on the still green grass, balancing on the balls of his feet. The late-afternoon sun didn't penetrate this corner of the cemetery where the Southern live oak's branches spread wide and reached toward the clear, blue sky. The tree provided shade over the marble headstone. And as he traced the etched lettering that hadn't yet faded after eight years, the stone was cool to the touch. If he closed his eyes and lost himself like he did in those nebulous, gray moments just before fully wakening, he could imagine another name inscribed on the marker.

Not Melissa Evangeline Drake.

Heaving a sigh that sounded weary to his own ears, he rose, shoving his hands into his pants pockets, never tearing his gaze from the monument that failed to encapsulate the woman who had once held his heart in her petite hands.

A name. Dates of her birth and way-too-soon death. Daughter, sister, friend.

Not *fiancée*. Not *the other half of Ezekiel Holloway's soul*.

And he didn't blame them. After all, he'd only had her in his life four short years, while they'd had twenty-two. She belonged to them more than she ever did to him. But for a while, she'd been solely his. His joy. His life. His *everything*. And she'd been snatched away by a man who'd decided getting behind a wheel while drunk off his ass had been a good idea.

One moment, they'd been happy, planning their future together. The next, he'd received a devastating phone call from her father that she was gone. The only merciful blessing had been that she'd died on impact when the drunk had plowed into the driver's side of her car.

And a part of him had died with her that night. The part that had belonged to her and only her.

"I can't believe it's been eight years to the day since I lost you," he said to the tombstone, pausing as if it could answer.

Most days, he struggled to remember what her voice sounded like. Time might not heal all wounds, but it damn sure dimmed the details he tried to clutch close and hoard like a miser hiding his precious gold.

"I have to tell you this is not the anniversary I imagined we'd have." He huffed out a humorless chuckle. "I tried to call your parents yesterday and this morning, but they didn't answer. I understand," he quickly added, careful not to malign the parents they'd both adored. "Losing you devastated them. And I'm a reminder of that pain. Still…" He paused, his jaw locking, trying to trap in the words he could only admit here, to his dead fiancée. "I miss them. I had Aunt Ava and Uncle Trent after Mom and Dad died, but your folks… They were good to me. And I hated losing them so soon after you. But yeah, I don't blame them."

They all had to do what they needed to move on, to return to the world of the living.

He'd thrown himself into work and any kind of activity that had taunted fate to come for him again—skydiving, rock climbing, rappelling.

And the women. The daredevil adventures might burn off the restlessness, but they couldn't touch the loneliness. The emptiness. Only sex did that. Even if it was only for those few blessed hours when he was inside a woman and pleasure provided that sweet oblivion. Adrenaline and sex. They were his sometime drugs of choice. Temporary highs.

When those were his ways of coping with the past, the loss, how could he hold it against the Drakes that they'd chosen to cauterize him from their lives?

"I know it's been several months since I've visited, and so damn much has happened since then—"

"Zeke?"

He jerked his head up and, spying the woman standing on the other side of the grave, blinked. Surely his brain had conjured the image to taunt him. How else could he explain Reagan Sinclair here in this cemetery?

Unbidden and against his will, his gaze traveled down her slender frame clothed in a pale-yellow dress that bared her shoulders and arms and crisscrossed over her breasts. For a second, he lingered over the V that offered him a hint of smooth, rounded flesh before continuing his perusal over the long, flowing skirt that brushed the tips of her toes and the grass. She resembled a goddess, golden, lustrous brown skin and long hair twisted into a braid that rested over one shoulder. And when he lifted his scrutiny to her face, he couldn't help but skim the vulnerable, sensual curves of her mouth, the almost haughty tilt of her cheekbones and the coffee-brown eyes.

Silently, he swore, yanking his regard back to the head-stone. And hating himself for detecting details about this woman he had no business, no *right* to notice. Especially standing over the grave of the woman he'd loved.

"Hey," she softly greeted him, blissfully unaware of the equal parts resentment and need that clawed at him.

"What are you doing here?" he asked, tone harsher than he'd intended. Than she deserved.

But if the question or the delivery offended her, she didn't show it. Instead, she moved closer, and even though he'd thoroughly scrutinized her only moments ago, he just noted the bouquet of vibrant blue-and-white flowers she held. She knelt, her skirt billowing around her, and laid the flowers in front of the gravestone. Straightening, she paused, resting a hand on top of the marble before stepping back. Only then did she meet his gaze.

And in that instant, he was transported back eight years. A lot about the day of Melissa's funeral had been a blur, but how could he have forgotten that it'd been Reagan who'd found him at this very same, freshly covered grave after everyone else had left for the repast at the Drakes'? Reagan who had slipped her hand into his and silently stood next to him, not rushing him to leave, not talking, just... refusing to leave him alone. She might've been his cousin's friend back then, but that day, in those long, dark moments, she'd been his.

He smothered a sigh and dragged a hand down his face, his beard scratching his palm.

"I'm sorry," he murmured. "This day—"

She shook her head, holding up her hand to forestall the rest of his apology. "I understand." She paused. "Does it get any easier?" she asked, voice whisper soft.

Did it? Any other place on any other day, he might've offered his canned and packaged reply of *yes, time is the great healer*. But the words stumbled on his tongue. Then died a defeated death. "Most days, yes. The pain dulls so it doesn't feel as if every breath is like a knife in the chest. But then there are other days when..."

His gaze drifted toward the other side of the cemetery. What his eyes couldn't see, his mind supplied. Two matching headstones, side by side. The people buried there together in death as they'd been determined to be in life.

I feel empty, he silently completed the thought. *Unanchored. Alone. Abandoned.*

He would've denied those words, those feelings if anyone vocalized them to him. Especially his older brother,

Luke. But in his head where he couldn't run from his denial?

Well…even if he had the speed of Usain Bolt, he couldn't sprint fast enough to escape himself.

"I forgot your parents were buried here," Reagan said, her voice closer. Her scent nearer, more potent. "I always wondered why they weren't with the rest of the Wingates in their mausoleum."

"Because they weren't Wingates," he replied, still staring off into the distance, squelching the clench of his gut at his explanation. Smothering the unruly and insidious thought that he wasn't one either. That in a family mixed with Wingates and Holloways, he and Luke were still… different.

"My father was a Holloway, Aunt Ava's older brother. He created a bit of a scandal in the family and society when he married my mother, a black woman. But in spite of the derision and ostracization they faced—sometimes within his own family—my parents had a happy marriage. Even if they remained somewhat distant from the rest of the Holloways."

"They were protecting their world," Reagan murmured. "I don't think there's anything wrong with that."

"They were very careful, sheltering. But they still taught us the value of family. When they died in that car crash eleven years ago, Aunt Ava and Uncle Trent took Luke and me in…even though by then, we were both in college and technically adults. They gave us a place to call home when ours had been irrevocably broken."

He turned back to her. "They might have taken us in, and we now work for the family company, but my parents didn't consider themselves Wingates, so Luke and I didn't bury them as ones."

She slowly nodded. Studied him in that calm-as-lake-waters way of hers that still perceived too much. Unlike most people, she didn't seem content with just seeing the charmer, the thrill seeker.

He didn't like it.

But damn if a small part of him didn't hate it either.

"Where will you choose to be buried? The Wingate side or the Holloways?" she mused. But there was nothing casual or easy about the question…or the answer. "God, that's a morbid question. I heard it as soon as I asked it. Still… can't be easy feeling as if you're split in two. Trying to figure out if love or obligation, a debt unpaid, holds you here."

His pulse thudded, echoing in his ears. And inside his chest, the arrow that had struck quivered in agitation.

"What are you doing here?" he asked, abruptly changing the subject away from his family. From his own discomfort and inner demons. "Can't be just to visit Melissa's grave."

That clear inspection didn't waver, but after several seconds, she released him from it, glancing over her shoulder. And he exhaled on a low, deep breath.

"No, my grandmother rests just over there. I come by every other week. It's only been a couple of months since we lost her, so being here…" She shrugged a shoulder. "It brings me more comfort than it does her, I'm sure. But I try to bring enough flowers for her and Melissa."

"Thank you," he said, his palm itching to stroke down the length of her dark brown braid. He slid his hand in his pocket instead. "And I'm sorry about your grandmother." The troubles with WinJet and the fire in the manufacturing plant had consumed him, and he'd been working like a madman since, so he hadn't heard about her death. "I didn't know her, but she must've been very special."

The brief hesitation might not have been caught by most people. But most people weren't paying attention to every breath that passed through Reagan's lips.

"We shared a close bond," she said.

"But?" Ezekiel prodded. "There's definitely a *but* there."

His light teasing didn't produce the effect he'd sought—the lightening of the shadows that had crowded into her gaze.

"But it's difficult to discover the one person you believed loved you unconditionally didn't trust you."

The tone—quiet, almost tranquil—didn't match the words. So one of them was a deception. From personal experience, he'd bet on the tone.

And against his better judgment but to his dick's delight, when he reached out, grasped her chin between his thumb and forefinger and tipped her head back, he had confirmation.

Her eyes. Those magnificent, beautiful eyes couldn't lie. If windows were eyes to the soul, Reagan's were fucking floor-to-ceiling bay windows thrown wide open to the world.

A man could lose himself in them. Step inside and never leave.

With a barely concealed snarl directed at himself, he dropped his arm and just managed not to step back. In retreat. Because that's what it would be. Flight from the need to fall into the pool of those eyes.

He'd had that sensation of drowning before. And he'd willingly dived in. And now the person who was supposed to be there to always keep him afloat lay in the ground at both of their feet.

Fuck it. He took that step back.

"Why do you think she didn't trust you?" he asked, focusing on Reagan and not the fear that scratched at his breastbone.

She released a short, brittle huff. "Think? I know."

Shifting, she gave him her profile, but he caught the slight firming of her lips, the drag of her fingertips across the left side of her collarbone. He narrowed his eyes on the small movement. She'd done that the night of the party. Was it a subconscious tell on her part? He catalogued the detail to take out and analyze later.

"Well, tell me why she didn't trust you, then," he pushed. Gently, but it was still a push. Something inside him—something ephemeral but insatiable—hungered to know more about this woman who had grown up right under his nose but remained this familiar, sexy-as-hell stranger.

"Did you know that I'm a millionaire?" she asked, dodging his question—no, his demand.

Ezekiel nodded. "I'm not surprised. Your father is a very successful—"

"No." She waved a hand, cutting him off. "Not through my father. In my own right, I'm a millionaire. When my grandmother died, she left each of her three grandchildren enough money to never have to worry about being taken care of. But that's the thing. She *did* worry. About me anyway." No breeze kicked up over the quiet cemetery, yet she crossed her arms, clutching her elbows. "She added a stipulation to her will. I can only receive my inheritance when I turn thirty—or marry. And not just any man. A *suitable* man."

Her lips twisted on *suitable*, and he resisted the urge to smooth his thumb over the curve, needing to eradicate the bitterness encapsulated in it. That emotion didn't belong on her—didn't sit right with him.

"The condition doesn't mean she didn't trust you. Maybe she just wanted to make sure you were fully mature before taking on the responsibility and burden that comes with money."

Not that he believed that bullshit. Age didn't matter as much as experience. Hell, there were days he looked in the mirror and expected to glimpse a bent, wizened old man instead of his thirty-year-old self.

"I could accept that if I weren't the only grandchild hit with that proviso. Doug and Christina might both be married, but neither of them had that particular restriction on their inheritance. Just me."

"Why?" he demanded.

Confusion and anger sparked inside him. He was familiar with Reagan's older brother and younger sister, and both were normal, nice people. Maybe a little too nice and, well, boring. But Reagan? She was the perfect image of a Royal socialite—composed, well-mannered and well-spoken, serving on several committees, free of the taint of scandal, reputation beyond reproach. So what the hell?

She didn't immediately reply but stared at him for several long moments. "Most people would've asked what I did to earn that censure."

"I'm not most people, Ray," he growled.

"No, you're not," she murmured, scanning his face, and then, she shook her head. "The why doesn't really matter, does it? What does matter is that at twenty-six, I'm in this holding pattern. Where I can see everyone else enjoying the lives they've carved out for themselves—and I can't move. Either I chain myself to a man I barely know and don't love to access my inheritance. Or I stay here, static for another four years while my own dreams, my own needs and wants wither and die on the vine."

Once more, she'd adopted that placid tone, but this time, Ezekiel caught the bright slashes of hurt, the red tinge of anger underneath it.

"I'm more than just the daughter of Douglas Sinclair. I'm more than just the member of this and that charity committee. Not that I'm denigrating their work. It's just… I want to…be free," she whispered, and he sensed that she hadn't meant for that to slip. For him to hear it.

What did she mean by *free*? Not for the first time, he sensed Reagan's easygoing, friendly mask hid deeper waters. Secrets. He didn't trust secrets. They had a way of

turning around and biting a person in the ass. Or knocking a person on it.

"Surely your father can find a way around the will. Especially if it seems to penalize you but not your brother or
sister," he argued, his mind already contemplating obtaining a copy of the document and submitting it to Wingate
Enterprises's legal department to determine what, if anything, could be done. Some loophole.

"My father doesn't want to find a way around it," she
admitted softly, but the confession damn near rocked him
back on his heels. "My grandmother did add a codicil.
She left it up to my father's discretion to enforce the stipulation. He could release the money to me now or respect
her wishes. He's decided he'd rather see me married and
settled. *Taken care of*, are his words. As if I'm a child to
be passed from one guardian to another like luggage. Or
a very fragile package." She chuckled, and the heaviness
of it, the *sadness* of it, was a fist pressed against Ezekiel's
chest. "That's not far off, actually."

Understanding dawned, and with it came the longing to
grab Douglas Sinclair by his throat.

"So that's what the introductions to man after man were
about?" he asked.

"The night of James Harris's party?" She nodded. "Yes.
And the not-so-subtle invites to our home for dinner. In the
last week, there have been three. I feel like a prized car on
an auction block. God, it's *humiliating*." For the first time,
fire flashed under that calm, and he didn't know whether he
wanted to applaud the emotion or draw her into his arms to
bank it. He did neither, retaining that careful distance away
from her. "I just want to yell *screw it all* and walk away
completely. No money, no husband I don't want. But..."

"But family loyalty is a bitch."

A smile ghosted over her lips. "God, yes. And a mean,
greedy one to boot."

"Ray." That smile. The awful resignation in it... He couldn't *not* touch her any longer. Crossing the small distance he'd placed between them, he cupped the back of her neck, drawing her close. Placing a kiss to the side of her head, he murmured, "I'm sorry, sweetheart. Family can be our biggest blessing and our heaviest burden."

Brushing his lips over her hair one last time, he dropped his arm and shifted backward again. Ignoring how soft her hair had been against his mouth. Or how his palm itched with the need to reshape itself around her nape again. How he resisted the urge to rub his hand against his leg to somehow erase the feel of her against his skin. "Whatever you decide, make sure it's the best decision for you. This life is entirely too short to deal with regrets."

Her lashes lowered, but not before he caught a glint of emotion in her eyes.

Oh yes. Secrets definitely dwelled there.

"Regrets," she repeated in her low, husky tone. "Yes. Wouldn't want those." Shaking her head, she smiled, but it didn't reach the gaze he stared down into. "I need to go. A meeting. Take care of yourself, Zeke," she said.

With a small wave, she turned and strode down the cemented path, her hips a gentle sway beneath the flowing material of her dress. Tearing his regard from her slender, curvaceous form, he returned it to the grave in front of him. But his mind remained with the woman who'd just walked away from him and not the one lying in the ground at his feet.

I chain myself to a man I barely know and don't love to access my inheritance.

I stay here, static for another four years while my own dreams, my own needs and wants wither and die on the vine.

Her words whirled in his head like a raging storm, its

winds refusing to die down. And in the midst of it was his own advice.

This life is entirely too short to deal with regrets.

He should know; he had so many of them. Not calling his parents and telling them he loved them more often. Not being more insistent that Melissa spend the night at his house instead of driving home that night. Not letting his uncle Trent know how much he appreciated all that he'd done for Luke and Ezekiel before he died.

Not being able to turn this WinJet disaster around for the company.

Yeah, he had many regrets.

But... The thoughts in his head spun harder, faster.

Reagan didn't want to shackle herself to a man she barely knew and didn't love.

Well, she knew him. Love wasn't an option. The only woman to own his heart had been taken from him. Now, he didn't have one to give. Love... He'd been down that road before and it was pitted with heartbreak, pain and loss. But Reagan wouldn't expect that from him. They had a friendship. And that was a solid foundation that a good many marriages lacked.

The idea—it was crazy. It bordered on rash. And his family would probably call it another one of his harebrained adventures.

None of them understood why he pursued those exploits. He'd been in control of precious little in his life. Not his parents' untimely demise. Not where he and Luke landed afterward. Not Melissa's death. And even though he enjoyed his job at Wingate Enterprises, that family loyalty, the debt he felt he owed Ava and Trent, had compelled him to enter into the family business.

And now he had to bear witness to the slow crumbling of that business.

He didn't need a psychologist to explain to him why he had control issues. He got it.

When he climbed a mountain or dived from a plane, his safety and success were in his own hands. It all depended on his skill, his preparation and will. He determined his fate.

And while his chaotic and uncertain life was beyond his power, he could help Reagan wrest control of hers. As he remembered the girl who had stood with him during one of his loneliest and most desolate moments, it was the least he could do to repay her kindness.

Yes, it could work.

He just had to get Reagan to agree with him first.

Four

It'd been some years since Reagan had been to the Wingate estate.

Five to be exact.

The gorgeous rolling hills and the large mansion sitting on the highest point brought back so many memories of a happier, much less complicated time.

Though Reagan was a couple of years older, she'd been good friends with Harley Wingate when they'd been younger. Some would say the best of friends, who stayed in each other's homes, wrote in diaries and then shared their secrets and gossiped about boys. Reagan smiled, wistful. Those had definitely been simpler times.

Before her miscarriage and Harley leaving the United States for Thailand. Reagan had never revealed her pregnancy to her friend, and then Harley had left with her own secrets—including who had fathered her own baby.

Sadness whispered through Reagan as she drove past the home where she'd spent so many hours. A mix of Southwestern and California ranch architectural style, it boasted cream stone and stucco with a clay tile roof and a wraparound porch that reached across the entire second story. Memory filled in the rest. Wide spacious rooms, a library and dining areas, an outdoor kitchen that was a throwback to the ranch it resembled. Several porches and patios stretched out from the main structure and a gorgeous pool that she and Harley used to while away hours beside. Expensive, tasteful and luxurious. That summed up the home and, in many ways, the family.

Reagan's father had been proud his daughter was friends with a Wingate daughter.

She'd ruined that pride.

Not going there today. Not when she'd received a mysterious and, she freely admitted, enticing voice mail from Ezekiel Holloway asking her to meet him at the guesthouse on the estate. What could he possibly have to discuss with her? Why couldn't they have met at his office in the Wingate Enterprises building just outside of Royal?

And why had her belly performed a triple-double that would've had Simone Biles envious just hearing that deep, silk-over-gravel voice?

She shook her head, as if the action could somehow mitigate the utter foolishness of any part of her flipping and tumbling over Ezekiel. If the other reasons why he was off-limits—playboy, friend-zoned, he'd seen her with braces and acne—didn't exist, there remained the fact that he clearly still pined over his dead fiancée.

Eight years.

God, what must it be like to love someone like that? In her teenage folly, she'd believed she and Gavin had shared that kind of commitment and depth of feeling. Since he'd ghosted her right after the miscarriage, obviously not. And her heart had been broken, but she'd recovered. The scarred-over wound of losing her unborn child ached more than the one for Gavin.

Unlike Ezekiel.

It'd been a couple of days since she'd walked out of the cemetery leaving him behind, but she could still recall the solemn, grim slash of his full mouth. The darkness in his eyes. The stark lines of his face. No, he'd *loved* Melissa. And Reagan pitied the woman who would one day come along and try to compete for a heart that had been buried in a sun-dappled grave almost a decade ago.

Pulling up behind a sleek, black Jaguar XJ, Reagan shut off the engine and climbed from her own dark gray Lexus. Like a magnet, she glided toward the beautiful machine. Her fingers hovered above the gleaming aluminum and chrome, hesitant to touch and leave prints. Still those same fingertips itched to stroke and more. Grip the steering wheel and command the power under the hood.

"Am I going to need to get you and my car a room?"

So busted. Reagan winced, glancing toward the porch where Ezekiel leaned a shoulder against one of the columns. Unless he lounged around the house in business clothes, he must've left the office to meet her here. A white dress shirt lovingly slid over his broad shoulders, muscular chest and flat abdomen, while dark gray slacks emphasized his trim waist and long, powerful legs.

"You might," she said, heading toward him but jerking her all-too-fascinated gaze away to give the Jaguar one last covetous glance. "V8 engine?"

He nodded. "And supercharged." She groaned, and he broke out into a wide grin. "I didn't know you were into cars," he remarked, straightening as she approached.

Reagan climbed the stairs to the porch, shrugging a shoulder. "My brother's fault. He started my obsession by sharing his Hot Wheels with me when we were kids, and it's been full-blown since then. We make at least two car shows a year together."

"What else are you hiding from me, Reagan?" Ezekiel murmured, those mesmerizing green eyes scanning her face.

Heat bloomed in her chest, searing a path up her throat, and dammit, into her face. Ducking her head to hide the telltale reaction to his incisive perusal, she huffed out a small laugh. "Hiding? Please. Nothing that dramatic. I'm an open book."

He didn't reply, and unable to help herself, she lifted her head. Only to be ensnared by his gaze. Her breath stuttered, and for a slice of time, they stood there on the edge of his porch, staring. Drowning. At least on her part.

God. Did the man have to be so damn hot?

Objectively, she understood why so many women in Royal competed to have him in their arms, their beds. Even if it were just for hours. Oh yes, his reputation as a serial one-night monogamist was well-known. Was the rumor about him never actually sleeping with a woman true as well? Part of her wanted to know.

And the other?

Well, the other would rather not picture him tangled, sweaty and naked with another woman, period. Why just the thought had her stomach twisting, she'd rather not examine.

"C'mon in," he invited, turning and opening the screen door for her to enter his home.

Nodding, she slipped past him and stepped into the guesthouse he and his brother shared. *Guesthouse.* That brought an image of a garage apartment. Not this place. A towering two-story home with a tiled roof, wraparound porch, airy rooms with high ceilings and a rustic feel that managed to be welcoming, relaxing and expensive—it provided more than enough room for two bachelors.

It wasn't the first time she'd walked the wood floors here. After Luke and Ezekiel's parents died, they'd moved here, and she'd visited with Harley. But then, she hadn't been personally invited by Ezekiel. And they'd never been alone.

Like now.

"I have to admit, I've been dying to find out what all the cloak-and-dagger mystery is about," she teased as he closed the front door behind them. "I've narrowed it down to plans for world domination or spoilers for the next superhero movie. Either way, I'm in."

A smile flashed across his face, elevating him from beautiful to breathtaking. *That's it*, she grumbled to herself, following him into the living room. She was only looking at his neck from now on. That face elicited silly and unrealistic thoughts. Like what would that lush, sensual mouth feel like against hers? Did he kiss a woman as if she were a sweet to be savored? Or a full-course meal to be devoured?

God, she had to stop this. The man might as well be her big brother. No, scratch that. There were moral and legal rules against lusting after your brother like she did Ezekiel. Still, it was all shades of inappropriate and wrong. Mainly because while she didn't see him as a sibling, he definitely viewed her as one.

The reminder snuffed out the embers of desire like a dousing of frigid water.

Ezekiel snorted, gesturing toward the couch. "As if I would ever share spoilers. Now world domination…" He shrugged a shoulder. "I can be persuaded."

"I'm not even touching that," she drawled. "But your questionable values don't deter my curiosity one bit." She lowered to one end of the sofa. "So dish."

Rather than taking a chair or joining her on the couch, Ezekiel sat on the mahogany coffee table in front of her. His white dress shirt stretched across the width of his broad shoulders as he leaned forward, propping his elbows on his muscular thighs. All the teasing light dimmed in his eyes as he met hers.

Unease slid inside her, setting beneath her breastbone. Unease and a niggling worry.

"What's wrong?" she whispered. "What's happened?"

Harley? Her parents? Something else with Wingate Enterprises? She, like everyone else in Royal—hell, the nation—had heard of the trouble at their jet manufacturing plant. Unlike the gossip swirling around the Wingates proclaimed, she didn't believe the allegations of corruption. They didn't coincide with the people she'd known for years. And she absolutely didn't believe that Ezekiel would've gone along with something so nefarious. They might not have been close, but the boy and man she'd called a friend had a core of integrity and honesty in him that wouldn't have abided any fraudulence or deception. Especially any that could potentially cost people their lives.

"Reagan," he said, pausing for a long moment. A moment during which she braced herself. "Marry me."

The breath she'd been holding whooshed out of her. She blinked. Blinked again. Surely, he... No, he couldn't have possibly...

"E-excuse me?" she stuttered, shock slowing her mind and tongue.

"Marry me," he repeated, his jade gaze steady, his expression solemn. Determined. "Be my wife."

Oh God. His determination slowly thawed the ice that surprise had encased her in, permitting panic to creep through. He'd lost it. He'd finally cracked under the pressure from the trouble at Wingate. What other explanation could there be?

"Ezekiel..."

"I'm not crazy," he assured her, apparently having developed the talent of reading minds. Or maybe he'd interpreted her half rising from the couch as a sign of her need to escape. He held out a hand, stalling the motion. "Reagan, hear me out. Please."

He sounded sane. Calm, even. But that meant nothing. The man had just proposed to her—if she could actually call his demand a proposal. Who just commanded a woman to marry him? As if she were chattel—hold up. Now *she* was the one losing *her* mind. Demand, ask, send a freak-ing telegram… Nothing could change the fact that she'd suddenly plummeted into an alternate universe where Ezekiel damn Wingate had ordered her to become his wife.

All manners flew out the window in extreme circumstances like this.

"What the hell, Zeke?" she breathed.

The man nodded, still cool. Still composed. "I understand your reaction. I do. But just let me explain. And if you say no and want to leave, I won't try to stop you. And no hard feelings, okay?" She couldn't force her lips to move, and he evidently took her silence as acquiescence. "I've been thinking about our conversation at the cemetery for the last couple of days. Your situation with the will and not wanting to give in to your father's matchmaking campaign."

"Siege is more like it," she grumbled.

A corner of Ezekiel's mouth quirked. "Yes, we'll go with that. *Siege.*" Once more, his face grew serious, and she barely smothered the urge to wrap her arms around herself. To protect herself from the words to come out of his mouth. "The stipulation in your grandmother's will is you have to marry a suitable man in order to receive your inheritance. You also said you didn't want to marry a man you didn't know. A man who would try to control you." He released a rough, ragged breath. "We've been acquainted, been friends for years. And I have no interest in overseeing you or your money. As a matter of fact, I'm willing to sign a contract stating that your inheritance would remain in your name alone, without any interference from me."

"Wait, wait." She held up a hand, palm out, silently asking him to stop. To let his words sink in. To allow her the time to make sense of them. "Are you telling me you want to marry me just so I can access my grandmother's money?"

"Yes."

"But why?" she blurted out.

Unable to sit any longer, she shot to her feet and paced away from him. Away from the intensity he radiated that further scrambled her thoughts. Striding to the huge picture windows on one wall, she stared out, not really seeing the large stables or the horses in the corral in the distance. This time, she surrendered to the need to cross her arms over her chest. Not caring if the gesture betrayed her vulnerability, her confusion.

"Why?" she repeated, softer but no less bemused. In her experience, no one in this world did something for nothing. What did Ezekiel want from her? How did he benefit from this seemingly altruistic offer? "I've had no indication you were even interested in marriage." Only forty-eight hours earlier he'd been holding a vigil over the woman he'd wanted to pledge himself to for life. "Why would you voluntarily tie yourself to a woman you don't love?"

"I'm not looking for love, Reagan." She sensed his presence behind her at the same time his words reached her.

The quiet finality in that statement shouldn't have rocked through her like a quake, but it did. She wasn't looking either; that often deceptive emotion required too much from a person and gave too little back. But hearing him say it…

"I don't want it," he went on. "Love isn't included in the bargain, and you should know that upfront. Because if you need that from me, then I'll rescind the offer. I can't lie or mislead you. And I don't want to hurt you."

"I don't need it," she whispered. "But that still doesn't answer my question. Why?"

His sigh ruffled her hair, and as he shifted behind her, his chest brushed her shoulder blade. But rather than feel cornered or smothered, she had to battle the impulse to press back into him, to bask in the warmth and strength he emanated.

So she stiffened and leaned forward.

"Would it be advantageous for the world to believe that

you, a member of the upright Sinclair family, are in my corner during this WinJet shit storm? Yes. Do I find the thought of companionship appealing? Yes. Is it hard admitting that not only am I sometimes lonely, but that it's an ache? Yes. They're all true, but not the biggest reasons for my proposition," he said.

Proposition, she noted, not proposal. Yet, she didn't latch onto that as much as him being lonely. God, she knew about the hole loneliness could carve. And how you might be willing to do anything to alleviate it.

"Freedom," he said. "That's what you whispered. Maybe you didn't mean for me to hear it, but I did. You long to be free. I don't know of what, and I won't pry and ask if you don't want to enlighten me. But it doesn't matter. I can give it to you. If you accept me, you'll have access to your inheritance and all those dreams and goals you mentioned won't remain stagnant for four more years."

She closed her eyes, a tremble working its way through her body before she could prevent it. He'd listened to her. That was a bit of a lark. Having someone pay attention, consider and not dismiss her needs, her desires. *Her.*

"I still don't think it's fair to expect you to legally commit yourself to me. Marriage isn't something to be taken lightly," she maintained, although, dammit, her arguments against this idea were weaker.

"It won't be forever," he countered. "A year, eighteen months at the most. Just long enough for you to receive the money. Then we can obtain an amicable divorce and go our separate ways, back to being friends. Ray." He cupped her shoulders and gently but firmly turned her around to face him. He waited until she tipped her head back and met his unwavering but shadowed gaze. "Besides the obvious reasons, I understand why you might be hesitant to agree. I might be related to the Wingates, but with the fire and the bad press, our reputation isn't as clean as it used to be. And you might very well be dirtied by association—"

She cut him off with a slice of her hand between them. "As if I care about that," she scoffed. "No, my concern stems from this smacking of something out of an over-the-top TV drama. And that no one will believe it since we've never even been seen together as a couple. Or that all of this will seem like a stunt and only have more aspersions thrown your way."

"You let me worry about appearances and spinning this. I'm a VP of marketing, after all," he said, a vein of steel threading through his voice. "The only person we need to convince and impress is your father since he holds the reins to your inheritance. If he approves, we can have a quick wedding ceremony and start the ball rolling toward him releasing your money."

Reagan studied his beard-covered jaw. Jesus, she was really considering this propo—no, *proposition*. This was more akin to a business arrangement. Complete with a contract. Except with a ring. And a wedding.

And a commitment. A commitment without...

She lifted her gaze to his and found herself locked in his almost too intense stare. Which was going to make this all the more difficult to vocalize.

"I know you, uh..." Fire blazed up her neck and poured into her face, and she briefly squeezed her eyes shut. "I know you enjoy female company. Won't marrying me, um, interfere with..." She trailed off.

"Are you trying to ask me if I'm going to be able to endure going without sex?" he asked bluntly.

Damn. "Yes," she pushed forward. Because although she threatened to be consumed in mortification, she needed this point to be clear. "If I agree to this—and that's a big *if*—we have to appear as if we're in love even though it's not true. And that includes not going out on," she paused, "*dates* with other women while we're married."

She didn't even consider suggesting sex as part of their bargain. Ezekiel saw her as his cousin's best friend, not a desirable woman. Offering him the option would only embarrass both of them, and she'd tasted rejection and humiliation enough to last her a lifetime. There were only so many times a woman could be told she was unwanted in words and action before she sympathized with the turtle, afraid to stick out her head from her shell in fear of it being lobbed off.

"Ray, look at me." She did as he demanded, a little surprised to realize her gaze had dipped to his chin again. "I control my dick, not the other way around."

Oookay. Hearing him utter *that* shouldn't have been sexy. It should've offended her. But it was, and it didn't. If the flesh between her legs had a vote, she should have a mix tape made with him saying dick over and over again.

Proposition. Platonic. Friend. No sex.

She wasn't sure, but her vagina might have whispered, *Spoilsport.*

"I'm taking that as a yes, that other women would be out of the picture for the duration of our…arrangement," she said, arching an eyebrow.

"Yes, Ray." A smile curved his mouth, and she cursed herself for again wondering how he would feel, taste. Good thing sex was off the table. She probably wouldn't survive it with this man. "Now, your answer. Or do you need more time to consider it? Will you be my trust fund fiancée?"

In spite of the thoughts whirling through her head, she almost smiled at his phrasing. Did she need more time? His arguments were solid. His reasons for sacrificing himself to her cause still remained nebulous, but if he was willing…

She allowed herself to imagine a future where she was independent. Where her work at the girls' home in Colo-

nial County would no longer have to be a secret she kept
to herself out of fear of hurting her parents. A future where
she could build a similar home here in Royal that supported
teenage pregnant mothers who didn't have the family support, health care or resources they so desperately needed.

She should know. She had been one.

And this would solve her dilemma with honoring her
grandmother's request even if the stipulation continued to
hurt Reagan. She feared estrangement from her father, her
family, and marrying Ezekiel would prevent that as well.
Once, her father had been delighted about her friendship
with a Wingate. Now she had the opportunity to marry into
the family. Maybe he might even be...proud of her again?

Blowing out a breath, she pinched the bridge of her nose.
Then lowered her arm and opened her eyes to meet the pale
green scrutiny that managed to see too much and conceal
even more.

"Yes, I'll marry you."

Five

"Are you sure about this?" Reagan questioned Ezekiel for, oh, probably the seventeenth time since she'd agreed to his…bargain. "It's not too late to back out," she said as he cut the engine in his car. Even riding in the Jaguar hadn't been able to banish the nerves tightening inside her. Which was a shame. The car rode and handled like a dream.

Long, elegant fingers wrapped around the fist she clenched in her lap, gently squeezing. He didn't speak until she tugged her scrutiny from their joined hands to his face.

"I'm sure, Reagan. Just like I was sure the last time you asked. And the time before that. And the time before that." Chuckling, he gave her hand one last squeeze before releasing her and popping open his car door. In seconds, he'd rounded the hood and had her own door open. He extended a hand toward her, and with a resigned sigh, she covered his palm with hers.

And ignored the sizzle that crackled from their clasped hands, up her arm and traveled down to tingle in her breasts. She'd better get used to doing nothing about her reaction to him. It was inconvenient and irritating.

Not to mention unwelcome.

He kept their hands clasped together as they walked up the steps to her home. Ezekiel had advised that they shouldn't waste any time getting the ball rolling on their plan. So she'd called the administrator of the girls' home and let them know she wouldn't be in today. Though she hated missing even one shift, Reagan agreed with Ezekiel. The sooner the hard part of telling her family was over with, the better.

Next, she'd called her parents to ensure they would both be home this evening for an announcement. Forcing a cheer she didn't feel into her voice as she talked to her mother had careened too close to lying for Reagan's comfort, and even now, her belly dipped, hollowed out by the upcoming deception. Necessary, but still, a deception all the same.

"Sweetheart, look at me."

Reagan halted on the top step, her chest rising and falling on abrupt, serrated breaths. But she tipped her head back, obeying Ezekiel's soft demand.

She didn't flinch as he cupped her jaw. And she forced herself not to lean into his touch like a frostbite victim seeking warmth. His thumb swept over her cheek, and she locked down the sigh that crept up her throat.

"Everything's going to be fine, Reagan," he assured her, that thumb grazing the corner of her mouth. "I'll be right by your side, and I promise not to leave you hanging."

She just managed not to snap, *Don't make promises you can't keep*, trapping the sharp words behind her clenched teeth. Of course he would leave. Whether it was at the end of this evening if it didn't go well or at the termination of their "marriage." All men left, at some point. Gavin had. The affectionate, warm father she remembered from her childhood had, replaced by a colder, less forgiving and intolerant version.

As long as she remembered that and shielded herself against it, she wouldn't be hurt when Ezekiel eventually disappeared from her life.

"We should go in. They're expecting us." Stepping back and away from his touch, she strode toward the front door of her family home. A moment later, the solid, heated pressure of his big hand settled on the small of her back. "So it begins."

"Did you just quote *Lord of the Rings*?" he asked, arching a dark brow. Amusement glinted in pale green eyes.

"The fact that you know I did means we might actually be able to pull this 'soul mate' thing off," she shot back.

He gave an exaggerated gasp. "What kind of animal doesn't know Tolkien?"

"Exactly."

They were grinning at each other when the front door opened, and her father appeared in the entrance.

"Reagan." He paused, studying Ezekiel, his scrutiny inscrutable. "Ezekiel." He stretched a hand toward him. "This is a nice surprise."

As the two men shook hands and greeted one another, Reagan inhaled a slow, deep breath. *I can do this. I have to do this.*

Because the alternatives—a parade of men, more disappointment as she turned them down, trapping her in this half life—were hard for her to stomach.

"Well, come on in. We've held up dinner to wait on you." Her father shifted backward and waved them inside. "I'll have Marina add an extra setting for our guest."

"Thank you, Douglas. I appreciate you accommodating me on such short notice," Ezekiel said, his hand never leaving Reagan's back, his big frame a reassuring presence at her side.

"Of course."

Douglas led the way to the smaller living room where her mother waited. As soon as they entered, she rose from the chair flanking the large fireplace. At fifty-five, Henrietta Sinclair possessed an elegance and beauty that defied time. Short, dark hair that held a sweep of gray down the side framed her lovely face in a classic bob. Petite and slender, she might appear on the fragile side, but to play

mediator and peacemaker between Reagan and her father
for all these years, she contained a quiet strength that was
often underrated. Admittedly, by Reagan herself.

"Well, you said you had a surprise, and this is definitely
one," Henrietta said, crossing the room toward them. "Welcome, Ezekiel." She held both her arms out toward him,
clasping his hands in hers. He lowered his head and kissed
each cheek. "It's so good to see you."

"You, too, Ms. Henrietta," Ezekiel said. "Thank you
for having me here." He gently extricated his hands from
hers and returned one back to the base of Reagan's spine.

And her mother's shrewd gaze didn't miss it.

"None of this 'Ms. Henrietta' stuff. Please, just Henrietta," she admonished with a smile. "And you look beautiful
this evening, Reagan." She scanned her daughter's purple
sheath dress and the nude heels. "Any special reason?"

"Very subtle, Mom," Reagan drawled, shaking her head.
Relief tiptoed inside her chest, easing some of the anxiety
that had resided there since she and Ezekiel had left his
home. Maybe this wouldn't be as difficult as she'd imagined. "Actually, Zeke and I would like to talk with you and
Dad before dinner."

Her father moved to stand beside her mother, and his
impenetrable expression would've made the Sphinx cry
in envy. Reagan's nerves returned in a flood, streaming
through her so they drowned out the words that hovered
on her tongue.

Jesus, she was a grown woman. Why did her father's
approval still mean so much to her?

Because it's been so long since you experienced it.

So true. In ten years, she'd tasted disappointment,
glimpsed censure, felt his frustration. But it'd been so very
long since his eyes had lit up with pride. A part of her—
that sixteen-year-old who'd once been a daddy's girl—still
hungered for it.

Maybe Ezekiel sensed the torrent of emotion swirling inside her. Or maybe he was just a supreme actor. Either way, he shifted his hand from her back and wrapped an arm around her shoulders, gently pulling her farther into his side, tucking her against his larger frame. Like a shelter.

One she accepted.

If only for a few moments.

"Douglas, Henrietta, as you know, Reagan and I have been friends for years. Since we were younger," Ezekiel said, his deep voice vibrating through her, setting off sparks that were wholly inappropriate. "In the last couple of months, we've rekindled that friendship and have become even closer. I've spoken to her, because it is ultimately her decision, but I also wanted to obtain your blessing to marry your daughter."

Silence reigned in the room, deafening and thick. Reagan forced herself not to fidget under the weight of her father's stare and her mother's wide-eyed astonishment.

"Well, I—" Henrietta glanced from the both of them to her father, then back to them. "I have to admit, I was expecting you to tell us you two were dating, not..." She trailed off. Blinked.

"I know it seems quick, Mom," Reagan said, stunned at the evenness of her tone. When inside her chest twisted a jumble of emotion—trepidation, fear...uncertainty. "But considering how long Zeke and I have known each other, not really. We just fell for one another, and it felt right."

Good God, how the lies just rolled off her tongue. She was going to hell with a scarlet *L* for *Liar* emblazoned across her breasts.

"Is that so?" her father asked, finally speaking. "Then why is this the first time we've heard of this...*relationship*?"

Reagan hiked her chin up, straightening her shoulders and shifting out from under Ezekiel's arm to meet her father's narrowed gaze. This was their vicious cycle. His censure. Her hurt. Her defiance. Next, their mother would step in to soothe and arbitrate.

"Because we decided to keep it to ourselves until we were ready to share our personal business with everyone else. The only thing faster than Royal's gossip grapevine is the speed of light. We wanted to make sure what we had was solid and real before opening ourselves up for the scrutiny that comes from just being a member of the Wingate family and a Sinclair. There's nothing wrong with that."

"Speaking of that," Douglas added, his attention swinging to Ezekiel. His expression hardened. "With all that Wingate Enterprises is embroiled in right now, you didn't consider how that might affect Reagan?"

"Dad—"

"Of course I did, Douglas," Ezekiel cut in, his tone like flint. "I would never want to expose her to any backlash or disrespect. Believe me, I've suffered enough, and I don't want to subject her to that. Protecting her is my priority. But if my own past and this situation has taught me anything, it's that life is too short and love too precious to allow things such as opinions and unfavorable press to determine how we live. Then there's the fact that we are innocent, even if the court of public opinion has judged us. Family, our true friends and members of the Cattleman's Club believe in and support us. And they will support and protect Reagan as well. As a member yourself, you understand the power and strength of that influence."

Her father didn't immediately reply, but he continued to silently study Ezekiel.

"And I believe the Wingates are innocent as well, Dad," Reagan said. "We've known them for years, and they've always proven themselves to be upstanding, good people. The incidents of the last few weeks shouldn't change that." She inhaled a breath, reaching for Ezekiel's hand, but before she could wrap her fingers around his, he was already entwining them together. "*He's* a good man. An honorable one. I wouldn't choose a man who didn't deserve my heart and your trust."

As soon as the words left her mouth, she flinched. Wished she could snatch them back. But they were already out there, and from the twist of her father's lips, and the lowering of her mother's lashes, hiding her gaze, she could read their thoughts.

The last one you chose was a real winner, wasn't he? Got you pregnant, then abandoned you.

We don't trust your judgment, much less your capability of picking a worthy man.

Fury flared bright and hot inside her. And underneath? Underneath lurked the aged but still pulsing wounds of hurt and humiliation. *I'm not that girl anymore. When will you stop penalizing me for my mistakes? When will you love me again?*

"And this sudden decision to marry wouldn't have anything to do with your grandmother's will?" her father retorted with a bite of sarcasm.

Hypocrite. Her fingers involuntarily tightened around Ezekiel's. How did he dare to ask her that when he'd been throwing random man after man in front of her to marry her off? The only difference now was that she'd found Ezekiel instead of her father cherry-picking him.

"Dad, I don't need—"

"Excuse me, Douglas," Ezekiel interjected, his grip on her gentle but firm. "I'm sure I don't have to tell you about your daughter. She's not just beautiful, but kind, selfless, sensitive, whip smart, so sensitive that at times I want to wrap her up and hide her away so more unscrupulous people can't take advantage of her tender heart. That's who I want to be for her. A protector. Her champion. *And* her husband."

It's fake. It's all for the pretense, she reminded herself as she stared up at Ezekiel, blinking. And yet…no one had ever spoken up for her, much less about her, so eloquently and beautifully. In this small instant, she almost believed him.

Almost believed those things of herself.

"I don't appreciate you cutting me off, but for that, I'll make an exception and like it," she whispered.

Again, that half smile lifted a corner of his mouth, and when he shifted that gaze down to her, she tingled. Her skin. The blood in her veins.

The sex between her legs.

No. *Nononono.* Her brain sent a Mayday signal to her flesh.

"I don't know if I deserve Reagan, but I will do everything in my power to try," Ezekiel said, squeezing her fingers.

Affection brightened his eyes, and it wasn't feigned for her parents' benefit; she knew that. He *did* like her. "I know you have doubts, and I can't blame you for them. But not about how I will care for your daughter."

Her father stared at Ezekiel in silence, and he met Douglas's stare without flinching or lowering his gaze. Not many men could do that. And she caught the glint of begrudging respect in her father's eyes.

"You have our blessing," Douglas finally said. He extended his hand toward Ezekiel.

And as the two men clasped hands, her mother beamed.

"Well, thank God that's out of the way. Goodness, Douglas, that was so dramatic," Henrietta tsked, moving forward to envelop Reagan in her arms. The familiar scent of Yves Saint Laurent Black Opium embraced her as well, and for a moment, Reagan closed her eyes and breathed in the hints of vanilla, jasmine and orange blossom. Pulling back, Henrietta smiled at Reagan. "Congratulations, honey."

"Thanks, Mom," she murmured, guilt a hard kernel lodged behind her breastbone.

"Have you two thought about a date yet?" her mother asked, and Reagan swore she could glimpse the swirl of wedding dresses, flowers and invitations floating above her head. "What about next spring? The clubhouse is usually reserved months in advance, but your father has donated enough money to this community that they would definitely fit you in. And we should probably send invitations out now..."

"Mom." Reagan gently interrupted her mother's full steam ahead plans with a glance at Ezekiel. "We were actually thinking of just a small affair in a couple of weeks."

"What?" Henrietta gasped, and her horrified expression might have been comical under different circumstances. "No, no, that just won't do. What would everyone say? Your sister had a big wedding, and so did your brother. So many people will want to attend, and they need advance notice. I won't have my daughter involved in some shotgun wedding as if she's—" Her voice snapped off like a broken twig, her eyes widening as suspicion and shock darkened them. "Reagan, are you... You can't be..."

"No," Reagan breathed. "No, Mom, I'm not pregnant."

And as relief lightened Henrietta's eyes, anger washed through Reagan. Despair swept under it like an undertow. When would she stop being the sum of her mistakes with her parents?

"Well, then, what's the rush?" her father asked, his head tilting to the side, studying her. There was a shrewdness there that she refused to fidget under as if he'd just caught her sneaking in after curfew.

"We want to begin our lives together," she replied. "There's nothing wrong with that."

"A wedding in two weeks is...unseemly," her mother complained, shaking her head, her mouth pursed in a distasteful moue. "Six months. That's not too much time to ask. It's still short notice, but we can plan a beautiful winter wedding befitting my oldest daughter and have it right here on the estate. It'll be perfect." She clapped in delight.

God, this wasn't going how she'd expected at all. If it were up to Reagan, she would hightail it to the Royal courthouse, sign the marriage license and have a bored judge legally tie them together. It seemed more fitting to this situation. Definitely more honest.

Weddings with arches made of roses and the finest crystal and favors in the shapes of rings and a towering cake—those were for couples who were truly in love. Who looked forward to a life together filled with devotion, family and golden years together.

Weddings weren't for people who had based their temporary union on desperation, pity and money. Who looked forward to a year from now when they could be free of obligation and each other.

Besides, this wasn't fair to Ezekiel. He hadn't signed up for all of this. Hell, she wasn't even his wife yet, and her parents were acting like interfering in-laws. Waiting six months to marry would only extend their agreed-upon timeline. He'd only counted on auctioning away a year of his life, not a year and a half, possibly two.

She shook her head. No, she wouldn't do this to him. It was one thing to allow her parents to pressure her, but another to subject Ezekiel to it.

But before she could tell them that the modest, small ceremony was their final decision, Ezekiel released her hand and looped an arm around her waist, pressing a kiss to her temple. Her belly clenched. Hard. Just a simple touch of his lips and desire curled inside her, knotting into something needy, achy. Stunned by her body's reaction, she froze, a deer with its hoof suspended over the steel teeth of a trap.

"I don't want to rob Reagan of having this experience

with you, so if it's okay with her, we can wait six months," Ezekiel said. "I don't want her to look back years from now and regret anything. Her wedding day should be special."

How many times could a woman be struck speechless in the matter of minutes? Countless, it seemed.

"Zeke," she finally murmured, tilting her head back. "You don't have to do that…"

"It's no trouble," he replied softly. "Not for you."

She heard his gentle assertion, but she read the truth in his eyes. *Don't rock the boat.* Don't cause—what had been his word?—trouble. *Go along to get along.* That had been her mantra since she was sixteen. While before it had worked for her, now? Now it felt…wrong.

"Stop worrying, sweetheart. It's fine. *I'm* fine." The low, barely-there whisper reached her ears, and with a jolt, she opened her eyes, only then realizing that she'd closed them.

She searched his face, seeking out any signs of his frustration, his disappointment, his *pity*. God, which would be more like a dagger sliding into her chest? Each would hurt for different reasons. No matter how many times she glimpsed them in her family's eyes, they still pierced her.

But only understanding gleamed in his gaze. Understanding and a resolve that both confused and assured her.

For now, she'd concentrate on the assurance. Because if she permitted herself to become any more curious about Ezekiel Holloway—or worse, give in to the urge to figure him out—she might never be able to back away from that crumbling, precarious ledge.

"Okay," she whispered back.

"Wonderful," her mother crowed with another delighted clap of her hands. "We'll start planning right away. And we'll start with a date. How about…"

Her mother continued chatting as they all headed toward the formal dining room for dinner, but Reagan only listened with half an ear.

Most of her focus centered on the palm settled at the base of her spine and currently burning a hole through her dress.

The rest of it? It'd been hijacked by all the thoughts spinning through her head like a cyclone. And foremost in those thoughts loomed one prominent question...

What the hell have you just done?

Six

Ezekiel glanced at his dashboard as he shifted into Park.
9:21 p.m.

Late, but as he pushed open his car door and stepped out into Wingate Enterprises's parking lot, he knew Luke would still be in his office. Ever since the shit had hit the fan with the fire at WinJet, the resulting lawsuits, bad press and plunge in business, his older brother had been damn near killing himself to create new areas of investment, including new hotels and the best corporate jet. As vice president of new product development, he seemed to view saving the company and jobs of their over two hundred employees as his white whale.

Ezekiel worried about him.

Usually, the roles were reversed. When their parents died, Luke had been the one to look out for Ezekiel, to care for him even though he'd only been twenty-one and grieving himself. And when Ezekiel had lost Melissa, Luke hadn't left his side, even moving a small couch into his younger brother's room to make sure if Ezekiel needed him, Luke would be right there.

So yes, Ezekiel was used to being the one on the receiving end of the concern. But now, every time he passed by his brother's room at the house and his bed remained unslept in, that apprehension dug deeper, sprouting roots. Being a creative genius had its pros and cons. Luke could come up with amazing ideas and projects. But he could also become obsessive over them, everything else—including his welfare—relegated to the it'll-take-care-of-itself class.

Ezekiel trekked across the lot, approaching the six-story building that sat right outside of Royal in a large industrial park. The unassuming, almost bland exterior of the structure didn't scream family empire, but inside… He pulled free his wallet and waved his badge across the sensor beside the door, then entered. Inside, the modern, sleek and masterfully designed interior projected wealth, professionalism and power. Aunt Ava had chosen every painting, every piece of furniture and fixture herself. Anyone walking into this building could never doubt the success of those inside its glass walls.

Striding across the empty lobby, he took the elevator to the sixth floor. As soon as the doors slid open, he headed directly for his brother's office. Unsurprisingly, he noted that Kelly Prentiss, Luke's executive assistant of five years, sat at her desk, even at this late hour. Dedicated to his brother, she ensured he ate and took at least minimal care of himself when no one else could.

"Hey, Zeke," she greeted, smiling at him, warmth brightening her green eyes. The redheaded beauty still looked composed and fresh as if it were after nine in the morning instead of at night. "You know where he's at." She nodded her head toward the partially closed door adjacent to her desk.

"How's he doing?" he murmured, aware his brother had the hearing of a bat and wouldn't appreciate them talking about him behind his back. But if he asked Luke the same question, the inevitable "Fine," would tell him exactly zero.

"He's…" She paused, narrowing her eyes in the direction of his office. "Luke. Still trying to shoulder all of this. But I'm watching over him. And I'll make sure he gets home tonight instead of pulling another all-nighter."

"Thanks, Kelly. I'm going in. If you hear yelling, just ignore it. That'll just be me, wrestling him to the floor and trying to knock some sense into him. Y'know, business as usual."

She laughed, turning back to her computer. "I hear nothing and know even less. I'm practicing my speech just in case I'm called as a witness for the defense."

He grinned and forged ahead into the lion's den.

Luke perched on the couch in the sitting area, papers strewn all over the glass table. A disposable coffee cup teetered too close to the edge, a takeout container next to it. He glanced up from his study of the documents long enough to pin Ezekiel with a glare.

"You have never, nor will you ever be able to take me," he grumbled.

Ezekiel snorted. They'd both wrestled in high school and college, and though it pained him to admit it, he'd never been able to pin his brother. Of course, Luke had been in the 182 weight class, and Ezekiel had been in 170. But Luke had never let him forget his undefeated status.

Ass.

"What are you doing here?" Luke muttered, his focus returning to the work spread out before him.

Knowing he possessed a short window before he lost his brother's attention completely, Ezekiel dropped to the armchair flanking the couch.

"Since going home and talking to you wasn't an option, I had to come here. I mean, telling your big brother you're getting married isn't something you should do over the phone."

Luke froze, his hand stilling over a paper. Slowly, his head lifted, and astonishment darkened his eyes, his usually intense expression blank. He didn't move except to blink. A couple of times.

Ezekiel should've felt even a sliver of satisfaction at

shocking his brother—a remnant of the younger sibling syndrome. But only weariness slid through him, and he sank farther into the cushion, his legs sprawled out in front of him.

"What?" Luke finally blurted.

"I said, I'm getting married." Sighing, Ezekiel laced his fingers over his stomach. "It's a long story."

"Start at the beginning," Luke ordered. "And don't skip a damn thing."

Instead of bristling at the curt demand, Ezekiel sighed and filled his brother in on his very brief "courtship" of Reagan Sinclair. When he finished, ending with the tense dinner at his future in-laws' house, Luke just stared at him.

Jesus, what if he'd broken his brain with this too-unbelievable-for-a-TV-sitcom story?

"So, wait," Luke said, leaning back against the couch as if Ezekiel's tale had exhausted him. "You mean to tell me, you're willingly entering an arranged marriage—arranged by yourself, I might add—so a woman you barely know can receive her inheritance? And that woman happens to be the daughter of Douglas Stick Up His Ass Sinclair? My apologies for offending your future father-in-law, but not really, considering you're the one who gave him that particular moniker."

"Reagan is hardly a stranger. She and Harley are best friends—"

"How many years ago?" Luke interrupted.

"*And* we have always been acquainted," Ezekiel continued despite his brother's interruption.

"Right," Luke drawled, his shock having apparently faded as that familiar intensity entered his gaze again. "But there's 'hey, great to see you at this nice soiree' acquainted, and then there's 'hey, be my wife and let's get biblical' acquainted."

"First, *soiree*? How the fuck old are you? Eighty-three?"

Ezekiel snorted. "And second, I don't plan on getting 'biblical' with her. This is a purely platonic arrangement. I'm helping her out."

Purely platonic arrangement. Even as he uttered the words, *liar* blared in his head like an indictment. Yes, he didn't plan on having a sexual relationship with Reagan. But the images of her that had tormented his nights—images of her under him, dark eyes glazed with passion, slim body arching into him, her breasts crushed to his chest, her legs spread wide for him as he sank into her over and over... None of those were platonic.

In his case, not only was the flesh weak, but the spirit was looking kind of shaky, too.

But he hadn't popped the question to land himself a convenient bed partner. When it came down to it, his dick didn't rule him. He could keep his hands—and everything-damn-else—to himself. Sex just muddied the already dirty waters.

Reagan had claimed to understand that he wasn't looking for love, couldn't give that to anyone else. But she couldn't. Not really. It wasn't as if he longed to climb into that grave with Melissa anymore; he didn't pine for her. But her death—it'd marked him in a way even his parents' hadn't. At some point all children have to face the inevitability of losing a parent. And they even think about how that time will be. His mom and dad's death had been devastating and painful, and to this day he mourned them. But he'd known it would come, just not so soon.

Losing a young woman who not only had her whole future ahead of her, but he'd imagined would be part of his future, had, in ways, been more tragic. More shattering. Because she shouldn't have died. According to statistics, she should've outlived him. But she hadn't. And part of her legacy had been a deeply embedded fear that nothing lasted forever. Anything important, anything he held onto too tightly could be ripped from him. Oh, there existed the possibility that it might not. But he'd played those odds once and his heart had been ripped out of his chest, and he didn't believe he would survive the pain. Not again.

Melissa had taught him that he was no longer a betting man.

So while Reagan might claim to understand why she shouldn't expect love and some happily-ever-after with him, sex would potentially change that. Women like her... She wouldn't be able to separate satisfying a base, raw need from a more emotional connection. And he loathed to hurt her, even unintentionally. Though he'd never caught wind of her being seriously involved with anyone, something in those soft brown eyes hinted that she'd experienced pain before. And he didn't want to add to it.

So for the length of their "marriage," his dick would remain on hiatus.

"And what do you get out of it?" Luke asked, dragging him from his thoughts and back into the present. "Other than canonization for sainthood?"

Ezekiel shrugged. "Companionship. The knowledge that I'm helping a woman I respect and like achieve her goals. Plus, you can't deny that news of a Wingate family engagement and wedding would definitely detract from the gossip and bad publicity surrounding us and the company at the moment. Who doesn't love a whirlwind romance, right?" He sighed, leaning forward and propping his elbows on his thighs. "I know this doesn't make sense—"

"No, to the contrary, it makes perfect sense," Luke cut him off. "At least to me. I'm just wondering if it isn't as clear to you."

Ezekiel frowned. "What the hell is that supposed to mean?"

Luke leaned forward, mimicking his pose. "It means you couldn't save Melissa, so you're trying to rescue Reagan."

"That's bullshit," Ezekiel snapped, anger sparking hot and furious in his chest. "One has absolutely nothing to do with the other." He shot to his feet, agitated. Too fucking...exposed.

He paced away from his brother, stalking across the office to the windows that looked out over Royal. Seconds later, he retraced his path, halting in front of Luke, the coffee table separating them like a tumbleweed blowing across a dirt street. "You accuse me of having a savior complex, but I'm not the one who's basically moved into his office, assuming the responsibility of saving this company all on his own. Analyze yourself before you decide to play armchair psychiatrist with me."

The silence between them vibrated with tension and anger. *His* anger. Because instead of getting in Ezekiel's face and firing a response back at him, Luke reclined back against the couch and stretched an arm across the top of it.

"Hit a nerve, did I?" he murmured, arching an eyebrow.

"Shut the hell up," Ezekiel snapped.

That shit his brother had spouted wasn't true. After Melissa, Ezekiel went out of his way to avoid becoming deeply involved with people outside of his family. He wasn't arrogant enough to think he could rescue people like a superhero in a suit instead of in a cape and tights.

"Zeke." Luke's sigh reached him moments before he stood and circled the coffee table. "What you're doing for Reagan? It's a good thing. I didn't mean to imply it wasn't or that you shouldn't do it. I'm just...concerned." He set a hand on Ezekiel's shoulder, forcing him to look into the face that was as familiar to him as his own. "I need you to be careful, okay? I don't want you to get hurt again."

Ezekiel shook his head. "This is more of a business arrangement than a relationship. We both understand that. You don't have to worry about me. Everything is going to be fine."

Luke nodded, but the skepticism darkening his eyes didn't dissipate. And for the moment, Ezekiel chose to ignore it. Just as he'd chosen to disregard the unexpected urge to protect Reagan from her father's censure tonight. To put her happiness before his own preferences when he'd agreed with her mother's wishes to extend their engagement from two weeks to six months.

Reagan had never come across as fragile to him; though slim and petite in stature, she possessed a confidence and self-assuredness that made her seem unbreakable...untouchable. But tonight? There'd been moments when he could've sworn her bones had been traded for glass. And he'd fought the insane urge to wrap her up and cushion her from the strange tension that had sprung up at moments between her and her parents.

Luke squeezed his shoulder. "Telling me not to worry is like telling the Cowboys not to pass Amari Cooper the football. Ain't going to happen."

Ezekiel snorted, and Luke returned to the couch and his spread of papers. Before he lost Luke's attention completely to work, Ezekiel followed and swept up the empty coffee cup and takeout container. He crossed the room and tossed them in the trash can.

"Thanks, Luke," he said, heading for the office door.

"For what?" his brother muttered absently.

"For being there."

Luke's head snapped up, his light brown eyes focused and sharp.

"Always."

He was right about that, Ezekiel mused, letting himself out and closing the door shut behind him. Through everything, Luke had always been there for him. Had never failed him.

Even when Ezekiel failed himself.

Seven

Reagan stepped off the elevator onto the executive floor of the Wingate Enterprises building. She barely noticed the tasteful, expensive furnishings or exquisite decor that prevented the office from feeling *corporate* but instead exuded welcome and competence.

She did notice the silence.

And not like the peaceful stillness of the cemetery where she and Ezekiel had encountered each other weeks ago.

No, tension reverberated in this quiet. It stretched so tight, screamed so loud she curled her fingers into her palms to prohibit her from reverting to her six-year-old self and slapping her hands over her ears.

She strode past the desks with people bent over them, hard at work, and the office doors shutting out the world. The anxiety that seemed to permeate the air like a rancid perfume twisted her stomach into knots.

She'd seen the news this morning. Had blankly stared at the screen as words like *DEA*, *drugs* and *smuggling* were thrown at her by solemn-faced news anchors who were unable to hide the inappropriate glee in their eyes over a juicy story. Her first thought had been to get to Ezekiel. To see if he was okay. To...*protect him.*

Reagan shook her head as she approached the circular, gleaming wood desk that sat outside his shut office doors. There was no protecting him or his family from this latest development in what had become a perpetual shit storm that circled the Wingate clan and their company. And he didn't need or want that from her anyway. No, she was here to make sure her friend/fiancé wasn't reeling.

Pausing in front of the desk, she met the curious gaze of the pretty woman behind it. Recognition dawned in her brown eyes seconds later, and she smiled.

"Good morning, Ms. Sinclair. How can I help you?"

Glancing down at the gold nameplate on the desk, Reagan returned the woman's smile. "I'm well, Ms. Reynolds. I don't have an appointment, but is Ezekiel free for a few minutes? I need to speak with him."

"Of course. I'm sure he would love a visit from his fiancée this morning. It also happens he's in between meetings, so it should be fine." She lifted the phone from its cradle and punched a button. "Mr. Holloway, Ms. Sinclair is here to see you." She paused. "I'll send her right in." Replacing the phone, she nodded. "He's waiting on you, and belated congratulations on your engagement."

"Thank you," Reagan murmured, heading for Ezekiel's office.

Would she ever get used to being called someone's fiancée? No, not someone. Ezekiel Holloway's. She doubted it. Three weeks had passed since they'd announced their intent to marry to her parents, and sometimes it still felt like a dream. Or a nightmare. There were days she couldn't decide which.

Even though he expected her, she still rapped the door, then turned the knob. She entered and scanned the office, finding Ezekiel perched behind his desk, dark brows furrowed as he studied the computer monitor in front of him. For a moment, she entertained spinning around and exiting as quickly—and impulsively—as she'd made the decision to come here.

But Ezekiel glanced up, and she halted midstep, her heels sinking into the plush carpet.

God, he looked…exhausted. His brown skin pulled taut over the sharp slashes of his cheekbones, lending his already angular face more severity. Stark lines only enhanced the almost decadent fullness of his mouth, and guilt coiled inside her for noticing. Faint, dark circles bruised the flesh under his eyes as if it'd been some time since the last time he and sleep had been acquainted.

The news about the DEA investigation had apparently dropped sometime yesterday even though she'd just seen it this morning. That had probably been the last time he'd visited a bed. Weariness dulled his usually bright green eyes, and her fingertips tingled with the need to cross the room, kneel beside him and stroke the tender skin under his eyes, to brush her lips across his eyelids. Anything to remove the worry, anger and fear from those mesmerizing depths.

Instead, she remained where she stood. First, Ezekiel wouldn't appreciate her noticing those emotions in his gaze—would most likely deny their existence. And second, that wasn't what they were to each other. Business partners and friends, yes. But lovers kissed and comforted each other to ease pain. And they were most definitely not, nor ever would be, lovers.

Still… God, she wanted to touch him.

Inhaling a deep breath and cursing the madness that had brought her here, she moved forward until reaching the visitor's chair in front of his desk. She didn't sit but curled her fingers around the back of it and studied him some more.

"You look terrible," she said without preamble. Blunt, but preferable to *do you need a hug?*

A faint smirk tilted the corner of his mouth before it disappeared. "Thank you for that. But I doubt you drove all the way out here just to critique my personal appearance. What's going on?"

"I—" Damn. Now that she was here, awkwardness coursed through her. She smothered a sigh. "I saw the news this morning. I wanted to make sure you were…okay."

"Am I okay?" he repeated, loosing a harsh bark of laughter. She tried not to flinch at the sound but didn't quite succeed. "Drugs were found at the WinJet plant. Now, on top of falsifying inspection reports and causing injury to our employees, we're being accused of drug trafficking. The DEA has been called in. And we're the subject of a drug smuggling investigation. No, Reagan, I'm far from *okay*."

He shoved his chair back and shot to his feet.

"Dammit." He cupped the back of his neck, roughly massaging it. He stalked to the floor-to-ceiling window that offered a view of the Wingate Enterprises property and the town of Royal. It was picturesque, but she doubted he saw anything but his own demons. "I'm sorry," he rasped several seconds later. "I didn't mean to snap at you. It's been a rough couple of days."

"I can only imagine," she murmured. After a brief hesitation where she silently ordered herself to stay put, she disobeyed her better judgment and crossed the floor to stand next to him. "No, actually, I can't imagine. And I'm sorry. The last few weeks must have been hell for you and your family."

"The workers who were injured in the fire sued, and we decided to settle the lawsuit. Just when we believed the worst had started to blow over, *this* happens. I can't—" He broke off, his jaw clenching so hard, a muscle ticked along its hewn edge. "It's like we're cursed. Like one of those bedtime stories where the family lives this golden, blessed life and then an evil witch decides to strike them with trouble from every turn." Emitting another of those razor-sharp laughs, he shook his head. "Goddamn, now I'm talking in fairy tales."

Her chest squeezed so hard, she could barely push out a

breath. Ezekiel's big frame nearly vibrated with the strength of his tightly leashed emotions. His frustration, his confusion, his...helplessness reached out to her, and she employed every ounce of self-control to stop herself from reaching back out in return.

"I'm sorry," he breathed, rubbing his palm down his face, the bristle of his trimmed beard scraping in the silence. "Thank you for coming by. That was sweet of you, and though I didn't act like it, I appreciate it."

"It's what friends do," she replied, reminding herself out loud why she couldn't touch him.

"And fiancées?" Ezekiel asked, a hint of teasing underneath the weariness in his voice.

"Of course," she added with a casual shrug of her shoulder. "A real one would offer sex to comfort you, but the way our arrangement is set up..." *Oh hell.* Had she really said that? She'd been joking, but... Oh. *Hell.* "I was just kidding..."

She trailed off as he stared at her, the fatigue in his green gaze momentarily replaced by an intensity that vaporized the air in her lungs. The tension in the room switched to a thickness that seemed close to suffocating. She should say something, try to explain again that she was kidding. But was she? If he asked her for it, would she give her body to him? Let him lose himself for just a little while with her?

No.

Yes.

Images crowded into her mind. Images of them. Of him surrounding her, his thick, muscled arms encircling her and grasping her close as his large body surged inside her. Her thighs trembled, and her suddenly aching sex clenched. Hard. She swallowed a gasp at the phantom sensation of being possessed by him, stretched by him. Branded by him.

"But you're not my real fiancée, are you, Ray?" he finally said, and if his tone sounded rougher, well, she ignored it. She had to.

"No," she whispered. "I'm not."

"Because we're friends and you don't want me like that, right?" he asked, that dark gaze boring into her. As if he could see the truth behind her careful lies.

"Yes, we're friends," she agreed, raising a hand to her collarbone and rubbing the scar there through her thin blouse.

"And you don't think of me like that. Do you?" he pressed in that same deep, silken voice.

"No," she lied. Even as her subconscious shamed her for breaking a commandment.

He didn't say anything to that, but something inside her made her suspect he agreed with her subconscious. Did he *want* her to desire him? Or was he just making sure she understood where their boundary lines were drawn?

The latter. Definitely the latter.

"What's next for you? For Wingate Enterprises?" she asked, desperately turning the conversation back to the reason she'd come here.

He shifted his gaze from her and back to the window. "I don't know," he admitted on a gruff whisper. Again, he rubbed the nape of his neck. "Once the DEA gets involved that could mean anything. They could freeze our assets. Confiscate anything they believe is related to the accusations. Lock the doors of the building. Arrest anyone they consider involved... *Fuck*," he snarled. "How did we get here?"

"It's just been a couple of days, Zeke. They'll find out who planted the drugs, and Wingate will be cleared."

He shot her a sharp glance. *"Planted?"* he demanded. He shook his head. "You would be the first person who suggested they were, and that we're not responsible for smuggling or trafficking."

She sliced a hand through the air. "That's nonsense. Your family would never be involved in something like that. There's an explanation, but you being a drug kingpin isn't it." She snorted. Because yes, the idea of it was just that ridiculous.

"God, Ray," he said. And for the first time, his chuckle wasn't a humorless, jagged thing that scraped her raw. "Thank you," he whispered. "Thank you for the first real laugh I've had in days." He lifted his arm, and it hovered between them for a couple of seconds before he brushed the backs of his fingers across her cheek. "Thank you for not turning and hightailing it at my bark and braving my bite."

"Yes, well, I don't appreciate being snapped at. But for that apology, I'll make an exception and like it," she mumbled, echoing the same thing she'd said to him at her parents' home.

He obviously remembered because he smiled. But then his hand dropped away, and he sobered. "Ray," he said, his voice lowering. "If you're having second thoughts about marrying me, I understand. You don't have to be afraid to tell me."

"What?" Surprise rocked through her, and she frowned. "Why would I have second thoughts?"

He sighed, and the exhaustion crept back into his face. "The terms of your grandmother's will state you need to marry a suitable man. And when your father gave us his blessing, he didn't know that my family would soon be accused of being a criminal enterprise. There's no way he can be pleased with this turn of events. Or with his daughter becoming involved with it merely by association."

"I'm not tainted by you, Zeke," she snapped, offended. And yes, her father could be old-fashioned and stuck in his ways, but even he drew the line at convicting a man until he'd been proven guilty. "And I resent the implication that my being connected to you would. I'll handle my father. I'm not calling off the engagement. Are you?"

He hesitated, that springtime gaze roaming her face as if searching for the truth behind her words. Finally, he said, "No, I'm not calling it off."

"Good," she said, tone brisk. "Now, I need you to do something for me." She didn't wait for his acquiescence but strode across the room and settled down on the chocolate leather couch in his sitting area. "Come here. Please," she belatedly tacked on.

He slowly walked toward her, his forehead creased in a frown. "What's going on? Why?"

She patted the cushion next to her. "I meant what I said," she said, plucking up one of the brown-and-red-patterned throw pillows and placing it on her lap. "You look terrible. Like you haven't slept. Or eaten. I can't do anything about the food part, but I can make you take a nap. Here." She tapped the pillow. "Just for a little while."

"Ray…" he protested, halting at the foot of the couch. "I'm not a kindergartner. I can't just take a time-out. I—"

"Will fall down in exhaustion if you don't take care of yourself. This situation is only going to get worse before it's cleared up. If you're not going to watch out for yourself, as your friend, I will. So get over here. Now." She injected a steely firmness into her tone that she didn't quite feel. And part of her burned with pent-up desire. But God, she couldn't touch him. Definitely couldn't sex the worry away. But she had to do something. Had to give him…something.

"Seriously, Ray. I have a ton of work to do and fires to put out. And, dammit, I feel ridiculous," he grumbled.

"Can you just shut up and humor me? I did abandon a beautification committee meeting and poked the wrath of Henrietta Sinclair to drive all the way over here and see you. The very least you can do is give me a couple of minutes," she insisted, throwing a glare in just for good measure so he knew she meant business.

"For God's sake…" he muttered, lowering to the couch and reclining back, setting his head on the pillow across her lap. "One day you're going to make an excellent mother, seeing how well you have the guilt trip down."

His words punched her in the chest, and she couldn't control the spasm that crossed her face. With his eyes closed and his arms crossed over his chest, he didn't glimpse it, and for that, she was grateful.

Reagan pushed through the hollowness his innocent words left behind and pressed her fingertips to his temples. Slowly, she massaged the tender areas, applying just enough pressure to soothe. Over the years, when her father had come home tense from a hard day at work, her mother had sat him down and done the same. And he would release a rumble of pleasure just as Ezekiel did.

Gradually, his big body relaxed, and his arms loosened, dropping to his sides. His beautiful lips parted on a heavy sigh, and he turned his head toward her. It didn't skip her attention, that if not for the pillow, his face would hover dangerously close to the part of her that harbored no confusion about what it wanted from this man.

Even now, tenderness mixed with longing. With a languorous desire that wound its way through her like her veins were tributaries for this need. His wind-and-earth scent drifted up to her, and she just gave up and soaked in it. Here, under the guise of friendship and offering the little bit of comfort she could allow and he would take, she could lower her self-imposed barriers and just…bask in him. Soon enough she would have to raise them again.

For both of their sakes.

"Ray?" came his drowsy mumble.

"Yes?"

His thick, black lashes lifted, and she stared down into his eyes.

"Thank you," he murmured.

"You already said that," she reminded him.

"I haven't thanked you for being my friend."

"Oh," she said. "You're welcome, Zeke."

And damn if that reality check didn't sting.

Eight

"I'd have to say your engagement party is a success," Luke observed.

Ezekiel had to agree. Tuxedoed and gowned guests crowded into the great room of the Texas Cattleman's Clubhouse. Their chatter and laughter filled the air, and yes, by all appearances, his and Reagan's engagement party was going off without a hitch.

When he'd asked his cousin Beth to help him organize the party three weeks ago, she'd taken over, arranging to have it in the clubhouse where several people in the family were members. Several years ago, the club had undergone a major renovation, and now it was lighter and airier with brighter colors, bigger windows and higher ceilings. Tonight, floor-to-ceiling French doors had been thrown open to the July night, and the warm, flower-scented air filtered into the room, making the already cavernous area seem larger.

Flowers, white, tiny fairy lights and even a beautiful arch decorated the space, and the dark wood floors seemed to gleam. Tall lamps had been placed on the patio beyond the French doors and more of the lights had been entwined around the columns and balustrades. Linen-covered tables, with elegant hurricane lamps and more flowers adorning them, dotted the room and bordered a wide area for dancing.

Everything was sophisticated, luxurious and gorgeous. His cousin had managed to pull off the impossible in a matter of weeks.

Yet, Ezekiel hadn't taken a single easy breath all evening. Like that other shoe just hovered above his head, ready to plunge into the room at any moment.

"Even Aunt Ava seems to be pleased with your choice of fiancée," Luke continued. "Considering her higher-than-God standards, that's a minor miracle."

Ezekiel snorted, sipping from his tumbler of whiskey. Luke wasn't wrong. His aunt might be a thin, somewhat fragile-looking woman, with her dark blond hair brushed with the lightest of gray, but one look into those shrewd gray-green eyes, and all thoughts of frailty vanished. She was a strong, driven woman who had been a wife, was a businesswoman and mother. And if you asked her children, they might tell you in that order. The death of Uncle Trent had been a severe blow to her. But she'd begun to return to her old, exacting, often domineering self just before the issues with WinJet hit.

"I'm glad she came tonight," Ezekiel said, studying his aunt and the man next to her. "I see she brought Keith."

"Since when is Keith Cooper going to let her go anywhere without him?" Luke muttered, the dislike Ezekiel harbored for the man evident in his brother's voice. "I swear, it would be almost laughable how obvious he is if it weren't so pathetic."

As his uncle's best friend, Keith Cooper had been in their lives for years. On the surface, the man with the thinning brown hair, dark eyes and athletic build that had softened from one too many bourbons was an affable, laid-back man with an easy laugh. Married and divorced three times and with no children, he'd adopted the Wingates as his family. Or rather he'd inserted himself into their family.

And maybe that was what rubbed Ezekiel the wrong

way. Keith was always there. Like a snake. The big, toothy smile didn't hide how he watched Aunt Ava with an avarice that made Ezekiel's skin crawl. No, Keith hadn't done anything overt to earn his dislike, but Ezekiel didn't trust him.

Not at all.

"So you know, I have my speech prepared," Luke drawled, tugging Ezekiel's attention from his aunt.

He frowned. "What speech?"

"The best man's speech. Beth set aside a time for toasts after dinner. With everything that's going on, I figured you just hadn't gotten around to asking me yet." Luke slid him a sidelong glance. "But I knew you would ask so I came ready."

"Well, that was subtle as hell." Ezekiel laughed. "Of course you're my best man. Besides, Sebastian said no." At Luke's scowl, he barked out another laugh. "Kidding. Damn. I'm going to need to ask Kelly to schedule an enema to get that stick out of your ass."

"Hilarious. You're so fucking hilarious," Luke grumbled, but a grin tugged at the corner of his mouth. "It must be that pretty-boy face that Reagan is enamored with because it sure as hell isn't your sense of humor."

"Oh, I disagree. I'm quite fond of both," Reagan interjected, appearing at Ezekiel's side and sliding an arm around his waist.

She tipped her head so it rested on his shoulder, and the casual observer would believe this woman, with her radiant beauty and equally bright smile was blissfully in love. Hell, he almost believed it. But apparently one of Reagan's many talents included acting. She didn't flinch or stiffen when he stroked her arm or held her close to his side. Instead, she'd flirted with him, gifting him with affectionate glances and warm smiles.

Reagan was an enigma.

A gorgeous, sensual enigma that he wanted to cautiously

step away from before the obsession of figuring out her many pieces consumed him.

The same woman who appeared to be the perfect daughter bravely entered into a business arrangement of a marriage so she could quietly defy her family and claim her own future. The same woman who lived her life on the center stage of Royal society, but whose eyes glimmered with sadness when she didn't think anyone noticed. The same woman who went rigid when he just brushed a tender caress over her cheek but invited him to lay his head in her lap to offer comfort.

Who was the real Reagan Sinclair? And why did desperation to discover the truth rip and claw at him?

This curiosity, this need to... To what? He knew what. And it—she—was forbidden to him.

Yet...when she'd drawn his head to her lap, had rubbed his temples with such care, he'd inhaled her delicious, intoxicating scent. Had locked down every muscle in his body to prevent himself from tearing away that pillow and burying his face between her slim, toned thighs to find out if her delectable perfume would be more condensed there. He'd closed his eyes against staring at the beautiful, firm breasts that had thrust against her blouse, fearful of seeing her nipples bead under the white silk. If he had, he might not have been able to stop until he had them clasped between his teeth, tugging, pinching...

Jesus Christ.

He lifted the whiskey to his mouth once more and took a healthy sip. Even now, with her hip pressed to his thigh, he wanted to hike her in his arms and show her and everyone else in the room how well they would fit together.

In truth, Reagan deserved a man who could give her all of his heart. A man who didn't view love as a trap with razor-tipped jaws. A man who could offer her security and a name that was above reproach.

He wasn't that man.

And yet, here he stood beside her, claiming her in front of family, friends and all of Royal.

When had he become so fucking selfish?

Luke cleared his throat, his eyebrows arching high. Laughter lit his brown eyes. And something told Ezekiel that Luke's humor was at his expense.

"What?" He frowned.

"Your fiancée asked you a question. But you seemed so engrossed in your drink, I think you missed it," Luke drawled.

A growl rumbled at the back of Ezekiel's throat, but he swallowed down the curse he itched to throw at his brother. He harbored zero doubts Luke at least had a clue where Ezekiel's thoughts had been.

"I'm sorry, sweetheart," Ezekiel apologized, glancing down at her. "What did you say?"

"I asked you to go ahead and confess the truth," she said, shooting him a chiding glance. "You hired a battalion of party planners to carry all of this off. And they worked all day and through the night like shoemaking elves."

He smiled, cocking his head to the side. "I help run a hugely successful, national conglomerate. You think I can't handle the planning and execution of one party?"

She mimicked his gesture, crossing her arms for good measure. His smile widened. Since that day in his office a couple of weeks ago, they'd become a little closer. Friendlier.

And that was both heaven and hell for him.

"Okay, fine. I begged my cousin Beth for help. She and Gracie Diaz attacked it with a competency that frankly scares the hell out of me. And all I had to promise in return was that you'd help with this year's TCC charity masquerade ball. See? I'm a problem solver."

"So in other words, you pimped me out for a party.

You're lucky I'm marrying you," she muttered, but ruined her mock-annoyance with a soft chuckle. "With Dad being a TCC member, I've assisted with past charity balls, so I'd be happy to help."

"I'm glad to hear that," he drawled. "Especially since Beth told me if I don't learn to ask my future wife for her opinion instead of just arbitrarily volunteering her for things, I might need to start Googling for a large dog-house now."

"Beth always was brilliant." Reagan laughed. "Oh, I met your cousins Sebastian and Sutton. And I have no idea how you can tell them apart. They're identical twins, but wow."

"Oh I know. I've known them all my life, and it's sometimes still hard for me to tell them apart if I'm not looking close enough."

Luke snorted. "They used to get into all kinds of shi—I mean, trouble—when they were younger, playing tricks on people."

"I can only imagine. And it's okay, Luke." She grinned. "I've heard the word *shit* before. You won't offend my sensibilities."

Luke chuckled, holding his hands up in the age-old sign of surrender. "Yes, but even though my mother is no longer here, I think she would come down and smack the back of my head for saying it in front of you."

"He's not wrong," Ezekiel added with a laugh. Nina Holloway had been a stickler for manners. "As far as telling my cousins apart, Sebastian has a scar on his lower back from when we were kids. Whenever they tried to play jokes on us and switch places, I would always grab one of them and look for the scar. I wouldn't advise doing that here though."

"I'll save that for the wedding reception then," she promised, and both he and Luke chuckled. God, she was sweet. And in ways, too damn innocent for him. "Are you about ready to head into dinner?"

"Yes." Because this piece of theater allowed him to, he stroked a hand down her long, lustrous waves. Then because he'd already admitted his selfishness, he tangled his fingers in the thick strands and tipped her head back. He noted the flash of wariness in the chicory depths, but she didn't turn from him, didn't playfully admonish him and pull away.

Granting her time to do either, he lowered his head and brushed his lips across her forehead. And because the feel of her under his mouth proved to be more of a temptation than he could resist, he repeated the caress over the gentle slope of her nose. Her soft but swift intake of breath echoed between them. "Lead the way," he murmured.

Slowly, she nodded and as he loosened his hold on her hair, she stepped back. The smile she flashed him trembled before firming. An apology for crossing boundaries lurched to his tongue.

But then he caught the heat swirling beneath the shadows in her eyes seconds before her lashes lowered.

That unintended glimpse arrowed straight to his dick.

Now it was his control that he clenched instead of her hair.

And when she reached back and entwined his fingers with hers as they headed across the room, he clung to the reasons why he couldn't escort her out of this party to the nearest dark room and fuck her senseless.

"Can you believe their arrogance? Being investigated by the DEA and throwing this party as if nothing is happening. Their gall is astounding. Even for Wingates."

Ezekiel's steps faltered and he nearly stumbled as the not-nearly-so-low whispers reached his ears. In front of him, Reagan stopped, her slim shoulders stiffening.

But another ugly voice piped up just behind them.

A disgusted snort. "I wonder if drug money is paying for all of this. Or blood money, as I like to call it."

"Goddammit," Luke quietly spat beside him.

Rage, pain, powerlessness and shame. They eddied and churned inside him, whipping and stinging. A howl scraped at his throat, but he trapped it, unwilling to give anyone more to gossip and cackle over.

"If you'll excuse me for a moment," Reagan said, her voice hard in a way he'd never heard from her. Not until she firmly disentangled her hand from his did he realize how tightly he gripped her.

Unmoving, he and Luke watched as she turned and crossed the short distance to the two older women who had been maligning them. Reagan smiled at them, and as if they hadn't just been ripping his family apart with their tongues, they returned the warm gesture. Hooking her arms through theirs, she led them through the crowd and toward the great room exit. She tipped her head to the club's security who unobtrusively stood vigil at the door, and in moments, the two men escorted the women out.

Ezekiel gaped at her as she retraced her path toward him and Luke.

"Holy shit," Luke marveled. "That might've been the hottest thing I've ever witnessed in my life."

"Watch your mouth," Ezekiel muttered. "That's my future wife you're talking about." But damn if Luke wasn't right. That take-no-shit act had been hot.

"Now," Reagan said, returning to his side, "we were headed into dinner." She clasped his hand again and moved forward as if nothing had interrupted them.

"I need to know, darlin'," Luke said, falling into step on her other side. Whether Reagan was his fake fiancée or not, she'd won his brother's admiration and probably his loyalty with her actions tonight. "What did you say to them?"

"Oh, I just thanked them for coming to celebrate our upcoming nuptials. But that I refused to feed mouths that could congratulate us out of one side and denigrate us from the other. Then I wished them a good night and asked security to escort them out."

Luke threw back his head on a loud bark of laughter that drew several curious glances. "Remind me never to cross you, Reagan Sinclair."

Pride, fierce and bright, glowed within Ezekiel, and even if their relationship was only pretense, he was delighted he could claim this woman as his.

And that scared the hell out of him.

Nine

"Reagan, I need a word with you, please."

Reagan paused midstep as she crossed her home's foyer toward the staircase, glancing at her father, who stood in the entrance to the living room.

Checking her thin, gold watch, she frowned. Just five fifteen. Douglas Sinclair routinely didn't arrive home until almost six o'clock from his law office. Had he been waiting on her?

"Sure, Dad. But will this take long? I have plans for this evening."

She'd agreed to accompany Ezekiel to a dinner at his family's estate at six tonight. But she'd lost track of time at the girls' home and was now running late. That had been happening more and more lately as her responsibilities at the home had expanded from administrative to more interaction with the girls.

Ezekiel didn't seem to mind when she called to apologize or reschedule dates. She should've told him by now where she spent the majority of her time, because after the engagement party three weeks ago, they'd grown even more comfortable with each other. Yet that kernel of fear that he would dismiss her efforts—or maybe worse, ask why she volunteered there—prevented her from confiding in him. As it did from admitting the truth to her parents.

But he wasn't her father. So maybe she would tell him

tonight after dinner. Not…everything. Still, she could share this. *Maybe.*

Her father didn't reply to her but turned and entered the living room, leaving her to follow. Her frown deepened. What was going on? Douglas's grim expression and the tensing of her stomach didn't bode well for this conversation.

"Sit, please," he said, waving toward the couch as he lowered to the adjacent chair.

Though she would've preferred to stand—easier to make a quick exit—she sank to the furniture. "What's wrong, Dad?"

He crossed one leg over the other and propped his elbows on the chair's arms, templing his fingers under his chin. That sense of foreboding increased. She and her siblings deemed this position his Thinking Man pose. Which usually meant he was about to lecture one of them or deliver an edict they probably wouldn't like.

"Reagan, I initially went along with this sudden relationship with Ezekiel Holloway and gave you my blessing for the engagement, but now I have concerns," her father said.

"About?" she pressed when he didn't immediately continue.

Her heart thudded against her chest, and she forced herself to remain composed. Douglas Sinclair despised theatrics. And the last thing she could afford was for him to accuse her of being too emotional to make an informed decision.

"The Wingate name used to be spotless and above reproach in not just Royal, but Texas. But now, with this scandal about dirty dealings at the jet plants, employee lawsuits and now drugs, for God's sake, I believe it's been dirtied beyond repair."

"Miles Wingate proved that the family wasn't responsible for the falsified inspection reports. Which makes me doubt everything else about the drugs," she argued. "You've known the Wingate family longer than I have, Dad. You have to know they couldn't be capable of trafficking or anything as reprehensible as that."

"I don't know anything of the sort," he disagreed. "People are not always who they appear to be. And while Trent Wingate might've been a trustworthy man, I cannot vouch for his family. Not personally." He lowered his arms and leaned forward, pinning her with a steady stare. "Besides, in the eyes of the public, they are guilty. Their reputation sullied. I don't believe it is wise to connect your name—or this family's name—with theirs at this time."

Her stomach bottomed out. She'd suspected this was where he'd been heading. But hearing him state it...

"James Harris, the president of the Cattleman's Club, as well as other TCC members all support the Wingates. They're not worried about their reputations being 'sullied,'" she said, imbuing her tone with her dislike over his elitist word choice. Hadn't she assured Ezekiel weeks ago that her father might be conservative but not arrogant or self-important? She shook her head.

"Maybe you're too blinded by your...*affection* for Ezekiel," Douglas continued. "But I think the right decision for not just you, but this family would be to break off this engagement. After all, how would it look if my firm was associated with people being investigated by the DEA for criminal behavior?" His mouth curled in distaste, eyes narrowing on her. "This doesn't only affect you. Your mother is also receiving the cold shoulder from some members of this community because her daughter is marrying into that family."

"That family?" she repeated, giving a short, harsh chuckle. Although she found nothing humorous about this conversation. "God, Dad, *that family* has been here in Royal for generations. They've done an immense amount of good for not just this community but outside the city with their philanthropic efforts. They're good people. And because of an accusation, of a rough period they're suffering through, you would abandon them?"

She huffed out a breath. "Before Ezekiel was my fiancé, he was my friend. Harley was my best friend. I refuse to just throw them away because people who indulge in rampant speculation rather than fact have nothing better to do than sit in judgment. I won't be one of them."

"You have no choice," he announced, tone flat and brooking no argument. "Your grandmother's will stipulates that you will receive your inheritance if you marry a suitable man. I determine the definition of suitable. And Ezekiel Holloway is not it. If you go through with this marriage, I won't release one penny to you until you're thirty. And don't try to convince me that the inheritance isn't the reason for this shotgun marriage. I went along with it at first, but no longer."

Fury blazed through her, and as she rose, her body trembled with it. Only respect bridled her tongue when she wanted to lash out at the father she loved. Since she didn't trust herself to speak, she pivoted and strode out of the room.

"You will end the engagement, Reagan," her father declared from behind her.

She didn't bother to turn around or glance over her shoulder at him as she pulled the front door open and walked out of her home.

Ezekiel buttoned the cuff of his shirt, frowning as he crossed the foyer of his guesthouse to answer the knock at the door. That had to be Reagan. He'd received her terse text about being on her way, but not only was she fifteen minutes early, they'd agreed yesterday that he was supposed to pick her up from her house. He hadn't needed to hear her voice to guess that something was wrong.

In seconds, he opened the door and his suspicions were confirmed. Though she was as lovely as ever in a pair of light green, wide-legged trousers and a white camisole, her customary smile didn't light up her face. Instead, her lush mouth formed a straight, serious line and shadows dimmed her pretty eyes. Unease slicked a path through him, and he stepped back, silently inviting her inside.

"What's wrong, Reagan?" he asked, closing the door behind her.

She whirled around, facing him, and thankfully didn't make him wait. "My father ambushed me when I arrived home." Her lips twisted into a bitter smile. "He's rescinded his approval of our marriage. Apparently, it wouldn't be good for his reputation or business. *God.*" She thrust her fingers through her dark waves and paced across the foyer, her strides fairly vibrating with her anger. Pausing in front of a painting depicting the Wingate estate, she stared at it for several long moments. But he doubted she was really seeing it. "I'm sorry, Zeke," she whispered. "I'm so angry. And ashamed."

"Ray, look at me," he quietly ordered. When she slowly spun around, he studied her gorgeous features, noting the conflict in her eyes, the sad downturn of her mouth. The slight slump of her shoulders. "Your father's not wrong."

Fire flashed in her gaze, replacing the distress. The breath snagged in his chest at the sight. Dammit, she was beautiful, and that passion only enhanced it.

Still... He couldn't blame Douglas. In the weeks since he'd visited the older man's home asking for his blessing, Wingate Enterprises had started to free-fall. In the wake of this latest scandal, stocks had plummeted, most of their jet contracts had been canceled and there had even been some boycotting of their hotels. They'd had to start laying off staff. With company assets frozen by the DEA, they couldn't even liquidate their holdings to plug up the worst of the bleeding.

So no, Douglas had the right to be concerned about his daughter marrying a man who might not even be able to provide for her. Whose name could bring her more harm than good.

"Of course he's wrong," she snapped. "And I would never abandon you just because of gossip and innuendo. What kind of person would that make me? What kind of friend would that make me?"

A smart one. Instead of voicing that opinion, he slid his hands into the front pockets of his pants and murmured, "You never did tell me what you needed your inheritance for, Ray. To go to such extreme measures like agreeing to marry me, you must have a reason, a purpose for the money."

Her expression smoothed, becoming the loveliest of masks. "I already told you. I want my freedom."

"I remember," he agreed, moving closer to her and not stopping until they stood only bare inches apart. "But over the course of the weeks we've spent together, I've also come to know a woman who wouldn't allow something like money to keep her from grabbing that freedom. No, there's something else."

He paused, cocking his head to the side. "Do you think I haven't noticed that you disappear during the day several times a week? As much as I remember the girl you used to be, the woman is still sometimes a mystery. You're keeping secrets, Ray. And your reason for needing this money is one of them." He slid a hand free and pinched a lock of her hair between his thumb and finger, rubbing the rough silk of it. "You can trust me with your secrets, sweetheart."

Indecision flared in her eyes before her lashes lowered,

hiding her emotion from him. But he caught the slight quiver of her lips before they firmed.

"Trust me," he damn near pleaded. His desperation for her to do just that shook him. But he didn't rescind the words.

The thick fringe of lashes lifted, and she stared at him. Weighing him. And relief flowed through Ezekiel when her lips parted because she'd obviously found him worthy.

"I plan to open a fully staffed and independent home for pregnant teen mothers here in Royal."

Shock quaked through him, pleasure rippling in its wake. Jesus. Of all the things he'd expected her to say, a haven for unwed mothers hadn't even been in the top ten. Admiration for her lit him up from within. Outside of his family, most of the socialites he knew served on boards or committees for charities, but very few desired to get their hands dirty.

Why *this* cause? Did she know someone who'd been pregnant, abandoned and homeless? The questions crowded onto his tongue, but rather than ask them, he cupped her face between his hands, stepping closer to her. "This is important to you, isn't it?"

Reagan nodded, and her lips parted as if to offer him an explanation, but after a hesitation, she closed them again, shifting her gaze over his shoulder.

"No, sweetheart, please don't look away from me." When she returned her regard to him, he swept his thumb over her cheek, and for a moment, he wished it was his mouth tracing the curve, tasting that soft, beautiful skin. "Thank you."

"For what?" she breathed.

"For trusting me with that information. I'm assuming your parents don't know about your plans?"

She shook her head, her hair caressing the backs of his hands and wrists. "No. They...wouldn't approve."

"Your secret is safe with me. And, Ray?" He settled a thumb under her chin, tilting her head back so she had no choice but to meet his gaze. His heart thumped against his sternum, and he viciously cursed himself for what he had to do. "Your project is also safe with me. Which is why I'm breaking off this engagement."

Hurt and anger flashed across her face. Her brows drew down into a frown as she settled her palms on his chest. She pushed at him, but he braced himself, refusing to be budged. Instead, he tightened his hold on her.

"Let me go, Ezekiel," she demanded. "If you don't want—"

"Want what, Ray?" he snarled. "Want you to have your freedom, your dreams sooner rather than four years from now? Want you to not damage your relationship with your family over me? Want you to have everything you deserve?" *Want you?* He ground his teeth together, trapping that last question. "I want all of that for you. And whether you admit it or not, your father, your mother—they're important to you. And I'm not going to let you risk that."

Not for me.

She sighed and the soft gust of air brushed over his skin. Like a kiss.

"It's not right. None of it," she whispered, the fingers that were trying to push him away seconds ago curling into his shirt. "I wish..."

Her voice trailed off, and he was grateful. Because a part of him hungered to know what she wished, what she desired. Maybe it was for the best—for both of them—that they were making a clean break. Before they crossed a line that neither of them could come back from.

That they would ultimately regret.

Giving in to a need that he refused to acknowledge, he lowered his head and pressed his mouth to her forehead. He inhaled her honeysuckle-and-cream scent, capturing it like a photograph. Her breath tickled his neck, and he stood still for a long moment, enjoying the sensation on his skin.

Lifting his head, he met her gaze. His gut tightened to the point of pain. Sadness swirled in those chicory depths. But so did a touch of heat, of desire. *Fuck.* It wouldn't require more than the barest of movements to take her mouth. To possess it. To find out if his dirtiest midnight fantasies about her texture, her taste came close to reality. With one tiny shift, he could satisfy his curiosity and just *know...*

He stepped back, dropping his arms to his sides. "You'd better go before your family starts to wonder where you are," he said, forcing a neutrality into his voice that didn't exist.

"Right," she agreed softly. "Take care of yourself, Zeke."

"You, too, Ray."

He turned to watch her leave, and though she paused on the threshold of the front entrance after opening the door, she didn't turn around or glance over her shoulder at him.

Only when she left and he stared at a closed door did he exhale and shut his eyes.

He should be grateful. Relieved. And he was. But damn if he could decide if he'd dodged a bullet or lost the one thing that had given him purpose these last few weeks.

Given him peace.

He shook his head and pivoted on his heel, heading for the staircase.

It didn't matter. She was gone.

And in the end, it was for the best.

For both of them.

Ten
***

Reagan stepped into the cool interior of the restaurant with a sigh, thankful to be out of the early September heat. It was only about three weeks from the official start of fall, but Texas didn't know it. Fixing a polite smile on her face, she strode to the maître d's stand.

"Hello," she greeted. "I'm meeting Douglas Sinclair. He should have already arrived."

"Of course," the young man said, nodding. "Please follow me."

She was ten minutes late for lunch with her father, but considering he'd sprung the "invitation" on her an hour ago, it couldn't be helped. He should be thankful she'd rearranged her plans to meet him anyway.

The only reason she had acquiesced to this impromptu lunch date was because he'd made it seem important, urgent even. It'd been two weeks since her father had demanded she end her engagement with Ezekiel, and a part of her still resented him for that. But maybe this lunch could be the start of healing that rift. Her father loved her; in her heart, she acknowledged he only wanted the best for her. Even if he could be overbearing and stubborn, she'd never doubted that...

"Reagan." Douglas stood from a table next to the large picture window that looked over downtown Royal. "We've been waiting on you. You look lovely."

She barely registered the kiss he pressed to her hair, focusing on the *we*. This was supposed to be a lunch for just the two of them. But as her attention snagged on the man also rising from his chair, a cold sliver of hurt and anger settled between her ribs.

Of course her father hadn't just wanted to spend quality time with her. He had his own agenda, and that trumped everything.

"Reagan, I'd like to introduce you to Justin McCoy. Justin…" he smiled broadly at the other man "…my beautiful daughter Reagan Sinclair."

Justin McCoy. The tall, handsome man with light blond hair smiled at her, his blue eyes quickly roaming over her before meeting her gaze again.

God, she needed a shower. She cut her father a sharp side glance.

"It's an absolute pleasure to meet you, Reagan," Justin said, grasping her hand although she hadn't offered it. He lifted it toward his lips, and her stomach lurched. If not for her father's eagle-eyed gaze, she would've snatched her arm back. Especially since she hadn't given Justin permission to touch her.

On second thought…

She tugged her hand back before Justin could touch her, ignoring her father's frown and Justin's shock. She didn't believe in the *ask forgiveness rather than permission* school of thought. And if neither this man nor her father respected her boundaries, then she didn't have to allow a man who was at best a gold digger to put his hands or mouth on her to spare their egos.

That simmering anger stirred to a boil, and she dragged in a breath before forcing a politeness to her tone that required Herculean effort on her part.

"Mr. McCoy, if you would excuse us for a moment. I need to have a quick, private word with my father."

Not waiting for either man's agreement, she whirled on the heel of her nude stiletto and stalked toward the exit. She pushed through the door and waited for her father on the sidewalk outside the restaurant.

She didn't have long to wait before he appeared.

"How dare you embarrass me like that, Reagan," he fumed, fury glittering in his narrowed glare. "You go back in there right now and apologize for your rude behavior."

"I will not."

His chin jerked up as if her words had delivered a physical slap, and his lips slackened. She'd shocked him. Hell, she'd shocked herself. Her heart drummed against her rib cage, and the tiniest sliver of fear slid through her veins. Since she'd returned to Royal and her family from that home without her baby, empty and ashamed, she hadn't once defied either of her parents. Especially her father. And she would be lying to herself if she didn't admit it scared her now. But no.

Just. No. Apparently, she had her limits, and she'd reached them.

"Reagan—"

"I'm not an idiot, Dad," she interrupted, slicing her hand through the air for emphasis. "I clearly see what this is. An ambush. Another setup. Well, I refuse to go along with it. Not this time. And definitely not with *him*."

"Yes, you will, Reagan," he hissed, his attention shooting over her shoulder. Most likely ensuring no one stood witness to her insolence, as he no doubt saw it. "I won't stand for this blatant disrespect. And I don't know what you think you know about Justin McCoy—"

"It isn't what I *think* I know," she shot back. "That man in there intentionally seduced an innocent girl and got her pregnant just so he could worm his way into a wealthy family. Considering our family history, you would think impregnating a girl would be at the top of your unworthy traits list," she sneered.

"Lower your voice this instant," he ordered, once more glancing around them. And that tore through her like a red-hot sword. Of course. They couldn't chance anyone over-hearing about their shameful family secret. "Wasn't it you who told me I shouldn't listen to rumors and conjecture?"

"Rumors?" She released a jagged bark of laughter. "It's not an opinion that he used Julie Wheeler only to aban-don her. It's not opinion that he tried to do the exact same thing with Beth Wingate. Ask Camden Guthrie or Bruce Wheeler. I promise you they will confirm that Justin Mc-Coy's complete lack of a moral compass is a fact. After all, it was Cam's dead wife and Bruce's daughter he betrayed."

"It is my job as your father to decide what is best for you, Reagan. And I might have failed once but never again," he ground out.

Had she thought he'd hurt her before? No, this…this was pain. Having him affirm that he believed he'd failed—that she'd been a failure.

Her breath shuddered out of her, and she blinked back the sting of hot tears.

She loved her father, but at this moment, he disappointed her just as she surely disappointed him. Douglas thought the purse strings controlled her, had kept her obedient and quiet for all these years. But he couldn't have been more wrong. Longing for his approval had. For her mother's, too, but more so his. There was no turning back the hands of time to that innocent period when she'd been a daddy's girl. She might never have what she desperately craved from him. The only difference between now and an hour ago was that she no longer cared.

"And the fact that you would believe he is a better man, a more *suitable* man than Ezekiel Holloway stuns and dis-heartens me." She shook her head. "I love you, Dad, but

I'm not going along with this anymore. I know you want what's best for me, but you've never asked me what that is. You don't care. And that saddens me even more."

She turned and walked away from him. And even when he called her name, she didn't stop.

She was through answering to him.

From now on, she would only answer to herself.

"Mr. Holloway, Reagan Sinclair is here to see you."

Ezekiel jerked his head up from studying a report at his executive assistant's announcement through the telephone's intercom. Alarm blared inside him, and he shot up from his chair, already rounding the desk and stalking toward the office door. There had been no communication between them since he and Reagan had broken off their engagement. What had happened to make her end the radio silence now?

Before he reached the door, it swung open and Reagan stepped in. The impact of her after weeks of not seeing her halted him midstride. Jesus, had he really somehow forgotten how beautiful she was? Or had he just tried to convince himself she wasn't so he could stop thinking about her? Either way, the attempt had been an epic fail.

He'd missed everything about her—her laugh, her quiet way of listening, the cultured yet sensual husky tone of her voice, her scent…her friendship. And hell yes, he'd missed just looking at her. Today, her sleeveless wrap dress molded to her slim but curvaceous figure like a secret admirer, and damn him, but he was jealous of the material that cupped her lovely breasts, slid over the flare of her hips and glided down those slender, perfect thighs. His fingers itched to follow the same paths, to explore that uncharted territory for himself. And to stake his claim.

But she wasn't his anymore. Not even for pretend.

What had been unattainable before had become even more of an impossibility.

Forcing his unruly thoughts and wayward body under control, he demanded, "Reagan, what're you doing here?" The worry at the obvious distress in her eyes and the slightly jerky movement in her normally smooth gait roughened his voice. "What's wrong?"

"Marry me."

He stared at her, struck speechless. Dozens of questions bombarded him, and he mentally waded through them, finally settling on the most important one. "What?"

"Marry me," she repeated, closing the short distance between them, not stopping until her hands fisted the lapels of his suit jacket, her thighs braced against his and that honeysuckle scent embraced him like a long-lost lover.

He swallowed a groan at her nearness, at the feel of her body pressed to his. Lust, hot and hungry, punched him in the gut, then streamed through him in a swollen flood. Desperate to place distance between them so he could fucking *think*, he gripped her hips to set her away from him. But touching her backfired. Instead of pushing her back, he held her close, his body rebelling and taking control. Two weeks. It'd been two *long* weeks.

"Reagan," he rumbled.

"No, Zeke. Don't give me all the reasons why we shouldn't. I don't care. Do you know where I just came from?" she asked, switching topics with a lightning speed that left him floundering. Between that and his dick finding cushion against her stomach, he couldn't keep up. "I just left a restaurant where my father arranged for me to have lunch with Justin McCoy."

"The *hell*?" His grip on her tightened. Douglas had set her up with that asshole?

"Yes." Reagan nodded as if reading his mind. "Apparently my father considered him a more suitable match than you. A man who uses and throws away women for his own gain rather than you, a man who has been nothing but honorable and unfailingly kind and respectful. I had enough. I walked away from him and his machinations. I'm through allowing him to run my life, to make choices for me out of guilt and loyalty."

Guilt? What the hell did that mean?

Shoving the questions aside for the moment, he refocused on her. "I understand your anger, believe me, I do, but take a moment and think this through before you make a mistake you can't take back. This decision will cost you your inheritance. It could damage your relationship with your parents. Is this rebellion worth that? Because you're not in…" He couldn't finish that sentence. Couldn't fathom it.

"No, Zeke, I'm not in love with you," she assured him, and he exhaled a heavy breath. Even as an unidentifiable emotion twisted in his chest. "And maybe this is a little bit of rebellion on my part, but it's so much more. I'm taking control—of my choices, my mind, my life. I respect you, Zeke. But this isn't about you. It's about me. About finally becoming the woman I've been too afraid to own. So, from now on, I'm making my own decisions," she continued. "And that includes you. I choose you, Zeke. And I want you to marry me."

Jesus, did she know what a delicious temptation she was? How he'd fought following after her that evening he'd let her walk out of his house? That had required strength he hadn't realized he possessed. Doing it a second time…

No, she might feel certain here in this office, but she was still upset. Could feel very differently in the morning, hell, hours from now. Maybe after they talked this out, she would see—

She rose on her toes and crushed her mouth to his.

Oh fuck.

His control snapped.

Like a flash fire, the press of her lips to his poured gasoline over the lust that had been steadily simmering. He took possession of that sweet siren's mouth, claiming it with a thrust of his tongue. Possessing it with a long, wet lick. Corrupting it with an erotic tangle and suck that left little to the imagination about what he wanted from her.

And he wanted it all. In this moment where the lines between platonic friendship and desire incinerated beneath his greedy mouth and her needy whimpers, he wanted everything she had to give him.

With an almost feral growl, he reached between them and grasped her wrists, tugging her arms behind her. He cuffed them with one hand and thrust the other into her hair, fisting the strands and jerking her head back for a deeper, dirtier kiss even as he pressed her curves flush against him. Her breasts, so soft, so full, pillowed against his chest and her belly welcomed his erection. His legs bracketed hers, and he shamelessly used the position to grind against her, letting her know without any question how much she affected him. How hard she made him.

Though he dominated her body, she wasn't submissive to him. God no. Her mouth moved over his as if he were her first or last meal. Her teeth nipped at his lips, and he knew when this feasting ended, his lips would be as swollen as hers. She met him thrust for thrust, lick for lick, sweep for sweep. She was his equal.

No. He shuddered as she drew on his tongue, sucking. He was her supplicant. And he would do any goddamn thing for her as long as she didn't stop.

The loud buzz of his intercom blared in the room like the blast of a horn, seconds before his assistant's voice intruded. "Mr. Holloway, I'm sorry to interrupt. But you asked me to remind you about your two-o'clock meeting with the marketing team."

Ezekiel stared down at Reagan, his chest heaving, his breath like a chain saw. Equal parts shock and grinding lust tore at him, and *fuck*, where had this need come from? How had it burned out of control so fast?

Anything that uncontrollable, that hot, that addictive wasn't good. Not for him. Not when he needed to maintain that careful emotional distance. Not when she would possibly want more from him then he was able to give.

Yet…she'd come to him; she needed him. Maybe he couldn't help her obtain her inheritance, but he could unconditionally support her, be that person she could finally lean on. *Still rescuing her*, a voice that sounded suspiciously like his brother whispered through his head. Possibly. Probably. But, she'd assured him she didn't desire more than he was capable of offering, that she didn't love him. Obviously, she craved him as much as he did her—that combustible kiss confirmed that. And, as she'd just stormed in here and told him, she made her own decisions, knew her own mind.

If she did, then they could go through with this marriage, maybe, once Douglas calmed down, still have a chance to obtain her inheritance and have scorching-hot sex, too. He could have her and when the time came, walk away.

Because there were no ifs about that. He *would* walk away. As she would.

Slowly releasing her, he returned to his desk. Planting a hand on the desk, he looked at Reagan again. She hadn't moved, but gazed at him, mouth wet and puffy from his kisses.

Ezekiel pressed a button on his phone.

"Laura," he said to his executive assistant, "please cancel the meeting as well as clear and reschedule my calendar for the next week. I'm going to be out of the office. If anyone asks, I'm getting married."

Eleven

Good God, they'd done it.

As of two hours ago, she was Mrs. Reagan Holloway, Ezekiel Holloway's wife. She stared out the floor-to-ceiling window of the luxury suite into the bright, dazzling lights of the Las Vegas strip. Ezekiel hadn't spared any expense for the place they would spend their honeymoon.

Honeymoon. She wrestled with the emotions twisting and tumbling inside her. Jesus. This was unreal. As unreal as the whirlwind trip to Las Vegas after leaving his office twenty-four hours ago. As unreal as the unexpectedly lovely and private ceremony under a candlelit and crystal-encrusted gazebo in the back of a chapel made of glass. As unreal as this elegant and richly appointed penthouse with its Italian marble foyer, sunken living room and lavish master bedroom.

Was it how she'd imagined her wedding and honeymoon to be?

No.

It was better because it was all *her* choice.

Somehow, it didn't seem possible that just yesterday she'd rushed into Ezekiel's office and demanded he marry her. She winced, her fingers tightening around the stem of her wineglass. Thinking back on her uncharacteristically rash act, she still couldn't believe she'd done it.

Or that she'd kissed him.

Her belly executed a perfect swan dive as she lifted trembling fingers to her lips. A day later, and the imprint of his mouth was still on hers. He'd branded her. Years from now, she would no doubt still feel the pressure, the slight sting, the hungry possession of that kiss. What a sad commentary on her love life that it'd been better than the best sex she'd ever had. Ezekiel Holloway could own a woman's soul with his mouth. No wonder he'd never lacked for company. No wonder women vied for a chance to spend just hours in his bed. Or out of it, for that matter.

She needed to stop thinking about him and other women.

Or that before this evening ended, she and Ezekiel would be swept up in the throes of passion.

Whispers of nerves and curls of heat tangled together inside her belly, and she exhaled, trying to calm both. If that kiss was any indication, Ezekiel was well versed in sex. She, on the other hand, not so much. There had only been a couple of men she'd been with in the last ten years. And while the experiences had been nice—God, how anemic *nice* sounded—the encounters hadn't melted her bones or numbed her brain as just a mating of mouths with Ezekiel had. What would actual sex be like between them? Would he find her lacking? What if she—

"Stop it."

She whipped around at the softly uttered command, a bit of the wine in her glass sloshing over the rim to dot the back of her hand. Silently cursing herself for her jumpiness, she lifted her hand to her mouth and sucked the alcohol from her skin.

Her heart thumped against her rib cage as Ezekiel's gaze dipped to her lips and hand. That green, hooded gaze damn near smoldered, and it seized the breath from her lungs.

Clearing her throat, she snatched her attention from him and returned it to the almost overwhelming sight of Vegas. Not that the view could abolish him from her mind's eye.

He'd ditched the black suit jacket he'd worn to their wedding, and the white shirt stretched over his wide shoulders, emphasizing their breadth. The sky blue tie had also been removed and the first few buttons undone, granting her a glimpse of the smooth brown skin at his throat and over his collarbone. The shirt clung to his hard, deep chest and flat, tapered waist. The black slacks embraced his muscled, long legs and couldn't hide their strength.

She would know that strength tonight. Intimately.

Her lashes lowered, and she blindly lifted the glass to her lips again as her fingertips rose to her own collarbone and found the small scar there, rubbing over the raised flesh.

"Stop what?" she belatedly replied, her voice no louder than a whisper.

He didn't immediately answer, but a stir of the air telegraphed his movement. A moment later, another touch from a larger, rougher finger replaced hers. She opened her eyes to meet his, even as he lightly caressed the mark marring her skin. She gasped, unable to hold it in.

Heat blasted from that one spot, spiraling through her like a blowtorch to her insides. It battled with the ice that tried to encase her. The ice of memories. Of pain beyond imagining.

His gaze lifted from just below her neck to meet her eyes, the intensity there so piercing, she wondered if patients going under the knife encountered the same trepidation. The same sense of overwhelming exposure and vulnerability.

"I've noticed you touch this place here..." He stroked the scar, and she couldn't prevent the small shiver from working its way through her frame. Fire and ice. Arousal and shame. They intertwined like lovers inside her stomach, mating in a dirty dance. "You did it that night on the balcony and at the cemetery. At your parents' home. And again in my office the day you came to see me. It's your tell, Ray. Whenever you're uncomfortable. Or nervous. Possibly even scared."

He swept one more caress over her skin before dropping his arm. But he didn't move back out of her personal space, didn't grant her breathing room. Every inhale carried his earthy but fresh scent—like a cool, brisk wind through a lush forest. She wanted to wrap herself in it. But his too perceptive observation froze her to the spot.

"So whatever you're thinking that has you feeling any of those emotions, stop it. Or tell me so I can take the fear away."

Her attempt at diversion hadn't worked last time, so she stuck to a believable half-truth. At least he hadn't asked her how she got the scar. That, she could never admit to him. Because it would involve telling him her most carefully guarded secret.

"Why?" she murmured.

"Why what?" he asked. "Why do I want to take away your fear?"

She nodded.

"Because I've seen it one too many times in your eyes in the last few weeks, and I don't like it," he said.

She stiffened, taken aback by his words. But he cocked his head to the side, his gaze narrowing on her.

"Are you offended because I said it or because I noticed?" He hummed in his throat, lifting a hand to her again. This time he traced the arc of her eyebrow, then stroked a teasing path down the bridge of her nose before sweeping a caress underneath her eye. "These gorgeous brown eyes? They tell everything you're feeling. Whether you're amused, irritated, frustrated, thoughtful or angry. In a world where people deceive and hide, you're a refreshing gift of an anomaly. Except..." He exhaled roughly, still brushing the tender skin above her cheekbone. "You have secrets, Reagan. Your eyes even betray that. I don't need to know what they are to know they hurt you, make you guard this beautiful heart."

He pressed two fingertips to her chest, directly over the pounding organ. The organ he called beautiful but one that had caused her so much pain and disillusionment.

The organ that even now beat harder for him.

Taking several moments, she studied the dark, slashing eyebrows, the vibrant, light green eyes that seemed to miss nothing, the sensual fullness of his mouth, the silky facial hair that framed his lips and covered his rock-hard jaw. Beautiful. Such a beautiful man.

And hers. At least for the next year.

Hers to touch. To take into her body. To lie next to.

But not to love. His heart belonged to a dead woman, and he had no intention of trying to reclaim it. He'd warned her of that early in their bargain. And this heat between them—this heat that threatened to incinerate rational thought and sense—it warned her that if she wasn't careful, she could once again be that reckless sixteen-year-old willing to throw caution to the wind for love.

She'd vowed never to be that girl again.

Once more she skimmed a finger over the scar at her collarbone. The one she'd earned just before she miscarried and lost her baby.

She courted danger now, with this arrangement with Ezekiel. But if she held tightly to the reminder that pain and love were two sides of the same coin, she wouldn't cross that line into heartbreak. Because she refused to give him her heart.

But her body? Oh, that he could have.

Meeting his unwavering gaze, she slowly set the glass of wine on the glass table behind her. She moved forward, circling around him and heading out of the room toward the luxurious master suite. A huge king-size bed dominated the middle of the room while a wall of windows granted a sprawling view of Vegas and the desert beyond. The small sitting area with two ornate chairs and a small glass table occupied one corner, and a dainty vanity filled the other. A closed door hid the cavernous and opulent bathroom with its double sinks, Jacuzzi tub and glass shower big enough to accommodate an entire sorority.

Yet, as she spun around to face the door, nothing in the bedroom captured her attention like the man in the entrance. With one shoulder propped against the frame and his hands in his suit pants pockets, he silently watched her. Waited.

They hadn't discussed consummating their marriage; she'd avoided the conversation, unsure if it would be wise to go there with him. No, it wasn't wise. But God, she wanted it.

Even though she trembled with nerves and foolish excitement, she stared at him as she slowly dragged down the side zipper on her simple but elegant sleeveless gown. The white satin loosened, and she slid the skinny strap down one arm, then removed the other. Heart thudding almost painfully in her chest and her breath so loud it echoed in her head, she pushed the material down until it bunched at her hips. A small shimmy, and the dress flowed down her legs to pool around her feet.

The urge to dive for the bed and hide beneath the covers rose strong and hard inside her, but she forced herself to stay still, clad only in a nude strapless bra, matching thong and sheer, lace-topped thigh-high stockings. Then, notching her chin up, she silently ordered her arms to remain by her side, her fingers to remain unclenched.

She couldn't do anything about the shiver that worked its way through her body though. Or the throbbing of her pulse at her neck. Or the gooseflesh that popped up along her arms.

Or the moisture that even now gathered in her sex, no

doubt drenching her barely-there panties. All he would have to do was lower that penetrating gaze down her torso and center it between her thighs to see the evidence of his affect on her.

That knowledge both thrilled and unnerved her.

She lifted her gaze from the solid width of his chest, where she'd focused all of her attention while she'd performed her impromptu striptease. And, *oh God*, what she spied there.

Raw, animalistic lust. Those green eyes burned bright with it. An answering coil tightened low in her belly, and she pressed a palm to the ache. His gaze dropped, and when it flicked back up to hers, she couldn't contain the whimper that escaped her. So much heat. So much hunger.

Had anyone ever looked at her as if she were their sustenance, sanity and survival?

No. No one had. Not the few lovers she'd had.

Not even Gavin.

What did it say about her that Ezekiel owned her with that look? That if she'd harbored even the tiniest of doubts about giving herself to him, that needy, ravenous, *necessary* stare undid every snarled tangle of doubt?

Slowly, he straightened, removing his hands from his pockets, and stalked forward, eliminating the distance between them. He didn't stop until not even a breath could've slid between them.

The wall of his solid chest brushed her nipples, sending arcs of sizzling pleasure from the tips to the clenching, empty flesh between her damp thighs. His muscular thighs pressed to hers, and against her belly... She shuddered, desire striking her middle like a lightning bolt. His thick, hard cock burrowed against her belly, and before she could think better of tempting the beast, she ground herself against his mouthwatering length. More than anything, she wanted him to possess every part of her.

"Playing with fire, Ray?" One of his big hands gripped her hip. But not to control her. To jerk her closer. To roll those lean hips and give her more of what she'd just taken.

Her teeth sank into her bottom lip, her lashes fluttering. But when his fingers dived into her hair, clenching the strands and tugging so pinpricks scattered across her scalp, she opened her eyes, meeting his. He didn't handle her with kid gloves, didn't treat her like this demure, sheltered socialite or a fragile girl. And God, *she loved it*. Wanted more.

"I'm not playing," she breathed, stroking her hands up his strong back and digging her nails into the dense muscle there. "No games between us."

"No games," he repeated in that same grit-and-granite voice. "How novel an idea." He lowered his head and nipped at her bottom lip. Then soothed the minute sting with a sweep of his tongue.

She groaned, leaning her head back into his grasp.

"You've showed me this pretty little body, almost making me come with just the sight of you. But I want the words, sweetheart. Tell me you want this—*me*—in your bed. In your body. Tell me..." He bent his head, pressing his forehead to hers. His breath pulsed against her lips, and she could almost taste the dark delight of his kiss. "Tell me you won't regret this in the morning."

Rising on her toes, she grazed her mouth over his. Returned for a harder, wetter taste. His lips parted over hers, and their tongues tangled, curled, took. When she pulled free, their heated pants punctuated the air, resounded in her ears.

"I want you. In my bed. Beside me. Over me. Inside me. This is my decision, Zeke. Eyes wide open. I'll have no regrets about giving myself to you." *My body, but not my heart.* She silently added that vow as a promise to herself and to him. He wanted no strings attached with their union, so when they divorced in a year, no emotional entanglements existed.

Well, she wanted the same. She *needed* the same.

His groan rolled out of him, and his fingers fisted in her hair again, tugging her head back. He slid his mouth over her jaw, down her neck and gently bit the tendon that ran along its length. She clawed at his back, arching into him. Craving more of that primal touch. As if reading her mind, he raked his teeth along her shoulder, retracing the path with the smooth glide of his lips.

Desperation invaded her, and she slid her hands around his torso, attacking his shirt buttons. She'd released the top four when his mouth passed over the scar on her collarbone.

Stiffening, she curled her fingers around the sides of his shirt, the air snagged in her throat. Every instinct in her screamed to jerk away from both his caress and the memories. But when the tip of his tongue traced the raised flesh, she closed her eyes and a half cry, half sigh escaped her throat. He didn't pause in his ministrations, but his hold on her tightened, as if lending her his strength.

The urge to recoil evaporated, replaced by the need to lean into him, press her cheek to his chest. Let him all the way in, past her heavily guarded secrets and into her heart. She ruthlessly squelched that longing under the bootheel of reality, but she did withdraw just a bit and dip her head to seek his mouth. Lose herself in the wildness of him.

His palms cradled her face, taking while she gave and gave. A new urgency roiled within her, and she hurriedly finished unbuttoning his shirt and removing the offensive material from his shoulders and arms. Offensive because it barred her from touching all that glorious, taut skin.

Once more she tore her mouth away from his, this time so she could watch her hands smooth over his broad shoulders and wide chest with something close to wonder. So much strength, so much power. And vulnerability, she mused, scraping her nails over his small, dark brown nipples. He shivered, his clasp on her face shifting to her hips.

"Again," he ordered, grinding his erection into her belly. "And use your teeth this time."

The echo of dominance in that order had flames licking at her. She could do nothing else but obey. Not because he'd demanded it…but because she wanted it.

Lowering her head, she opened her mouth wide over the small, beaded tip, swirled a warm, wet caress around it, then raked her teeth on him. Gently biting and teasing. His rumbled curse pierced the air as a big hand cupped the back of her head and pressed her closer. Emboldened, she sucked and nipped, torturing both of them. She switched to the other tip, delivering the same caresses. By the time she drew on him one last time, fine tremors quaked through his big frame.

"Payback, sweetheart." He strode forward, forcing her to backpedal.

When the backs of her knees hit the edge of the mattress, she sank to the bed, and he immediately dropped to his knees in front of her, wedging himself between her legs.

Embarrassment flashed through her for a quick instant. In this vulnerable position, he had a clear shot of what he did to her. Her thong would hide nothing from him, and even now the cool air in the room kissed the dampness on her sex and high inside her thighs.

But all thoughts of modesty shattered into dust as he scattered hard, burning kisses to her stomach, the tops of her sensitive breasts and the shadowed valley between. He cupped her flesh with both hands, squeezing and molding, and pleasure howled through her. Tilting her head back, Reagan closed her eyes, savoring his sure touch. She curled her fingers into the covers beneath her hips, seeking purchase in this lust-whipped storm.

Peeling away the cups of her bra, he wasted no time tasting her just as she'd done him. His diabolical tongue curled around her nipple, stroking, sucking. Was it possible to be driven insane with pleasure? If so, the trip was more than halfway over for her.

Unable to *not* touch him any longer, she gripped his head in her hands, pressing him to her, staring down at him as he tormented her with that beautiful, wicked mouth. It was erotic—almost too sexual to behold. But she couldn't drag her gaze away.

As he shifted to her neglected breast, he whisked the pad of his thumb over the aching, wet nipple, teasing it. His attention shifted from her quivering flesh up to her face, and their gazes locked. He didn't release her from the visual entrapment as he pursed his lips and pulled her into his mouth. Kept her enthralled as he lapped at her before drawing so hard the tug reverberated in her sex.

Too much. Too much.

She closed her eyes, but that was a mistake, because the lack of sight only enhanced the sizzling sensations crackling along her nerve endings.

With one last suck on her tip, he abandoned her breasts and trailed a blazing path down her stomach, briefly pausing to dip into her navel with a heated stroke, then continuing down, down, *oh God*, down.

His breath bathed her soaked flesh, and she tumbled back on the mattress, pressing the heels of her hands to her eyes. Instinct had her squeezing her thighs, but his palms prevented the motion. He spread her wider, and though she didn't look down, she swore she could *feel* his gaze on her. The heat of it. The intensity of it.

Pushing herself up, she balanced her weight on her elbows. Stared down her body as he hooked his fingers in the thin band of her panties and drew the scrap of material down her legs. Leaving her bare, exposed and completely vulnerable. But the fierce, undiluted hunger darkening his face banished those emotions. How could she feel vulnerable when he focused on her as if she were his sole purpose of existing in this moment? No, no. She didn't feel weak, she felt…empowered.

He wanted her just as much as she wanted him.

His thumb stroked between her folds, and she glimpsed how it glistened with the proof of her desire. Lifting his gaze to hers, Ezekiel brought his thumb to his mouth and licked it clean. If possible, his magnificent features tightened further, and an almost animalistic sound rumbled from him. Then he put his mouth on her.

A keening wail tore free from her throat as he dived into her sex. His tongue licked the same path his thumb had taken. Again and again, lapping at her. Devouring her. Destroying her. His hum of pleasure vibrated against her sensitive, swollen flesh, and she writhed beneath him. He left no part of her undiscovered, staking his claim on her as thoroughly as if he'd branded her. His lips closed around the bundle of nerves at the top of her sex, and he carefully drew on her, his tongue swirling, rubbing and teasing.

Desperate and coming undone, she settled her heels on the edge of the bed, widening her thighs and grinding into his relentless mouth. Electrical currents danced up and down her spine, and for a moment, she feared the power of this looming orgasm. Even as the pleasure swelled, she mentally scrambled back from it. Both wanting it to break and fearing the breaking.

But Ezekiel didn't grant her any quarter. He slid a finger and then another through her folds, then slowly pushed them inside her. Her sex immediately clamped down on them, and she cried out, arching hard, her hips twisting, bearing down. Pleading for more of that invasion. That fulfillment. Again, her mind whispered *too much*, but this time she didn't run from it but embraced it. She worked her hips, sexing his fingers even as she pushed into his mouth.

More. More. More.

"Take it then, sweetheart," Ezekiel encouraged her, and she realized she'd chanted the demand aloud. "Give it to me."

His urging and the stroking of his fingertips over a place high and deep inside her catapulted her into orgasm. She exploded, her cries bouncing off the walls, and he didn't stop, not until she weakly pushed at his head, her flesh too sensitive.

Lethargy rolled over her in a wave, and she sprawled on the mattress, unable to move. She could only stare as Ezekiel surged to his feet and quickly stripped himself of his remaining clothes.

Her breath stuttered as he bared that big, hard, gorgeous body. She'd already caressed and kissed his wide chest. But his lean hips, that V above them designed to drive women wild with lust, his powerful, muscular thighs, and God, his dick. Long, thick and wide, the swollen tip reached to just under his navel. Maybe she should feel some kind of trepidation at taking him inside her. But no, with the renewed rush of desire flooding her veins, she craved having him fill her. She ached for it. Maybe then this emptiness would dissipate.

Ezekiel paused to grab his wallet from his pants before tossing them aside. From the depths of the black leather billfold, he withdrew a couple of small square foils and tossed one on the bed before ripping open the other.

She waited for him, equal parts eagerness and nerves. There was no turning back—not that she wanted to. She didn't fool herself into believing there wouldn't be consequences for this decision. For both of them.

Yet, as he sheathed himself and climbed on the bed, crawling over her body, she didn't care about the costs. Not when his gaze burned into hers. Not when he settled between her thighs. Not when he cradled her face between his large palms.

Not when his cock nudged her entrance and slowly penetrated her.

She gasped at the welcome, coveted intrusion. Whimpered at the low-level fire of the stretching. Clutched his shoulders at the unmistakable sense of being claimed.

"Zeke," she whispered, burrowing her face into the nook between his throat and shoulder. "Please."

She shifted restlessly beneath him, unsure how to alleviate the pressure that contained both pleasure and the barest bite of pain. It'd been so long for her, that as he pushed, steadily burying himself inside her, she couldn't remain still. Had to find the position, the place that would relieve the ache…or agitate it more.

"Shh," he soothed, tilting her head up and brushing his mouth across hers. "Relax for me, Ray." Another stroke of his lips even as he continued to gain more access to her body, drive farther inside her. "Relax and take me. That's it," he praised, momentarily closing his eyes as she lifted her legs around his waist, locking her ankles at the small of his back. Allowing him to surge deeper. "Fuck, that's good, sweetheart. So good," he ground out.

He held himself still above her, only his mouth moving over hers, his tongue mimicking his possession of her body. She returned every kiss, losing herself in him. Gradually, the hint of pain subsided, and only pleasure remained. Pure, mind-bending pleasure.

On a gasp, she arched her neck, pressing her head back into the mattress. Savoring him buried so deep inside her. Impatience rippled through her, and she rocked her hips, demanding he move. Demanding he take her.

Levering off her chest, he stared down at her, green eyes bright, expression dark.

"Ready?" he growled.

"Yes," she murmured, curling her hands around his strong upper arms. "Please."

With his attention pinned on her face, he withdrew his length, the weightiness of it dragging over newly awakened nerves. She groaned, twisting beneath him. Needing more. Hating how empty she felt when she'd just been so full. But a jerk of his hips granted her wish. He plunged back inside her with a force that stole the air from her lungs, the thoughts from her head.

Over and over, he took her, thrusting, driving, riding. On the end of each stroke, he ground his hips against her so he massaged that swollen bundle of nerves cresting the top of her sex. She'd become a sexual creature void of rational thought, only craving the ecstasy each plunge inside her promised. She raced after it, writhing and bucking beneath him, demanding he give her everything, hold nothing back from her.

And he didn't.

Crushing his mouth to hers, he reached between their straining, sweat-slicked bodies and circled her clitoris, once, twice, and before he could finish the third stroke, she shattered.

She came with a scream, throwing her head back, body quaking with wave after wave of release. For a second, she fought the power of it. But as he continued to thrust into her, riding out the orgasm so she received every measure of it, she submitted to the pleasure, to the loss of control.

And as she dived into the black abyss, she didn't hesitate or worry.

Because she knew, at least for the moment, she wasn't alone.

Twelve

As Ezekiel steered his Jaguar up the quiet Pine Valley street, he glanced at his wife. *His wife.* He rubbed a hand over his beard before returning it to the steering wheel. Part of him still couldn't believe he could call Reagan Sinclair— no, Reagan Holloway—by that title. Not just bride. That ship had sailed when she led him to their master bedroom and stripped for him in a private show that had him nearly begging to put his hands on that pretty body. Stroke all that smooth, beautiful skin. Taste her mouth and the sweet flesh between her thighs.

He probably shouldn't be thinking about sex with his wife while driving down the road to his in-laws' house to drop some unwelcome news.

Especially when just the thought of Reagan naked beneath him, eyes glazed over with pleasure, her sensual demands for *more* pouring from her kiss-swollen lips, had him shifting uncomfortably in his seat.

Two days. He should've been back to Royal and Wingate Enterprises two days ago. They were supposed to fly to Vegas, tie the knot, then fly back. But after that first night with Reagan, drowning in an unprecedented lust that had seared him from the inside out, he'd extended their "honeymoon." They'd spent it in the suite. Talking. Laughing. Eating. Fucking.

And sleeping.

For the first time since Melissa, he'd slept beside a woman instead of leaving her bed or guiding her from his. And the guilt he'd expected to flay him alive had been absent. Which had only stirred the flood of conscience and shame that had been missing.

But not enough to drag him from his wife's bed or make him uncurl himself from around her warm, naked body to sleep on the couch. Because then she wouldn't be within easy reach when he woke up throbbing and hard for her.

It appeared he couldn't get enough of his new wife. In and out of bed. Although to be fair, they hadn't gone very far from the bed.

He smothered a sigh. Okay, so they'd crossed the platonic bridge and burned it in a blaze of glory behind them. But he hadn't lost complete control over this situation. They could carry on with their plan of living separate lives without emotional entanglements. Sex did blur the line a little, but it didn't obliterate it.

He and Reagan had set those boundaries for very good reasons.

And neither of them could afford to forget those reasons.

A kernel of unease wiggled into his chest. She'd already made him forget his priorities—saving Wingate Enterprises. He couldn't allow this kind of slip to become a habit.

Beside him, Reagan fidgeted. And not for the first or fifth time. Glancing down, he noticed her clenched fists on her lap. Before he could question the wisdom of it, he covered her hands with one of his and squeezed.

"It's going to be okay," he murmured.

She shook her head, a faint, wry smile tipping the corner of her mouth. "I ran off to Vegas with a man my parents disapprove of. I don't know which will send my mother into a coronary faster—the elopement or Vegas. And my father..." She shook her head, releasing a humorless chuckle. "I don't even want to imagine his reaction right now. I started all of this to take my inheritance and keep my family. But it might turn out that I lose both."

"You're borrowing trouble, Ray," Ezekiel said softly. "Your father might be stern and overbearing, but he loves you. He'll stand by you."

She huffed out a breath. "You don't know Douglas Sinclair. Not like I do. If there's one thing experience has taught me it's that he doesn't handle disappointment well. And he never, *ever* forgets."

He jerked his gaze from the road to throw her a sharp look. Something in her voice—bitterness, sorrow, pain... It wasn't the first time he'd detected that particular note, just as he'd noted her habitual stroking of that scar just below her neck.

Secrets. And if he was staring into her eyes, he would see the shadows of them there.

Moments later, her parents' home loomed into view and he steered the car up the driveway, pulling to a stop in front of the mansion.

"Reagan." He waited until she switched her gaze from the side window to him. "Whatever you face in there, I will be right beside you. I won't leave you."

Her lips twisted into a smile that in no way reached her eyes. They remained dark. Sad. The urge to demand she pour out her pain onto him, to insist she let him in swelled within him, shoving against his chest and throat. But before he could speak, she nodded and reached for the door handle.

"We should go in," she murmured, pushing the door open and stepping out.

Silent, he met her in front of the car and took hold of her hand. The warning to not muddy the boundaries rebounded against his skull as he raised her hand to his lips and brushed a kiss across the back of it. She glanced at him, and a glint of desire flickered in her eyes. Good. Anything to chase away the shadows.

Just as they cleared the top step, the front door opened, and Douglas Sinclair stood in the entrance. He stared at them, his scrutiny briefly dropping to their clasped hands before shifting back to his daughter.

He didn't greet them but moved backward and held the door open wider. Yet, nothing about his grim expression was welcoming. More likely he didn't want the neighbors to have a free show.

Settling a hand on Reagan's lower back, Ezekiel walked inside, lending her his strength. He valued family loyalty and acceptance. Understood the drive to give one and crave the other. Yet he hated how even while Reagan strode ahead, shoulders soldier-straight, head tilted at a proud angle, she did so with a fine tremor that echoed through her and into his palm.

"Reagan." Henrietta rose from the couch as soon as they entered the small salon. She crossed the room and cupped her daughter's shoulders, pressing a kiss to her cheek. "Where have you been? We've been calling you for days now. Honey, we were all so worried."

"I'm sorry, Mom," Reagan said, covering one of her mother's hands and patting it. "I had my phone turned off. I didn't mean to scare you."

Henrietta studied her daughter for a long moment before shifting her scrutiny to Ezekiel. "Ezekiel," she greeted with a nod. "It's good to see you again."

"You, too, Henrietta," he replied, slipping his hand up Reagan's spine to cup the nape of her neck.

"Mom, Dad, I have news," Reagan announced. "Zeke and I—" She broke off, and he squeezed the back of her neck, silently reassuring her. "Zeke and I are married. We eloped to Las Vegas. I'm sorry that you're finding out after the fact, but we—"

"I asked her to come away with me, and she did," he

interjected, but she shook her head, giving him a small but sad smile.

"No, he didn't. I asked him, and I know you're probably disappointed in my decision to elope, but it was my decision." She squared her shoulders. "*He* is my decision."

Surprise and no small amount of hurt flashed across her mother's face, but the older woman quickly composed her features. She shifted backward until she stood next to Douglas, who hadn't spoken. But his stern, forbidding frown might as well as have been a lecture.

Every protective instinct buried inside Ezekiel clawed its way to the surface, and he faced the other man, moving closer to Reagan. Letting it be known that she was his. And dammit, whether that claim had an expiration date or not, he would protect what was his.

"You deliberately went against my wishes, and now you show up here for, what?" Douglas demanded, his voice quiet thunder. "For our blessing? Our forgiveness? Acceptance? Well, you have none of them."

"No, not your blessing," Ezekiel said evenly, but he didn't bother hiding the steel or the warning in it. "And she nor I require forgiveness for a choice we made together as two consenting adults. Would your acceptance of our marriage be important to your daughter? Yes. But it's not necessary."

"It is if she—or you—want access to her inheritance," Douglas snapped. "Which isn't going to happen. Her grandmother gave me final say over who I deem suitable, and you are not it. Reagan knew that and yet she still defied my wishes, regardless that it would bring hurt and shame onto her family."

"Douglas," Henrietta whispered, laying a hand on her husband's arm.

"No, Henrietta, this needs to be said," he said. "I—"

"No, it doesn't," Reagan quietly interrupted. "It doesn't

need to be said, Dad, because I already know. You've made it very clear over the years—ten to be exact—that I have only brought disappointment, embarrassment and pain to this family. God knows I've tried to make up for it by being the respectable, obedient daughter, by following every rule you've laid down, by placing your needs and opinions above my own. But nothing I've done or will do will ever make up for me being less than worthy of the Sinclair name. For being less than perfect."

"Honey," Henrietta breathed, reaching a hand toward her daughter. "That's just not true."

That sense of foreboding spread inside Ezekiel, triggering the need to gather Reagan into his arms and shield her from the very people who were supposed to love her unconditionally. Because this was about more than an elopement or an inheritance. This—whatever it was that vibrated with pain and ugliness between these three—was older, burrowed deeper. And it still bled like a fresh wound.

"It's true, Mom," Reagan continued in that almost eerily calm voice. "We've just been so careful not to voice it aloud."

Ezekiel looked at Douglas, silently roaring at the man to say something, to comfort his obviously hurting daughter. To climb down off that high horse and tell her she was loved and accepted. Valued.

"If you think this 'woe is me' speech is going to change my mind about the inheritance, you're wrong." The same deep freeze in Douglas's voice hardened his face. "I hope your new *husband*..." he sneered the word "...with his own financial and legal troubles can provide for you. Although, that future is looking doubtful."

Fury blazed through Ezekiel, momentarily transforming his world into a crimson veil.

"Watch it, Douglas," he warned. "No one smears my family name. And since your daughter now wears it, she's included. I care for mine… I protect them above all else. And before you throw that recklessly aimed stone, you might want to ask yourself if you can claim the same."

"Don't you dare question me about how I protect my family," Douglas snapped. "All I have ever done, every decision, is for them. You, who has had everything handed to you merely because of your last name, know nothing about sacrifice. About the hard work it takes to ensure your family not only survives but thrives. About rising above what people see in order to be more than they ever believed you are possible of. You don't know any of that, Ezekiel *Holloway*. So don't you ever question my love for them. Because it's that love that convinces me that my daughter marrying you is the worst decision she could've ever made."

Anger seethed beneath Ezekiel's skin, a fiercely burning flame that licked and singed, leaving behind scorch marks across his heart and soul.

"I may be a Holloway, but I'm still a black man in Royal, Texas. You don't corner the market on that. When the world looks at me, they don't see my white father. They see a black man who should be grateful about being born into a powerful, white family. When they find out where I work and my position, they assume I'm only there because I'm Ava Holloway Wingate's nephew, not because I earned it by busting my ass working my way up in the company while attending college and receiving my bachelor's and master's." He huffed out a breath. "So don't talk to me about hard work or sacrifice, because I've had to surrender my voice and my choice at times so others can feel comfortable about sitting down at a table with me. I've had to work ten times harder just to be in the same place and receive the respect that others are given just because of the color of their skin."

He forced his fingers to straighten from the fist they'd curled into down by his thigh. "And I never questioned your love for your family. I just have reservations about the way you show it."

"Zeke," Reagan whispered, leaning into him. Offering support or comfort, he didn't know. Maybe both.

"Please, if we can all just calm down for a moment," Henrietta pleaded, glancing from her husband and back to Ezekiel and Reagan. "Before we all say something we can't take back."

"Mom, I'm afraid it's too late for that," Reagan said, a weariness that Ezekiel detested weighing down every word. "And I'm sorry for hurting you. Again." Inhaling a deep breath, she dipped her chin in her father's direction. "You, too, Dad."

She turned and walked out of the room, and Ezekiel followed, not giving her parents a backward glance. His loyalty belonged to the woman they'd just selfishly, foolishly rejected.

Fuck it. He would be her family now.

She had him. And no matter that their union was temporary, he would give her a family to belong to.

Thirteen

Funny how a person could have pain pouring from every cell of their body and still walk, breathe, *live*. Since arriving at her parents' house, she'd become the embodiment of agony, grief and rage. Yet, she managed to grab an overnight bag, descend the front steps, climb into Ezekiel's car, buckle up and not break down as he drove away from a house that had been her home all her life.

Like a horror-movie reel, the scene in the informal parlor played out across her mind. Only to rewind when it finished and start again.

Reagan squeezed her eyes shut and balled her hands in her lap. But all that did was twist the volume up in her head. She'd known deep down that her father blamed her for her past mistakes, had never forgiven her for them. And his accusations as well as his stony silence confirmed it. But still, oh God, did that *hurt*. It hurt so badly she longed to curl up in a ball on the passenger's seat and just disappear.

Be strong.

Never show weakness or emotion.

Be above reproach and avoid the very appearance of impropriety.

Those had been rules, creeds she'd lived by as a Sinclair. And except for when she'd fallen so far from grace at sixteen, she'd striven to live up to that hefty responsibility. But now, after living with so many cracks and fissures because of the pressure placed on her, she just wanted to break. Break into so many pieces until Reagan Sinclair could never be formed again.

Then who would be left? Who would she be?

God, she didn't know. And how pathetic was that?

"Reagan." Ezekiel's voice penetrated the thick, dark morass of her thoughts, and she jerked her head up. He stood in the opening of her car door. A car she hadn't realized he'd stopped and pulled over, and a door she hadn't heard him open. "Come on out."

He extended his hand toward her, his green eyes, so full of concern, roaming over her face. Slowly, she slid her palm over his and allowed him to guide her from the vehicle. Only then did she notice he'd parked on the side of a quiet, deserted road.

She recognized it. Several country roads twisted through Royal, some leading to the ranches that dotted the town and others leading to rolling fields filled with wildflowers. This one lay several miles outside her parents' gated community. A bend in the road and a thick copse of trees shielded them from anyone who might travel past the end of it. As Ezekiel closed the door behind her, turned her so he rested against the Jaguar and pulled her into his arms, she was thankful for the semi-privacy.

"Go ahead, sweetheart," he murmured against her head as he wrapped his arms around her, one big hand tunneling through her hair and pressing her to his chest. "Let it go. No one can see you here. Let it go because I have you."

The emotional knot inside her chest tightened, as if her body rebelled against the loosening storm inside of her. But in the next moment, the dam splintered, and the torrent spilled out. A terrible, jagged sob wracked her frame, and she buried her face against Ezekiel's chest as the first flood of tears broke through.

Once she started, she couldn't stop. How long she wept for that sixteen-year-old girl who'd been abandoned by the boy she'd loved and her family, Reagan couldn't say. It seemed endless, and yet, seconds. Fists twisted in his shirt, she clung to him, because at this moment, he was her port in a storm that had been brewing for years.

Eventually, she calmed, her harsh cries quieting to silent tears that continued to track down her cheeks. And even they stopped. Ezekiel cupped one of her hands and pressed a handkerchief into it.

"Thank you," she rasped, the words sore against her raw throat.

He stroked her back as she cleaned up the ravages of her weeping jag.

"I'm here if you want to talk. Or if you don't want to talk. Your choice, Reagan," he murmured.

The self-preservation of her family's demand for secrecy—as well as her own guilt—battled the urge to unload. But God, she was tired. So tired. Yes, she struggled with trusting people, in trusting herself. Maybe, just maybe, she could try to take a little leap of faith and trust him…

"When I was sixteen, I was involved with a boy—well, he was nineteen years old. My parents didn't approve of him. And in hindsight, I understand why. But back then, I was just so hopelessly in love with him and would've done anything for him. And I did. I rebelled against Dad and Mom. I saw him behind their backs, sneaked out at night to see him. He consumed my world as a first love usually does. But…" she swallowed, closing her eyes "…I ended up pregnant."

Ezekiel stiffened against her, and she braced herself for his reaction. Shock. Disbelief. Pity. Any or all of them would be like a punch to her chest.

He shifted, settling more against his car and drawing her between his spread thighs. Pulling her deeper into his big, hard body. Gentle but implacable fingers gripped her chin and tilted her head back.

"Open your eyes, sweetheart. Look at me."

She forced herself to comply, and her breath snagged in her lungs. Compassion. Tenderness. Sorrow. But no pity. No disappointment.

"You have nothing to be ashamed of, so don't look down while you give me your truth."

She stared at him. *Nothing to be ashamed of.* No one—not her parents, not her brother or sister—had ever said those words to her. But this man did. Against his wishes, she briefly closed her eyes. That or allow him to glimpse the impact of his assurance. He'd said her eyes reflected her feelings, and she didn't even want to identify the emotion that had her mentally backpedaling. Had fear rattling her ribs and clenching her stomach.

Shoving everything into a lockbox deep inside her, she drew in a breath and lifted her lashes, meeting that piercing green gaze.

"As you can expect, my parents didn't react well to the news. And yes, I was terrified. Yet I also believed my boyfriend when he said he would never leave me. What I hadn't counted on was that dedication not measuring up against the check my father waved in front of his face. Dad paid him off, and he disappeared. And my parents... They sent me away. To a girls' home in Georgia."

"I remember," Ezekiel said. "It was just before the school year ended, and Harley was upset because you wouldn't be with her for the summer. She never mentioned—"

"She didn't know," Reagan interrupted, shaking her head. "No one except my family did. My parents didn't want anyone to find out. I was supposed to go to the home, have the baby and adopt him or her out. I didn't want to give my baby up, but they were adamant. They were embarrassed and ashamed." The words tasted like ash on her tongue. "Especially my father. Before, we'd been close. I was a self-admitted daddy's girl, and there was no man greater than my father in my eyes. But afterward… He couldn't even look at me," she whispered.

"And this?" He gently pushed her fingers aside—the fingers that had been absently rubbing the scar on her collarbone.

"When I was about fourteen weeks, I started cramping. I didn't tell anyone for the first couple of days. But the third morning, pain seized my lower back so hard I doubled over and almost fainted. I did fall, and on the way down I clipped myself on the dresser." She again stroked the mark that would forever remind her of the worst day of her life. "I lay there on the floor, curled up, bleeding from the wound when I felt a—a wetness between my legs. I was miscarrying."

"Oh, Ray," Ezekiel whispered, lowering his forehead to hers, and his breath whispered across her lips. "I'm sorry."

"Spontaneous miscarriage, they called it," she continued, needing to purge herself of the whole truth. To cleanse herself of the stain of secrecy. "They told me there was nothing I could've done to prevent it, but I still felt responsible. That it was my punishment for disobeying my parents, for not being the daughter they deserved, for having unprotected sex, for not being good enough for my boyfriend to stay around, to love me—"

"Sweetheart, no," he objected fiercely, his brows drawing down in a dark frown as his head jerked back. "None of that is true. It happens. My mother suffered two miscarriages. One before me and one after me. It happens to good people, to women who would've made wonderful, loving mothers. It was biological, not penal." Worry flashed in his eyes. "Were you hurt more than you're telling me?"

"Do you mean can I still have children? Yes." Relief swept away the concern from his expression, but she shook her head. "But do I want to? I—I don't know." It was a truth she'd never admitted aloud. "It may have happened ten years ago, but the pain, the fear, the grief, the terrible emptiness..." She pressed a palm to her stomach. "I'll never forget it. And I'm terrified of suffering that again. I don't want to. Losing another child..." She turned her head away from his penetrating stare. "I don't know if I can."

"Reagan. Sweetheart. Will you look at me?"

Several heartbeats passed, but she returned her gaze to him.

He circled a hand around her nape, a thumb stroking the side of her neck while the other hand continued to cup her face. "You don't have to explain or justify anything to me. I get it. After my parents and then Melissa died, the thought of loving another person only to lose them to illness, fate or death paralyzes me. They don't give out handbooks explaining that one day that person might be snatched unfairly from us. No one prepared me for that, just as no one prepared you for the fact that you might lose your baby before you had the chance to hold him or her. And because no one did, we only get to dictate how we deal."

He stroked the pad of his thumb over her cheekbone, his gaze softening.

"Do I think you would one day make a beautiful, caring and attentive mother who would love your child as fiercely as the most protective mama bear? Yes. Do I believe you deserve to know the feeling of cradling a child in your arms, smelling their scent, hearing him calling you Mom? Yes, sweetheart. You deserve all of that and more. But I'm the last person to tell you you're wrong for being afraid of it. And Reagan...?"

He paused, his scrutiny roaming her face, alighting on her mouth, nose and finally eyes. She *felt* his tender survey like caresses on her skin. "If no one else has ever told you, I'm sorry. I'm sorry for the loss of your baby. I'm sorry the boy—because he's not worthy of the title of man—you believed would stand by you abandoned you instead. I'm sorry that you felt deserted by your family. And I'm sorry no one told you that in spite of—no, *because* of—your life lessons, you are even more precious."

The need to reassure him that he, too, deserved more trembled on her tongue. Ezekiel deserved a woman who adored him beyond reason. Who would be his soft place to land as well as the rock he leaned on in times of trouble. The thought of him alone, with the heart he so zealously guarded as his only companion, saddened her more than she could vocalize without betraying emotion either of them would be comfortable with.

So instead, she rose on her toes and pressed her mouth to his. Tried to convey her gratitude for his compassion and kindness. Attempted to relay everything she was too confused to say aloud.

Immediately, his lips parted under hers. His hold on her cheek slid into her hair, and his fingernails scraped her scalp, arrowing shivers of heat directly to her breasts, belly and lower, between her thighs.

Sorrow and hurt morphed to heat, kindling the desire inside her that never extinguished. Not for him. For Ezekiel Holloway, she was a pilot light that never went out.

His groan vibrated against her chest, then rolled into her mouth. She greedily swallowed it, the emotional turmoil of the last hour spurring her on to drown in him and this overwhelming pleasure that bore his personal stamp of ownership.

"Ray." He moaned her name, but his hands dropped to her shoulders as if to push her away. "Sweetheart."

"No," she objected. Stroking her hands over his hips and up his back, she curled her fingers into his shirt. Held on and pulled him tighter against her. "I want you. I want this. Don't deny me, Zeke," she said.

Demanded.

Pleaded.

His gaze narrowed on her, studying her. After the longest of moments, he shifted, spinning them around so she perched on the hood of the Jaguar and he stood between her spread thighs.

He flattened his palms on the metal beside her, leaning forward until she placed her hands next to his and arched her head back.

"I won't deny you anything," he growled.

Then his mouth crushed hers.

He hated the words as soon as he let them slip. Wanted to snatch them back. They revealed too much, when he should've been protecting his tender underbelly from exposure.

But with lust a ravenous beast clawing at his insides, he couldn't care right now. Not when her tongue dueled with his, sucking at him as if she couldn't get enough of him. Nipping at him as if she wanted to mark him. Licking him as if he were a flavor that both teased and never satisfied.

He should know.

Because as he sucked, nipped and licked her, all three were true for him.

This woman… *Goddamn.* She was ruining him with her sinful mouth, wicked tongue and hungry moans. Even now, he couldn't remember another's kiss, another's scent. Another's touch. And that traitorous thought should anger him, fill him with guilt. And maybe later it would. But now? Now, all he could do was dig his fingers through her hair, fist the thick strands and hold her steady for a tongue-fucking that had his dick throbbing for relief.

Nothing else mattered but her and getting inside her.

With fingers that were miraculously steady, he swept them over her jaw, down her throat, lingered on the scar that carried such traumatic memories for her and lower to the simple bow at her waist that held the top of her wrap dress together. He tugged on the knot, loosening it, and didn't hesitate to smooth his palms inside the slackened sides to push the material off her shoulders and down her arms to pool around her wrists.

Reagan started to lift her arms, but he stilled the movement. Instead, he gripped her wrists and pulled them behind her back. Trapped by her dress and his firm fingers, back arched, she was a gorgeous, vulnerable sacrifice for him. Only, as he lowered his head to drag his tongue down the middle of her chest to the shadowed, sweetly scented valley between her breasts, he was the one eager and willing to throw himself on the altar of his need for her.

God, he couldn't get enough of her taste. That honeysuckle scent seemed entrenched in her smooth, beautiful brown skin, and he was a treasure hunter, constantly returning for more.

Tracing the inner curve of her breast, he couldn't resist raking his teeth over it and satisfaction roared through him at the shiver that worked through her body. He'd earned a PhD in the shape and map of her body in the last few days, and yet, every time he discovered a new area that caused her to quake or whimper, he wanted to throw back his head and whoop in victory. He'd never get tired of eliciting new reactions from her, of giving her new things to shatter over.

And that was a problem since he was letting her go in a year.

Smothering the thought that tried to intrude on the desire riding him, he refocused all of his attention on the flesh swelling above the midnight blue lace of her bra. And the hard tip beneath it. Bringing his free hand into play, he tugged down the cup, baring her breast to him. Then, pinching and teasing the silk-and-lace-covered nipple, he drew its twin into his mouth.

He couldn't contain his rumble of pleasure as he stroked, lapped and sucked on her. Part of him believed he was obsessed with her—the last four days pointed toward this. His preoccupation now further emphasized it. How he took his time circling the beaded nub, relearning her although he'd just had her before they left their suite that morning to board the plane home.

The other part of him wanted to get down on his knees and beg her to push him away, ban him from her bed so he could wean himself off an addiction that could only destroy them both in the end.

"Zeke," Reagan gasped, twisting and arching up to him, thrusting her flesh into his mouth. Demanding her pleasure. "I need you," she said on the tail end of a whimper.

Fuck if he didn't love that sound from her. Every needy, insatiable sound that telegraphed her hunger for him.

As he'd said before, he couldn't deny her anything.

Shifting his head, he freed the other breast and reintroduced it to his mouth. Over and over he tongued the tip, swirling and teasing, pulling and worshipping.

Because she *deserved* to be worshipped.

And not just because of this body that could make a grown man find religion. But because she had a strength of spirit and character as well as a spine of steel underneath the genteel socialite demeanor. Because she'd taken her own tragedy and now planned to offer a safe haven to girls who faced the same difficulties.

Because she was just *good*.

Inexplicably, desperation surged through him, and he reached around her to unhook her bra and then rid her of both it and the top still trapping her wrists. He didn't question the need to feel her arms wrapped around him; he just surrendered to it.

He didn't even know how to begin to articulate the request—but simply grasped her hands and drew them forward, clasping them behind his neck. Then he buried his face in the crook between her throat and shoulder, inhaling her scent, opening his mouth over that sensitive spot, savoring the crush of her chest to his.

Yes, he'd been with more women than he could place names and faces to, but none had *held* him. He hadn't allowed it. And now, with Reagan, he craved it as much as he needed to be buried balls-deep inside her. And that need had him backing away from her mentally and physically, his ingrained self-protective instinct kicking him in the chest.

"Zeke?" she murmured, but he stopped the question with his mouth, and anything she would've asked translated into a groan.

As their mouths engaged in a hot, dirty battle, she gripped the front of his shirt and tackled his buttons. Within seconds, she tossed his shirt onto the hood behind him and raked her nails down his bare chest. Over his nipples. Down his abs. To the waistband of his pants.

The air in his lungs sawed in and out as she tugged at his leather belt, loosening it, then opened the closure tab. He didn't stop her—could barely drag in a damn full breath, much less move—when she lowered his zipper and dipped her hand inside his black boxer briefs.

He hissed as her fingers closed around his length, bowing his head so his cheek pressed to hers and he fisted the skirt of her dress. Pleasure spiked up his spine, locking his body. Gritting his teeth, he dipped his head lower, staring at the erotic sight of her slender, elegant fingers curled around his dick. The tips nearly-but-not-quite met around his width, and the brutish, swollen head peeked above her hand. As both of them watched, his seed pearled, and he damn near choked as she spread the drop over his flesh.

Ezekiel almost came on the spot when she lifted her thumb and slid it between her lips.

"What are you trying to do to me, Reagan?" he grunted,

taking her mouth and licking deep. "You want this to end before I even get inside you?" He nipped her full bottom lip in punishment. "You want to see me lose it?"

The question sounded close to an accusation, and a small, utterly wicked smile teased her lips. "Yes. I want you to come *undone* for me."

And then she took him in her hand again, stroking him from tip to base. Squeezing. Up and down, her fist rode him, dragging him to the edge. Undoing him just as she'd claimed.

His stomach caved with each tight caress, each twist of her fist. Bolt after hot bolt of lust attacked him, sizzling through his veins and gathered in his sac. So close. So fucking close.

But he didn't want to spill on her hand. When that happened, there was only one place he wanted to be.

Deep inside her.

Grabbing his wallet from his back pocket, he removed a condom and, in record time, sheathed himself, gritting his teeth against the pressure rapidly building inside him. With hands that should've been rough and hurried but were instead reverent and gentle, he swept higher and higher up her thighs until he reached her lace-covered sex.

For a moment, the lust almost overwhelmed him, drove him to grab, tug and claim. *Possess.* But his affection for her tempered the urge, and he eased her underwear from her with exquisite care. His concern for her had him slip his discarded shirt under her back to protect her skin from the warm metal of the car. His longing for her had him palming her thighs, holding her wide for his ravenous gaze and hard flesh as he pushed inside her. Watching her open for him, welcome him.

He glanced up her torso, over her trembling breasts to her face. And had to grab ahold of his frayed control with a desperate grip when he found her gaze trained on them joined between her legs, too.

"You see how you're taking me, sweetheart?" he whispered. Her eyes flicked to his and the heat there set a match to the already blazing conflagration in his body. "Perfect. You were made to do it. And I was created to fill you."

He didn't speak anymore...couldn't. Everything in him—every muscle, tendon, cell—focused on burying himself in the tightest, sweetest flesh. Tremors quivered through him, and he fought the need to thrust like a wild animal.

"Don't hold back from me, Zeke," she breathed, lying back on the hood and smoothing her palms down her body to cover his hands over her toned thighs. "Come. *Undone.*"

Her wish, her order snapped the cord tethering his control. He fell over her, pulling a taut nipple into his mouth as he thrust inside her over and over. Her legs and arms cradled him, her hips rising and bucking to meet each stroke. And her hoarse, primal cries for *more* spurred him on as he rode her.

Thank God.

He hoped if she'd asked him to stop, he would be able to. He prayed he would've managed it. But with her nails digging into his bare shoulders, the heels of her shoes pressed into his ass, he was so goddamn glad that fortitude wouldn't be tested. Not when sweat dotted his skin, lust strung him tighter than a drum, and pleasure barreled down on him like a train with greased tracks and no brakes.

"Let go, sweetheart," he rumbled, levering off her to reach between them and rub the swollen little nub at the top of her clenching sex.

She bowed hard, and seconds later, her core clamped down on him, nearly bruising him in her erotic embrace. She milked him, coaxing his release, and with several short, hard thrusts, he gave it to her.

Gave it to *them*.

A bone-deep lethargy swept through him, and right under it hummed a satisfaction that burrowed even deeper. Easing off Reagan, he took care of the condom, helped her dress and then righted himself. They didn't speak, but they did communicate. She clasped his hands in hers, brushing her lips over his chin and jaw. And he took her mouth, relaying how beautiful and desirable he found her.

Long moments later, he held the car door open and guided her inside before closing it behind her and rounding the hood. Jesus, he would never be able to drive the Jaguar again and not think of what happened on top of it today. And the fact that a smile eased onto his face at the thought should've alarmed him. Maybe when his body wasn't loose and relaxed after the best sex he ever had, it would.

His cell phone rang as he slid behind the steering wheel. Silently groaning, he reached for it. Damn. He'd forgotten that he'd powered his phone back on a couple of hours ago for the first time since leaving for Vegas. Yes, he'd been out of the office and unavailable for longer than, well, ever, but he wasn't ready to face everything head-on yet. He glanced at the screen, intending to note the caller ID and then send the call to voice mail. But when his brother's name popped up, he hesitated.

It was Luke. And he was most likely worried.

Shit.

Swiping the answer bar, Ezekiel lifted the phone to his ear. "Hey, Luke."

"Where the hell have you been?" his brother roared.

Pinching the bridge of his nose, he glanced over at Reagan to find her studying him, eyebrows arched.

"Vegas. I instructed Laura to let everyone know I would be out of town and to reschedule anything that came up," he said calmly. "I'm a married man, by the way."

"Congratulations," Luke said, even if it seemed to

emerge through gritted teeth. "But Laura said a couple of days, not four."

"Yes, I took two more days," Ezekiel ground out, trying not to snap. "What's the big damn deal, Luke? Yes, we're in trouble, but the company isn't going to collapse while I take some vacation time."

Silence greeted his outburst.

An ominous silence that sent dread crawling down his spine. "Luke?" His grip on his cell tightened until the case bit into his palm. "What's going on? What's wrong?"

A heavy sigh echoed down the line. "I'm sorry, Zeke. Sorry for coming at you like I did." Luke paused, and because they were so in tune with each other, Ezekiel could easily imagine his brother scrubbing a hand over his head in frustration. "And wish I could've called you with better news when you just returned from your honeymoon, but... Zeke, the shit has hit the fan."

"What?" Ezekiel snarled, his heart pounding so loud against his chest he could barely hear his brother above the din. "Dammit, tell me, Luke."

"With our assets frozen, the company hasn't been able to cover debts. One of them being the estate." Luke's voice thickened, and Ezekiel's throat closed in response. "Zeke, the bank foreclosed on our home. Everyone's been forced to move out. Harley is living with Grant until their move back to Thailand. Beth's gone to live with Camden. Sebastian and Sutton are renting a house together, and I'm crashing with a friend for now. But Aunt Ava..." Again Luke paused, and his dark rumble of anger reverberated in Ezekiel's ear. "She's moved in with Keith."

"Goddammit," Ezekiel snarled. Out of his peripheral vision, he caught Reagan's head snapping toward him. Her arm stretched across the console and she clasped his free hand in hers. "He's taking advantage of her, Luke, and using the situation to get her under his thumb. Just when

we were starting to get her back to her old self after Uncle Trent's death. Now she's…" He trailed off, squeezing his eyes closed. "How is this all happening?" he whispered. "Why is this…"

"I don't know, Zeke," came his brother's solemn answer. "I really don't."

Fourteen

"Reagan, can I just say again how much I appreciate you agreeing to help with the masquerade ball?" Her pretty green eyes shining, Beth Wingate reached across the table in the small meeting room in the Texas Cattleman's Clubhouse and squeezed Reagan's hand. "Especially since Zeke volunteered you without asking first. I hope you know I warned my cousin against making that a habit in your marriage," she drawled.

Reagan laughed, waving away the other woman's concern. "It's no problem at all, really. With Dad being a member of the club for so long, I'm no stranger to helping out with the events they've sponsored. Honestly, I'm happy to help out in any way I can."

"Good, I'm glad." Beth gave Reagan's hand one last squeeze. "And since I haven't yet had the opportunity to congratulate you on your new marriage, congratulations." Her smile dimmed a little, shadows entering her eyes. "I know this wasn't the homecoming you were expecting though. And I'm sorry you had to return to this...mess."

Reagan didn't have to ask to what *mess* Beth referred. Until two weeks ago, the oldest Wingate daughter had been living on the estate with her family. But now she resided with her fiancé, Camden Guthrie, due to the foreclosure on the family properties.

Beth, lovely and elegant with a slim build and dark blond

hair, had always been the epitome of composure and grace. But even she appeared a little tired and strained despite re-uniting months ago with her first love. The trials the family faced obviously weighed on her. And having to continue to organize the TCC's charity masquerade must be one more added pressure.

"The masquerade ball is next month, in October, and even though a few people have regrettably returned their tickets because of our...association with the event, ticket sales are still steady. At least most folks are more interested in attending the social event of the year than in shunning the Wingates." Beth's mouth straightened into a grim line before she shook her head. "Anyway, I really hate that our family issues are overshadowing your marriage, Reagan."

"Please don't apologize, Beth. Our vows included 'for better or worse.' We're just experiencing a bit of the worse right now." Reagan shrugged a shoulder, the relaxed gesture belying the tangle of knots in her stomach. "Besides, it's not like we have the most conventional of marriages."

"Do any of us?" Harley chimed in from next to her. Her childhood friend tipped her head to the side, her long, straight brown hair falling over her shoulder as she studied Reagan. "I mean, Beth reunited with her long-lost love after a ton of lies and secrets. I had a whole secret baby scandal. But the point is we ended up with the men we love and who love us in return."

"Isn't that just like happy couples? You're in love so you see it everywhere." Reagan huffed a chuckle. As delighted as she was to have her old friend back in Royal after five years—even if it was only until after her upcoming wedding—she'd forgotten about Harley's stubbornness. "I adore you like a sister, Harley, but I don't want you to start making Zeke and me into the next fairy tale. We married so I could receive my inheritance, that's all." Even though that goal didn't look obtainable at the moment.

Harley waved away Reagan's objection. "I know, I know, that's the party line between you and Zeke. Regardless of the hows and whys, I'm just glad my best friend and my cousin are together. You make a great couple. And I believe you're good for each other."

Before Reagan could reply, Gracie Diaz swept into the meeting room. "Hey, everyone. I'm so sorry I'm late," she said, the apology slightly breathless.

Reagan remembered Gracie Diaz from her time spent at the Wingate estate. Only a couple of years older than her, Gracie had been the daughter of a family ranch hand, and later, hired by Beth as an assistant for the various charities she managed. Even though there'd been a difference in their statuses, she and Beth were very good friends. But more recently, Gracie had become a national celebrity for winning the sixty-million-dollar Powerball lottery. She was Royal's own rags-to-riches story.

As the stunning brunette pulled out one of the chairs and sat—no, collapsed—onto it, Reagan narrowed her eyes, studying her. Nothing could detract from the beauty of Gracie's thick, dark hair and lovely brown eyes, but Reagan still couldn't help but notice the faint circles under slightly puffy eyes, as if she'd recently been crying.

"No problem, Gracie." Beth frowned, scooting to the edge of her seat and wrapping an arm around her friend's shoulders. Pulling her close for a quick hug, she said, "Now don't take this the wrong way, hon, but you look terrible." Gracie snorted, and Beth grinned at the other woman. "The masquerade plans can wait. What's going on?"

Gracie propped her elbows on the table and pressed her palms to her forehead. "I swear, since winning the lottery and all that money, I've vacillated between being eternally thankful and cursing the day my numbers pulled up." She sighed, and the sound contained so much exhaustion, Reagan winced in sympathy. "Growing up, I never did understand the saying *more money, more problems*, because we never had money. But now…"

"Gracie, what's happened?" Harley pressed, leaning forward and clasping her upper arm.

"You must not have seen the news today," Gracie said, tunneling her fingers through her hair, then dragging the thick strands away from her face. "Apparently my cousin is claiming he bought the lottery ticket, and I stole it from him. Now he's insisting I turn more than half the winnings over to him. Which is ridiculous. I haven't seen my uncle's son in years, but now suddenly I'm a thief who steals from family."

Reagan snatched her phone from her purse, and in moments, brought up the local news' website and viewed the clip posted at the top of the home page. Apparently Gracie's family drama had temporarily replaced the Wingates as the newest scandal. Silently, she watched as a reporter interviewed Alberto Diaz outside Royal's town hall. He claimed that he was devastated and angry that his own cousin could betray him. Convincing sorrow etched his features as he gave his forgiveness to Gracie, but still demanded half of the money.

The sound bite skipped to the same reporter racing to reach Gracie as she opened her car door. Understandably, Gracie was angry at the accusation and refuted the lie before ducking into her car and driving off.

"He's lying," Reagan declared, dropping her phone onto the table.

"Of course he is," Harley agreed fiercely, her eyes blazing. "I can't believe they even gave him airtime for that. They're no better than a tabloid spreading that garbage."

"Yes, well, unfortunately, people thrive on that kind of trash. And it's easier for them to believe the salacious things than the truth." Gracie lifted her hands, palms up. "I'm sorry. I didn't mean to unload this on all of you. There's nothing I can do about it right now."

"You're going to fight him, aren't you?" Beth demanded.

"Oh, you're damn right," Gracie seethed. "I don't mind helping family out. I'm buying Mom a new home in Florida so she can be closer to her sister, and I'm paying for my brother to attend a private school so he can achieve every one of his dreams. So, if Alberto would've asked me for help, for money, I would've gladly given it to him. But this? Accusing me of a crime and trying to extort half of my winnings? That's blackmail, and I'm not giving in to it."

"Good for you!" Reagan praised, admiring this woman's grit and backbone. "And if there's anything we can do, just let us know. You got us in your corner ready to fight."

For the first time since she entered the room, Gracie smiled. "Thank you, Reagan. All of you." She pressed her palms to the tabletop. "Okay, enough about my unscrupulous family woes. Where are we with the masquerade ball?"

Beth covered her friend's hand and squeezed before picking up a paper and passing it to Harley. "I was just about to tell Harley and Reagan about the Cinderella Sweepstakes."

"Anything with Cinderella in it, I'm for it," Reagan teased, accepting the sheet Harley held out to her.

"I know, right?" Beth grinned. "You have the details there, but the gist of it is the local radio station offered a free makeover and ticket to one lucky winner. And considering each ticket is a thousand dollars, this is a wonderful opportunity. The station came up with the name Cinderella Sweepstakes. Isn't that perfect? The contest should bring more publicity and money to the ball. Fingers crossed. With all of us working together, it's going to be a wonderful success this year."

The meeting continued for the next couple of hours, and by the time Reagan left the clubhouse and pulled up outside the small town house rental she and Ezekiel had moved into, satisfaction was a warm glow inside of her. Satisfaction and excitement.

Working with the Wingate women and Gracie had stirred ideas about a possible fundraiser for the girls' home where she volunteered. With her father withholding her inheritance, Reagan might not be able to build her own home anytime soon, but that didn't mean she couldn't come up with an alternative to support the unwed and pregnant girls who needed help. And that included investing her time.

But with Ezekiel and his family feverishly working to salvage what was left of Wingate Enterprises, that time might be reduced as she needed to look for a job. She refused to just stand by while her husband exhausted himself to support her.

An agenda other than love might've been behind their marriage, but she meant what she'd told Beth earlier. For better or worse. And though their union had a time limit, she would stand beside him for however long she wore his last name.

Longer.

Climbing from the car, she shut the door behind her and strode up the short walk to the front door.

"Reagan," someone called behind her.

Lowering the key she'd been about to slide into the door, Reagan turned and smiled as Piper Holloway, Ezekiel's aunt, approached her, carrying a large brown-paper-covered parcel.

"Here, let me get that for you," Reagan said, hurrying toward the other woman.

But Piper laughed. "No need. I'm fine. Believe me, running an art gallery as many years as I have has given me muscles you probably can't see." Reaching Reagan, she leaned over and brushed an airy kiss over her cheek. "I have a little housewarming gift for you and my sneaky nephew." She tsked, shaking her head. "Running off to get married without a word to any of us. If I wasn't so happy for both of you, I'd be more than a little upset I didn't get to stand beside you two on your wedding day."

"It was a little spur-of-the-moment, otherwise I know he would've wanted you there," Reagan murmured. It was true. While Ava Wingate could be a little standoffish, her younger sister Piper was incredibly open and warm. Harley, at least, had preferred her aunt's company and easy affection to her mother's frequent criticism. "And thank you for the gift. You didn't have to travel all the way from Dallas to bring it."

"My pleasure. I wanted to congratulate you two in person anyway."

"Well, I know Zeke will be pleased to see you," Reagan said, turning back to the door and unlocking it. "Come on in."

She stepped back and allowed Piper to enter first. "Hey, Zeke, I'm back," Reagan announced, shutting the door behind her. "Look who I found outside—" She drew to a halt, spying that Ezekiel wasn't alone. "Oh, I'm sorry. I didn't know you had company."

"Hey, sweetheart," Ezekiel greeted, striding forward. He pressed a quick kiss to her lips, then, removing the package from his aunt's grasp, drew her in for a one-armed hug. Reagan's lips tingled, and she forced herself not to touch them. *Part of the show,* she reminded herself. *It's all for show.* "Aunt Piper, I didn't know you were coming over."

"I'm that impolite guest that just drops by unannounced," she joked, wrapping an arm around her nephew's waist and squeezing.

Ezekiel chuckled. "Never impolite or unwelcome. Have you met Brian Cooper?" He turned toward the tall, dark-haired man standing next to the living room couch. "Reagan, Aunt Piper, this is Brian Cooper, an attorney from the Dallas area. His uncle is Keith Cooper."

Surprise winged through Reagan at that bit of news. Why would Keith's nephew be here at their home? Especially considering how Ezekiel felt about the man his aunt Ava had moved in with.

"Brian," Ezekiel went on, "I'd like to introduce you to my wife, Reagan, and my aunt, Piper Holloway."

"It's nice to meet you both." Brian crossed the small room and shook hands with both of them.

Although, his gaze lingered on Piper.

O-kay.

With sharpened interest, Reagan studied the other man and woman. Piper, slim, tall, with her edgy, short cut and dark green eyes, was an older, beautiful, sophisticated woman. And apparently Brian, who couldn't look away from her, seemed to agree. They did make a striking couple. And from the way Piper tried—and failed—not to study the younger man from under her dark lashes, she had to notice how handsome the attorney with the athletic build was.

As if he could sense her thoughts, Brian glanced at her, and Reagan arched an eyebrow, a smile tugging at the corner of her mouth. "So you're from Dallas, too?" she asked. "Piper owns one of the most influential and prestigious art galleries there."

"Holloway Gallery downtown?" Brian asked Piper.

"Yes, that's me," Piper acknowledged. "Have you been in before?"

"Yes, I've been to a couple of shows there." He slid his hands into the front pockets of his pants. "The gallery isn't far from my office. Maybe we could get together for a cup of coffee soon."

"We'll see," she murmured, then switched her attention to her nephew. "Since I didn't get an invite to the wedding—and don't think I'm letting you off the hook for that anytime soon—I brought by a painting for your new home."

The next half hour flew by, and when Piper and Brian

left, Reagan closed the door behind them, then whipped around to face Ezekiel.

"I think your friend has a crush on your aunt," she teased.

He snorted. "I hate it for him if he does, because even I felt that brush-off."

"Yeah, it was kind of obvious. Why do you think she did? Piper tried to hide it, but she kept peeking at him." Reagan frowned. "You think maybe she's self-conscious about the age difference? Which is silly. He is younger, but she's a gorgeous, vivacious and successful woman. Any man, regardless of age, would be lucky to have her look their way."

"Sweetheart, are you really asking me to think about my aunt's dating habits? As far as I'm concerned, she's a virgin," Ezekiel drawled.

Laughing, Reagan strode across the floor to him. After a brief hesitation, she pressed against him and circled her arms around his neck. Rising to her toes, she kissed him, and the desire that never banked for him flickered into higher, hotter flames.

They hadn't drawn up rules dictating this new turn in their relationship. Part of her was okay with it—no rules meant she couldn't break them when she just wanted to casually touch him like this. But the other part of her needed to know what they were doing. Because every time she kissed him, touched him, woke up next to him, she couldn't stop craving more. Even if her mind warned her against that greed, that it could only end in heartache, her heart didn't seem to be heeding the memo.

Because somewhere along the line, her heart had chosen him. Maybe when she'd come upon him visiting his ex-fiancée's grave. Maybe when he'd laid his head in her lap and allowed her to help ease some of his burden. Maybe when he hadn't judged her after she'd revealed her past.

Did it really matter when? Her stupid, never-learn-its-damn-lesson heart had thrown itself at him, and he was Teflon. At sixteen, her reckless, headfirst dive into love could be chalked up to immaturity. But this dizzying, terrifying leap? She was going in knowing Ezekiel didn't want her future, her affection outside of the bedroom, and most certainly not her love.

And yet...

Yet he had it. All of her.

"How was your day?" Ezekiel asked, planting one last kiss against her mouth.

"Good." She forced a smile to her lips even though it trembled. "I spent time at the girls' home, then headed over to the clubhouse for a meeting with Beth, Harley and Gracie about the masquerade ball. I bought tickets for us, by the way. I wanted to get ours before they were sold out—what? What's wrong?"

"Nothing. Go ahead with what you were saying." Ezekiel shrugged, stepping back and heading out of the small foyer toward the living room.

No, she hadn't imagined that flicker of unease in his eyes or the tightening of his mouth. Something had triggered his reaction. Running her words through her head, she stared at his back and the tense set of his wide shoulders.

"Zeke, if it's about the tickets... If you'd prefer not to attend the ball because of everything that's going on, I fully understand. It's just that the rest of your family is going, and I thought you'd want to be there as well. But I can—"

"Ray," he said, voice soft but firm. "We're going to the ball. Please drop it. Everything's fine."

No. Everything *wasn't* fine, but he wouldn't share with her. Since returning from Vegas, Ezekiel had grown increasingly distant. Not physically—he was as passionate and insatiable with her as ever. Even more so in some ways. As if an element of desperation had crept into the sex. But a wall had sprung up around his emotions. Like now. He stood mere feet away from her, but he might as well as be on the other side of Royal. Or at the office, where he spent hours and hours into the night trying to salvage his family's business.

Speaking of...

"What are you doing home so early?" she asked. "It's only six, and usually you're still at the office. Did something happen?"

He shook his head, a faint smile playing at the corner of his sensual lips. "No, sweetheart. Everything's fine. I just asked Brian to meet me here instead of at the office. I wanted to talk with him about the legal issues with your inheritance. And I didn't want to do that at the office."

"I wondered about that. Are you sure you can trust him? I know how you feel about his uncle."

Ezekiel rubbed his bearded jaw. "I really like him in spite of who he's related to. I've met him before, and he's always struck me as a good guy. And a damn good attorney. He promised to look into your grandmother's will and see if there's a way to get around your father's hold on your inheritance."

"That's good," she said. "Do you think maybe you could ask him to look into something else as well?" She relayed the circumstances around Gracie and her cousin. "Maybe knowing what legal claim her cousin actually has will give her some ammunition going into this battle."

"Damn, I hate that for Gracie. This money should be a blessing, not a curse." Ezekiel pulled his cell phone from his pants pocket, then tapped out something on the screen. "I have something even better. I'll ask Miles if he can find out anything on this cousin. If he isn't able to, then it can't be found."

Miles Wingate, Ezekiel's cousin, owned Steel Security, a company that protected high-powered clients both physically and online. No doubt he could unearth any information on Alberto Diaz.

"Thanks, Zeke. I'm sure Gracie would appreciate it."

"She's family," he said simply, and for him, that was it. Family took care of family.

"Oh, I have some potentially good news," Reagan announced, circling around Ezekiel and picking up the coffee cups and saucers on the table in front of the couch. "I let the supervisor over at the home know that I would be cutting back on my volunteer time since I would be looking for employment. And she said an administrative position might be opening with the organization, and she would put my name in for it. With my experience there, she thinks I would be a good fit. So not only would I have a job but at a place I love."

"That's wonderful, sweetheart," he murmured. "I hope it works out."

There it was again. That note in his voice. That flash of emotion across his face and in his eyes.

"Zeke," she said, the cups and plates suddenly weighing down her arms.

"Reagan." He stepped closer, cradling her face and tilting his head down. He placed a tender kiss on her forehead, then nudged her chin up to look into her eyes. "Seriously, with your passion for their project, they would be fools not to snatch you up." He took the cups and saucers from her. "How about going out for dinner tonight?"

With a kiss to her temple, he left the living room for the kitchen, leaving her to stare behind him.

He couldn't fool her. Something *was* bothering him.

But why didn't he share it with her? What was he *not* telling her?

And why did the thought of it have unease curdling in her stomach?

Fifteen

Ezekiel sipped from his glass of whiskey as he stared out the dark window of his new living room. This late at night, he couldn't see much, but he knew what lay beyond the glass. And the view of the tiny, fenced-in backyard with its postage-stamp-size patio couldn't be more different than the rolling, green hills of the ranch where he'd lived for so many years.

I would be cutting back on my volunteer time since I would be looking for employment.

I bought tickets for us, by the way.

He lifted an arm, pressed a palm to the wall and bowed his head. But that did nothing but amplify the words ricocheting in his head. *Dammit.* Straightening, he tipped his glass back and downed the rest of the alcohol. As it blazed a path down his throat, he welcomed the burn when it hit his chest. Anything was better than the dread and hated sense of inevitability that usually resided there these days.

God knows, he wasn't one of those men who preferred that their women not work. They needed to feel fulfilled and purposeful, too. But that wasn't why Reagan was seeking a job. *He* was the reason. The scandal and the resulting fallout that threatened his family's company and reputation and his own investments. They were living off his savings right now, and they weren't anywhere near the poorhouse, but to Reagan…

He huffed out a hard, ragged breath.

Her father had been right. Ezekiel might be able to provide for her, but he couldn't protect her from the whispers, the condemnation, the scorn. He'd married her so she could have freedom and all he'd given her was a prison sentence to a man and family scarred by scandal. He'd failed her in every way that counted. At least to him as a man, a husband. Hell, he'd had to call another man and ask him for help to solve his wife's problem. Because he couldn't do it himself.

Just today, they'd had to lay off more employees from Wingate. Employees who depended on him, on his family, for their livelihoods. And all he could do was sit in his office with his thumb up his ass futilely trying to figure out a way to help. To do fucking *something*.

If he couldn't save his family's company, how could he possibly help Reagan save her inheritance, help her achieve her dream of a home for unwed, pregnant teens here in Royal? Help her have the life, the future she wanted?

The answer was simple.

He couldn't.

He'd failed Melissa so many years ago. He'd failed the Wingates.

He'd failed Reagan.

And with her beautiful, wounded heart, her indomitable spirit and strength, she deserved better. So much better.

Better was a man who could protect her from the ugliness of life and follow through on his promises.

Better was a man who was brave enough to love her without fear.

Better was not him.

"Zeke?"

Lowering his arm, he pivoted to find Reagan standing in the hall entrance, a black nightgown molding to her sensual curves. The sucker punch of desire to his gut wasn't a surprise. By now, he accepted that he wouldn't be able to look at her, to be in the same damn state as her, and not want her.

He turned back to the window.

"What're you doing up, Reagan?" He'd waited until she'd fallen asleep, their skin still damp from sex, before he'd left their bed.

"I should ask you that same question. And I am. What's wrong, Zeke?" Moments later, her fingers curled around the hand still holding the empty tumbler. She gently took it from him, setting it on the table behind them. "And don't tell me nothing again. I can see how stressed you are. How tired. It's Wingate, isn't it?"

He didn't immediately reply, mentally corralling and organizing his words. But when he parted his lips, nothing of the pat, simple reply emerged.

"When I told Luke about our engagement, he accused me of trying to save you. Because I failed with Melissa."

"Failed with Melissa?" she repeated. "Zeke, she died in a car accident."

"Yes." He nodded, images of that night so long ago flashing across the screen of his mind. "But what you don't know is I was supposed to be in the car that night. I was supposed to be driving. If I had been, maybe..." He didn't finish the thought, but he didn't need to. He'd repeated the words so often over the years, they were engraved on his soul.

"Then maybe you would both be dead," Reagan said, grasping his upper arm and tugging until he turned from the window and looked down at her.

Dammit. He hadn't wanted to do that. Would've avoided staring down into her beautiful face if he had his way. Because those espresso eyes, elegant cheekbones and lush mouth unraveled his already frayed resolve.

"There is no guarantee that you would've been able to save her. The only person responsible for her death is the drunk driver who crashed into her. This isn't your burden to bear, Zeke."

He heard her—had heard the same from Luke, Harley and Piper over the years. But the guilt remained. It burrowed down deep below bone and marrow.

"You know, when I first told Luke I asked you to marry me, he accused me of having a savior complex—of trying to rescue you, because I couldn't do the same with Melissa. I told Luke that wasn't true," he continued, not addressing her assertion of his innocence. "And at the time, I believed it. Melissa had nothing to do with you, and I wasn't trying to save you. But now..." He gently removed her hand from his arm. "Now, I think he had a point, and I was fooling myself into believing I could help you. Provide for you. *Protect* you. I can't, Reagan. Your father was right, and we both know it."

Shock blanked her eyes and parted her lips. Her soft gasp echoed in the room, and he locked his arms at his sides to keep from wrapping her in them. When he'd suggested this arrangement those months ago, his goal had been to avoid the pain that gleamed in her gaze. But now, to be the cause of it... He closed his eyes, yet seconds later reopened them. He did this; it would be a coward's move not to face it.

"When I asked you to marry me—when you agreed— this wasn't the life you envisioned, and it wasn't the one I promised you. Your father said I couldn't take care of you, that I would only bring you hardship and scandal, and he was right. I took away the life you've known, the one you deserve. Because of me, you're estranged from your family and still don't have access to your inheritance."

"You don't know what you're saying, Zeke."

"Yes... I do," he ground out. "I failed you, Reagan, and all I can offer you now to make it right is a divorce. Then you can have your relationship back with your parents and a chance at the money your grandmother wanted you to have.

You can have your dreams and the girls' home you were meant to build. I refuse to take all that away from you."

"Am I so easy to toss aside, Zeke?" she whispered, her fingers lifting to that scar on her collarbone.

"Ray, no," he murmured. Nothing about this was easy. It was ripping him to shreds inside. "That's not true." He reached for her, to draw her hand away from that mark that represented so much tragedy for her, but she stumbled back, away from his touch.

"My ex. My parents. You. What is it about me that's so easy for people to walk away from?" She paced away from him, dragging fingers through her hair. Her hollow burst of laughter reverberated in the room. "No, I take that back. This isn't on me. It wasn't ever on me," she said softly, almost as if to herself.

Spinning around, she faced him again, and he was almost rocked back on his heels by her beauty and the fury in her eyes. "For too long I've blamed myself for whatever deficit in me permitted people to abandon me. I'm through with that. And you don't get to use me as an excuse for running scared and not owning your own shit."

"What do you think I'm doing now, dammit?" He took a step toward her before drawing to an abrupt halt. "Do you think it's easy for me to admit that I've failed you? That I couldn't give you everything I promised? That I wasn't—"

He bit off the rest of that statement, hating to think it much less state it aloud. But she didn't have that problem.

"*Enough?* You weren't enough to save Melissa. You aren't enough to save Wingate. And you aren't enough to save me?" For a moment, her expression softened, but then it hardened into an icy mask. One he hadn't seen on her before tonight. "News flash, Zeke. I didn't ask you to. It isn't me you're so concerned with protecting—it's yourself. I threaten that pain and guilt that you've become so comfortable carrying around it's now a part of you. Because to admit that I'm more than a charity case to you means you would have to deal with the reality that you stand in your own way of finding acceptance and love. You'll have to face the truth that you've been lonely and alone out of choice, not cruel fate."

Anger sparked inside him, flicking high and hot. As did fear. But he fanned the flames of his anger, smoking out that other, weaker emotion. He wasn't *afraid*. She didn't know him. Didn't know all he'd suffered, lost. How could he not throw up shields around his heart? To protect himself from that kind of devastation? Even now, knowing he was letting her go, damn near pushing her out the door, had pain pumping through his veins instead of blood. But the thought of how much worse it would be if something happened to her...

No. Fuck it. Call him a coward. Selfish.

He couldn't do it. Not again.

"Zeke."

He dragged his gaze from the floor and returned it to her face.

The fury that saturated her features thawed, leaving behind a sadness that cut just as deep as her hurt. She sighed, shaking her head. "You *are* enough. You're more than enough. But I can't make you believe or accept it, so I'm leaving. Not because of some perceived stink of association with you. I'm leaving because the first time you 'released' me for my own good, I let you. Then I returned and begged you to marry me. I won't do it again, and I won't stay with a man who doesn't want me enough to fight for me. For us. And I damn sure won't beg him to let me stay."

She strode forward and past him. He lifted an arm in a belated attempt to reach for her, to try to make her understand why he was a bad bet. Why he was putting her before his wants and needs. Because she was wrong—he did want her. Too much.

But either she didn't see his hand or she didn't want his touch, because she blew past him and headed toward the hall leading to their bedroom. He parted his lips to call after her, but then she stopped in the opening without turning around, her slim back straight, her shoulders drawn back.

"I didn't need you to be my superhero. I am fully capable of saving myself. I needed you to be my friend, my lover, my husband. I needed you to love me more than your fear of opening your heart up again. Just like I love you more than my fear of being abandoned again. And for the record, you were—you *are*—worth the risk. But this time? I'm walking away. Because I'm worth the risk, too."

Then she walked away. Just like she'd promised.

Sixteen

Reagan climbed the steps to her parents' home and, twisting the knob, pushed the front door open. Since her mother was expecting her for lunch, there was no need to knock.

Standing in the quiet foyer, she surveyed it as if she hadn't been there in years instead of weeks. Since that confrontation with her father, she hadn't stepped foot in the home that had been hers since birth. The only reason she did so now was because of a phone call from her mother, asking her to please come over so they could talk. The *I miss you* at the end had sealed Reagan's fate. It was difficult to tell Henrietta Sinclair no on the best of terms. But when she tacked on the emotional warfare? Impossible.

The familiar scent of lemon and roses enveloped her, as comforting as a hug. Funny to think there'd been a time when she'd hated the scent of roses. But now? Now she missed it as much as she missed her family.

Especially now, when she didn't have anyone.

Well, that wasn't exactly true. She had Harley, who was graciously letting her stay with her and Grant until her new apartment came available next week. She had Beth and Gracie, who had been so saddened when she'd told them a week ago about the breakup with Zeke. But had quickly assured her she was still family to them.

And of course, and most important, she had herself.

That night with Ezekiel had been a revelation of sorts.

A revelation that though her past might have shaped the woman she'd become, she was not the sum of her mistakes. Just as she'd told Zeke, she didn't need saving; she wasn't some damsel in distress. And her dream of a girls' home here in Royal wouldn't crumble to dust just because her father held her inheritance hostage. Her dream hadn't been birthed by either her father or Ezekiel, so neither one could—or would—be the death of it.

She loved him… *God*, did she love him. That love was rooted in friendship, admiration, respect and a desire that even now her soul-deep hurt hadn't banished. But she valued who she was and what she brought to the table of their marriage more. That he couldn't see how she possessed the strength to carry him just as he did her… She shook her head. Maybe it was good their relationship ended when it did. That lack of regard for her would've surely poisoned them long before he decided the expiration date on their arrangement had come due.

Inhaling a breath, she shoved away those thoughts and the pain they resonated through her body for the time being.

"Mom?" she called, walking toward the rear of the house and the smaller salon her mother usually occupied this time of day, working on her numerous charitable events and committee responsibilities.

"In here, Reagan."

That was *not* her mother. Shock ricocheted through her like a Ping-Pong ball, and she skidded to a stop on her heels, frozen. After several moments, she unglued her feet and reversed course toward the formal living room. She'd heard her father's voice but seeing him standing there in the middle of the room pelted her with more icy shards of surprise.

"Dad," she said, amazed her voice remained calm when inside she was the exact opposite. "What are you doing here? I was supposed to meet Mom for lunch."

He cleared his throat and locked his hands behind his

back. And oh, how she'd missed him. Reserved, domineering and often stern to the point of being implacable. But he was also protective, loving in his own way and willing to lay down his life for his family. They were all what defined Douglas Sinclair, and the distance between them had left a hollow, empty place in her heart.

"I apologize for the deception, but I asked her to arrange this…" he waved a hand between them "…meeting. Otherwise, I didn't know if you would agree to come."

It was on the tip of her tongue to say she would've, but at the last moment, she swallowed the words. Because she might not have, given that it might've meant subjecting herself to another blistering lecture.

"Well, I'm here now," she said, moving farther into the room. "What's going on, Dad?"

Instead of answering, he reached inside his suit jacket and removed an envelope. He crossed the short distance separating them and handed it to her. She tore her gaze away from him and glanced down at the piece of mail.

"Please," he insisted. "Open it."

With a frown, she acquiesced. And minutes later, the paper trembled in her shaking hand. Unsure that she could've read the single sheet correctly, she scanned it again. But no, the terms remained the same. Her grandmother's inheritance had been released to her.

He'd released it to her.

"Dad," she breathed, stunned at the enormity of this. But then an ugly idea crept into her mind, and she lowered the paper to her side. "Is this because I left Zeke?" she demanded. "Because I don't want to be 'rewarded' for that. It had nothing to do with—"

"No, Reagan," Douglas interrupted her. "It has nothing to do with that. I'd decided to give you the inheritance a couple of weeks ago. It's just taken me this long to get past my pride to speak to you." He sighed, and once again, astonishment paralyzed her. Outward displays of emotion—sadness, pain, regret, which he usually kept so sternly in check—softened his eyes and turned his mouth down at the corners. Her heart thudded against her sternum. "The love a parent has for their child…" He shook his head. "It's so hard to explain, but I want to try."

He paced to the large fireplace and silently studied its dark depths before turning back to her. And though his familiar, serious expression was firmly in place once more, his voice shook with the feelings she'd spied only seconds ago.

"Being black in Texas was…rough for your mother and me. Especially in the time we came of age in. And infiltrating the business world carried its own set of hindrances and injustices. But for you, your brother and sister and mother, I would endure it all again. You all are worth every ugly name, every snub, every racist hurdle I had to climb or break through. Still, I swore to myself my children would never have to suffer that kind of pain, struggle and discrimination. I wanted better for you…because I love you so much.

"I guess you could call it an obsession of mine—making sure you were all right. Especially after the pregnancy when you were sixteen. I felt so…helpless. My baby girl was hurting, had been taken advantage of, and I felt like I'd failed in protecting you. And I know I didn't handle the situation right. I don't regret paying off that boy because he was no good for you, but I do regret that in the middle of my pain and powerlessness I made you feel like I didn't love you anymore. That somehow you were less in my eyes. When in truth, I wanted to wrap you up and shield you more."

He paused, then shifted, his profile facing her as he stared out the huge picture window. The view of Pine Valley was lovely, but she doubted he saw it. And she couldn't focus on anything but her father and the words that both hurt and healed.

"Since I failed in protecting you—"

"Dad, that's just not true," Reagan objected fiercely.

He shook his head, holding up a hand. "To me, I didn't do my job as your father. All I wanted for you was a life where you didn't experience that ever again. If something should happen to me tomorrow, I wouldn't have to worry because I'd know you were taken of. Which, for me, meant a husband who could provide for you, care for you, insulate you with his name, his wealth and connections so you wouldn't ever know being poor, disdained or abandoned. Never know mistreatment or mishandling of your precious heart again.

"But nearly losing you because of my own agenda and shortsightedness revealed to me that I took it too far. I was so concerned with you being hurt by society, by this world, that I ended up being the one who hurt you. In my drive to protect you out of love, I forgot compassion. Understanding. Forgiveness. Mercy. All of those are elements of the love I touted. I also forgot that struggle often shapes a person, makes them stronger. It helps us be better. And while I detest what you went through, it did make you into a better, stronger person, and..." He shifted back to her and tears glistened in his eyes. "I love you. And I'm proud of you."

He lifted his arms, slowly opening them to her, and without hesitation she flew into them.

And in that moment, as her arms wrapped around his waist, her cheek pressed to his chest, the sixteen-year-old girl and the adult woman converged into one. "I love you, too, Dad."

Seventeen

"What the hell?" Ezekiel stared at the email from his personal accountant. More specifically, the numbers inside the email. There were a shit ton of zeroes in that number. "This can't be..."

But even as he murmured the objection, he reread the message again, and there it was in black and white.

He was a millionaire.

For the first time since Reagan walked away from him and out of his house, he felt something other than a pain-infused grief. Like a death. Only difference, there wasn't a tombstone to visit.

You did the right thing. The only thing you could do.

He repeated the reminder that had become a refrain in his head over the last week. Whenever he teetered on the edge of giving in, yelling, "Fuck this," and going after her, he remembered that he was doing what was best for her.

Best for you.

The taunt whispered across his mind, and he flipped that voice a mental bird.

"What can't be?" a familiar and unexpected voice asked.

Ezekiel jerked his head up and watched Luke close Ezekiel's office door behind him and cross the floor to his desk. Even though the workday was only a couple of hours old, Luke had rolled the sleeves of his dress shirt to his elbows, undone the top button, and his tie knot was loosened.

Concern momentarily overshadowed Ezekiel's shock. No one in this company was working harder than Luke to save it. And it showed in the faint bruises under his brother's eyes denoting lack of sleep, the hollowed cheekbones and firm lines bracketing his mouth.

"When was the last time you went home and had a decent night's sleep?" Ezekiel demanded.

Luke dismissed his question with a flick of his hand. "What can't be?" he repeated. "You receive some good news?"

"Yes," Ezekiel said, struggling against badgering Luke into answering his question. Shaking his head, he shifted his attention from his brother's weary features to the computer screen and the open email. "I just received a message from my accountant." He huffed out a breath, disbelief coursing through him once more. "I have a few personal investments outside of Wingate and apparently, one of the companies I invested in just sold for billions. Billions, Luke. And I'm a millionaire because of it."

Joy lit up his brother's light brown eyes, eclipsing the exhaustion there.

"Holy shit, Zeke!" Luke grinned, rounding the desk to pull Ezekiel up out of his chair and jerk him into a back-pounding hug. "That's wonderful. Damn, I'm glad we finally have some good news around here."

"I'm still in shock. I don't even know what to do right now," Ezekiel murmured.

"I do. Go get Reagan back."

Ezekiel's chin jerked up and back from Luke's verbal sucker punch. "What?" Just hearing her name... It scored him, leaving red-hot slashes of pain behind. "What the hell are you talking about?"

"I'm talking about going to find your wife, get down on your knees if need be and beg her to come back to you," Luke stated flatly. "I love you, Zeke, but you fucked up."

A growl vibrated in his chest, rolling up into his throat, but at the last moment, he didn't let his angry retort fly. Luke loved him and meant well. But still... Ezekiel didn't want to hear this. "Luke, I appreciate—"

"No," Luke interjected with a hard shake of his head. "You're my brother and the most important person in the world to me. Which is why I can tell you the brutal truth even though you don't want to hear it. And I can do it knowing it won't hurt our relationship."

Ezekiel almost turned away, but only his love for his brother kept him from walking away. Well, that, and he harbored zero doubts Luke would drag him back to make him listen.

Luke sighed, rubbing a hand over the back of his neck. "I know I warned you against marrying Reagan when you first told me about the engagement. I was worried for both of you. But when I saw you two at the engagement party, I changed my mind. You belong together... You belong *to* her. And I say this remembering how you were with Melissa. I loved her—she was sweet, kind and loved you. But Melissa is gone, and you have the chance for a future with a woman who not only fiercely defended you like a lioness but who challenges you. Who makes you better. Who loves you. And you, whether you want to admit it to yourself or not, love her."

"Love?" Ezekiel laughed, and the serrated edge of it scraped his throat. "You say that when we have so many examples around us of people who have been gutted by love. Like when you love someone, they don't leave," he snarled.

He snapped his lips shut, hating that he'd let that last part escape. But now that it had, he couldn't stop the images of those he'd lost and the people they'd left behind from careening through his head.

Uncle Trent. His parents. Melissa.

"Besides," he ground out, "my reasons for divorcing

Reagan stand. I'm doing her more harm than good remaining married to her. This way she won't be ostracized by *polite* Royal society or separated from her family. She'll have the chance to obtain her inheritance."

"Bullshit."

Ezekiel glared at his brother, who aimed one right back at him.

"I call bullshit," Luke repeated through clenched teeth. "You're running scared. Like you have for the last eight years. You speak of Melissa and Mom and Dad like they were cautionary tales. Mom and Dad's marriage is a goal, not a warning. Their love was the epitome of courage, of sacrifice and love. And you shit all over that when you use them to justify your fears. Zeke." Luke clapped a hand over Ezekiel's shoulder and squeezed. "You're about to throw your future away over something that you have no control over. You're so worried about what could possibly happen. Yes, God forbid, Reagan could *possibly* die in a tragic accident like Melissa and Mom and Dad. But you could also possibly have a wife and family and be complete in a way you've never known or could dream of. She's worth the risk. *You're* worth the risk."

Ezekiel stared at his brother, but it was Reagan's words echoing in his ears.

You don't get to use me as an excuse for running scared and not owning your own shit.

I threaten that pain and guilt that you've become so comfortable carrying around it's now a part of you. Because to admit that I'm more than a charity case to you means you would have to deal with the reality that you stand in your own way of finding acceptance and love.

Jesus. Ezekiel closed his eyes, and Luke gripped his other shoulder, holding him steady.

He loved her.

He loved Reagan Sinclair Holloway with his heart. His whole being.

Because if he didn't, he wouldn't be so damn terrified of being with her. She was right. She threatened his resolve, his beliefs about himself, his determination to forbid anyone from getting too close. From loving too hard.

Yes, he'd failed.

But not by marrying Reagan.

He'd failed in keeping her out of his carefully guarded heart.

At some point, she'd infiltrated his soul so completely that she owned it. He couldn't evict her. And…he didn't want to.

Did he suddenly believe he was worthy of her? No, but her strength, her warrior spirit made him want to strive to be worthy.

Was he suddenly not afraid? No. He'd believed a man should be brave enough to love her without fear, and that man wasn't him. But he'd been wrong. A man should just be brave enough to love. The fear of losing her might not ever go away, but he couldn't let it rule his life.

That man, he could be.

Starting now.

"You're going after her, aren't you?" Luke asked, a smile spreading across his face.

"Yes," Ezekiel said, as a weight he hadn't even been aware of bearing lifted from his chest. "And if she'll have me, I'm bringing her home."

Eighteen

Reagan stood in the back of the long line that bellied up to the funky but trendy food truck Street Eats. Of all the trucks hawking their fare, this one had a constant stream of people, ready and eager to grab the upscale street food. The sign next to the menu proudly declared the owner Lauren Roberts's focus on organic and farm-to-table produce.

Lauren herself helped serve the food, and even through the serving window, Reagan could easily see the businesswoman's loveliness. The Cinderella Sweepstakes included a makeover for the charity ball along with the free ticket, but she didn't need one. Smooth, glowing skin, pretty brown eyes, dark hair that was pulled back into a ponytail at the moment, and curves that Reagan envied completed the picture of a beautiful, confident and successful woman.

Reagan waited until the line had dwindled to a couple of people before joining it. Once she reached the window, Lauren smiled at her.

"Hey there. How can I help you?"

Reagan returned the smile. "Actually, I was wondering if I could have a couple of minutes, Lauren? My name is Reagan Sinclair," she introduced herself. "I'm on the planning committee for this year's Texas Cattleman's Club masquerade ball. And it's my pleasure to tell you that you're the winner of the Cinderella Sweepstakes radio contest."

Surprise widened Lauren's eyes. "You're kidding?"

"No, all true. You've won a ticket and a free makeover," Reagan assured her.

"Hold on a second. I'll be right out."

True to her word, Lauren emerged from around the truck moments later holding two cups.

"Sweet tea on the house," she said, offering Reagan one of the drinks. Sipping from her own tea, Lauren shook her head. "I still can't believe I won! Can I be honest?"

"Of course." Reagan tasted her beverage and savored the cool, refreshing tea with a hint of mint. Good Lord, it was delicious. "Wow, this is good."

"Thanks." Lauren grinned. But the wattage of it dimmed a little as she led Reagan to a nearby bench. Sitting, she curled a leg under the other and twisted to face Reagan. "I'm a little embarrassed to admit this, but I didn't even enter. A friend did it for me." She huffed out a chuckle. "Still, I'm excited to win. I never expected to. And I can't really pass up this opportunity to network with potential customers and investors. And shoot." She held up her hands, that grin tugging at the corner of her mouth again. "What woman doesn't enjoy a makeover?"

"A free one at that," Reagan teased. "Not that I think you need one. You're lovely just as you are."

"That's nice of you to say, but no." Lauren nodded, her eyes gleaming. "I'm looking forward to some changes."

"Well, then I'm glad I'm the one who could bring you the good news. And I'm looking forward to seeing you at the ball."

"Thanks, Ms. Sinclair," Lauren said, rising from the bench.

"Reagan." She stood as well, smiling. "Please call me Reagan. And thank you again for the tea."

"You're more than welcome." Lauren glanced over at the food truck where the line of customers had lengthened again. "I should get back. Thanks again, Reagan." Waving, she retreated back to her truck.

Reagan paused to finish her beverage, then headed toward her car across the street. A sense of accomplishment filled her. It was always awesome when good things happened to good people. And though she'd just met the other woman, Lauren seemed honest, hardworking and nice. Reagan looked forward to seeing her at the ball—

She stumbled to a halt. Shock swelled and crashed over her, momentarily numbing her.

Too bad she couldn't stay that way.

Already, the hurt and anger started to zigzag across that sheet of ice, the fissures growing and cracking. All at the sight of Ezekiel leaning against her car.

God, it wasn't fair. Not at all.

After the way he'd basically cast her aside, the only emotions bubbling inside her should be fury and disdain. She might have walked away, but he'd let her. Without the slightest fight. That, more than anything, relayed how he felt about her.

Yet beneath the fury, there was also gut-churning pain and grief, for how not just their marriage but their friendship had ended.

And the ever-present need... Just one look at his tall, powerful body wrapped in one of his perfectly tailored suits—this one dark blue—and that handsome, strong face with those smoldering green eyes... Just one look, and she couldn't stem the desire or the memories that bombarded her, both decadent and cruel.

Slowly, he straightened, and she forced her feet to move and carry her across the street. Over the short distance, the anger capsized all the other emotions roiling inside her like a late-summer Texas storm. If he'd come to see if she was all right after he'd broken her heart, he could go straight to hell. She didn't need his pity. And she refused to be a balm that he could smooth over his self-imposed guilt.

No, thank you.

She'd wanted to be his wife, not an act of reparation.

"What are you doing here, Zeke?" she asked, voice purposefully bland, even though it belied the knots twisting in her belly or the constriction of her heart.

"Looking for you," he said simply, his gaze roaming over her face. Almost as if he were soaking in every detail.

Mentally, she slapped down that line of thinking. It could only lead to the seed of hope she'd desperately tried to dig up sprouting roots.

"After handing my ass to me in a sling, Harley told me where you were."

Okay, so Reagan and Harley needed to have a serious *come to Jesus* talk about consorting with the enemy. Or since the enemy was Harley's cousin, at least giving the enemy classified information.

"Well, you've seen me." Reagan sidestepped him and reached for the door handle. "Now if you don't mind, I have a meeting." Not a lie, she had an appointment with a realtor to find land for the girls' home she planned on building.

"Reagan," Zeke murmured, lifting a hand toward her. But when she arched a brow, daring him to complete the action, he lowered it and slid it into his pocket.

Self-preservation demanded he not touch her in any way. Her mind asserted she could withstand the contact, but her heart and her body? No, they were decidedly weaker when it came to feeling those magnificent hands on her.

"Reagan," he said again. "I know I don't have the right to ask you for it, but can I have just a couple of minutes? I want—"

"Let me guess. You want to apologize. You never meant to hurt me. And you would like to find a way to be friends again." She inhaled, bracing herself against that wash of fresh pain. But damn if she would let him see it. "Apology accepted. I know. And no. Not right now."

She went for the door handle again. But his fingers covered hers, and she stilled, the *don't touch me* dying a quick and humiliating death on her tongue. She couldn't speak, couldn't move when her nerve endings sizzled as if they were on fire.

He shouldn't affect her like this. Shouldn't ignite this insatiable, damn near desperate need for him. How many years before it abated? Before her body forgot what it felt like to be possessed by him?

She feared the answer to that.

"Please, sweetheart," he murmured, removing his hand, then taking a step back. "Hear me out, then I'll leave you alone."

"Fine," she bit out, conceding. Only because she suspected he wouldn't budge before having his say. And the sooner they got this done, the sooner she could drive away and pretend she didn't ache for him. Both her heart and her body. Just to be on the safe side though… She took another step back. "Just…don't touch me again."

"I won't," he promised.

She pretended not to see the flash of pain in his eyes.

"Reagan." He shifted his gaze away from her, squinting in the distance before refocusing on her. "I wanted you to know that Miles contacted Gracie. He was able to track her cousin's credit card purchases, and he found one at a convenience store for the same time the winning ticket was sold. That transaction was made out of state, not here in Royal. Miles managed to recover the store's video footage, and Alberto was there, on camera, paying for his purchase. Since it's scientifically impossible for him to be in two places at one time, he quickly dropped the claim against Gracie when Miles presented the evidence to him. So she's good."

"That's wonderful, Zeke. Thank you for having Miles look into it. I know Gracie has to be so delighted." Relief for her friend flowed through her, and she made a mental note to call her. But fast on the heels of that thought nipped another. "Is that what you wanted to tell me?"

It was *not* disappointment that crashed against her sternum. It wasn't.

"No," he said. "That was me stalling while I tried to gather my courage and ask you, no, beg you, to forgive me."

Beg. She blinked. No matter how hard she tried to conjure the image, she couldn't envision Ezekiel Holloway begging for anything.

"And though I'm asking for your forgiveness, I'm having a hard time extending it to myself. I was so wrapped up in my own pain, my own fear and guilt that I convinced myself I was doing what was best for you. When really, I was doing what was best for me. Well, what I believed was best for me. I couldn't have been more wrong."

Reagan sighed. "I've had twenty-six years of people making decisions based on what they think is best for me. And yet no one bothered asking my opinion on my life. Granted, I accept some of the blame for that, because I was afraid of rocking the boat, of not being loved. But I can't and won't allow that anymore, Zeke. From anyone. And I can't be with someone who respects me so little they think me incapable of making choices for myself."

"And you shouldn't settle for that, Reagan. Anyone who underestimates you is a fool. Like I was," he added softly. "Not that I ever underestimated your strength, your intelligence or drive. No, I misjudged your affect on me, my life…my heart."

"I… I don't understand."

"I didn't either. Until today. I thought I could put you in this box and compartmentalize you in my life. But you…" He breathed a chuckle. "You can't be contained. You're this force that's fierce and powerful but one people usually don't see coming because it's wrapped in beauty, grace and compassion. I didn't stand a chance against you, Ray. And that's what had me running scared. I fought against the hold you had on me with everything in me because, sweetheart, you scare me. Loving you, having everything that is you, then possibly losing you? I couldn't bear it."

Loving you. Those two words echoed in her head, gaining strength like a twister. Wrecking every possible thought in its path except one. *Loving you.*

Oh God, no. Hope, that reckless, so-damn-stubborn emotion, dug in deep, entrenched itself inside her. She closed her eyes, blocking out his face. But she couldn't shut her ears. And they listened with a need that terrified her.

"I took the coward's way out before," he continued, shifting forward and erasing some of the space between them. "But now, I'm here, telling you that I'm no longer living in the past. Not when you're my future."

"Zeke, stop," she whispered, opening her eyes. Because she couldn't take any more. Love for this man pressed against her chest, threatening to burst through. No fear. That had no place between them anymore. She just wanted...him. He'd taken a risk by coming to find her and lay his heart out for her. And she could do no less but the same. Life, love—they required risk. Because the reward... God, the reward stared her in the face.

"Okay, sweetheart," he murmured, dragging a hand over his head. "I'll go, but one more thing. Some investments paid off for me, and they were substantial. Enough to no longer put your dream of a girls' home here in Royal on hold. Half of those earnings are yours. It's not a settlement. If we're going to divorce, you'll have to file the papers. I'll respect whatever you decide, but I can't let you go not knowing what I want. You. A real marriage. A family."

"I don't want your money, Zeke," she said. Pain flickered in his gaze, but he nodded. "No, you don't understand. I don't need it. All I need—all I want—is you. Us."

"What?" he rasped. "You mean..."

"Yes, I love you. With everything in me, I love you," she whispered.

"Sweetheart." He stared at her, his breath harsh and jagged. "Please give me permission to touch you."

"Yes. God, yes."

Before she finished speaking, he was on her, his hands cupping her face, tipping her head back. A heady wave of pleasure coursed through her as his mouth crushed hers, seeking, tasting…confirming.

"I thought…" He groaned, rolling his forehead against hers. "I thought I'd lost you. I love you, Reagan Holloway. You're mine, and I'm never letting you walk away from me again."

"Promise?"

"Promise," he swore, pressing a hard, passionate kiss to her lips.

"Then take me home and prove it," she said, laughing, unable to contain the joy bubbling inside her. And she didn't even try to contain it. "But we have to make a stop first. I'd love to have you with me for it." She couldn't imagine beginning this project of love without the love of her life.

"Fine," he agreed, grasping her hand and tugging her away from her car. "We'll take my car, then come back for yours." When they stopped next to the Jaguar, he tossed her the keys.

She gaped at him. Then at the metal she'd reflexively caught. Then back at him.

"Oh my God. You must really love me," she gasped.

Laughing, he rounded the hood of the car. The hood that he'd made love to her on.

"Forever, Ray."

* * * * *

THE ITALIAN'S DEAL FOR I DO

JENNIFER HAYWARD

To my editor Laura McCallen and fellow authors
Michelle Smart, Andie Brock, and Tara Pammi who
made the Columbia Four such a joy to write!
Memento vivere!

And for Valentina and your invaluable help with the
beautiful Italian language! *Grazie*!

CHAPTER ONE

"HE WILL NOT make it through the night."

The grizzled old priest had served almost a century of Mondellis in the lakeside village of Varenna. He rested his gnarled, weathered hand on the ornately carved knob of the inches-thick, dark-stained door of Giovanni Mondelli's bedroom and nodded toward the patriarch's two grandchildren. "You must say your goodbyes. Leave nothing unsaid."

His gravelly tone was somber, weighted with the grief of an entire village. It cut through Rocco Mondelli like a knife, severing a lifeline, rendering him incapable of speech. Italian fashion icon Giovanni Mondelli, son of the Italian people, had been the father he'd never had. He'd been Rocco's guiding influence when he'd taken his grandfather's place as CEO of House of Mondelli and brought it kicking and screaming into the twenty-first century. Transformed it into a revered global couture powerhouse.

He could not be losing him.

Rocco's heart sputtered to a stop, then came back to life in a brutal staccato that pounded against the walls of his chest. Giovanni was everything to him. Father, mentor, friend… He wasn't ready to let him go. Not yet.

His sister, Alessandra, grasped his arm, her knuckles white against the dark material of his suit. "I—I don't think I can do this," she stumbled huskily, her glossy brown hair tangled around her face, eyes wide. "It's too sudden. I have too much to say."

Rocco ignored the desire to throw himself on the floor and cry out that it wasn't fair, like he had at age seven when he'd stood on the deck of a boat outside this window on Lake Como in a miniature-size suit, his big, brown eyes trained on his *papa* as he tossed his mother's ashes into the brilliant blue water. Life wasn't fair. It had nothing to do with fair. It had given him Alessandra, but it had taken away his beloved mother. Never could that be considered a fair compromise.

He turned and gripped his sister by the shoulders, breathing through the searing pain that gripped his chest. "We can and we will, because we have to, *sorella*."

Tears streamed down Alessandra's face, negotiating the crevices of her stubborn mouth. "I can't, Rocco. I won't."

"You *will*." He pulled her into his arms and rested his chin on her head. "Gather your thoughts. Think of what you need to say. There isn't much time."

Alessandra soaked his shirt with silent tears. It had always been Rocco's job as much as it had been Giovanni's to hold this family together following the death of his mother and his father's subsequent descent into gambling and drink. But he did not feel up to it now. He felt as though one of the breezes wafting in from the lake might fell him with a single, innocent, misplaced nudge. But giving in to weakness, into emotion, had never been an option for him.

He set Alessandra away from him and slid an arm around her shoulders to support her slight weight. His gaze went to the short, balding doctor standing behind the priest. "Is he awake?"

The doctor nodded. "Go now."

His strong, sometimes misguided, but always confident sister trembled underneath his fingers as he led her into Giovanni's bedroom. If the saying was true you could smell death in the air, it was not the case here. He could *feel* the warmth, the vital energy Giovanni Mondelli had worn like a second skin. That he had infused into every single one of his designs. He could *hear* the caustic bite of his grandfather's laughter before it turned rich and chiding and full of wisdom. *Smell* the spicy, sophisticated scent that clung to every piece of clothing he wore.

It was Rocco's eyes, however, that stripped him of any shred of hope. The sight of his all-powerful grandfather lost in a sea of white sheets, his vibrant olive skin devoid of color, snared his breath in his chest. This was not Giovanni.

He swallowed past the fist in his throat. "Go," he urged Alessandra, pushing her forward.

Alessandra climbed onto the massive bed and wrapped her slim arms around her grandfather. The sight of Giovanni's eyes watering was too much for Rocco to bear. He turned away, walked to the window and stared out at the lake.

He and Alessandra had flown the fifty kilometers from the House of Mondelli headquarters in Milan via helicopter as soon as they had heard the news. But his stubborn grandfather had been ignoring pains in his chest all day, and by the time they'd got here, there was little the doctors could do.

His mouth twisted. If he knew his grandfather, he'd probably decided this was the cleanest way to go. Giovanni Mondelli was not beyond manipulating the world to his advantage. What better way to go out then in a blaze of glory on the eve of Mondelli's greatest fall line ever?

But then again, Rocco conceded, Giovanni had been ready to join his beloved wife, Rosa, in the sweet afterlife, as he called it, for almost twenty years. He had lived life to the fullest, refused to fade after her passing, but there had been a part of him that yearned for her with every waking breath.

He would have her back, he'd promised.

Alessandra let out a sob and rushed from the room. Rocco strode to the bed, his gaze settling on his grandfather's pale face. "You've broken her heart."

"Sandro did that a long time ago," his grandfather said wearily, referring to Rocco's father, who Alessandra had been named for. His eyes fluttered as he patted the bed beside him. "Sit."

Rocco sat, swallowed hard. "Nonno, I need to tell you…"

His grandfather laid his wrinkled, elegant, long-fingered hand over his. "I know. *Ti amo, mio figlio.* You have become a great man. Everything I knew you could be."

The lump in Rocco's throat grew too large for him to forge past.

His grandfather fixed his dark eyes on him, staring hard in an act of will to keep them open. "Trust yourself, Rocco. Trust the man you've become. Understand why I've done the things I've done."

His eyes fluttered closed. Rocco's heart slammed against his chest. "Giovanni, it is not your time."

His grandfather's eyes slitted open. "Promise me you will take care of Olivia."

"Olivia?" Rocco frowned in confusion.

His grandfather's eyes fluttered closed. Stayed closed this time. A fist reached inside Rocco's chest and clamped down hard on his heart. He took his grandfather's shoulders in his hands and shook them hard. *Come back. Do not leave me.* But Giovanni's eyes remained shut.

The spirit of the House of Mondelli, the flame that had burned passion into brilliant, groundbreaking collections for fifty years, into his own heart, was extinguished.

Rocco let out a primal roar and rested his forehead against his grandfather's lined brow.

"No," he whispered over and over again. It was too soon.

* * *

The emotion he had exhibited upon the death of his grandfather was nowhere to be seen in the week following as Rocco negotiated the mind-numbing details of organizing Giovanni's funeral, now reaching state-like proportions, and the settlement of his estate. The Mondelli holdings were vast, with properties and business interests spanning the globe. Even with his own intimate knowledge of the company and its entities, it would take time.

Alessandra helped him plan the funeral. Everyone, it seemed, wanted to come—public and government figures, heads of state and celebrities Giovanni had dressed over his forty-five years in the business. Weeding them out was their challenge.

And, of course, the remainder of the Columbia Four were coming: the three men Rocco had met and bonded with during their first week at Columbia University. Not a mean feat given the intense, grueling schedules of Christian Markos, Stefan Bianco and Zayed Al Afzal. Athens-born Christian was a financial whiz kid and deal maker who divided his time between Greece and Hong Kong. The inscrutable Sicilian, Stefan Bianco, preferred to make his millions masterminding the world's biggest real-estate deals on his private jet rather than in his hometown of Manhattan, but then again everyone knew Stefan had commitment issues. The final member of the group, Sheikh Zayed Al Afzal, would have the longest to travel from his home in the heart of the Arabian desert—a tiny country named Gazbiyaa.

It comforted him as he sat down with the Mondelli family's longtime lawyer, Adamo Donati, to review Giovanni's will, to know the men he considered more brothers than friends would be by his side. The bond he shared with those men was inviolate. Impenetrable. Built from years of knowing one another's inner thoughts. And although his life was not the only one that was tumultuous at the moment, his friends would not miss such an important event, including Zayed, whose country was embroiled in rising tensions with a neighboring kingdom and teetering on the verge of war.

Memento vivere was the Columbia Four's code. Remember to live. Which meant living big, risking big and always having one another's back.

"Shall we begin?"

Adamo, Giovanni's sage sixty-five-year-old longtime friend, who was not only a brilliant lawyer but a formidable business brain, tilted his chin at him in an expectant look. Rocco nodded and focused his attention on the lawyer. "Go ahead."

Adamo glanced down at the papers in front of him. "In terms of the properties, Giovanni has split them between you and Alessandra. I'm sure this is no surprise, as you've talked to him about it. Alessandra will receive the house in St. Barts and the apartment in Paris, while you will take ownership of Villa Mondelli and the house in New York."

Rocco inclined his head. Alessandra, a world-class photographer who traveled the world doing shoots, had always joked Villa Mondelli was too big for her, that she'd rattle around its sprawling acres by herself, while it was the only place on earth Rocco felt he could truly breathe.

He cocked a brow at the lawyer. "My father?"

"The current arrangement will continue. Giovanni left a sum of money in Sandro's name for you to administer."

Like a child unable to manage his own pocket money. Rocco had long given up on the idea that his father could manage anything, but he wondered if somewhere inside him he was waiting for the day Sandro would apologize for gambling away their family home. For handing them over to Giovanni when he could no longer cope. That someday he might step forward and shock them all. Until then, his father had been provided with an apartment in the city, a weekly shipment of groceries and a limited amount of spending money that inevitably went to gambling rather than to his own personal grooming.

When that ran out, he would slink back asking for more, and when he was told no, he did things like showing up drunk and disheveled at Alessandra's twenty-fifth birthday party, embarrassing them all.

Mouth set, he gestured for Adamo to continue.

The lawyer looked down at the papers. "There is another apartment in Milan. Giovanni purchased it a year ago. It is not accounted for in the will."

"Another apartment?" Rocco frowned. His grandfather had never liked to stay in the city. He preferred to drive to the villa each day or take the company helicopter.

The lawyer's olive skin took on a ruddy hue, his gaze glancing off Rocco as he looked up. "It's in Giovanni's name, but a woman has been living there. I had someone look into it. Her name is Olivia Fitzgerald."

Rocco sucked in a breath. "Olivia Fitzgerald, the model?"

"We think so. It took some digging. She's not using her real name."

He stared at Adamo as if he'd just told him the Pope was turning Protestant. Olivia Fitzgerald, one of the world's top supermodels, signed to a competitor five years ago and unattainable to the House of Mondelli, had dropped off the face of the earth a year ago. Hadn't worked a day since, reneging on a three-million-dollar contract with a French cosmetics company. And Giovanni had been keeping her in an apartment in this city? While the tabloids scoured the earth for her...

His gaze met the lawyer's as he came to the inevitable conclusion.

"He was involved with her."

Adamo's cheeks flushed even darker. "In some way, yes. The neighbors say he spent time with her in the apartment. They were seen arm in arm, going for dinner."

Rocco pressed his hands to his temples. Giovanni, his seventy-year-old grandfather, had taken a twenty-something-year-old mistress? One of the world's great supermodels... A party girl extraordinaire who'd apparently frittered her way out of her million-dollar bank balances as fast as she'd filled them. It seemed preposterous. Was he even living on the same planet he had been a week ago?

Promise me you will take care of Olivia.

Cristo. It was true. Blood rushed through his head, pulsing at his temples. As if he would continue to allow his grandfather's former lover to live on Mondelli property now that Giovanni was gone. A woman who had taken up with him in a transparent attempt to avail herself of his fortune.

He leveled a look at the lawyer. "Give me what you have on her. I'll deal with Olivia Fitzgerald."

Adamo nodded. Ran a hand over his balding head and gave him another of those hesitant looks, so uncharacteristic of him.

Rocco arched a brow. "*Per favore*, tell me there are no more mistresses."

A faint smile crossed Adamo's lips. "Not that I know of."

"Then, what? Spit it out, Adamo."

The lawyer's smile faded. "Giovanni has left you a fifty percent stake of House of Mondelli, Rocco. The remaining ten percent controlling stake has been allocated to Renzo Rialto to manage until he sees fit to turn it over."

Rocco blinked. Attempted to digest. Giovanni hadn't left him a controlling stake in Mondelli? Prior to his grandfather's death, the Mondelli family had held a 60 percent share in the company, with outside shareholders holding the remaining 40 percent, leaving the family firmly in control of the legendary fashion retailer. Giving him the power he had needed as CEO to guide Mondelli forward. Why would Giovanni have taken that power out of his hands and given it to Renzo Rialto, the chairman of the board, who had always been Rocco's nemesis?

Adamo read his dismay. "He didn't want you to feel overwhelmed without him. He wants you to be able to lean on the board for support. Find your feet. When the board feels you're ready, they'll hand over the remaining shares."

"Find my feet?" White-hot rage sliced through him, rage that had been building since his grandfather's death. Steel edged, it straightened every limb, singed every nerve ending, until it escaped out his fingertips as he slapped his palms down on the desk and brought himself eye to eye with the lawyer. "I have built this company into something *Giovanni* could never have envisioned. Taken it from prosperous to *wildly successful.* I don't need to find my feet, Adamo. I need what's rightfully mine—control of this company."

Adamo lifted a hand in a placating gesture. "You have to consider your personal history, Rocco. You have been a renegade. You have not listened to the advice the board has tried to give you."

"Because it was *wrong.* They wanted to keep Mondelli languishing in its past glory when it was clear it needed to move with the times."

"I agree." Adamo shrugged. "But not everyone felt that way. There is a great deal of conservatism within the board, a nostalgic desire not to strip away what made the company great. You're going to need to use more finesse to work your way through this one."

The blood in his head tattooed a rhythm against his skull. *Finesse?* The only thing that worked with the board was to whack them over the head with a big stick before they all retired in a wave of self-important glory.

Adamo eyed him. "There is also your personal life. You are not what the board considers a stable, secure guiding figure for Mondelli."

Rocco reared his head back. "Do not go there, Adamo."

"It was a…delicate situation."

"The one where the board castrated me for an affair I didn't even know I was having?"

"She was a judge's wife. There was a child."

"Not mine." He practically yelled the words at Adamo. "The DNA is in."

"Not before the entire affair caused Mondelli some considerable political difficulties." Adamo pinned him with a stern look of his own. "You weren't careful enough about which playgrounds you chose to dip into, Rocco. You play too fast and easy sometimes, and the board doesn't like it. They particularly worry now that Giovanni isn't here to guide you."

So his grandfather had thought it a good idea to handcuff him to the chairman of the board? To assign him a *babysitter*? He eyed the lawyer, his temper dangerously close to exploding. "I am CEO of the House of Mondelli. I do not need guiding. I need for a woman to *tell me* when she's still married. And if you think I'm going to sit around while the board rubber stamps my every decision, you and they are out of your minds."

Adamo gave a fatalistic lift of his shoulder. "The will is airtight. You have a fifty-percent share. The only person who can give you control is Renzo Rialto."

Renzo Rialto. A difficult, self-important boar of a man who had been a lifelong friend of Giovanni's, but never a huge fan of him personally, even though he couldn't fault what he'd done with the bottom line.

He would relish pushing Rocco's buttons.

He scraped his chair back, stood and paced to the window. Burying his hands in his pockets, he looked down at Via della Spiga, the most famous street in Milan where the House of Mondelli couture collection flew out the door of the Mondelli boutique at five hundred euros apiece. *This* was the epicenter of power. The playground he had commanded so magnificently since his father had defected from life and his path had been chosen.

He would not be denied his destiny.

And yet, he thought, staring sightlessly down at the stream of chicly dressed shoppers with colorful bags in their hands, his grandfather was making him pay for the aggressive business manner that had made Mondelli a household name. For an error in judgment, a carelessness with women that had never *once* interfered with his ability to do his job.

Understand why I've done the things I've done... Giovanni's dying words echoed into his head. Was this what he'd been talking about? And how did it fit with everything else he'd said? *You have become a great man... Trust the man you've become.*

It made no sense.

Anger mingled with grief so heavy, so all encompassing, he leaned forward and rested his palms on the sill. Did this have to do with his father's legacy? Had Sandro made his grandfather gun-shy of handing over full responsibility of the company he'd built despite Rocco's track record? Did he imagine he, as Sandro's flesh and blood, was capable of the same self-combustion?

He turned and looked at the lawyer. "I am *not* my father."

"No, you aren't," Adamo agreed calmly. "But you do like to enjoy yourself with that pack of yours."

Rocco scowled. "The reports of our partying are highly overblown."

"The women part is not. You forget I've known you since you were in *pannolino*, Rocco."

He crooked a brow at him. "What would you have me do? Marry one of them?"

Adamo held his gaze. "It would be the smartest thing you could do. Show you have changed. Show you are serious about putting Mondelli first. Marry one of those connected Italian woman you love to date and become a stable family man. You might even find you like it."

Rocco stared at him. He was serious. *Dio.* Not *ever* happening. He'd seen what losing his mother had done to his father, what losing Rosa had done to Giovanni. He didn't need that kind of grief in his life. He had enough responsibility keeping this company, this family, afloat.

"I would not hold my breath waiting for the silk-covered invitation," he advised drily. "Do you have any more bombshells for me, or can I pay Renzo Rialto a visit?"

"A few more items of note."

They went through the immediate to-dos. Rocco picked up his messages after that, went to his car and headed to Rialto's offices. The retired former CEO of a legendary Italian brand was a thorn in his side, but manage him he would.

He swung the yellow limited edition Aventador, his favorite material possession, onto a main artery, attempting to corral his black temper along the way. He would deal with Rialto, then he would take care of the other complication in his life. Olivia Fitzgerald was about to find her very fine rear end out on the streets of Milan. Just as soon as he found out what kind of game she was playing.

CHAPTER TWO

ROCCO HAD EXPECTED Olivia Fitzgerald to be beautiful. She had, after all, a face that had launched a dozen brands to stardom. A toned, curvaceous body that regularly graced the cover of America's most popular annual swimsuit magazine. Not to mention a tumbling swath of silky golden hair that was reputed to be insured for millions.

But what threw him, as he sat watching her share drinks with her girlfriends at a trattoria in Navigli in the southwest of Milan as dusk closed in over the city, was *his* reaction to *her*.

He was seated at a tiny round table close enough that he could hear the husky rasp of her voice as she ordered a glass of Chianti, the textured nuance of it sliding across his skin like a particularly potent aphrodisiac. Close enough that he could see her catlike, truly amazing eyes were of the deepest blue—the color of the glacially sculpted lakes of the Italian Alps that met his eyes when he opened his curtains in the morning.

Close enough to observe the self-conscious look she threw back at his stare.

And wasn't that amazing? Surely a woman of such world-renowned beauty knew the reaction she elicited in men? Surely she'd been well aware of it when she'd ensnared Giovanni and had him purchase a three-million-euro luxury apartment for her in the hopes of continuing within the style to which she'd become accustomed?

Surely she knew the combined effect of it all was somewhat like a sucker punch to the solar plexus of just about every man on this planet, which he, to his chagrin, was also not immune to.

His mouth twisted into that familiar scowl of late. Olivia Fitzgerald—the Helen of Troy of her time.

Her girlfriends, two beautiful dark-haired Italian girls, giggled and glanced his way. He pulled his gaze back to the menu, sighed and ordered a glass of wine from the *cameriera*. The private investigator who'd helped Adamo uncover who was living in the apartment in Corso Venezia had been a gold mine of information on Olivia Campbell, as she'd been calling herself. She didn't socialize much, spent most of her days holed up in her luxury abode, but she did have a faithful yoga date with her girlfriends on Thursday nights, followed by drinks at this popular spot on the canals in Navigli.

It had been a stroke of luck that the café that sat on the water of the picturesque canals was owned by an old family friend of the Mondellis... No problem obtaining a prime location to study the flaxen-haired sycophant.

He had thought of waiting until she was at the apartment to confront her, but in his current black mood, he wanted the woman who'd taken his grandfather for a ride out on the street. *Yesterday.*

He sat back and crossed one long leg over the other. Watched as the three women engaged in animated conversation. She hadn't, he observed grimly, been struck down with grief at the loss of her lover. Was she even now out hunting her next conquest before her life of luxury was unceremoniously cut off? Was that what the self-conscious looks were about?

A wave of hostility spread through him, firing his blood. He forced out a smile as the *cameriera* set his drink down in front of him, wrapped his fingers around the glass and took a long swallow. Maybe this hadn't been such a good idea, hunting Olivia Fitzgerald down when his emotions were so high. His meeting with Renzo Rialto had not gone well. The arrogant bastard was convinced Rocco was a loose cannon without a guiding force now that Giovanni was gone, and had suggested exactly what Adamo had anticipated. "Settle down, Rocco," he'd encouraged. "Show me you are ready to take on the full responsibility of Mondelli and I will give it to you."

He growled and slapped the glass back down on the table. It was going to take more than an overblown bag of wind to make him say, "I do." Hadn't the Columbia Four vowed "single forever?" Weren't women the source of every great man's downfall? Wasn't it far more rewarding to have your fill of a female when you craved it, then leave her behind when you were done?

He thought so.

In a salute to the missing three, he lifted his glass and downed a healthy gulp of the dark, plum-infused wine. His gaze moved over Olivia Fitzgerald, registering the rosy glow of attraction in her perfect, lightly tanned skin as she stole another look at him.

A plan started to form in his head. He liked it. He liked it a lot. It was perfect for his reckless, messy mood.

He was watching her. Flirting with her.

Olivia tried to smother the butterflies negotiating wide, swooping paths through her stomach, but it was impossible to remain unaffected by the Italian's stare. It was like being singed by a human torch. Hot. Focused. *On her.* And why? He was undoubtedly the most attractive man she'd ever seen in her life, and given she'd traveled the world working with beautiful men of all backgrounds, that was saying something. *She*, on the other hand, was dressed in jeans, a scrappy T-shirt with a zip-up sweatshirt over it, had no makeup on and had thrown her sweat-dampened hair into a ponytail after her yoga class—virtually unrecognizable as the top model she'd once been.

She averted her gaze from his rather petulant pout, sure women threw themselves at his feet at the slightest hint of it. For the whole package, really. But the impression he made lingered. He seemed familiar, somehow, the broad sweep of his high cheekbones framing lush, beautifully shaped lips, a square jaw and an intense dark gaze.

She frowned. Was he a model she'd worked with? Had he recognized her? But even as she thought it, she knew she would have remembered him. How would you ever forget *that* specimen of manliness? *Impossible.* His utter virility and overt confidence were of the jaw-dropping variety.

Violetta yawned, threw her hair over her shoulder and drained her wineglass. "I need to go home and study. And since *he*," she lamented, giving the gorgeous stranger a long look, "is eating *you* up, I might as well go home and pout."

"That's because Olivia is stunning." Sophia sighed. "She is blonde and exotic."

"I wish I had *your* olive skin," Olivia pointed out.

"We trade," Sophia said teasingly, reaching for her bags. "I bet the minute we leave, he's over here, Liv. And about time, too. You haven't even looked at a man since we met."

Because she'd been treasuring her stress-free escape from reality... Because she was only just now feeling like herself again...forging a new identity. Because getting close to a man had meant he might recognize her, and she didn't want to be Olivia Fitzgerald right now.

Also, because none of them had made her pulse flutter like it was at this moment.

Violetta got to her feet and threw some euros on the table. Sophia followed suit.

"You can't leave me here," Olivia protested.

"We live on the opposite side of town," Violetta countered cheerfully. "And honestly, Liv, if we don't go soon, he's going to glare the table down."

"He could be a criminal," Olivia muttered. "I'll only leave."

"A criminal who wears a twenty-five-thousand-euro Rolex," Violetta whispered in her ear. "I don't think so. Enjoy yourself, Liv. Call with the juicy details."

Olivia had no intention of offering up any details, because she wasn't staying. The only reason she was out tonight was to take her mind off Giovanni and how much she missed him. She felt completely adrift without the one person who had been her anchor in this new life, where she was truly alone. Without the mentor who had spent the past year working on her fashion line with her, teaching her. And now that the girls had lifted her spirits a bit, it was time to go.

Violetta and Sophia ambled off in the direction of the metro. Olivia fumbled in her bag for money, the meager amount in there reminding her how desperate her situation was. Her job at the café paid for her spending money, but it would never be enough to afford her own place, let alone the stunning apartment Giovanni had lent her.

Biting her lip, she dug around her change purse for coins. She would figure it out. She always did.

A shadow fell over the table. She registered the rich gleam of the handsome stranger's impeccably shone shoes on the pavement before she lifted her head to take him in.

"Ciao."

He was even better looking up close, his deep brown eyes laced with a rich amber the candlelight picked up and caressed. Big. Six foot two or three, she'd venture with her model's eye. Well built—with more hard-packed muscle than the average Italian she'd seen on the streets. *Heavenly.*

"May I sit down?" he asked in perfectly accented English, taking advantage of her apparent inability to speak.

"Actually," she muttered, "I was just on my way home."

"Surely you can stay for one more drink?" He flashed a bright, perfectly white smile that drew her attention back to his amazing lips. "I stopped to enjoy the lights and a drink and found myself staring at you instead. A far worthier pursuit, I would say."

Her chest heated, the flush that started there traveling slowly up to her cheeks. It was a line, to be sure, but the best she'd ever been handed. And somehow in her vulnerable state, because he was just *that* attractive, it was difficult to say the words she knew she should.

She forced herself. "I really should go… It's getting late."

"You really should stay," he murmured, his sultry brown eyes holding hers. "Nine o'clock is early in Italy. One drink, that's all."

Perhaps it was the way he stayed on his feet and gave her the space to say no. Or maybe it was the fact she just so very much wanted to say yes, but she found herself nodding slowly and gesturing toward the seat across from her. "Please."

He sat, lowering his tall frame into the rather frail-looking chair. The waitress fluttered to his side the minute he crooked a finger, as if sent from above. He ordered two glasses of Chianti for them in rapid-fire Italian accompanied by one of those wide smiles, and the waitress almost fell over herself in her haste to do his bidding.

"Are you a regular here?" Olivia asked, amused, his behavior oddly relaxing, as if that type of confidence simply had to be obeyed and she might as well go with it.

"The café belongs to an old family friend of mine." The words rolled off his tongue, smooth as silk as he leaned forward and held out his hand. "Tony."

"Liv." She allowed her fingers to curl around his. The fact that he had not recognized her sent a warm current of relief through her. Or perhaps that was more a by-product of the heated, somewhat electric energy he imparted through his strong grip.

"Liv." He repeated the word as if trying it on for size and sat back, crossing his arms over his chest. "Your friends left rather suddenly. I hope I didn't chase them away."

A smile curved her lips. "You *meant* to chase them away."

He spread his hand wide. "Caught in the act. I so appreciate that about you Americans. So direct. It's refreshing."

"The New York accent is that obvious?"

"Unmistakable. I lived there for four years doing my business degree at Columbia."

The reason his English was so perfect... She gave him a long look. "If we're being direct, I'd ask you what you're doing here alone without a beautiful woman on your arm. Asking a complete stranger to have a drink with you."

His gaze darkened with a hint of something she couldn't read. He flicked a wrist toward the lights glimmering on the water. "I was looking for a little peace. Some answers to a question I had."

That intrigued her. "Did you find them?"

His mouth quirked. "Maybe."

She felt the inquisitive probe of his gaze right down to the lower layers of her dermis, the indolent way he looked at her suggesting he had all the time in the world to know her. "So what do you do, then, beautiful Liv, when you aren't sitting here?"

She couldn't help but feel like she was being led somewhere he wanted her to go, but the casually issued compliment had a much more potent effect than it should have.

"I'm a designer." She called herself that for the first time since she'd come to Milan a year ago to pursue her dream, somehow tonight needing to assert it as fact in the wake of her mentor's demise. "I'm working on my debut line."

Which hopefully would still see the light of day with Giovanni gone.

He lifted a brow. "You will partner with one of the design houses here?"

"That is the plan, yes."

"Did you study fashion in school?"

"Yes, at Pratt in New York."

His gaze turned inquisitive. "Why not stay there and start your career where you have roots?"

Because she was running from a life she never intended to return to.

"I needed a change…a fresh start."

"Milan is certainly the place to do that if you are a designer." He smiled at the waitress as she arrived with their drinks, then waited until she'd left before raising his glass. "To new…*friendships*."

Her pulse skittered across her skin like hot oil in a pan. She lifted her glass and pointed it at him. "And to you finding answers."

A slow, easy smile twisted his lips. "I think maybe meeting you was exactly what I needed."

That turned her insides completely upside down. She took a sip of her Chianti, discovered it was a significantly nicer vintage than the one she'd ordered and took some extra fortifying sips.

He crossed muscular arms over each other and sat back in the chair. "Have you had success with any of the design houses here?"

"I had made some inroads, yes, until something beyond my control happened. Now I'm not so sure it's going to work out."

"Why is that?"

She lifted her chin, fought the burn of emotion at the back of her eyes. "Life."

He was silent for a moment, then dipped his head. "I am sure you will find alternate avenues."

She nodded determinedly. "I intend to. You do what it takes, right? To make your dreams come true?"

His mouth twisted, a strange light filling his dark eyes. "You do indeed."

It was like a coldness had enveloped the warm Navigli night, the way the warmth drained from his expression. Olivia shifted in her seat, wondering when the breeze had kicked up. Wondering what she'd said or done to bring the mood change about—because everyone had dreams, didn't they? They were good things, not bad.

She took another sip of her wine. "So," she murmured in an attempt to lighten the mood, "you know what I do. Your turn to spill."

He arched a brow at her. "Spill?"

"Confess. Tell me your secrets… At least, what you do for a living."

"Aah." His mouth tilted. "I push money around. Make things profitable. Ensure the *creatives* don't bring the ship down."

She gave him a look of mock offense. "Where would the civilized world be without us?"

"True." His half smile sent a frisson of awareness through her. Made her hot all over again. She had a feeling he did that easily. Ran hot and cold. Turned it on and off like a switch.

His gaze probed hers. "What?"

"You do that easily."

"Do what easily?"

"Run hot and cold."

An amused, slightly dangerous glint filled his eyes. He set his wineglass down with a deliberate movement, his gaze on hers. "Possibly very true. Out of curiosity, Liv, which would you like me to be?"

Her heart skipped a beat. "I think I'll abstain from answering that."

"Forever or just for now?" he jibed.

"For now," she said firmly. She focused on the inch of ruby-red liquid left in her glass. She hadn't flirted with a man since the beginning of her unspectacular, long-term relationship with Guillermo Villanueva, a photographer she'd met on a job and eventually lived with. They had been finished for over a year now, and she was sorely out of practice when it came to flirting.

"Have you eaten?" He lifted an inquiring brow as she glanced up at him.

"I was going to eat when I got home."

He picked up the menu and scanned it. Ordered a selection of appetizers without consulting her. Surprisingly, for a woman who valued her independence above all else, she found it a huge turn-on. Found everything about him a huge turn-on. And it only seemed to get worse as they chatted about everything from French and American politics to books and music. He was clearly way above average intelligence, sophisticated and seemed to have vast amounts of knowledge housed under that compelling facade.

"Why Columbia?" she asked as she snared the last piece of bruschetta. "Did you have family in America?"

He shook his head. "I wanted a change of pace like you did. To spread my wings. New York as the epicenter of it all made sense."

"So are you a financial genius, then? Million-dollar deals and all that?"

A glitter entered his eyes. "The genius part is debatable, but yes, sometimes there are big deals."

She found herself staring at his mouth again. It really was lush. Spectacular. What would it be like to kiss him? What would it be like for him to kiss *her*? Oh, God. She pushed her empty wineglass away with an abrupt movement. Enough of that.

He inclined his head toward the glass. "Another?"

She shook her head. "I should get home. I have a lot I want to accomplish tomorrow."

"I'll drive you, then." He lifted his hand to signal the waitress.

She wanted to say yes. Wanted him to drive her home so he could kiss her good-night. But that was utter madness. She *didn't* know him. He *could* be a criminal. A high-end one with a Rolex and great shoes.

He looked up at their server as she took his credit card and ran it through the machine. "I would like to drive this young woman home, Cecilia. Can you offer me a reference?"

The brunette let out a husky chuckle, her gaze moving to Olivia. "He is perfectly respectable. If uncatchable."

Olivia had no doubts about that. She got to her feet, gathered her gym bag and purse and allowed Tony to guide her through the crowded little trattoria, his hand on the small of her back electrifying. They walked a short distance down a side street to where his insanely expensive-looking yellow monster of a car was parked at the curb.

He tucked her inside with a sure hand. She felt her heart rev to life as the engine rumbled beneath them, snarling like the beast it was. Pressing a palm to her throat, she gave him the directions to her apartment and tried to remember the last time she'd felt this alive. Like herself... The past year had been about finding herself again, stopping the nightmares, ending the pain.

Who was she now? She didn't even know.

Tony was quiet in the car, his elegant, eminently capable hands guiding the powerful vehicle through the streets to the aristocratic neighborhood that bounded Corso Venezia and Via Palestro, her home for the past year. Her chest pulsed with a funny ache as they passed the stunning examples of baroque and neoclassical architecture that lined the streets, the elegant exclusive avenues of Milan's fashion district. The beautiful palazzo that lay only a stone's throw from her window. Every day she sat there drinking coffee, dreaming up designs and feeding the voraciously hungry birds that knew her now. It was *hers*, this neighborhood. She'd finally found a sense of belonging and she didn't want to give it up.

Tony turned into the driveway of her modern building located in one of the neighborhoods tucked in behind Corso Venezia. When Giovanni had shown it to her, she'd instantly fallen in love with its wrought iron balconies and wall-size liberty windows. With its feeling of lightness after the prison New York had become...

Tony brought the car to a halt in the rounded driveway. "Do you have a parking spot? I'll see you to your door."

Her already agitated heartbeat sped up. She knew exactly where this was leading if he accompanied her up to her apartment, and for a woman who had never done this, never invited a man back to her apartment on a first date, it was like someone had dropped her onto one of those death-defying loop-the-loop roller coasters that promised equal amounts of terror and exhilaration.

She shook her head, dry mouthed, realizing he was waiting for a response. "It's underground," she told him huskily, pointing to the entrance at the end of the driveway.

He guided the car into the garage, parked in her spot and followed her to the elevators. They rode the glass-enclosed lift up to her tenth-floor apartment.

"An awfully exclusive apartment for a struggling artist," Tony commented, leaning back against the wall.

Olivia pressed damp palms against her thighs as the cityscape came into view. "A friend was helping me out."

His brow rose. "A *friend*?"

"A *nonromantic* friend," she underscored, absorbing the aggressive, predatory male in him. It wasn't helping the state of her insides.

His raised brows arced into a slashing V. "Men just don't *lend* multimillion-euro apartments to a female unless they have other intentions, Liv."

The insinuation in his words brought her chin up. "This one did," she rasped. The elevator doors swung open. She stalked out of the car and headed down the hallway to her apartment, her head a muddled, attracted mess.

Tony caught up with her at her door. She turned to face him, confused, her stomach a slow burn. "I think you don't know me at all."

"My mistake," he came back laconically, tall and daunting. "It's a natural question for a man to ask."

Was it? They'd only had a drink. She was so confused about the whole evening, about what was happening with this beautiful stranger, her head spun. She stood there, heart hammering in her chest. Tony put a hand to the wall beside her, keeping a good six or seven inches between them, his gaze pinned on her face. Her stomach dropped as if she was headed toward the steepest plunge on that scary roller coaster, the part where one had big, huge second thoughts.

Something glimmered in his gaze. "Aren't you going to invite me in for an espresso to cap the evening off?"

"I don't know," she answered honestly, knees weak.

"Oh, come on, Liv," he chided, that glimmer darkening into a challenge. "Men are territorial. Would you expect a man like me not to be?"

No. Yes. Her head swam.

He closed the gap between them until he was mere inches from her. His palm came up to cup her jaw, his gaze dropping to her lips. Her own clung shamelessly to that lush pout she'd been staring at all night, had been wanting to kiss all night. And he knew it.

He lowered his head and rocked his mouth over hers. Smooth, questing, he exerted just the right amount of pressure not to frighten her away, and that mouth, *that mouth*, was sensational. She anchored her palms against the solid planes of his chest, her bones sinking into the hard line of the wall as he explored the curves of her mouth. He kissed her so expertly she never had a chance. All she could do was helplessly follow his lead. When he delved deeper, demanded entrance to the heat of her mouth, she opened for him.

Their tongues slid along each other's in an erotic duel that rendered her knees useless. She dug her fingertips harder into his chest, breathing him in, registering how delicious he smelled. He was a potent combination of heady male and tangy lime, and she was completely and irrevocably lost.

He pulled back, his gaze scouring her face. "Your key," he prompted harshly.

Her brain struggled to process the command. Blood pumping, head full, she rummaged through her purse, found her keys and handed them to him.

The sane part of Rocco told him he didn't need to carry the charade any further. It was obvious Olivia Fitzgerald was not above falling into the arms of a man with a beautiful watch and a nice car if it meant rescuing her from her precarious position. Whether she displayed an irresistible vulnerability along with it was inconsequential. It was likely a well-rehearsed act.

The less-than-rational part of his brain wanted to see how far she'd let him take it. How desperate she was.

He tossed her keys on the entryway table. Watched her sink her small white teeth into her perfectly shaped bottom lip.

"I'm not so interested in coffee," he admitted harshly, watching her pupils dilate. "Do you mind if we skip it?"

She shook her head, eyes wide. Worried her lip with

those perfect teeth. He closed the distance between them, the heat they created together rising up to tighten his chest. He swallowed hard at the swift kick of lust that rocketed through him as he brought his palms to rest on either side of her where she stood, back against the door. It was inconceivable to him that he could feel such desire for her given who she was, what she had been to his grandfather, even if this was a deliberate experiment to extract the truth. But she was undeniably exquisite.

Her cheeks, tanned to a light golden brown from the hot Milanese summer sun, were flushed with desire. Her chest under the worn purple T-shirt was rising and falling fast, her nipples erect against the soft fabric. Her hands lay limp at her sides, as if she had no idea what to do with them.

He did. He wanted them on him, sliding over every inch of his hot skin until he rolled her under him and made her his. *Dio.* This was insanity.

He dipped his hands under the frayed edge of her T-shirt and sought out the silky-soft bare skin beneath. She was enough to tempt a levelheaded man to mad acts, even his rigidly correct grandfather who had never looked at another woman after his Rosa had died. Her swift intake of breath echoed in the silent apartment as he trailed his fingers over the bare skin of her flat stomach, her midriff, the muscles of her abdomen tensing beneath his touch. Her head dropped back against the door, eyes almost purple as she waited for his kiss.

"You could bring the strongest man to his knees," he muttered roughly, almost angrily, as he brought his mouth down to hers. "But then you know that, don't you, Liv?"

Her brows came together in a frown, her lips parting to answer him. He didn't let her get that far, his mouth taking hers in an insistent kiss that allowed no hesitation. She was rigid under his hands for a moment, as if teetering in indecision. He took her tongue inside his mouth, drawing her back into the heat. She was soft and perfect and he could not resist the lure of her flesh, bare beneath the T-shirt.

He pushed her jacket off her shoulders, letting it drop to the floor. "Lift your arms."

She did, her gaze on his as he pulled the threadbare T-shirt over her head, tossed it to the floor and drank her in. She was slim, perfect, with high, firm breasts and rose-colored nipples that were tautly aroused.

It was like being in the Garden of Eden and told not to touch. He just couldn't do it.

Bending his head, he palmed her breast, taking the rosy tip into his mouth. Her swift intake of breath made his blood heat. He sucked on her, laved her, until she was moaning, moving restlessly against him, then he transferred his attention to the other rounded peak. The feel, the taste of her underneath his mouth, was like forbidden fruit. *Irresistible.* The sound of their connection filled the hot Milanese night, breathy, seeking. He slid his thigh between hers and filled his hands with the rounded, toned curves of her bottom, seeking relief for his aching flesh.

Her gasp filled his ear. *"Tony."*

One word, one softly uttered admission of surrender, was all it took to bring him crashing back to earth. To know he had proved what he had come here to do.

He lifted his head, sank his hands into her waist and pushed her away.

"The name is Rocco."

Her eyes widened, darkened. A frown furrowed her brow as her hands came up to cover herself. "Rocco? Why did you tell me your..." Her voice trailed off as the color drained from her face.

"That's right, Liv," he said harshly, taking great pleasure in her look of horror. "Antonio is my middle name. How does it feel to sink your hooks into two generations of Mondellis?"

Her look of complete confusion was award worthy. She shook her head, gaze fixed on his. "What are you talking about? Giovanni and I were not like that."

"What were you, then?" His tone was savage. "You expect me to believe a man buys you a three-million-euro luxury apartment out of the goodness of his heart? Because you're *friends*? My grandfather has not talked about you *once*, has never even mentioned you in passing conversation. And yet you were *together*?"

"Because I didn't want anyone to know I was here." She snatched her T-shirt up from the floor and pulled it over her head. "Giovanni was protecting my privacy. He was my mentor. My *friend*. He was not my lover. How could you even think that? It's preposterous."

Fury lanced through him. He stepped forward until they were nose to nose. "No more than a seventy-year-old man thinking *you* could be interested in him." He waved a hand at her. "You must be good, I'll hand you that. What man could resist you servicing him? Moaning his name as if you can't wait to get into bed?"

She was in front of him so fast, her palm arcing through the air, she almost got it to his face before he snatched it away and yanked it down to her side.

"You bastard," she snarled at him, her catlike eyes spitting fire as he held her hand captive. "How *dare* you make accusations about something you know nothing about?"

"Because I *know* him," he raged. "Giovanni was hopelessly, irrevocably in love with my grandmother. There is no way he would take a twentysomething lover unless he was completely *taken in. Brainwashed with lust*."

She glared at him. "He didn't. I keep trying to tell you that."

He kept his fingers manacled around her wrist as she tried to tug her hand free. "Why are you hiding out from the world here? Why not use your name to build your line, if that was the truth—if that is your dream?"

"It *was* the truth." She wrenched her arm free, her show of strength taking him off guard. "Everything I said tonight was the truth. I needed to get away from modeling, from *everything*, so I came here."

"To escape your creditors?"

"To escape *my life*." She pointed to the door. "Get the hell out of my apartment. *Now*."

"*My* apartment, you mean." He gave her a searching look. "Why Giovanni, Olivia? Why choose a seventy-year-old man as your lover when you could have anyone? Any rich man on this planet would welcome you into his bed. Pleasure you with the youth of a much younger man. All you would have to do is snap your fingers."

Her hands curled into fists by her sides. "You are so unbelievably wrong."

"Then why the checks? Why was Giovanni doling out cash to you on a regular basis? Was that also *friendship*?"

Her mouth flattened into a defiant line. She closed her eyes, a long silence stretching between them. When she opened them, her eyes glimmered with a wealth of emotion he couldn't read.

"We were building a line together. The money was for fabrics. For suppliers."

He gave her an incredulous look. "I am the CEO of House of Mondelli, Olivia. I know every project Giovanni was working on because he was a creative and he tended to go off half-cocked with new ideas without exploring their viability. There was no line."

She stalked around him and headed down the hallway. He followed her into the bright, large room at the back of the apartment. Dozens of designs hung from a rack along the back wall. A sewing machine sat on a table. Stacks of illustrations lay scattered across a table.

He walked over and fingered some of the designs. They were beautiful, ethereal creations that even the noncreative in him could see were sensational, different, stamped with a unique sense of freedom of fabric and color that was distinct from anything he'd seen before. But they also featured a Giovanni-like sense of symmetry.

An odd emotion stirred to life inside of him. Riled him. "This doesn't prove anything. All it proves is that you were using my grandfather to further your ambition. What did you say in the café? You do what it takes to make your dreams come true?"

Some of her newly found color drained from her face. "You're taking that way out of context."

"I think I've got it just right. You have a drink with a complete stranger, a man with an expensive watch who clearly does well, you see your opportunity for another rich benefactor and you make your move." He tossed his head in disgust. "I could have had you against that door. You were ready to replace Giovanni *seven days after his death.*"

Her pallor took on a grayish tinge. "You set that all up tonight to see if I was a gold digger?"

"And wasn't it telling?" He gave her a mirthless, half smile. "The idea actually didn't come into my head until I sat there watching you and your *fidanzate* laughing and giggling as if your lover hadn't just passed away. I wanted to see what kind of a woman you were before I tossed your beautiful little behind out on the street and now I know."

Her head reared back. "I was out tonight to try to take my mind off Giovanni. I can't expect to understand how much you must be grieving him. I know you were close. But *I* am grieving him, too. I cared for him. And I will not permit you to sully what we had with your wild accusations."

"It's the truth," he gritted.

"It's far from it."

"Then spit it out. I am craving a little honesty here."

She took a deep breath. Pushed stray strands of hair that had escaped her ponytail out of her face. "Your grandfather was in love with two women. Madly, fully in love with two people. One of those women was my mother, Tatum."

He stared at her. "What the hell are you talking about?"

She sucked her bottom lip between her teeth. "When my mother modeled for Mondelli in the eighties, she had an affair with Giovanni. Giovanni was torn between her and Rosa, agonized over the decision, he said. In the end, he chose Rosa and severed all ties with my mother. Rosa knew about the affair, but neither she nor Giovanni spoke of it afterward."

He gave her a look of disbelief. Giovanni in love with Tatum Fitzgerald? While he'd been married to his grandmother? He may not have much of a belief in the concept of true love, but the one person he'd seen have it was his grandfather with Rosa. They'd conceived Sandro when his grandmother was just eighteen, had been each other's first loves and had remained deeply enamored until Rosa had passed away.

An affair? It was inconceivable.

He leveled a gaze at her. "How do you know all this?"

A nerve pulsed in her cheek. "I was going through a rough time in my modeling career. Giovanni approached me at an industry function in New York. I think he felt guilty about what happened to my mother's career after he ended things. She fell apart after he left her. She went on to marry my father, but she never got over Giovanni and they divorced. Giovanni told me the whole story that night."

He attempted to absorb the far-fetched tale. "So he decided to *befriend* you? Put you up in a luxury apartment in Milan and mentor you because he felt guilty over a relationship that ended *decades* ago?"

She lifted her chin. "He knew I needed a friend. Someone I could count on. He was there for me."

"What about your own family and friends?"

"They aren't something I can turn to." Her gaze dropped away from his. "I left my whole life behind when I came to Milan."

Because she'd known she had a free ride. He smothered a frustrated growl and paced to the window. "So Giovanni is just your friend, you were out tonight missing him, and that thing with me just now was what? The way you treat all men who chat you up in a café?"

"You *deliberately* tried to seduce me."

He swung around. "And *how* seducible you were, *bella*. You made it easy."

Her expression hardened. "If you choose not to believe a word I say, you can leave. I'll be out within the week."

"Tell me the truth about you and Giovanni and I'll give you a month. I'm not an unreasonable man."

Her eyes flashed. "Get out."

He thought that might be a good idea before he lost what was left of his head. Putting his hands on Olivia Fitzgerald, *coming here*, had been a mistake driven by his grief and his desire to know what had been in Giovanni's head these past months. And now it was time to rectify it by getting the hell out.

He swept his gaze over the racks of clothes. She was going to have an issue finding a place she could afford that could accommodate all of *this* without Giovanni bankrolling it. And even he wasn't without a heart.

"I'll give you a month. Then I expect the keys delivered to me."

She followed him to the door, looking every bit the angelic blonde damsel in distress that she was not. He walked through the door and didn't look back.

Giovanni had always been a bit of a romantic. Good thing Rocco was nothing like him.

CHAPTER THREE

ROCCO STOOD ON the tarmac of Milan's Linate Airport, Christian Markos at his side. The last of the Columbia Four to depart following Giovanni's funeral, Christian was headed to Hong Kong and a deal that couldn't wait. As always, when Rocco parted from his closest friends, there was an empty feeling in his heart. They had become so tight during those four years at Columbia. Watched one another grow into manhood and cemented their friendships as they took on the world.

Together they were an impenetrable force, greater than the sum of their parts. It was always difficult to return to their respective corners of the world, but they did so with the knowledge they would see one another soon—their four-times-a-year meet-ups a ritual none of them missed.

Christian wrapped an arm around him. "I may have a weekend off midmonth. Why don't we take your boat out? Catch up properly?"

Rocco smiled. "I'll believe it when we're drinking Peroni on the deck, *fratello*. Some big deal will come up and you'll be gone again."

Christian gave him an indignant look. "That last one was a megamerger. Out of my hands."

"And the brunette that came along with it?"

"Opposing pain in my behind," Christian grumbled. "Who was the blonde today by the way? Looked like a heated conversation."

It had been. Olivia Fitzgerald showing up at his grand-father's funeral had been an event he hadn't anticipated. Despite his objections, she'd insisted on staying. Not something he'd been willing to risk a scene over, particularly when his father had just made his own notable appearance, reeking of alcohol.

He looked at Christian. "Olivia Fitzgerald. She was not invited. I had an issue with it."

His friend lifted a brow. "Olivia Fitzgerald the model? I thought she was in hiding."

"She is, here in Milan. She knew Giovanni and wanted to pay her respects."

Christian looked curious. "What is your issue with her?"

"It's complicated."

"Everything is complicated with you." His friend shrugged. "You should sign her. The board would be kissing your feet."

"She doesn't want to be in the limelight." Why, he still didn't know.

An amused smile twisted the Greek's lips. "One of my senior deal makers had that photo of her nude on the beach in his office. I had to make him take it down. It's a little distracting when you're trying to crunch numbers."

"No doubt." Rocco knew exactly the shot his friend was talking about. The beach scene of Olivia kneeling in the surf, hands strategically covering herself, had graced the cover of an annual swimsuit magazine, then made the rounds as a wildly popular screensaver.

The engines of Christian's jet started to whir. "I'm so sorry about Giovanni," he said to Rocco. "I know how much he meant to you. And I'm sorry you had to deal with your father today. That can't have been easy."

"It was inevitable." The fact that Christian and Zayed

had had to remove his father from the proceedings—not so much.

He frowned. "I'm sorry you had to bear witness to that."

"It's not your cross to bear," his friend said quietly. "You take the weight of the world on your shoulders sometimes, Rocco. There's only so much of a burden a man can carry."

Rocco nodded. Except he'd been carrying the burden of his family for so long he didn't know how it could be any different.

"Go," he told Christian, clapping him on the back. "My boat and a case of Peroni are waiting when you come back."

His friend nodded and strode toward the plane. Rocco watched while he boarded the jet, the crew closed up the doors and the pilot taxied off to join the lineup of planes waiting to take off.

Even with everything he had on his plate, he couldn't get that night with Olivia out of his head. What she'd told him about Giovanni. Whether there was the slightest bit of truth in any of it. It sat in his brain and festered. Added to his confusion over his grandfather's decisions, the changes he'd seen in Giovanni of late. Had he been capable of cheating on his beloved Rosa? Sure, Giovanni had admired women for the pure aesthetic of them. He was a designer. But *unfaithful*?

He'd thought it had just been age softening his grandfather lately, the mellowing of his acerbic, grandiose personality. Had it instead been the influence of a woman? Olivia Fitzgerald?

Had he been in love with her? Did Olivia possess many of the same attributes as her mother, thus replacing the one woman he'd never been able to have? His stomach rearranged itself with a strange emotion he didn't want to identify. After witnessing the genius Giovanni and Olivia had created together in those designs, it was clear they had a connection.

And why did he care? What was it to him if his grandfather had fallen for a woman a third of his age? If he'd allowed himself to be made a fool of? *He* had done his job ensuring Olivia Fitzgerald would no longer take advantage of his family.

Because you almost lost your head. Over a beautiful blonde who'd had more of a master plan in *her* head than he'd ever had.

An image of Olivia's face when she'd walked into the church today flicked through his head. Fear she would be discovered even though she'd had a scarf over her head. Fear of *him* as she'd seen him. Stubborn defiance blazing in those amazing blue eyes as she'd stood her ground.

She'd also, he conceded, looked heartsick. Sad. And in his gut, he knew it was true emotion. He hadn't had the heart to toss her out. She had left as quickly as she'd appeared, not staying for the reception. He knew she was still in the apartment; he'd had the building supervisor keep him advised of her presence. He suspected she was having difficulty finding another place, but it wasn't his problem she'd lost her paycheck in Giovanni.

Christian's jet disappeared into the clouds. Rocco turned and headed toward the terminal, but his friend's words followed him. *You should sign her. The board would be kissing your feet...*

They *would* kiss his feet if he signed Olivia Fitzgerald. The worldwide press had been in a furor ever since her disappearance from modeling. She'd left on top, one of the most highly paid faces in the world. Everyone wanted her. Her disappearance had only added to the mystique.

He pushed his way through the terminal doors, strode through the tiny building and exited into the car park. There was only one problem with Christian's rather brilliant plan. Olivia didn't want to be found. Had wanted to escape her former life. And if it wasn't because she'd been bankrupt, as he'd suggested, then why? Why abandon a three-million-dollar contract when she could have just worked her way out of it, then gone into the career she'd desired?

She'd looked so miserable, so dejected, as she'd left the church today. She had no hope of launching that line without Giovanni. Her dream was done. Unless she found herself another benefactor.

He paused, his hand on the handle of the Aventador's door. Suddenly the path forward became clear. He had what Olivia needed as head of one of the most powerful design houses in the world. Olivia had what he needed if he could persuade her to come back to modeling for a year as the exclusive face of Mondelli. Her star power would turn Mondelli into a superstar brand, the couture house of the moment, the board would fall to its knees at such an acquisition and he would have control of his company again.

Adrenaline fueled his movements as he stepped into his car and brought it purring to life. Making Olivia an offer she couldn't refuse was an undeniably alluring play. But there was something else his mind was manufacturing that would be the icing on the cake. The pièce de résistance. Olivia Fitzgerald as the face of Mondelli and the brand-new fiancée of the CEO of House of Mondelli. A perfect union from all angles. And the perfect way to convince the board he had House of Mondelli as his top priority.

All his problems solved in one tidy little package.

A smile curved his mouth. Renzo Rialto would wet himself. How much more could he want? Now all he had to do was persuade Olivia Fitzgerald his plan was in both their interests.

Olivia was packing a box of design materials when the knocking sounded hard and insistent on her front door. Thinking it might be Violetta coming to help, and frowning at her exuberance, she got to her feet, dusted off her hands and went to answer it. Any distraction to take her mind off her rather desperate situation was welcome at this point.

When she saw who was standing in the hallway, she amended that thought. Any distraction *other* than a fully resplendent Rocco Mondelli clad in the dark suit he'd worn to the funeral that morning. Despite her vow to hate him, her heart pitter-pattered in her chest as she took him in leaning against the doorjamb, impatience written across his olive-skinned face.

"You said I had a month."

"You do." He walked past her into the apartment. "You'll find I'm a man of my word, Olivia. Have you had any luck yet finding another apartment?"

A man of his word? He'd deliberately seduced and misled her in this very apartment. She gave him a cool look and shut the door. "As a matter of fact, no, but I thought I'd better start getting packed up before you send in the goons."

"I won't have to." He waved a hand toward the kitchen. "This time I would like an espresso."

She stared at him in amazement. "You were ready to toss me out of that funeral this morning and now I'm supposed to make you coffee?"

He returned her stare, nonplussed. "I have an offer I think you'd like to hear."

Not in this decade.

His mouth curved. "Get me that coffee, Olivia."

Deciding she wasn't really in a position to argue because he *could* toss her out on her butt at this very moment, she walked past him to the kitchen, emptied the grinds from the espresso machine and did his bidding. He stood there, hands in his pockets, watching her.

"You were genuinely sad this morning."

She pressed the start button, turned and leaned back against the counter. "I loved Giovanni. Of course I was."

"So now it's love," he jibed. "Giovanni was madly in love with a woman and I hadn't a clue. How remarkable."

"You can walk right back out that door if this is the way this is going to go."

"*Nessuno*, Liv, it isn't." He crossed his arms over his chest and leaned back against the countertop. "I'm going to make you an offer that makes a whole lot of sense, you're going to take it and we're going to make the most of this difficult situation."

"There's nothing you could say that would convince me to have anything to do with you after what you did to me."

"I think you're wrong." He waved his hand toward the living room and the packed boxes littering every open space. "You are never going to be able to afford an apartment in Milan that will allow you to do your design work on a barista's salary. You've made it clear returning to your former life is not an option and you cannot rely on family and friends for help. So all you have left," he concluded, touching his chest, "is *me*."

"I don't want anything from you," she said pointedly, shoulders rising to her ears. "I will figure out a way."

His gaze darkened to a forbidding ebony. "What if I said I would honor the commitment Giovanni made to you? But I would take it even further. I would move the development of your line in-house at Mondelli, offer you all the design and marketing support we have and bring it to market for the fall of next year."

Her mouth dropped open. He would take the development of her line *in-house*? *Why*, when he clearly thought so little of her?

"Because you have something I want, Olivia." He answered her unspoken question with a twist of his lips. "I need a face to carry the House of Mondelli through the next year. Bridget Thomas's contract is up and I don't care to renew it. I would offer you a five-million-dollar contract for the year. You coming back to modeling would generate a great deal of excitement for the brand, make people stand up and pay attention again."

Her heart dropped. "I'm not modeling anymore. That part of my life is over."

He nodded. "I understand you want to design, that that's where your heart is. But surely one year, *twelve months of your life*, to secure your dream isn't such a hardship."

"No." The word flew out of her mouth, harsh, vehement. "I will never model again."

He pinned his gaze on her. "Why? What happened to make you give it all up?"

Her last appearance on a runway. Her best friend overdosing after walking that same runway months before... The memory of it slammed through her head, dark and terrifying. She reached back and gripped the counter, her fingertips pressing into the cold granite. She had completely lost it that night, her pressure-packed life finally eating her alive. And she was never going back.

She lifted her gaze to his. "It doesn't matter why. I left and I'm not going back."

"When the alternative is letting your dream die?" He stared at her, an incredulous look on his face. "If you debut a line with House of Mondelli you will *instantly* become a star of the design world. You won't have to build a reputation, you will have one immediately. And from there, all you need to do is choose your path. You would never have to set foot on a runway again after the twelve months."

She sank her palms into her temples and turned away. It was tempting, so tempting, to say yes. What he was saying was true. She'd thanked her lucky stars when Giovanni had taken her under his wing, because with his help she could succeed in a cutthroat industry that was almost impossible to break into. She could change her life and finally be happy. But return to modeling to make it happen? Acid inched its way up her throat. Not doable.

It would be the end of her this time.

She turned back to him, her features schooled into an expressionless mask. "I'm sorry. It's just not possible."

The incredulity on his face deepened. "I would wipe out the three-million-dollar debt you owe Le Ciel for the contract you broke."

She pulled in a deep breath. *Lord,* he was hitting all her weak spots. She would love to erase that blight on her track record. It would put her at peace with the world. But she couldn't do it. "No."

He lifted his shoulders, his gaze cool and calculating. "Then you'd better keep packing."

Desperation surged through her. "You saw the designs. They're amazing. Let me show them to you properly and you'll see how perfect they are for Mondelli's fall line. Let me bring them to market with you as Giovanni intended. The cachet of having my name attached to them, *Giovanni's* name, will give you that buzz you are looking for. It doesn't have to be me modeling."

He shook his head. "You have no cachet as a designer. I want you as the face of Mondelli. That is the only deal on the table."

"Then, no." She would rather beg on the street than go back to modeling.

"I would take some time to think about it," he advised, pushing away from the counter. "I won't ask again. And while you're at it, you might want to consider the other half of my offer."

She was almost afraid to ask what it was.

"I want to create huge buzz around our partnership. Therefore, if you accept my offer to be the face of Mondelli, we would also announce our engagement to the world at the same time. The marriage of two great brands."

Her mouth fell open, a dizzy feeling sweeping through her. *He was joking.* He had to be joking, except there wasn't one bit of humor on his beautiful face.

"That idea is preposterous."

"It's genius. A master publicity stunt."

She shook her head. "We hate each other. How would we possibly convince the world we are in love?"

A cynical smile twisted his lips. "Chemistry, Liv. We may hate each other, but neither of us would be being honest if we didn't admit that was one hell of a kiss against that door, *bella.*"

"And this engagement..." she ventured weakly. "Would it be real or pretend?"

"Real?" His gaze moved scathingly over her. "You think I would take the gold digger who used my grandfather for his money as a fiancée in the true sense of the word?"

Fury singed her veins, fisting her hands at her sides. "For the last time, I didn't use him."

"It doesn't matter." He waved a hand at her. "All of that is inconsequential now. I'm offering you a way out of your situation. Our engagement would cover the period of your contract with Mondelli. Once you've fulfilled it, we go our separate ways—*uncouple*, as it's fashionably put these days. You will have your line with Mondelli and my promise to support you every step of the way."

This time she *was* speechless. He wanted her to act as his fiancée? She'd had to acquire the skills of an actress to model, but this was way, *way* beyond her skill set.

"Absolutely not," she said firmly. "I will never return to modeling. If that's the only form your proposal will take, I'll have to decline."

He shrugged. "It's your decision. You have a week to come to me. After that the offer is off the table, this apartment is no longer yours and you, Olivia, better have a backup plan."

She watched as he turned on his heel and left, apparently not that interested in the espresso this time around, either. The sound of the door thudding shut made her wince. She had no backup plan. She had no plan at all. All she had was a beautiful apartment she desperately didn't want to leave, a life she'd built here she loved and an almost complete fall line that would make all her dreams come true if the House of Mondelli put its name behind it.

Everywhere she looked, she was out of options. Out of time. And that bastard knew it. He damn well knew it.

CHAPTER FOUR

OLIVIA SPENT THE rest of the week scouring Milan for apartments that would accommodate her work. She grew more dismayed with each visit. None of them were big enough, even if she did take on a roommate to afford one. The luxury apartment Giovanni had given her use of was palatial in comparison.

The end of her shift at the café at hand, she pulled her apron over her head, drew herself an espresso from the machine and sat down at one of the tables outside. She had to be out of the apartment tomorrow. The only thing she could do was pack up her designs, move into Violetta's already overcrowded house and pound doors to see if a local designer would take her on—which was unlikely, given how ultracompetitive the marketplace was.

Or she could go home, tail between her legs, and try to work some of her New York contacts. But New York wasn't going to be an easier nut to crack, and the thought of answering the inevitable questions when doors did open made her stomach knot. She wasn't ready to go back.

Panic rose up inside of her, her fingers curling tight around the handle of her cup. If she'd been more on top of her career, her finances, she wouldn't be in this situation. She never would have let her mother take control and fritter the money away. A *lot* of money. But preoccupied with pressure-packed million-dollar assignments and endorsements, traveling out of a suitcase more often than not, barely knowing what time zone she was in, let alone keeping her head above water, she'd had put her trust in the one person she'd thought she could.

Her mother had never been able to hold a real job when her career had fizzled out, and Olivia's father, Deacon Fitzgerald, had left when she was eight. A B-list photographer, her father had abandoned his career and started over with a new family and a new job at the transit company in a bid to erase the woman who had broken his heart. Olivia and her mother had sputtered along with whatever money her father could provide and her mother's spotty, on-again, off-again jobs until Olivia's career had taken off and Tatum had put the only skills she had, managing *her*, to work making her daughter a household name. But the more money Olivia had made, the faster it had gone, and the vicious, never-ending cycle was cemented.

The discovery she was broke on the heels of her best friend Petra Danes's overdose had sent her on a tailspin she'd never recovered from. The money had been her way out, and when that door was closed she'd quite literally self-destructed that last night in New York.

She took a sip of the coffee, the acrid brew harsh on her tongue. She'd come to Milan because she couldn't do it anymore. She was not healed; she needed time. That hadn't changed.

She watched as one exquisitely dressed Italian after another strolled by, the women in designer dresses even for a trip to the market. Turning to her father in her darkest time, for emotional support if not financial, hadn't been an option. She'd been so young when he'd left she'd hardly known him. And though they'd met regularly for a while until she was a teenager, each time she'd seen him it had grown more awkward and painful, as if her father had wanted to put as much distance between him and his old life as he could. So Olivia had stopped trying to see him, and he'd stopped calling except on big occasions like her birthday. And that was the way it had been ever since.

She bit her lip, refusing to get emotional over a parent lottery she'd lost a long time ago. A resigned clarity fell over her. She had only two choices: give up or accept Rocco Mondelli's offer. And since giving up her dream wasn't on the table, it left her only with the option to return to a career she'd vowed she never would. To an industry that had almost eaten her alive.

Her lashes fluttered down. Something Giovanni had said to her in those early dark days filled her head. *Passion is what makes life worth living,* ragazza mia. *If you don't have it in your soul, it dies a day at a time. Stop thinking of what you must do and start thinking of what will save you.*

And that was how she finally made her decision.

Olivia Fitzgerald showed up at his office forty-eight hours after Rocco had predicted she would. He instructed his assistant, Gabriella, to show her in. Gabriella appeared seconds later with Olivia at her side, an expectant look on his assistant's face.

"Go home," he instructed his PA. "I'm on my way out, as well. *Buona serata.*"

Gabriella echoed his farewell and disappeared. Olivia stood just inside the doorway, her carefully controlled expression veiling whatever thoughts were going on in her beautiful head. The tap of her toe on the marble was the only indicator she was apprehensive about what she'd come to do, and he liked that there was at least one outward sign filling him in on the inside picture.

The outside view was undeniably compelling. Her dark jeans made the most of her long legs, the cut of her clingy jersey shirt emphasizing her cool blonde beauty. Her hair was caught up in a ponytail once again, big dark sunglasses perched on her head as if to say she wasn't coming out of hiding until absolutely forced to.

He felt his nerve receptors react to her with that same layers-deep effect she'd had on him that night in Navigli. Even without makeup, she was still the most arresting woman he'd ever laid eyes on.

She lifted her chin as he brought his gaze slowly back up to her face. "If you're on your way out, we can do this another time."

"I'm on my way home." He got to his feet and reached for his briefcase. "I'm staying at my apartment in Milan tonight. We can talk there."

"This won't take long," she supplied hastily. "No need for that."

His mouth twisted. "I'm assuming you've come to take me up on my offer?"

Her lips pressed together. "Yes."

"Then we have lots to talk about. We can do it over dinner." He tossed the file he'd been working on into his briefcase, along with another pile of documents.

"I don't want to intrude on your evening. Why don't we…"

"Olivia." He lifted his head and pinned his gaze on hers. "Let's get something straight right off the top. In this relationship, I talk and you listen. I make the rules. You follow them. In no way is this going to be an equal, democratic partnership. Not for the money I'm paying you."

Her mouth dropped open. "I haven't signed your deal yet."

"But you will, because you're here." He dropped a last sheaf of papers in the briefcase and snapped it shut.

She sank her hands into her hips, her sapphire eyes a vivid blue beam blazing into him. "That night in Navigli must have been an aberration. Is *this* how you really treat your women? Favor them with a wild night in bed so they'll nip at your heels as required?"

He smiled at that. "Usually I have a bit more finesse, but in this case, it isn't necessary. Make no mistake about it, Olivia, Navigli was about me finding out what kind of a woman you really are. That was all."

Better she chew on that than the naked, unadulterated urge he felt to show her that wild ride in bed before he brought her to heel. Because this was a business arrangement. She had been Giovanni's lover. And rule number one for this particular business arrangement was to keep his hands off his soon-to-be pretend fiancée.

She flashed him a defiant look. "Helpful, then, for our little charade that you are such a magnificent actor. You fooled me with that kiss. It almost felt as if you meant it."

He lifted a brow, his gaze raking over her face. "As much as I'm loath to damage your ego heading into this very important assignment for both of us, I'm afraid my taste runs to sophisticated brunettes of a European bent. So you are quite safe, *cara*, from me."

She flinched, a tiny, almost indiscernible retraction he would have missed had he not been studying her so intently. *Bene.* The more they ignored the undeniable attraction between them, the better.

Her long, gold-tipped lashes came down to veil her eyes. "Too bad you're saddled with a very blonde, outspoken American fiancée for a year."

He gave her a slow smile. "I can handle you, Olivia, and you know it."

"You *think* you can because you are the epitome of arrogance." Fire lit the blue gaze she trained on him. "How is this going to work, then? Your overactive libido is well documented. Do we act as a joyous engaged couple while you engage in a discreet liaison or two on the side?"

He shifted his weight to both feet, widening his stance,

his laconic smile intensifying. "Who said I have an over-active libido? I would call it standard for a young, healthy male."

She lifted a shoulder. "Your reputation speaks for itself." Her gaze rested on him assessingly. "Giovanni thought it reflected a certain…emotional immaturity on your part. That you use it to avoid attachment."

"Emotional immaturity?" His head jerked back. "He said that?"

She nodded. "He thought you and Alessandra suffered from not having a direct parental influence while growing up. He said he did the best he could, but it's not the same as having your own parents to guide you."

He stared speechlessly at her, absorbing the look of satisfaction on her face. He'd started this war of words, yes. But *her* telling him his grandfather's innermost thoughts, thoughts that had apparently played a part in his decision to give Rocco a mere 50 percent stake in House of Mondelli? His fists itched to find the nearest wall and bury themselves in it. Giovanni had trusted his *twenty-six-year-old lover* enough to confide his thoughts in her, but not him?

He worked his jaw. Gathered his composure before he said something else to tip his cards. "What other confidences did Giovanni elect to illuminate you with?"

She gave him a wary look, as if realizing she might have gone too far. "He only made the odd comment here and there when we were talking about family. He was a private man, Rocco."

Apparently not that private. He jammed his hands in his pockets and impaled her with his gaze. "To answer your question, there will be no liaisons for either of us. This is a five-million-dollar partnership, Olivia, plus what I had to pay Le Ciel to break the contract you reneged on. We don't mess it up because we have to satisfy an urge. I can do that in the shower."

Her cheeks flamed a rosy pink. "That discussion was more for your benefit than mine. I'm just trying to understand the ground rules."

He picked up his briefcase and jacket. "They will become eminently clear as we discuss them over dinner. Shall we?"

She was silent as he drove them the short distance to the Mondelli penthouse, and he was glad for it, still steaming over the inside track she seemed to have on Giovanni's thoughts.

His frustration had abated, somewhat, by the time they reached the Galleria Passarella area in the heart of Milan. He should be *estatico*. He had exactly what he wanted after all. The perfect jewel to dangle in front of the board to cement his control of the company he'd helped build. He was no longer sporting the shorter end of the stick in this power struggle, and it felt good. More than good.

The penthouse occupied the top three floors of a graceful, modern building with superb views of the city. Rocco had chosen it because of the uniqueness of its design, the hidden jewel it contained. With the living quarters located on the ninth floor, the architect had used the tenth and eleventh floors to create a garden paradise that overlooked the city, including a terrace big enough to entertain fifty and a rock-pool retreat.

They stopped on the ninth floor, where he requested a light meal for him and Olivia from his housekeeper, then he led the way up the stone staircase to the roof garden. He could tell from the wide-eyed wonder in her eyes Olivia loved it instantly.

"It's hard to imagine this could exist up here."

"Exactly why I bought it. The heaters I had built in keep it the perfect temperature year-round." He opened his briefcase, pulled out her contract and tossed it on the soft-backed sofa near the pools. "Read through this while I get us a drink."

She gave the contract a rueful look. "You were that sure of me?"

"A dream is a powerful thing," he said simply. "So is desperation."

She opened her mouth as if to say something, then shut it after a long moment. *Bene.* She was learning.

"What can I get you to drink?"

"A glass of wine, thank you."

He pulled a bottle of rosé out of the wine fridge and tore off the foil.

"A toxicology screen?"

He had listed it as one of the up-front conditions. "Fairly standard, isn't it?"

"For a model with a history of *substance abuse.*"

He worked the corkscrew into the bottle. "This is a five-million-dollar deal we're negotiating, Olivia. When a formerly trustworthy top model starts showing up late for her shoots…reneges on obligations…blows off a three-million-dollar contract, there has to be a reason. I'm covering my investment."

Her chin lifted at a defiant angle. "There was no substance abuse problem. Unless you call one dirty martini too many on the odd night out an issue."

"Alcohol is a drug. If it interfered with your work, it was an issue."

"It did *not* interfere with my work."

"Then what did?" He poured two glasses of the rosé, put the bottle back in the fridge and carried the glasses over to her. "For all intents and purposes, you were a client's dream until that last year. You did your work, you did it exceptionally well and you were conscientious. What happened to change all that? Why the out-of-control partying near the end?"

A stubborn look crossed her face. "Maybe I was getting my bad-girl genes out of my system. I am my mother's daughter after all."

"You were for the first part of your career, as well." He handed her a glass and sat down beside her.

She lifted a shoulder. "Maybe the glow faded. Maybe it wasn't enough to hold my attention anymore."

And maybe she was lying through her teeth. A model didn't just walk away from a three-million-dollar contract because she was bored. She fulfilled her obligations, left on good terms and used the contacts she had made to build her reputation as a designer.

It made no sense. It was a mystery he intended to unravel.

He pointed his glass at her. "Did you leave New York to get away from a man? Were there issues with a relationship?"

She gave him an even look. "There was only one relationship—a long-term one I had that ended on good terms before I left."

"With Guillermo Villanueva..."

"Yes."

One of the world's most sought-after photographers, Venezuelan-born Guillermo Villanueva was known for his ability to put a twist, a different angle, on a face or a landscape that had been shot a thousand times. He was equally known for his swarthy good looks, which had models flocking eagerly to his shoots, putting their best foot forward as he reduced them to fluttery, feminine creatures that bent to his will.

Had Olivia been like that with him, too?

"How long was the relationship?" he asked to distract himself from a question that didn't matter.

She gave him a pointed look. "Does this really have relevance here?"

"*Sì*, Olivia, it does. We're about to be in the spotlight as a newly engaged couple. I need to know your personal history."

She sighed. "Three years. We were together three years."

He blinked. An eternity as far as he was concerned… For him, a two-month stint with a woman was an accomplishment. He wondered if Villanueva had been unfaithful to her. It wouldn't be surprising given the opportunities the photographer would have had working with beautiful women day in, day out.

"Was Villanueva the reason for the partying?" he asked.

A glimmer of emotion flashed in her brilliant blue eyes. "Guillermo was the most steadying influence I had in my life."

"Then why leave him?"

She was silent for a long moment, her gaze resting on the cascading pools of water. "I fell out of love with him," she said finally. "I wasn't with him for the right reasons."

Her quiet, level voice held a poignancy that made him look at her hard. It was a pattern, it seemed, that she was with men for the wrong reasons. With Giovanni, it had been money, a mentor. With Villanueva? Maybe a mentor, also. A stepping-stone to bigger and better jobs?

His rancor stirred anew. He was suddenly very sorry for Guillermo Villanueva. He had likely never seen it coming, so blinded with the radiance that was Olivia. She, on the other hand, had been done with him, ready to take those last steps to stardom. And Villanueva had been left in the dust.

Rocco had seen it happen to his brilliant Sicilian friend Stefan with a woman he'd sacrificed everything for, only to find out she'd been more interested in his bank account than him. A more trusting man than the rest of the Columbia Four initially, Stefan had subsequently become ten times harder than all of them.

He grimaced, taking a healthy swallow of his wine. Love was like that. It was never equally distributed between two people. And the poor fool who didn't recognize that got his heart torn out eventually.

"Finish reading the contract," he instructed. "We have much to discuss."

She picked it up and scanned it. He wasn't expecting her to have issues with it. It was a straightforward, clean contract. Olivia's face and body would be exclusive to the House of Mondelli for the next twelve months in a five-million-dollar endorsement deal, after which the second part of the contract, a design partnership agreement, would kick in.

After a few moments, she tossed the contract on the coffee table. "It's fine. Minus the tox screen."

"Olivia…"

"No." Her voice was harsh. "You need to trust me. This is a two-way street."

He trusted her as much as his rogue stallion on his best-behaved day. About a centimeter leeway on the reins… But he needed to get this deal done.

"Bene." He inclined his head. "But one sign that I need to and I will do it, regardless of your objections." He flicked a hand at the contract. "Can your lawyer look at it tomorrow?"

"Yes. That shouldn't be a problem."

"I've also had the paperwork drawn up to release you from your Le Ciel contract. You can show him that, too. It will clear you of any remaining obligations."

She drew her bottom lip between her teeth. "Thank you. That's a big weight off my shoulders."

The vulnerability glittering in her eyes caught him off guard. It was there when you peeled back the layers. When she forgot to hide it. He studied her for a long moment, then told himself he'd be a fool to overanalyze it. To buy in to it.

"See that you don't let me down," he advised tersely. "The eyes of the world are going to be on us. Millions of dollars are at stake. Screw up *once*, miss one shoot by ten minutes, blow off an appearance, however insignificant, fail to show up to any job with less than one-hundred-percent enthusiasm and I will make you rue the day you put pen to paper."

An emotion he couldn't read flashed in her eyes. Intimidation? Fear? Antagonism?

Her gaze tangled with his. "I will execute this contract to the best of my ability. You have my word on it. See that you keep yours."

"I intend to do so." He rose to his feet, walked over to the bar, procured the wine bottle and refilled their glasses. "How does working alongside Mario Masini sound?"

Her eyes widened. "You're serious?"

He sat down and stretched his long legs out in front of him. "I never say anything I don't mean."

"Wow." She looked dumbstruck. And rightly so. Mondelli's head designer was a legend in the fashion industry. He had joined the company to partner with Giovanni when the two men were in their early twenties. His classic yet inspired designs were the mainstay of high-profile personalities worldwide who wanted a streamlined vision that took its cues from beautiful materials and perfect cuts.

He allowed an inner smile as his plan came to brilliant, vivid life. "So now we talk details. We have one year. I want to move fast on this."

She nodded, looking a little overwhelmed.

"There is a design conference in New York next week the House of Mondelli is represented at. You will come with me and we will announce you as the new face of Mondelli at the press conference on the opening day."

Her face went gray. "That's very fast."

"It's the perfect opportunity. The eyes of the design world will be there."

She pushed her hair out of her face in what he was coming to recognize as a nervous tick. "And the engagement? When do we announce that?"

"My plan is to let the gossip hounds do it. We go ring shopping tomorrow, we show up in New York together with a massive rock on your hand and let the buzz take care of the rest."

The gray cast to her skin deepened. "And your family? When will we tell them?"

"We'll have dinner with Alessandra tomorrow night and tell her. You have met her, *sì*?"

She nodded. "We worked together on a shoot a few years ago."

"*Bene.* I am not intending on telling her the truth about us. She is too chatty, too apt to say the wrong thing to the wrong person. It's better she takes it for what it is."

She frowned. "Is our engagement really worth all this subterfuge? Wouldn't it be easier to simply announce me as the new face of Mondelli? It will generate a huge amount of buzz in its own right."

His gaze speared hers. "This is more than a publicity stunt, Olivia. This is the joining of two of the world's great brands. The creation of a dynasty, so to say. It will be a far more powerful story than you simply becoming the face of Mondelli."

"And when we *end* our engagement?"

"That will only increase the buzz. Everyone loves a heartsick, broken couple. It's great photography."

She looked at him as if he had an answer for everything. He did, in fact.

"I will have your belongings transferred to Villa Mondelli this week. I spend most of my time there commuting back and forth so it makes sense you are there with me. But we'll delay your actual move date until after we get back from New York. I have meetings in London later this week, and you likely won't want to spend your first days in the villa alone."

Her face lost the remainder of its color. "We're to live together?"

His mouth curved. "We're madly in love, Olivia. Of course we're living together."

"Yes, but—" she waved a hand at him "—we could position it as we're both so busy, I'm going to be traveling a ton, it just makes sense to keep it separate until we marry. I mean, living apart doesn't preclude…"

"A wild night in bed?" He shook his head. "Sorry to disappoint you, *bella*, but I'm not sleeping on your sofa to make this look real. You will move into Villa Mondelli when we get back."

She gave him an agitated look. "The apartment…"

He shrugged. "It's a good investment. If you can manage not to blow your money this time, maybe I'll allow you to buy it back."

Her mouth tightened. He plunged on relentlessly, "We have a lot of work to do before New York. Alessandra will be all about the big eyes for each other, but my Sicilian friend Stefan, who will undoubtedly want to toast us in New York, will be tougher. We'll need to know each other inside out."

She scrunched her face up. "What do you mean by tough?"

A wry smile twisted his mouth. "I went to Columbia with three other men I became very close with. We are all confirmed bachelors. For me to announce my engagement, to make such a quick, one-hundred-and-eighty-degree turn, we're going to have to make our feelings for each other convincing."

She slid a perfectly manicured nail in her mouth. "What will our story be, then?"

"I think we should say we met in a café and it was love at first sight."

She arched a brow at him, the humor of it all lost on her apparently. "And this was when?"

"A month ago. We've been staying out of the limelight, but now with your return to the modeling world, we're making our engagement public."

She chewed on the fingernail. *That* would have to stop, but he wasn't about to antagonize her further tonight. "Is there anyone you need to tell about the engagement?"

"My parents, eventually. I can do that in New York."

"You don't want to give them a heads-up?"

"We're not close," she said flatly. "It can wait."

"Siblings? Close friends? Anyone we should invite out the night we see Stefan?"

A shadow made its way across her face, intensifying the dark bags under her eyes. "No siblings," she said quietly. "And there are just the friends I've made here in Milan."

He nodded. "Any other details I should know?"

"No." She took a sip of her wine and lifted her gaze to his. "What else should I know about my fiancé other than the fact he is cynical and arrogant?"

"I work. A lot. Christian Markos and Zayed Al Afzal are my other two close friends I went to Columbia with. Christian is a financial genius based in Athens. Zayed has recently gone home to take the throne in his home country of Gazbiyaa."

"He's a *king*?"

"A sheikh. Gazbiyaa is in the heart of the Arabian desert."

"Okaaay." She rubbed a palm against her temple. "And Stefan? What does he do?"

"He's in high-end real estate. As in the deals that make

the *Wall Street Journal*... He doesn't touch anything under ten million."

She shook her head. "Quite the group of underachievers."

He lifted a shoulder. "We are all driven. But very different. More like brothers than friends. We even argue that way."

She smiled, and, *Dio*, when she did, it made the night sky light up. He'd have to make sure she didn't do that often. "You should know we run a charity together. It's a big thing for us. The Knights of Columbia was created to help disadvantaged youth overcome their backgrounds and succeed in business. It's based in New York, but we all do work in our home countries and funnel the kids through to various business programs in Manhattan." He took a sip of his wine. "We also personally mentor some of the kids."

Her eyes brightened. "It sounds amazing. Whose idea was it?"

"It arose out of work Christian was doing. He grew up on the streets of Athens, the child of a single mother. He never knew his father, had to fight his way out of poverty to take care of himself and his mother. It has defined him as a man, and he wanted to give back. We all loved what he was doing and wanted to be a part of it. Thus, the Knights of Columbia was born."

"I did charity work when I worked for Le Ciel," she murmured. "I miss it."

"We have a charity for young female designers who have suffered at the hands of men and have been forced to resort to shelters. It would be a great thing for you to get involved with if you have time."

"I would love to." She pressed her fingers against her mouth, her gaze uncertain. "You are so close to these men. How ever are we going to convince them this is real?"

An image of her plastered against the door of her apartment begging for more of him flashed through his head. His lip curled. "Act like you did that night in Navigli—act as if you want to devour me, as if you can't wait to get your hands on me. It doesn't get any more convincing than that."

A flush filled her cheeks. "That might be difficult," she drawled in response, "now that I know what kind of a man you are."

The insult bounced off him like the most ineffective of feints. "Fortunately, *cara*, pheromones aren't ruled by the brain. I'm sure you'll do just fine."

Her fingers tightened around the glass. He could tell she wanted to slap them across his face and tell him what to do with his deal. But she restrained herself because they both knew how important this was. For him, it was his chance to solidify control of House of Mondelli. For Olivia, her chance to take hold of her dream.

He only hoped he hadn't taken too big a risk on an asset that was a complete unknown. Because Olivia Fitzgerald was undoubtedly a wild card. She would either be the most brilliant play he'd ever orchestrated, or the one that would bring him down.

CHAPTER FIVE

OLIVIA TRIED TO maintain an air of enforced Zen as she and Rocco winged their way toward Manhattan in the Mondelli jet the following Sunday night, but with each mile the speedy little plane ate up toward the past she'd vowed to leave behind, her self-imposed calm faded further.

Her huge, square-cut, white-diamond engagement ring sat on her finger with an almost oppressive weight. It had already been pictured in tabloids and newspapers around the globe after she and Rocco had been spotted leaving an exclusive Via della Spiga boutique earlier that week. The taste of the media circus their engagement was about to become had already gone a long way toward ridding her of the ten pounds she needed to shed.

Technically, she was ready to face it. Her new wardrobe, courtesy of Mario Masini, was expertly packed in her suitcase stowed at the back of the jet. Her hair had been trimmed of its split ends, a shine added, her thoughts equally whipped into line by the Mondelli PR people, who'd key messaged her to within an inch of her life.

Outwardly she was perfect. Internally she was a mess.

She glanced over at her complex, stunning fiancé for a smidge of reassurance, but he had his head down working. Had been since they'd taken off seven hours ago.

She took advantage of the moment to study him. He may not be attracted to her, but she was to him, and he knew it. The way his tall, lithe body was too big for the streamlined airplane seat, the hard olive-skinned muscle visible where his shirtsleeves were rolled up to his elbows, the serious, intensely male lines of his face that always seemed to be furrowed in concentration, made her feel distinctly weak at the knees.

Pathetic, really, when he hadn't exercised any of those attributes on her since that kiss against her door, except for a few possessive touches during the dinner with Alessandra. She'd been sadly responsive to him, while he'd remained unaffected.

He also hated her. Let's not forget that. Reason number one to ignore him. He was an arrogant son of a bitch who thought she was a sycophant who'd bedded his *seventy-year-old* grandfather. She needed to get over him. *Now.*

She sighed and tapped her fingers on the glossy pages of the magazine lying on her lap. At least the massive amount of media coverage had negated the need to inform her parents of her engagement. Her mother had called her within minutes of reading the first tabloid piece, salivating over Rocco's money. Olivia had wanted to tell her she'd never see a penny of it, but Rocco had forbade her from revealing the truth to anyone. Which left her with exactly no one to confide in.

And God forbid she confide her feelings to her fiancé. Alessandra Mondelli, who'd been clearly fascinated with her brother's sudden engagement, clearly shocked to find Olivia hiding out in Milan and clearly determined to know all the details, had given her the lowdown on the man who seemed about as open as an ice cream shop on a bitterly cold February day.

"He's a driven perfectionist who's been forced his whole life to take charge," Alessandra had told her when Rocco had left their table in the busy Milanese restaurant to chat with a business acquaintance. "Of us when our father left, and of the company when Giovanni went running wild with his creative pursuits and left the business side of things in disarray." Alessandra had shaken her head. "He's hurting badly about Giovanni, but in typical Rocco fashion, he's internalized it all."

Alessandra's comments should have made Rocco seem more human, more approachable, but had instead only increased her insecurities. Yes, she was a world-famous beauty, but she was not her fiancé's type. He'd told her so.

That was supposed to help her heading into tonight's dinner with the formidable Stefan Bianco, who apparently had had his heart broken by a woman after his money?

Amazing.

She squirmed in her seat. Rocco glanced over at her, a sigh escaping his lips. "Are you always this distracted? You're like a six-year-old in need of toys…"

She rolled her eyes at how badly he read her. How completely inaccurately he'd judged her. To Rocco she was Mata Hari reincarnate.

"The paparazzi are going to be out in force looking for us," she murmured. "I'm anxious."

"Aren't you used to it by now?"

"Doesn't mean I have to like it." She pushed her hair out of her face. "I would have preferred an evening to acclimatize before I have to face it. It's intimidating enough having to convince one of your best friends we're mad about each other. Having a camera shoved in my face, I could do without."

His smile flashed white in the muted confines of the jet. "Worried you won't be able to control yourself?"

"From clawing your eyes out?" she came back tartly. "Yes."

The grooves on either side of his mouth deepened. "You know, I actually think we might pull this off. We argue like an old married couple."

She made a face. "Luckily this madness will end before that happens."

A curious gleam entered his eyes. "Do you ever intend to marry?"

"It isn't high on my list. I think I'll rely on my career as a designer instead."

His brow arched. "You don't want a big poufy dress and a veil? A lifetime commitment?"

"I'm not sure I'm capable of that kind of love."

Wow. She hadn't even realized she'd thought that until she'd said it.

He reclined back in his chair and fixed her with a speculative look. "That's an honest statement. One I can identify with."

"You don't think you are, either?"

His lips curled. "I don't *think* I'm not, I know I'm not. It's what makes this engagement of convenience just so very easy for me."

She wondered what had brought him to that conclusion. What was behind the cynicism Giovanni had spoken of when it came to his grandson... Despite his transgressions, Giovanni and his son had been madly in love with their wives. The Mondelli men clearly fell hard. So what had happened to Rocco? Had a woman burned him badly?

Their conversation was cut off as they made their final descent into Manhattan. The elegant little jet set down on the runway, they disembarked into the chill of a winter Manhattan night and were quickly ushered into a car operated by Rocco's driver and spirited to the Mondelli apartment in the heart of the city.

The insistent, pulsing energy of New York wrapped itself around her like a particularly deadly python with the ability to steal her breath. Her nerves began to shred as they navigated its busy streets and honking horns.

She had once adored this city, thrived on it as if it were

her lifeblood. Later, she had grown to hate it for what it had done to her, to the people she loved. Now her dominant emotion was fear. Fear of a debilitating variety.

Her chest as she stepped out of the limo in front of the Mondellis' exclusive Central Park West apartment building was so tight she felt as though they were on a smog alert times a million. She pressed a hand to the cool metal exterior of the car to steady herself. Rocco was by her side in a nanosecond, cupping her elbow.

"Are you all right?"

No, she wasn't all right. She'd never be all right again in this city.

But now was the time to pull herself together if she were to survive. She sucked in a deep breath, forced herself to nod and step away from the car. If she didn't think about Petra, if she didn't think about that last show at the Lincoln Center and how she'd disintegrated in front of her peers, she might just pull this off.

Rocco kept his hand under her elbow as he guided her into the limestone-faced building, notorious for its wealthiest-of-the-wealthy residents and the deal makers who anchored it with their vast fortunes. The doorman let them out on the twentieth floor, referring to Rocco by name as he wished them a good evening.

The apartment was beautifully decorated in muted caramels and greens, complementing the exquisite, original finish work the renovators had restored to a gleaming mahogany. Olivia headed straight for the long, narrow terrace that overlooked the park, braced her hands on the iron railing and sucked in big breaths, the chill in the air filling her lungs.

Rocco joined her, his jacket discarded, tie loosened. "What is it?" he asked quietly, throwing her a sideways glance. "What is it that upsets you so much about this city you were so triumphant in?"

The genuine concern on his face, the unusual softness in his voice, almost made her believe he cared. But letting her guard down around the man who held all the cards in this deal of theirs would be stupidity.

"It has some bad memories for me. I'm not the naive young girl making tons of money who couldn't see beyond the bright lights and the rush anymore."

His gaze rested on her face with that unnerving intensity he brought to everything. "Everyone has bad memories, Olivia. You can't let them control you."

"I'm not," she said brightly. "We're having dinner at an outrageously good restaurant, I get to meet the illustrious Stefan Bianco and I'm about to become a household name again. Who could ask for more?"

She spun on her heel and strode inside. The first thing she noticed upon further investigation of the luxury apartment was that there was only one bedroom in the suite.

They were sharing a bed.

Oh, Lord. She glanced around desperately. Maybe there was a pullout sofa.

"Only one bed," Rocco qualified, coming to a halt behind her. "Sorry, *princessa*. This apartment wasn't meant for entertaining."

Compartmentalize, she told herself. She needed to compartmentalize this problem and focus on the big one at the moment: getting ready for this dinner she so heartily didn't want to attend. She glanced at the grandfather clock ticking loudly in the lounge, and her queasiness dissolved into panic. They had to leave in fifteen minutes.

She hightailed it into the bathroom. Luckily she was adept at putting on her face in just under seven minutes. Her hair, a bit wild from the travel, would have to be put up in a quick chignon. And her dress...

Which dress?

She kicked off her jeans and top and raced into the dressing room. The breath was knocked from her lungs when she ran headfirst into a brick wall, otherwise known as Rocco searching for a tie. His hands closed automatically around her waist to steady her. Winded, she put a palm to his chest and caught her breath. The feel of warm, muscled male beneath her fingertips upped her pulse a point or two. *Damn.*

She unpeeled herself from him and put some space between them. "So sorry," she murmured with a self-conscious smile. "I'm working on eight minutes."

He nodded and stood back to give her space. The heightened color in his high cheekbones was a rare enough sight that she stopped and stared for a moment. *What's wrong with him?*

She followed his gaze like a detective searching for clues. Down over her chest it went, past her hips, down her legs. And it struck her then. She was wearing lingerie. Skimpy lingerie. It was so second nature for her to run around half-naked given her former profession—*current profession*, she corrected—that she hadn't given it a second thought.

The color darkening his olive skin deepened. Her brain mind-numbingly processed the facts in front of her. That was lust on his face. Unmistakable. He had been lying to her.

Her mind reeled with the realization. He didn't want to admit he wanted her because he didn't want to want her. And wasn't she an idiot for ignoring her instincts? She had *known* that night in Navigli the heat hadn't been one-sided. And yet he'd cruelly let her think he found her lacking in the face of his Italian brunettes!

"You…" She bit her lip before she tore a strip off him, her rational brain kicking in. Having one up on the man who held all the cards could be a good thing.

"Could you help me with my dress?" she asked sweetly instead, turning her back to him as she rustled through her suitcase for one of Mario's dresses that eluded wrinkles. "That would speed things up."

Rocco stood utterly still as Olivia bent over in front of him and rustled through the case. The lingerie she had on were not the skimpiest he had ever seen, but on his blonde bombshell of a fiancée they looked indescribable. Her rounded, toned behind made his head feel as tight as his groin. Her legs went on forever, ending in slim perfect ankles he could so clearly imagine wrapped around himself he almost groaned.

She spun around, holding up a silver-blue dress victoriously. "Just need you to do the hook at the back."

Or he could hang himself right now. That was a definite option. Better than seeing her perfect nipples outlined against the fine lace of her bra. Better than wondering how soft the skin was between those delectable thighs, showcased perfectly by the revealing cut of her panties...

"Rocco?" She waggled a brow at him. "Are you okay?"

"Perfetto." He waved a hand at her. "Put the damn dress on so I can do it up. The driver's waiting outside."

Mercifully, she slipped the dress over her head. It didn't get any easier, though, as she backed up against him and held her hair out of the way for him to do up the clasp. "That top tiny one please."

He found the tiny hook, his big hands fumbling over the minute closure. She squeezed closer to him, the silk of her dress swishing against his thighs, sending his blood pressure into dangerous territory.

"You smell good." She sighed. "What are you wearing?"

With her bottom perilously close to his raging erection, her lush body lining the length of his, there was only one thought in his head and it wasn't the name of the cologne he was wearing.

The hook slid into the clasp. He uttered a silent prayer of thanks. *"Finito."*

She turned around, a tiny smile playing about her lips. *"Grazie.* I may need help taking it off again later, though."

He would be conveniently getting ice for a nightcap at that moment. He grabbed the tie he wanted to wear, did it up with swift precision while Olivia did her hair, then ushered her out into the warm night air and to the car.

Stefan Bianco met them at the back entrance of the fusion restaurant he was part owner of in Chelsea. His friend's mouth curved into one of his signature lazy smiles when he saw them, the one that camouflaged one of the most ruthless, hard-edged businessmen Rocco had ever met.

He and Rocco embraced.

"Welcome to Tempesta Di Fuoco."

"Impressive, my friend." Rocco stood back and drew Olivia forward. "Olivia, meet Stefan. Not nearly as intimidating as he's made out to be."

Stefan carried the hand Olivia offered to his lips. "You are even more beautiful in person. I can see why Rocco lost his head."

A hint of color washed his fiancée's cheeks. "And you are even more...charismatic...than Rocco painted you."

Amusement gleamed in Stefan's eyes. "You will have to enlighten me on his description. I'm sure it would be entertaining."

Rocco curved an arm around Olivia's waist and pulled her into his side. "Nothing you haven't heard before, *fratello."*

They were seated at a quiet table in one of the alcoves of the exceedingly modern restaurant, done in chrome and steel and muted colors. Rocco and Olivia sat on one side of the table for four, while Stefan sat on the other, his hand lifting to summon the sommelier to bring them a very old, very fine bottle of cabernet.

"I trust that's fine?" he asked Olivia. "I can't tolerate champagne. Such a woman's drink. And French," he added caustically.

"I'm not a fan of champagne myself," Olivia observed, bestowing that high-wattage smile of hers on his friend. "And I do love a good Cab, thank you."

Stefan did a double take. There wasn't a man on this earth who would be immune to Olivia Fitzgerald when she used that smile on him, and Rocco would bet his stock portfolio by the end of this meal she would have his incorrigible friend eating out of her hand.

Stefan sat back and crossed his arms over his chest. "So how did you manage to work your way past my friend's considerable defenses? He has enough to man an army."

A smile curved Olivia's lips. "He picked me up in a café after scaring my girlfriends away... It was more... lust than love at first sight."

Humor darkened his friend's eyes. "That sounds more like him. What *isn't* like him is to fall flat on his face like this. He's usually much more careful. I always said *if* he'd ever marry, he would choose a blue-blooded Italian to carry on the Mondelli line and live a very premeditated life."

Olivia blinked at the backhanded compliment. Rocco put up his hand. "I'm still here, *fratello*, in case you'd forgotten."

His friend shrugged. "You have to admit, this is knee-jerk behavior for you. If we were in my wine cellar, you'd spend half an hour choosing the vintage, then decide perhaps it needed more thinking on."

Olivia put her water down with a deliberate movement, those amazing blue eyes of hers glittering as she recovered. Rocco almost jumped out of his seat when she curved her palm around his thigh underneath the table and squeezed. "Apparently we are compatible on other levels. Although Rocco attempted to deny it at first."

A muscle jumped in his jaw at the twin sensations of

Olivia's hand burning into his thigh like a brand and the anger emanating from her like a physical, living entity despite the smile plastered across her face.

"There was a slight miscommunication between us at first," he managed. "We moved past it."

Olivia's fingers splayed wider on his thigh, caressing muscles far too alert from that close encounter in the dressing room.

Stefan's gaze sharpened on his fiancée. "That was you at Giovanni's funeral."

Olivia nodded. "Rocco and I had had a lover's quarrel. Not the most appropriate place, I admit, but he was green with jealousy over my former relationship with Guillermo Villanueva. I managed to convince him there's simply nothing left there."

"There's a first." Stefan's mouth quirked. "I'm not sure I've ever seen Rocco care enough about a female to go running after her."

Rocco gritted his teeth, unable to remove Olivia's disturbing hand because *his* right hand was covering hers on the table. He squeezed it hard. "I did not *run* after you."

"Of course you did, sweetheart." She gave him a saccharine-sweet smile and closed her fingers over his thigh in another firm squeeze. "You showed up on my doorstep with flowers and poetry." She angled a look at Stefan. "Can you imagine big bad Rocco writing poetry? It was outrageously cute. Anyway," she said, looking adoringly back at her fiancé, "he really had nothing to worry about. He knows I only have eyes for him."

A hot flush spread its way across his cheeks. His brain was catching up with his groin now, and it hit him what was happening. Olivia had read his attraction in that dressing room, had figured out he was lying. And this was payback.

He released her hand and captured the one on his thigh,

bringing it to his lips. "I do know that, *amore mio.* Now stop spilling our secrets. I'll never be able to live them down."

"On the contrary," Stefan demurred, "I am highly entertained."

Rocco kept a firm grip on his fiancée's hand. "Olivia is enough to inspire any man to poetry." He couldn't mask the sarcasm in his voice. "I'm sure you can see how that is."

Stefan's green eyes danced. "I certainly can. Maybe you should read the poem at the wedding. I'm sure we'll all be wiping the tears away."

Rocco gave his friend a dangerous look. He was saved by the arrival of the sommelier, who presented the wine to Stefan. The Sicilian glanced at the label, nodded and indicated for it to be served.

"So when and where is this star-studded marriage expected to happen?" he asked. "Are you giving yourselves some time to enjoy your newfound *compatibility*, or should we expect an invitation?"

Olivia tucked in closer to Rocco's side and returned her hand to his thigh. "We haven't set a date. It's going to be an extremely busy year for both of us. Maybe the summer of next year."

Stefan nodded. "Nothing wrong with restraint. *Bambini* can come later."

Rocco almost choked on his mouthful of water. "I haven't totally gone off the deep end, Bianco. There's been no talk of *bambini* yet."

Olivia's fingers settled in a red-light zone between his thighs. His erection throbbed in his pants, begging for more. "Oh, but we don't plan to wait too long, do we, *cara*? I *am* twenty-six. These eggs of mine aren't getting any younger."

Rocco gave her a meaningful smile laced with warning. "They've plenty of life left in them, *bella*. You *are* only twenty-six. And believe me, I do want you to myself for a while."

Tonight. To strangle her. To find out what had happened to the nerve-racked woman he'd arrived in New York with.

Olivia stared innocently back at him, using her big doe eyes to full effect. "Oh, I want that, too. I know what we've agreed upon, sweetheart... It's just that when I think of little Roccos with dark curly hair and big brown eyes, I find it hard to resist."

"Who could?" Stefan drawled facetiously. "If we populated the world with millions of little Roccos, it would be a better place."

"And the hands..." Olivia picked one of his up and showed it off. "Rocco has great hands, but they'll be chubby little amazing ones to begin with."

Stefan nodded. "No doubt about it. Mondelli has great hands. Many a woman would attest to that, but now that he's taken, too bad for them, hmm?"

Rocco bit down on the inside of his mouth. Counted to three. "I am famished," he asserted in a blatant change of subject. "Should we look at the menu?"

"The chef has prepared a special celebratory meal." Stefan eliminated that distraction with a wave of his hand and a glimmer of laughter in his dark eyes. "Sit back and enjoy."

Rocco attempted to. The vibe in Stefan's new restaurant was high energy, the food as they tasted their appetizers superb, the easy familiarity of the conversation with his longtime friend enjoyable. It was Olivia who was the problem. If she'd been sitting any closer to him she'd be in his lap. Her spicy perfume, which he found he enjoyed a bit too much, kept invading his thinking processes. And her hands were *everywhere*... Caressing his fingers on the table, massaging his thigh. And now she'd slipped her shoe off and was—what did the Americans call it? *Playing footsie* with him!

Santo Cielo.

He frowned and focused intently on the idea Stefan was proposing for a Knights of Columbia charity basketball game fund-raiser. "I think it fits perfectly with our mission statement," he agreed. "And if you can get the players, we're golden. When were you thinking?"

Stefan lifted a brow. "I just told you—late September so we can play outside."

He closed his eyes briefly as Olivia's inquisitive fingers investigated the contents of his pocket, then slid back out again. "Right. Sorry."

"Can I help?" Olivia leaned forward, all halo-endowed innocence. "I'm in my element at a fund-raiser. I can cheer you on."

Rocco watched his friend keep his eyes above her plunging neckline. *Just.* "By all means," Stefan said wryly. "Half the men in New York would show up to see you." He passed his palm over the heavy stubble on his chin. "Would you consider doing a promotional poster for us?"

"No, she wouldn't," Rocco inserted. "My fiancée is not a pinup model."

"She was."

"It's true," Olivia offered. "I don't mind. Those were fun shoots."

"No." The word exploded out of his mouth as Olivia slid her finger up the zipper of his pants and traced the rigid length of him. He was on fire. Literally on fire. He reached down, picked up her hand and slapped it down on her thigh, then rose from the table.

"I need to make a call." He directed the words at Stefan. "Entertain my fiancée, would you?"

"That won't be difficult." Stefan's amused comment sidled through the air to him as he walked away.

He exited the front door of the restaurant and stood leaning against the facade of the building while he made his call, his only company on the street another diner in a designer suit smoking a cigarette. When he finished, he stayed there for a moment, breathing in the fresh air. Attempting to regain control over his tense, aroused body.

Stefan strolled out the front door and over to where he stood. "Cooling off? Where was her hand, by the way?"

Rocco gave him a dark look. "Where is she?"

"In the ladies'." Stefan moved his gaze over him and shook his head. "She has your number, my friend. You have it bad. I feel as if I'm watching Rocco unplugged."

He wanted badly to tell his friend it was a facade. That *she*, Olivia, was playing a necessary role. Trying to drive him mad while she was at it… But he couldn't risk everything he'd put into this investment by being anything less than fully committed. Blood brothers or otherwise.

He pulled on the cloak of aloofness he did every bit as well as Stefan. "She is a handful. But honestly," he challenged, quirking a brow at his friend, "would you want anything else?"

Stefan eyed him. "Perhaps not. I guess I'm wondering if the board's POV on you has anything to do with this sudden engagement."

His insides tensed. "You think I care what they think?"

Stefan leaned back against the wall beside him. "I'm just saying marriage is a big step. This is all very sudden." He waved a hand at him. "So she's beautiful. So she's good in bed. Those are a dime a dozen for you, *fratello*. Enjoy her, but think hard about what you're doing."

Rocco turned to face him. Wondered why he felt the unusual urge to put his fist through his friend's face. "She's a good choice for me and for the brand."

"Maybe. But you're grieving over your grandfather. Give yourself some time before you do something stupid."

"That's why we're planning a long engagement." Rocco

gave the Sicilian an assessing look. "When are *you* going to get over Serena? No one wants to say it, but it's time."

The guarded, impenetrable expression that seemed to be his friend's de facto look of late descended over his square-jawed face. "I've been over Serena for a long time."

"You think so?"

Stefan stared him down. "You think *you're* in control of your little situation in there?"

No. He decidedly was not. But he was about to fix that.

The deliberate twist of the key in the lock of the apartment door echoed excessively loudly in Olivia's ears after the loaded silence in the car coming home. The explosive look on Rocco's face as they'd driven through the relatively quiet streets of Manhattan made her wonder if she'd taken her exercise in distraction a bit too far.

He stood back for her to enter, his long, lean body taut, his face so blank that adrenaline pounded through her in a disconcerting rush. Hadn't she done her job? She'd really gotten into her role as fiancée. Even Stefan had seemed to enjoy himself... And she hadn't thought about tomorrow's press conference even once, which was an added bonus.

The door slammed shut. She winced and turned to face him.

"What the *hell* was that?" he growled, his stance open-legged and aggressive.

She touched her fingers to her throat. "I was having some fun. This really is a ridiculous situation, Rocco. Stefan wasn't going to believe it was love at first sight for one second. I was trying to make it believable."

His long strides carried him to her so quickly the room seemed to sway around her. He stopped mere inches from her, the heat pulsing from him so intensely she felt it singe her skin. "You weren't trying to make it *believable*. You were trying to drive me nuts. Stefan thinks I've lost it."

She bit her lip, her gaze skipping away from his. "I'm sorry. I might have taken it a bit too far."

"A bit too far?" Incredulity dug a furrow across his brow. "You had your hand on my crotch."

Heat rushed to her cheeks. "I said I went too far. I've apologized."

His gaze bored into hers. "Sorry isn't an effective response for what I'm feeling right now, *tesoro*. I am *way* past the line."

Of what? Her throat went dry, her stomach clenching in a knot. "You lied to me. You told me you weren't attracted to me that night in Navigli when you clearly were."

"For a *reason*."

Her hands clenched by her sides. "Because you think I was with Giovanni."

"Because you *were* with Giovanni."

She made a sound in the back of her throat. "Do you really know your grandfather *so little* you think he would have been having an affair with a woman young enough to be his granddaughter?"

"He was not in his right mind." A muscle ticked in his jaw, a flare of fury firing in his eyes. "He was off in some…fairy-tale land of late. Doubtless you perpetuated that."

Her head pounded with fury. "You are so wrong, you know that? So laughably wrong. And you know what else? You deserved that tonight, Rocco. And more, if I were to be honest. You can't even admit the truth to yourself about how you feel."

He stared at her, long and hard, his face contorting into an expression that made her want to head for the door and run. "Here I am, then, Olivia," he rasped, his gaze impaling hers. "About ten showers away from finding your payback amusing. And that *is* the truth." A muscle in his jaw ticked wildly. "You want to finish what you started? Put your hand back where it was, *cara*. In fact, put more than your hand there." His voice softened to a low purr. *"I dare you."*

The heat, the potent attraction that had been smoldering, building, between them all night wrapped itself around her like a shroud, seizing her lungs. Despite what he thought of her, despite what he'd done to her that night in Navigli, her body wanted him to finish what he'd started. Badly.

She raised her gaze to his. Dark color stained his high cheekbones, everything about him hard, masculine challenge. He would be spectacular in bed. All that intensity caged in an outrageously good body. She could almost taste how good he would be.

She nearly did it, too. Because numbing her brain as to what lay ahead just a little bit longer was high on her agenda. Then her rational brain kicked in. Short-term avoidance wasn't going to help her in reality. She stepped back, removed herself from all that heat and called it a brush with insanity.

"No, thank you, Rocco. I'm finally starting to learn the rules of your game, and I decline. This year is going to be hard enough without introducing sex into the mix."

She watched him process her response. The emotion that flickered through his volatile gaze. Watched him firmly slam a lid on it. "I tend to wholeheartedly agree. But push me again like that, Olivia, and I won't be responsible for my actions, deal or not. Count on that."

A shiver rocked through her. She turned and walked into the bedroom before the madness escalated. She should be focusing on the day ahead, figuring out how she was going to get through it rather than allowing herself to become hopelessly distracted with Rocco.

Not that anything could prepare her for returning to the life she'd left behind. Nothing ever could.

CHAPTER SIX

IT WAS A New York press frenzy at its finest, camera people crawling over one another to get a better position, journalists jockeying their way to the front of the room, extralarge coffee cups clutched in their hands. The buzz of a big story was in the air.

"No doubt way over the fire code," Savanna Piers, Mondelli's chic head of public relations, commented wryly, "but no one's going anywhere."

Olivia stood alongside Savanna and Rocco in the atrium of the hotel where the annual meeting of fashion designers was being held, the opening press conference about to begin. Standing beside them were spokespeople from the other represented manufacturers, but it was clear from the tone of the overheard conversations nobody wanted to talk to them. They all wanted to talk to *her*: Olivia Fitzgerald, the supermodel who had abandoned her career at its peak, defected on a three-million-dollar contract with a major French cosmetics company and disappeared from the face of the earth.

A sheen of perspiration blanketed her body. She felt a pool of it trickle down her back. Felt her breathing quicken as the oxygen in the room seemed to drain with every second...

The colors and movement around her faded into a detailless swirling gray. It reached out for her then, the panic, beckoning her, dark and familiar. She pulled in a desperate breath and fought it. Tried to hold it at bay, but the room grew darker around her.

"I need some air." She backed away and headed toward the hallway. Standing with her back against the wall in the corridor as catering staff bustled by her, she closed her eyes and made herself breathe in and out, deep long breaths like her therapist had taught her.

Eleven years she'd been having these panic attacks. Since she was fifteen. And they never got less terrifying. On the road in foreign countries with no support system in her emotionally unavailable parents and the stress of having to be the best every time she stepped onto a set, they'd started one night in Berlin. Debilitating, overwhelming, she'd been terrified of them. It had felt as though she was losing her mind.

Petra had finally made her see a doctor. Her therapist had helped her get the attacks somewhat under control, but when the pressure was high she couldn't fight them. Like that night at the Lincoln Center. It had ended her career.

"Olivia."

Rocco had joined her in the hallway. She opened her eyes to look at him, but the world kept swaying around her and she closed them again.

"There was no air in there."

He took her hands in his and pulled her down into a squatting position. "Head between your knees."

She pushed her head down and breathed. But it didn't seem as if she could get enough air into her lungs... The blackness was calling to her. Comforting. Easier than being here.

Rocco's hands tightened around hers. "No. Don't do that. Breathe, Olivia. Deep breaths, in and out."

His hands were tight around her ice cold ones. *Insistent.* She kept breathing, in and out. Deep, steadying pulls of air into her lungs. And slowly the blackness receded.

She brought herself upright. Rocco's gaze was pinned on her, dark and concerned. "Better?"

"Yes."

He glanced at his watch. "We're starting in five minutes. Are you okay to go back in?"

She nodded.

He brought her to her feet with a hand around her waist and kept a firm palm to her back as they walked back inside. Savanna led them to the side of the podium, her eagle-eyed gaze resting on Olivia's face. "Focus on the feel-good story of you and Rocco and your partnership. No one's going to choose mean over a picture-perfect story if they have any sense. You're America's sweetheart. Go with it."

Was. She had been America's sweetheart... Now she was afraid *sensational* was going to rule the day.

She straightened the hem of her dress as the president of this year's conference took the stage and made his opening remarks. By the time Mondelli was summoned forward, Olivia's knees were knocking against one another. Rocco captured her hand in his and started up the steps to the podium. The room blurred into a sea of faces and electronics as she climbed the steps, her clammy fingers clutching tighter to Rocco's as they ascended.

"Relax," he murmured out of the side of his mouth, giving her hand a squeeze. "I'm right here with you."

Despite her ever-present antagonism toward him, she *did* feel better with him by her side. Rocco was like that tree in a storm you knew would never come down. Its roots were too secure, its foundation too solid, to ever be unearthed by a mere media scrum.

Reporters began yelling questions even before they reached the microphone. Rocco held up a hand to silence them. "If you'll let me make my announcement, there will be plenty of time for questions."

When the din finally cleared, Rocco tugged on her hand

and drew her to the microphone. "I know you have all missed her, which is why I am thrilled to welcome Olivia Fitzgerald back to the modeling world as the new face of the House of Mondelli."

The room broke out in a fevered pitch. Rocco held up a hand and silenced them. "Combining the talents of one of the world's most famous faces with one of the globe's most venerable fashion houses is an undeniably exciting occasion to mark. But," he added, slipping an arm around Olivia's waist and tucking her into his side, "as many of you have speculated, there is another union we are even more happy to announce, and that is the forthcoming marriage of Olivia and I."

The noise in the room grew deafening. Savanna stepped forward and took control of the Q and A. "Francesca," she called out, pointing to an older blond-haired fashion reporter from one of the networks.

"First of all," Francesca began, "congratulations on your engagement and partnership." Her gaze shifted to Olivia. "The mystery we're all trying to unravel, Olivia, is why you disappeared at the peak of your career. Would you care to set the record straight?"

Olivia swallowed hard. *Why couldn't they just let the past lie?*

"It's very simple." She forced the words through excessively dry lips. "I just needed some time away. I was working on a project I'm going to be very excited to tell you about shortly."

The veteran reporter lifted a brow. "You reneged on a three-million-dollar contract with Le Ciel to *take some personal time?*"

Her heart dropped. *Here we go.*

"That contract has now been settled," she said huskily. "For legal reasons, I have to leave it at that."

"Word is," Francesca continued, undaunted, "Le Ciel is

furious. Do you think this will impact your career going forward?"

Olivia felt some of her old press savvy kick back in. "I was just named the face of Mondelli. Does it look like it?"

The veteran reporter inclined her head with a wry smile.

"Where were you hiding out?" The question came from the center of the room.

"I was in Milan." She threw a smile at her fiancé. "Where I met Rocco."

Savanna pointed to another veteran fashion reporter. "Dan."

"When will we first see Olivia in your campaigns?"

"In the spring," Rocco answered. "You'll see her back in New York for Fashion Week next month."

Savanna nodded at a redhead Olivia didn't recognize, wearing very fashionable purple glasses. "Tara?"

"How is the House of Mondelli going to move forward without Giovanni's genius at the helm? Some say Mario won't be enough to keep things afloat."

"We have half a dozen spectacular young designers Giovanni trained working with Mario," Rocco said smoothly. "No company can be content to rest on its laurels. We had always intended these designers to carry the torch forward. Giovanni was seventy after all."

"Olivia." A notoriously bigmouthed gossip reporter waved from the front. "How does it feel to land one of the world's most sought-after bachelors?"

Olivia relaxed back into Rocco's arm and turned to smile up at him. "Very lucky."

Eyes glittering with humor, Rocco lifted a hand to cup her jaw. "I am the lucky one to *land*, as you put it, Olivia."

"Since you've managed to elude us for the past week," the gossip reporter continued, "how about a kiss?"

Her fiancé let loose a good-natured smile. "I suppose that's only fair."

Her heartbeat picked up in a steady thrum as Rocco splayed his fingers wider around her jaw, leaned down and covered her lips with his own. Her lashes fluttered closed as he took her mouth in a thorough kiss that had the camera flashes going off madly like fireworks.

She was just off balance enough when he set her away from him to much applause from the scrum that the next question hit her from left field.

"Olivia. Can you tell us what happened that night at the Lincoln Center? What caused your meltdown?"

She froze, her face suspended midsmile. Frederic, the producer of the show that night at the Lincoln Center, an old personal friend of hers, had swiftly replaced her when she'd faltered and hadn't been able to take the stage. He'd forbidden any talk of what had happened afterward on pain of his influential wrath. But apparently someone had talked.

How much did they know?

The room started to sway dangerously around her, perspiration sliding down her back in rivulets now. Air got harder to pull in, but she sucked it in desperately, the question echoing over and over in her head. Scenes from that night flashed through her brain—ugly, paralyzing, stomach churning...

"Olivia?" Rocco set a supporting palm to the small of her back. The touch sent words tumbling out of her mouth.

"It was very hot backstage that evening," she rasped. "I was not feeling well."

Rocco started proactively detailing some of the key campaign elements they would see from Mondelli in the spring/summer. She managed to plaster a smile on her face as their time ran out and Rocco thanked the media. But it wasn't over. It was never going to be over.

Three hours and an excruciatingly boring reception later, Rocco shoved a glass of brandy into the hand of a still blank-faced Olivia in the quiet stillness of their apartment salon, and tried to contain his growing frustration. Neither he nor Savanna had been able to get his fiancée to talk after the press conference, despite their repeated attempts to discover what she was hiding. No one thought it was going to end there, and preempting whatever was to come was the best strategy. Unfortunately, his fiancée wasn't talking.

Can you tell us what happened that night at the Lincoln Center, Olivia? What made you have a meltdown?

The reporter's question rang in his head. No doubt Olivia hadn't been the most reliable model in the final couple of years she'd worked, but she'd never been billed a prima donna. So what had the reporter meant? What had happened that night?

He had a feeling it was the key to everything, the key to Olivia, yet no one was talking, not even Frederic Beaumont, the man who had produced the show that night, deflecting Rocco's inquiry at tonight's reception with a lifted brow. "As your fiancée said, it was extremely hot backstage. A lot of the models were struggling."

Closing ranks. He didn't believe him for one minute.

He glanced at his mute fiancée, grabbed his own tumbler and paced the room. "I can't help you if you won't talk to me."

Olivia pushed the brandy aside, her face white and pinched as she sat curled up in his favorite reading chair. "I don't want your help. It's ancient history."

"In case you hadn't noticed," he disputed heatedly, "it came back to life today. You are a very expensive asset of mine, Olivia. You think they're going to let whatever it is lie? Tell me what it is and we'll deal with it together."

She gave him another one of those blank looks. "You heard what I said. I wasn't feeling well. End of story."

He eyed her with growing ire. "The reporter referred to it as a meltdown."

"Reporters like to make things dramatic that aren't."

He muttered an oath beneath his breath. "And the reason you fell apart when the question was asked?"

She pressed her lips together. "I am frustrated. I just wish people would leave it alone and stop prying into my personal life when it's none of their business."

His free hand fisted at his side, his five-million-dollar investment pounding in his head. He counted to three, forced out a long breath and went to kneel by her chair. "I want to help you, Olivia. Give me *something*. It can't just have been the heat that night."

She pushed her spine back into the chair, recoiling away from him. "You want to protect an *asset*. Rest assured, Rocco, I will not renege on our deal, and I will perform the duties of my contract *to the letter*."

"This isn't just about you being an asset. You are struggling... I can help."

Her sapphire eyes heated to a dark blue flame. "Like you wanted to help me when you seduced me that night in Navigli to find out what kind of a woman I was? Like you wanted to help me when you coerced me into a return to modeling you knew I didn't want? Better we both do our jobs, Rocco, and refrain from pretending we care when we don't."

He almost would have bought her bravado had it not been for the wounded, vulnerable glint in her eyes. The pallor in her skin. The look she'd had all day that a slight breeze might knock her over. Her fiery gaze spoke of fear and pain and, most of all, a bone-deep sadness that got to him despite his efforts to remain detached.

He rose, sat on the edge of the chair and caught her chin in his fingers to turn her gaze to his. *"Tell me."*

He was surprised at the tenderness in his voice. At an empathy he hadn't known he possessed. She blinked and stared at him. *Dio*, this woman did something to him. It didn't matter she had been his grandfather's, that Giovanni's body wasn't even cold in his grave and still he wanted to comfort her. Touch her. He wanted to carry her to bed and make love to her and banish those demons from her eyes.

Madness. Pure madness.

The far too perceptive Stefan Bianco had had it right. Olivia did have his number. She had always had his number, right from that first night in Navigli.

Her gaze connected with his and read what lay there. Confusion darkened her vibrant blue orbs.

"Rocco…"

Her husky, hesitant tone prompted the return of his sanity. She had never been, nor would she ever be, his. *Impossible.*

He stood up with an abrupt movement. "Drink the brandy," he muttered roughly. "I will order us dinner."

When he'd finally sent an exhausted Olivia to bed and sat on the terrace with a final brandy in his hand, he was glad for the city that never slept. The honking horns and peeling ambulances kept him company, floodlit Central Park a feast for the senses as he tipped his head back and drank it in.

The silence, the solitude, grounded him as it always did. Made his present situation crystallize like the stars emerging from the silvery haze in the cloudy night sky above.

The more distance he kept from the woman inside who was driving him mad, the better. It had taken him hours last night to wrestle his body into an acceptable enough state to get into bed, after which the scent of her had driven him half-crazy. He'd been out of bed at 5:00 a.m. out of the pure need, *not* to look at his sultry fiancée splayed across his bed, glorious hair everywhere.

But it was more than that. This restlessness in him came from a place he was loath to face. He was bitterly afraid he had been wrong about Olivia. Very wrong.

She had clearly been lying just now, as she had during the press conference. The shut-down, blank look on her face had said it all. Which pointed out an uncomfortable fact. He'd never seen that look on her face before. Not when she'd denied Giovanni was her lover that night in Milan after he'd seduced her. Not through this past trying week when he'd plied her with a million questions to get their stories and backstory straight. She had always told him the truth, however painful, or she hadn't said anything at all.

Until tonight. Until today at the press conference. He could tell the difference. He could read her now.

Do you really know your grandfather so little you think he would have been having an affair with a woman young enough to be his granddaughter?

He ran his palm over the stubble on his jaw, a jolt of unease slicing through him. Giovanni not giving him sole control of Mondelli had shaken him, made him question how well he knew the man who had raised him, who had been his heart and soul. But Giovanni was also a complex man with many layers. Perhaps there were facets of him he hadn't known. Perhaps he *had* had an affair with Tatum Fitzgerald.

Tonight when he'd had that chat with Frederic Beaumont, the wily old Frenchman had congratulated him on capturing the "most enchanting creature he'd ever worked with" in Olivia, and made a veiled comment about Mondelli men having a thing for Fitzgerald women. When Rocco had lifted a brow at the comment, Frederic had only said sagely that Tatum Fitzgerald had been one of Giovanni's great muses, but his eyes had said much more.

He took a swig of the brandy, closing his eyes as its warmth heated his insides. If his grandfather had engaged in an out-of-character affair with Tatum Fitzgerald, that was one thing. But to have an affair with her daughter, as well? It didn't sit right in his chest. Maybe it never had.

He'd been so angry at his grandfather's death when he'd confronted Olivia, he'd wanted to lash out, and she had been the most convenient target. Brand her a gold digger and make himself feel better by solving the problem.

The uneasy feeling inside him intensified. Propelled him out of his chair and to the railing, Manhattan glistening below in all its finery. What if he'd been wrong? What if he'd branded the woman sleeping in his bed an opportunist when she had really been Giovanni's inspiration in the most innocent sense? When perhaps *she* had been the one to reinvigorate a creativity that had begun to fail the aging genius? He had seen it in those designs...

He took another sip of the brandy. The spirit blazed an undeniable path of self-awareness through him. Had he wanted to think the worst of Olivia because of just how very much she got to him? How she'd managed to penetrate the ironclad exterior he'd adopted the day he'd realized his father as he'd known him was never coming back? When he'd decided no one would ever get to him emotionally again?

Sandro had only been twenty-seven when his wife of the same age had died giving birth to Alessandra. Suffering from severe preeclampsia, Letizia had delivered him a healthy baby girl, but stolen his one true love in the process. His father had fallen apart, descended into a grief so raw it had scared his two children witless and left them with no one but each other.

At first, Giovanni had been patient with his son. Had turned a blind eye to Sandro's drinking, to his gambling, but after a time, when he'd decided enough was enough, that Sandro's children needed a father and he needed his son back at Mondelli, Sandro had said he'd needed more time. Then more. Until it became clear he couldn't mentally handle a return to the family business, until he'd gambled Rocco's family home away and it had become apparent he wasn't capable of taking care of his children, either. Of himself.

Rocco could remember the day vividly when Giovanni had arrived at their house, soon to be taken by creditors, and ordered him and Alessandra to gather their things. He'd only been seven and a half at the time, but he would never forget the anguish in his father's eyes as his grandfather had scooped them up and took them home to Villa Mondelli, his disappointment in his son palpable in the older man's demeanor.

Rocco had absorbed his father's anguish, the hint of madness that losing his mother had instilled in him, and although he had been too young to understand it all, he had known one thing—love meant making yourself vulnerable. Love meant pain. And he would never do that to himself willingly.

He tipped his head back and took a long swallow of the brandy. The lights from the park cast an otherworldly glow over the high rises that soared behind it. It was as mystifying a view of New York as his behavior had been tonight. Because even if he had been wrong about Olivia, even if Giovanni *had* been mentoring her as a way to pay back what he owed to her mother, even if she *was* that vulnerable, frightened creature he'd witnessed tonight that his grandfather had elected to shelter and protect, it didn't change anything. What he and Olivia had was a business deal. He was no white knight to ride in on a steed and save the day.

He finished off the brandy and set the glass down. Whatever crazy thing drew him to Olivia, whatever it had been between them from the start, was precisely what he needed to avoid. His only interest should be preserving his family legacy. In doing what had always been paramount for him. Allowing himself to care for anything beyond that had never been in the cards.

CHAPTER SEVEN

A WEEK INTO his and Olivia's return to Milan, every aspect of Rocco's plan seemed to be falling into perfect strategic place. The announcement of his fiancée as the new face of Mondelli was making waves across fashion circles, her sudden return to modeling an angle it seemed no media outlet could resist. And although some media chose to speculate on the reason behind Olivia's disappearance from modeling, most were universally positive about the union, choosing, as Savanna had predicted, to focus on the glamorous engagement of two high-profile personalities and brands rather than speculate on a story for which they had no answers.

He glanced down at the front page of the weekly gossip magazine that typically featured royalty on the cover, but instead this week featured *the kiss*, as the press had dubbed it. The one he and Olivia had shared at the press conference.

He'd seen more of the vivid, easy smile on Olivia's face the tabloid had featured in the after shot since they'd returned to Milan, his fiancée seeming to relax as soon as they'd cleared New York airspace. The staff at Villa Mondelli appeared to love her, and she seemed at peace roaming the beautiful grounds. It was only at night when they retired to the master suite that the tension ratcheted up between them. He'd taken to going to bed even later than he normally did, working in his office until he was sure Olivia was asleep. Because to do otherwise was asking for trouble.

He took the last sip of his espresso and pushed the cup away. His efforts to harness his potent attraction toward his pretend fiancée had been successful. If he didn't see, touch or hear her, he was okay. And he intended to keep it that way. Particularly when he was now sure he'd been right. His grandfather would never have had a relationship with her. He must have been out of his head to think it possible.

The knowledge removed a barrier he instead needed to be ten times thicker.

Gabriella stuck her head in his office. "You need to leave now if you're going to make it to your lunch."

His mouth curved. "Even with my driving?"

"Even with your driving," she acknowledged drily.

"On my way."

His nemesis was seated at a prime table near the windows when Rocco entered the popular seafood restaurant, the chairman's quick glance at his watch as he sat down indicating he was five minutes late. Rocco didn't bother to acknowledge it. Rialto pointed at his glass. "I've ordered a bottle of merlot. I thought we could toast your very successful week."

A satisfied rush blanketed him. "I thought it so."

"Landing Olivia Fitzgerald as a face and a wife? I almost feel you've taken my advice to heart. Although I am surprised given your thoughts on the matter the last time we spoke."

"I've reconsidered." Rocco waited while the *cameriera* uncorked then served their wine, before fixing Renzo with an even look. "You wanted me to think about what is best for Mondelli. I have."

"It's the speed with which you have done so that worries me," the chairman said drily. "This is not a chess match, Rocco. This is the future of the company your grandfather built. When we spoke last time about witnessing some long-term stability with you, I was asking for a true commitment, not smoke and mirrors."

Rocco's blood heated to a dangerous level. "You forget it was *I* who quadrupled the market value of Mondelli. I *do* have this company's best interests at heart. Which is why I have executed a strategic merger that is pure brilliance."

Renzo eyed him. "Olivia Fitzgerald is undeniably breathtaking, and I'm sure provides a wealth of distraction in the bedroom, but not necessarily what I intended when I suggested marriage. She is unpredictable given her recent past. A wild child."

"It is a perfect union from every angle," Rocco countered flatly. "A dynasty of two great brands."

Renzo took a long, deliberate sip of his wine, set his glass down and sat back, arms folded across his chest. "You don't see it, do you?"

"See what?"

"The Mondelli men's weakness when it comes to women. *Pensare con quello che hai in mezzo alle gambe al posto della testa...*"

Thinking with what's between your legs and not your head... Rocco ground his back teeth together. "That..."

Renzo waved a hand at him. "Giovanni made a fool out of himself over Tatum Fitzgerald. He forgot his priorities, let his head get swelled by having her even though he was a happily married man, and the company stuttered. Your father's career imploded over the love of a woman." He shook his head. "Make a smart decision, Rocco, not one in which you're thumbing your nose at all of us."

Blood thudded through his head in a deafening rush. He leaned forward, rested his elbows on the table and met the chairman's gaze. "I am not my father, nor my grandfather, Renzo. I am the man who took a struggling company and raised it to a higher level. You *need* me. Don't forget that important fact."

"And you need me," Renzo countered deliberately. "You have taken Mondelli to great heights, Rocco. No one can dispute that. I'm simply giving you some advice."

Rocco sat back in his seat. "So you have. Are we done on this subject?"

"Set a date."

Rocco frowned. *"Mi scusi?"*

"If you want to convince the board you are truly a changed man, set a wedding date."

The blood thumping against his temples converged in a pool of disbelief. "You're joking?"

Renzo's mouth twisted. "It is my job to ensure control is turned over to you when you are well and truly ready. *I* am responsible to the shareholders, and in this day and age, perception is as important as reality. *They* think you are a question mark, Rocco—unpredictable at best. So if Olivia Fitzgerald is the choice, marry her. Show your intentions."

Rocco thought he must be hallucinating. "Olivia and I are far too busy to plan a wedding right now."

"Undoubtedly." Renzo's gaze narrowed on him. "But I suggest you do it. The sooner you prove to the board you can run Mondelli with the measured, mature perspective of a man who's sown his wild oats, the quicker we will be to hand over control."

Rocco absorbed the unyielding glint in the chairman's eyes. "You are *actually* telling me to speed up my wedding date to pacify shareholder perception?"

The older man's eyes glittered back at him with something like unmediated glee. "We all sacrifice things, Rocco. I don't love my wife. I married her because she was the perfect partner for a CEO. Power comes with sacrifice, and if you don't realize that by now, you will learn."

He bit back the response that rose in his throat. He didn't

have to explain to Renzo he'd known sacrifice since he was a teenager bringing up his baby sister. Since he'd been fresh out of school, deep in over his head, running a company so vast he'd lain awake at night in the early days, his mind reeling on how to corral it. How to fix it.

He picked up his wine and took a long sip. It was a bitter pill to swallow, but Renzo was right. At the end of the day what mattered was what the analysts said about him. And they thought he was a maverick.

He'd never intended on marrying for love—so why *not* marry Olivia? It didn't do anything but cement the plan he'd already put into place.

His hand tightened around the glass as he set it down. Renzo was also right about Olivia. He might think he was in control, but she was a danger to him. He *had* thought and acted with what was between his legs and not his head. Just like Giovanni had done.

He would not repeat history. He would not be that weak.

Olivia was chatting over some designs with a gregarious Mario Masini when her fiancé deigned to make an appearance in the design studios. He had pretty much disappeared since they'd returned home from New York, thrown himself into his ridiculous fourteen-hour days and communicated with the short verbiage of a man too busy to converse when they eventually sat down at the dinner table together at the villa.

She was aware he was deliberately putting space between them after their close encounters in New York, and she got it. She was glad for it. So why did she feel barefoot and rejected? Because for *one* second there, a voice in her head jibed, she'd thought he actually cared. Some delusional part of her brain had conjured that up. When what she really was was an asset to be managed. That was all.

Mario moved to embrace Rocco, his lined old face softening. Her fiancé was drool worthy again today in a silver gray suit and blue tie that never seemed to wrinkle. Elegant and earthy all at the same time, he was a man with so much sex appeal he was drowning in it.

"Ciao," she murmured as casually as she could, waving a hand to the designs spread out on the table. "Mario and I were just chatting over fabrics. Is it that time already?"

His mouth curved. "Thirty minutes past. It isn't a problem. We're eating in tonight. Take your time."

She almost wished they were staying at Villa Mondelli, where she could put a literal and figurative distance between them at the formal dining room table. Instead, they were staying at the apartment so she could make her 7:00 a.m. photo shoot with Alessandra tomorrow without getting up obscenely early.

Mario pointed at the designs on the table. "She is brilliant, this woman of yours. It's as if she brings the light inside with her."

Rocco nodded. "That's a very apt description."

Mario smiled broadly. "We are going to make her a star of the design world."

Olivia's heart swelled. Instead of accepting her warily into the fold, Mario had seemed incredibly enthusiastic over her designs, as if he, too, welcomed the infusion of creativity as Giovanni had.

She couldn't help the smile that stretched her lips. It was happening. Her dream was actually happening.

Rocco flicked a look at her. "Do what you need to do. I'll answer some emails."

But he didn't. She tried to concentrate on her conversation with Mario, but with Rocco roaming the room, pulling her pieces off the rack, flicking sketches apart and staring at them with that trademark intensity of his, she was hopelessly distracted. A few minutes later, Mario made an amused comment about her attention span and "young lovers" and announced they were done for the day.

Rocco waited until the older man had left the studio before his gaze slid over her face. "Either your acting skills have kicked in, or my presence is making you nervous."

She lifted her chin. "You're looking at my designs properly for the first time. My future rests in your hands... Wouldn't you expect me to be heart in mouth?"

His mouth twisted. "I thought that was just the general effect I had on you, *bella*."

She rested her hands on her hips. "I'm not the one working until 1:00 a.m. to avoid being in a bedroom together. Are your control-freak tendencies on red alert?"

His ebony gaze darkened. "As a matter of fact, they are. Your little stunt in New York wasn't exactly a cure for a man practicing abstinence. Nor is the provocative way you sleep splayed across my bed." He shrugged an elegant shoulder. "I keep thinking maybe it's just easier to get it over with. How simple it would be to slide a hand under the small of your back, tempt you with what I know you've been dying to have, then take you long and hard until all you'd be doing is *begging* me to come to bed. *Then* maybe we could snuff this out."

Her insides dissolved into a river of fire, his taunt sending the intimate flesh at the heart of her into an excited, heated pull. She could not believe he'd just said that.

A hard glitter entered his eyes. "But of course, that will never happen."

She sank her teeth into her bottom lip as her brain crashed rapidly back to earth. Turning, she stacked the designs on the table into neat piles, anger pulsing through her. "Oh, I get it, Rocco. You won't put a hand on me because you think I was your grandfather's lover, that I am soiled goods. But you want to, so you use your shock value to send me running." She straightened the last pile, leaned back against the table and looked up at him. "Have I got it right?"

The in-your-face arrogance faded from his face. "I owe you an apology."

That caught her off guard. "For what?"

"For assuming things that were not true. I was angry and I made accusations I shouldn't have about your and Giovanni's relationship. But the facts were staring me in the face."

Antagonism replaced her confusion. "What facts? The fact he'd *loaned* me an apartment?"

"*Bought* it for you. The fact that he was writing you checks for large sums of money. That he never mentioned you at all. It was not normal behavior for Giovanni. Even your neighbors thought you were lovers."

"Because he would come visit me at night to work?" She sank her hands deeper into her hips and glared at him. "You assumed a great deal of things, Rocco, and you were dead wrong on all of them."

He inclined his head. "I was angry. Grieving. To accept that the Giovanni I knew would have cheated on Rosa, that he could be anything but the intensely loyal man I knew him to be, was exceedingly difficult."

Undoubtedly. Her mouth flattened. "It still didn't give you the right to treat me like you did."

His face tightened. "I am apologizing."

She'd bet he rarely, if ever, did it. It probably made him want to choke. But the relief flaring through her was undeniable. That finally he believed her. It had been like a palpable force between them, stirring mistrust on every level.

She eyed the conflicting emotions shimmering in his eyes. He needed to understand.

She crossed her arms over her chest and held his gaze. "Giovanni told me Rosa was his first love. That he couldn't imagine ever being with anyone else. Then he met my mother and he was blindsided. She did one of his break-through shows in New York. He was on a high from his success, higher than he'd ever been, and my mother was the glittering jewel he couldn't resist."

"He should have," Rocco growled.

"He knew that. He said being with her was like some inescapable force he couldn't resist. And he wondered if he'd married too early."

"Rosa was pregnant with my father at eighteen. They had no choice but to marry."

She nodded. "It was a very different kind of love he had with Rosa—the inviolate pureness of it. What he felt for my mother was passionate, intense. And he was torn."

"Because he was *married*," he ground out, eyes flashing. "Because my grandmother *lived for him*."

Her heart constricted. "Giovanni seemed like some mystical force, but he was human, just like we all are. I get how you feel, I do. I watched my father fall apart because his wife was in love with someone else. I *lived* through it. I hated my mother for my entire teenage years for doing that to us. I still hate her a bit for it. And I wanted to hate Giovanni, too... But when he explained how it was between them, I finally got it. It was never about them deliberately trying to hurt other people. It was about feelings beyond their control."

His lip curled. "A lovely reiteration of a modern-day Romeo and Juliet story, Liv. Believe me, I do get it—the idea of temptation, how that temptation, that depth of love, can destroy everything around you. It is my father's life. It's why I go to such lengths to never let it rule me. It's a weak man's poison."

She frowned. "Giovanni was not weak."

"I don't know what he was anymore." The admission was torn from him in a low, gravelly tone. "But I know he couldn't have been your lover. That was me projecting my anger onto you."

She expelled a long breath.

"Who ended it, then?" he asked abruptly. "How did he choose?"

"Rosa. She found out about the affair, told Giovanni he had to choose and, when he did, forbade him ever to see my mother again."

"It was never in his head to go back to your mother once Rosa died?"

A poignant smile twisted her mouth. "I asked him that. He said once you travel through some doors, you can never go back."

He was quiet for a long time. Then he walked over to the racks where her designs hung and pulled a couple out. "Mario is right. You are insanely talented."

For a moment she actually didn't know what to say. "Thank you," she said finally.

He came back to lean against the table beside her. "There is a change we have to make in the deal."

Her heart stuttered. Being so close to her dream and having it be plucked away from her would kill her.

"I met with the chairman of the board today. There is a general sentiment among the board and shareholders that I am a wild card in the wake of Giovanni's death. My tendency to want to do things my way ruffles feathers. My bachelor persona fails to keep those invested in the company tucked securely in their beds at night with sweet dreams of dollar figures running through their heads. They want to see me stable. Married."

A flicker of unease slanted through her. This made the reasons for their engagement clear. Given the Columbia Four's rather wild reputation, she could understand why the board might be uneasy with such a young, strong-minded CEO.

"We just announced our engagement," she said haltingly. "How much more could they want?"

A cynical smile twisted his lips. "They want a date. A marriage."

Her knees went weak. "As in us walking down the aisle?"

"Exactly like that, *cara*." She didn't like the premeditated look that stretched his olive-skinned face as he turned the full force of his will on her. "Nothing changes, except we tie the knot in six weeks. Our one-year agreement is still in place and Mondelli brings your designs to market just as we said."

"Six weeks?" The words came out as a high-pitched squeak.

He shrugged. "You told me yourself you never planned to get married. A quick, uncontested divorce with all the terms outlined will be painless."

Painless? Her fingers caught the side of the table in a death grip. So this was why he'd been softening her up. Complimenting her designs...

She shook her head. "Oh, no. You are not bullying me into this, Rocco. I am not walking down the aisle with you, lying to the world in six weeks. It's too much."

"Ah, but you are, sweet Liv." The smile that curved his lips was far from reassuring. "It's inconvenient, I agree. The last thing either of us needs to be doing right now is planning a wedding. But it is what it is. And we both continue to get what we want."

The media circus of last week's press conference flashed through her head. The horrible, paralyzing, *naked* feeling of being in the spotlight again. Her stomach swirled with nausea at the thought of it—*ten times worse*.

"You are out of your mind," she breathed. "Tell the board I won't hurry my wedding for them. Tell them whatever you like. But this is *not happening*."

This time he wasn't getting his way.

CHAPTER EIGHT

FASHION PHOTOGRAPHERS WEREN'T known to be the most subtle of breeds. The ones Olivia had worked with in the past had ranged from sophisticated persuaders, like her former lover Guillermo, to the completely indifferent, to full-out beasts who yelled at you and told you you had half the talent the last model had.

In this regard, Alessandra was a breed apart. She was incredibly patient, encouraging and had an amazing eye for the composition of a great shot. Unfortunately for the talented young photographer, Olivia hadn't given her anything to work with over the morning, and they both knew it. She was stiff, awkward and without her usual grace, struggling to find her groove.

Close to lunchtime, Alessandra finally pulled her camera over her head and set it on a table. "Let's take a break," she suggested. "We'll start again in fifteen."

Come back when you're able to give me something to work with. Alessandra didn't say it, but her eyes did. Olivia's shoulders sagged. The shot Alessandra wanted for the fall/winter catalog was one of her leaning on a fence in a fabulous crepe dress, reeking of dreamy impatience as she waited for her lover to pick her up.

The mood just wouldn't come. Maybe because the last kiss she and Rocco had shared was that almost one in the New York apartment when she'd nearly made a fool out of herself over him. Again.

Not inspirational.

"I'm assuming my brother has something to do with the shadows under your eyes," Alessandra guessed mischievously. "For any number of reasons."

True, but not when it came to the wild romps in the sack Alessandra was undoubtedly referring to. Rocco's outrageous suggestion they get married had kept her awake until the early hours of the morning.

She frowned. "Is he always such a browbeating autocrat?"

Alessandra laughed. "A well-meaning one, yes. He gets what he wants."

"He *wants* us to get married in six weeks."

"Six weeks?" Alessandra looked horrified. "Why so soon?"

"The board is asking us to speed up our wedding. They want to see Rocco married before they put their full confidence behind him."

Rocco's sister pursed her lips. "I guess it makes sense given Giovanni didn't leave him a controlling stake in Mondelli. Rocco's bachelor behavior has always antagonized the board, but without a controlling stake, they can dictate what they like and tie his hands." Her gaze turned sympathetic. "Not that *you* should have to speed up your wedding because of it."

Olivia's mouth dropped open. "Mondelli is your family's business. How could Giovanni not have left Rocco a controlling stake?"

"Giovanni put Renzo Rialto, the chairman of the board, in charge of the controlling ten percent of Mondelli to give Rocco some time to find his feet without him. My brother is brilliant and responsible for building Mondelli into a global powerhouse, but Giovanni was always there to keep him in check."

Olivia rocked back on her heels. It all made sense now.

Why Rocco hadn't told the board to go to hell with its demands. Because he couldn't.

She shook the haze out of her head. "I think I'll get that air."

Rocco told himself he wasn't checking up on Olivia, but he knew he was. She'd been so tight-lipped and unapproachable this morning, he actually wondered if she was going to refuse to marry him. And since that couldn't happen, since Mondelli's fall/winter Vivo campaign for which Alessandra was shooting today was worth ten million dollars, here he was at her shoot when he should be going over the monthly numbers with the CFO.

Alessandra gave him a warm hug. "Couldn't stay away?"

"You could put it that way. How is she doing?"

"She's been a bit of a stiff mess." She frowned up at him. "That isn't the same woman I shot two years ago, Rocco. What happened to her?"

He lifted a shoulder. "She won't talk about it. To anyone. I have tried, believe me."

"Can you go talk to her? Nothing we've taken this morning is going to work. If this continues, it's going to be a total waste of a day."

He nodded and made his way out onto the terrace, where Olivia was standing at the railing staring down at the courtyard below. She looked like an exotic bird perched for flight.

The guilt inside him ratcheted a layer deeper. *Per l'amor di Dio.* He did not need to be walking around with a living, breathing case of remorse. They were both getting what they needed out of this.

He joined her at the railing. Surprise wrote its way across her beautiful face. "I thought you had a packed day."

"I wanted to check on you. You seemed off this morning."

She turned to face him, blue eyes flashing. "You are railroading me into marrying you. You are asking me to stand in front of a priest and *lie* about my feelings for you. Forgive me if I think this is taking things a bit far."

He inclined his head. "I agree that part isn't easy. But it's necessary."

"Necessary for *you*." She crossed her arms over her chest. "You are right about my dream, Rocco. I want it badly. Badly enough to marry you. With one condition."

He lifted a brow.

"I want my own line. My own signature line at Mondelli. *I* want to control my destiny."

He frowned. "Mario has to okay those decisions."

"Then get him to. Or find yourself another fiancée."

He studied her for a long moment. Read her determination. "All right," he said quietly. "I'm sure we can come to some agreement. Anything else bothering you?"

Her mouth twisted wryly. "Alessandra told you I was a disaster."

"Not a disaster. Just not yourself."

She turned and looked out at the rooftops. "I'm afraid I've lost my touch. That I don't have it anymore. It used to come so easily to me, and this morning was…a disaster."

"Olivia." He slid a hand around her waist and turned her to him. "Whatever happened to you a year ago, whatever it is you won't talk about, *is* ancient history. Go in there and be the model you are. I guarantee you will be jaw-dropping."

Her brilliant blue eyes darkened into a deep, azure blue. "What if I can't?" she asked huskily. "What if I can't get it back and you've wasted five million dollars on me?"

He shook his head. "You don't lose that kind of talent. What you're fighting is in your head."

Doubt flickered in her eyes, her gaze dropping away from his. He slid his fingers under her chin and made her look up at him. "You know I'm right."

"What would you know about it?" she asked tartly. "You've probably never had an unsure day in your life."

"That's where you're wrong, *cara*. When I was young, when I first took over as CEO of Mondelli, I thought I had it all figured out. I spearheaded this big deal, overrode Giovanni's protests that it wasn't right for the company and brought us close to bankruptcy."

Her eyes widened. "And you know what Giovanni said to me? He didn't berate me. He didn't say, 'I told you so.' He told me to learn from my mistake. To never make the same one again." He shrugged, a wry smile twisting his mouth. "It rocked me, to be sure. For months I was wary, afraid to take any big steps, but eventually I learned to trust my judgment again. To trust my instincts. And so will you."

She blinked. "You really almost bankrupted Mondelli?"

"Sì." He gave her a reprimanding look. "So go back in there, relax and figure it out. You haven't lost your talent, it's just lying dormant."

He thought he saw some level of understanding in her eyes. But she was too tense, too stiff, to ever make this work, and it *had* to work. Ignoring his better judgment, he slid his palms down over her hips to cup her derriere, pulling her flush against him. Her eyes flew wide. "What are you doing?"

"Solving this problem the only way I know how."

She was midway through a reply when he claimed her lips. Their sweet softness under his sent all his good sense out the window. Turned what had been a deliberate quest to loosen her up into a seduction of himself instead. His body seemed to be programmed with a particular weakness for her. For the taste of her. For how she felt under his hands…

And his thirst for her consumed him. He wanted what he couldn't have so badly it was like a fever in his blood.

He slid his hands into the weight of her silky hair and took what he wanted. She responded this time, as if she couldn't fight it any more than he could. An animal sense of satisfaction rumbled through him as he imprinted her with the need that had been consuming him for weeks. The soft contours of her body melted into his, invited him closer. He closed his fingers tighter around a mass of satiny hair and arched her head back to deepen the kiss. To stake complete ownership.

Her lips parted beneath his, an invitation he couldn't ignore. He dipped his tongue into the heat of her. Her taste mingled with his, the absolute perfection of what they created together rocking him to his toes.

That night in Navigli hadn't been an aberration. It had been a foregone conclusion.

He ran his hands down her back, sought out any remaining tension with the sweep of his fingers, kneaded a knot free with a press of his thumbs.

A discreet cough came from behind them. They whirled around in unison to find Alessandra had joined them on the terrace, an amused look plastered across her face. "Sorry, you two, but we need to get started."

Olivia nodded jerkily, wiping her palm across her mouth. Alessandra went back inside.

"I can't believe I just did that," Olivia said, staring at the lipstick on her palm. "Which point were you trying to prove this time, Rocco? That you are irresistible now that the spoiled-goods sign has been lifted from me?"

Anger at himself, at her, welled up inside of him. "Actually, Liv," he muttered, "I was trying to comfort you. To be there for you. Like it or not, we are in this together."

Color bled into her cheeks. "A team? I seem to remember you proclaiming me a purchased asset."

He raked a hand through his hair. "I might have been a bit overbearing. We are marrying now. It would be nice if we can be there for each other. Call a truce to this war of ours."

She shook her head. "Forgive me if it's not so easy for me to process your one-hundred-and-eighty-degree turns."

The bustling movements of the crew moving around inside captured his attention. "They need you in there," he advised roughly. "Go channel how much you hate me. You'll do just fine."

She studied him warily for a moment, then walked back inside. He stayed at the railing. What was wrong with him? He had to stay away from her. But something about Olivia, something about who she was inside, how vulnerable she was, seemed to waltz right past his defenses every time.

And wasn't that *insane*? He felt like finding a mirror and double-checking this was still him. Because wasn't it enough to know Tatum Fitzgerald had torn his steadfast, larger-than-life grandfather in two? Did he even have to question what allowing himself to feel emotion for Olivia would do to him?

He had told himself not to cross the line. Not to let himself feel. Yet he had just crossed so far over the line he couldn't pretend not to be emotionally involved anymore.

He swore and pushed away from the railing. That absolutely, positively could not happen. Not when Renzo Rialto and the board wanted to eat him alive, and that was the only place his focus should be.

He strode back inside, avoiding the controlled chaos on the set as he headed toward the elevators. He was shutting this thing with Olivia down. Finding another strategy, because this one obviously wasn't working.

Olivia watched Rocco disappear into the elevator, her equilibrium smashed to pieces. She had no idea what had just happened. Was Rocco just as confused about his feelings for her as she was of hers for him, or was he just using her again? She was tempted to think he really did care, that what she'd sensed that night in New York was real. But that was dangerous thinking for a woman about to marry him for show. For a woman he was clearly using to regain control of his company.

As for him suddenly asserting they were a team in this? She shook her head as she sank down in the makeup chair. That would be a foolish, *foolish* thing to believe.

But as she walked back onto the set after her makeup had been repaired, she couldn't help but remember what Rocco had said. She *had* once been phenomenal at this. At creating an illusion. It *was* all in her head. She just had to bear down and do it.

She would never have admitted it, but when Alessandra tried again with that pose of her leaning against a fence with her baby finger in her mouth, the heat from Rocco's kiss filled her head. And she wondered what would happen if she were ever stupid enough to let him take her to bed.

Complete and total annihilation.

When Alessandra finally put her camera down and announced them finished, Olivia gave her an apprehensive look. "Did you get everything you needed?"

Alessandra quirked a finger at her. "These five shots are worth the day."

They were, of course, the photos of her leaning against the fence, her finger dangling innocently from her mouth, Rocco's stamp written all over her. The look on her face stole the breath from her throat.

"Exactly," Alessandra said with satisfaction. "You look utterly, delectably, madly in love."

CHAPTER NINE

NEW YORK DURING Fashion Week was a frenetic exercise in seeing and being seen. Anyone who was anyone in the fashion world descended on the city like a swarm of locusts ready to make their mark. Press coverage was massive, celebrity sightings in an already star-encrusted city even more frequent and thousand-dollar bottles of Cristal ran like water in the dozens of warm-up parties held across the metropolis.

There was, however, no partying going on at the Mondelli suite at Fifteen Central Park West on the afternoon of the Italian fashion house's show, Olivia's first appearance on a runway in over twelve months. The show, combined with the details of planning the society wedding of the year, had Olivia hurtling close to the edge. She was wearing the face of Medusa. Rocco was afraid if he touched her, she would snap in half.

She stood, hands on jean-clad hips, in the salon, blue eyes shooting fire at him. "I told you I don't care," she muttered in response to his question about the wedding color scheme. "Maybe we should make it a black-and-white theme—the light and the darkness."

"Perfetto," he murmured. "You would be the darkness and I would be the light."

"As if." She shoved the guest list back at him. "I told you. Violetta, Sophia, my mother and my father. That's it. And my father is not walking me down the aisle."

"Why?"

"Because he has his own family now, and who knows if he'll be able to take the time off work. He works long hours for the transit company."

Rocco frowned. "So I'll send him some money to cover the week. Maybe he and his family can even make a vacation out of it."

"You will not." Heat flared in her eyes. "He hasn't wanted anything to do with my mother and me for years. Leave him alone."

"Let's talk about your mother, then. If you've forgiven Giovanni and her for the affair, why the animosity?"

"Forgiving her for the affair has nothing to do with my general feelings for my mother."

"Which are?" He lifted a brow. "I'm going to be meeting her tonight. Maybe you should give me a heads-up as to what I'm walking into."

"Like you did with Stefan?" She shook her still-damp hair back over her shoulders. "All she cares about is status. Keeping up with the Joneses."

He frowned. "It must have been hard for her when her career fell apart. When she lost Giovanni and your father."

"She brought it on herself. And then she made everyone pay." Olivia got down on her hands and knees and peered under the coffee table. "Have you seen my sneakers? We have to be out of here in five minutes."

He shook his head and shrugged on his jacket. "What do you mean 'made everyone pay'?"

"Dammit, I need those sneakers." She crawled over and looked under the sofa. "They're my lucky ones. Are you sure you haven't seen them?"

Rocco walked to the door, found her sneakers jammed under a pair of his dress shoes and fished them out. He carried them over to her but held them out of reach.

"Tell me."

She got to her feet and grabbed the running shoes out of his hands. "When I began to have success with modeling, my mother latched on to me as if I was her saving grace. Her career was done, and she had a hard time holding a normal job. So she spent my money like it was cheap wine. Went on living her life like she had in the good old days. The more she spent, the more I had to work to pay the bills. I was exhausted, in a different city every week. But it never stopped. It was an endless vicious cycle of wanting to cut back and not being able to."

His brows came together. "Are you saying she spent all your money?"

She sat down and tugged a shoe on. "I'm saying that when I returned home from a trip to Europe where my credit card was declined, the bank manager told me I was broke. As in *zero* dollars in the bank. She had spent it all."

His stomach lurched. "On what? What could she have spent that much money on?"

She yanked the other shoe on. "An apartment, a car, trips to visit her friends in the south of France. I was so busy working I had no idea."

"And you trusted her," he concluded grimly.

"Who would you trust more with your life than your mother?"

Or your father. The uneasy feeling in his stomach intensified. The way he had read this woman wrong from the very beginning on every point shamed him to his core. She hadn't been out partying away her money. She had been attempting to support her family, just as he had had to.

"Mi dispiace," he said quietly as she stood there, a vulnerability emanating from her he now knew to be utterly authentic. "I have judged you completely wrong from the beginning, Olivia. I owe you an apology."

She stared back at him for a long moment, surprise

etching its way across her face. Self-disgust kicked in his gut. He had really been a first-class ass this entire time.

Her gaze fell away from his. "We should go. I need to be backstage in half an hour."

Olivia tried to ignore the seismic shift that seemed to have occurred in her and Rocco's relationship as they walked the short distance to the Lincoln Center. It had been there ever since that kiss during the photo shoot. Ever since he'd told her he believed her about her and Giovanni's relationship. He may have been avoiding her even more the past couple of weeks, but he was different with her. His respect for her showed. He'd stopped treating her like a high-priced show horse he'd purchased, his to bend to his will.

Rocco came backstage with her to greet the designers and models. Frederic, who was producing the show, gave her a hug and a kiss on the cheek. "Put that face away," he scolded. "You are going to shine tonight. They can't wait to see you."

That made her stomach squeeze into an even tighter ball.

"By the way," Frederic said quietly as models and crew members flowed past them, "Guillermo is shooting backstage tonight."

"Oh." She caught her lip between her teeth and considered that. She hadn't seen Guillermo since the night she had walked out on him, her own heart broken in two. "Thanks for the heads-up," she said huskily. "How is he?"

"Fine. Single. Here any minute." He gave her an affectionate push toward the makeup room. "They're ready for you."

She was made up, desperately trying to distract herself from the way the mood had shifted backstage from one of industrious, purposeful action to an electric, anticipatory tension that sizzled in her veins, when a familiar voice rang out. She turned around and saw her designer-clad mother making her way toward her with Rocco in tow. *Great.*

She rose and gave her an awkward hug. "I thought we were going to meet at the reception afterward?"

"And wait to meet your delicious fiancé?" Her mother wrinkled her nose. "You're on the runway again, sweetie. It's so fabulous. I wanted to come and wish you good luck."

"That's very sweet of you. But would you mind giving me some space before the show?"

Her mother peered at her. "Are you okay, hon? You look nervous."

She *was* nervous. She wanted to throw up. She wanted to put her clothes back on, run out of here and never come back.

Rocco curved a hand around her mother's shoulder. "Why don't I show you to the seat beside mine and we can all catch up after the show?"

Her mother beamed. "That sounds wonderful."

Olivia almost loved him in that moment. Almost.

Tanya, one of the designers, appeared with her first outfit, an ultrachic emerald-green cocktail dress. Olivia shrugged out of her robe and slid it over her head, every movement mechanical, born of years of practice. Tanya fussed around her for a few minutes, making sure the dress fell perfectly, then pronounced her ready.

She walked out into the wings, joining the other models clustered there, her pounding heart a raging contrast to the ice in her limbs. *You can do this*, she told herself. *You can.*

"Livvie." Guillermo materialized in front of her, two cameras slung around his neck. He was as dark and devilishly handsome as ever, his swarthy skin a perfect foil for his amazing green eyes. He drank her in, gaze full of affection. "You look incredible."

"Gui." She stepped forward and pressed a kiss to both his cheeks. "It's so good to see you. How have you been?"

His smile was wry. "Since I've recovered from your heart smashing and disappearance? I was worried about you, Liv. You could at least have let me know you were okay."

She bit her lip. "I thought maybe a clean break was better for us."

A flicker of something she knew she had put there glimmered in his eyes. "Maybe so." He frowned. "Do you think we could talk afterward? I know you're engaged to Mondelli, it's not that. I just want to make sure you're okay."

Her teeth sank deeper into her lip. She was starting to realize what it was like to be hopelessly besotted with someone and not have those feelings returned. "Gui…"

A flash of platinum blond flew past her. She turned and stared at the model joining the line, her wildly excited expression marking her new in the business. Something contracted deep inside of Olivia at the sight of the young girl's pert nose and ridiculously high cheekbones.

Petra. But Petra was dead…

The bottle of water she held slipped from her fingers and fell to the floor.

Guillermo picked it up. "It's Natasha," he murmured quietly. "Petra's sister."

The image of Petra's vibrant young sister, an almost identical younger version of her friend, giggling with the other models, collided with Olivia's last memory of her best friend. Petra had been lying prone across her living room sofa, her face chalk white, her expressive eyes vacant. Olivia's fingers had stumbled over the keys of her phone, desperately dialing 9-1-1. But it had been too late.

She wasn't aware the wounded, animallike sound had come from her until Guillermo reached for her arm, an alarmed expression on his face. "Liv…"

"No." She shook him off and started walking. Anywhere but here, looking at *that*. She was dimly aware of Frederic announcing it was ten minutes to showtime.

She kept walking past him. His eyes widened and he followed her.

"Liv." He tugged on her arm. "What the hell are you doing? You're starting the show."

She broke free and kept walking. "I'm sorry. I can't. I just...can't."

In the back of the wings, she sat down in a chair and put her head between her legs. The frantic sounds of a show about to happen filled her ears. Haunted her with her biggest failure... She put her fingers to her temples as the world swirled around her, darker and darker. Beckoned her with its beguiling promise of escape. She'd thought she was strong enough to do this. But she wasn't.

"Liv." Rocco's voice penetrated the darkness. "What's wrong?"

She shook her head. Shook him away.

He knelt down in front of her and captured her jaw in his hands. "Look at me."

She shook him off. "Go away."

"Nessuno." He captured her jaw again, this time tighter, his fingers digging into her flesh. "I will not allow you to destroy yourself like this. Tell me what's wrong."

She wrenched herself free. "*I can't do this.* My best friend overdosed after she walked off this stage, Rocco. Because she couldn't handle the pressure anymore. It's why I left. *I can't do it.*"

His eyes widened. "I'm so sorry. I had no idea."

A lone tear broke through the wall she had built around herself. "I loved her. She was my rock. She was the *strong* one. And *I* allowed that to happen to her."

"You didn't *allow* anything," he countered roughly. "She was suffering, Olivia. That type of suffering requires professional attention. You couldn't have stopped it."

She squeezed her eyes shut. "I can't go out there. Tell Frederic to replace me."

"Yes, you can. *Look at me, damn you.*" She kept her eyes squeezed tightly shut. He took hold of her shoulders and shook her. *"Look at me."*

She opened her eyes. His gaze held hers. "All that is out there is a walk, Liv. A walk down a runway. *It* doesn't define you. Your extraordinary talent does. And if you don't go out there tonight, if you turn your back on all those people, you are alienating everyone who matters. Everyone who will decide whether those beautiful designs you and Giovanni created together will touch the world." His expression softened, dark and sure. "And they will touch the world because they are genius, *cara. You* are a genius. But you have to let them see it."

Another tear burned a hot track down her cheek. "You don't have to say that."

"Do I ever say anything I don't mean?" He pressed his forehead against hers. "Make this the night you leave the darkness behind. Because you are light, Olivia. Everything about you is radiant. Don't let them win."

The tears fell harder. She wanted to. She wanted to let them win. She had already done that when she'd left the first time. But her dream hadn't been on the line then...

The pounding music and the MC's voice as he opened the show made her blood turn to ice. She drew back and stared blindly at Rocco. "I can't."

"Yes, you can." The quiet conviction in his eyes held her, wound its way around her insides. "Just you walking down a runway, Liv. That's all this is. Nothing more. You've done it hundreds of times. Let's do it together."

She swallowed hard. Felt his words penetrate the numbness. If she walked now, she *was* giving up everything. Everything she had created with Giovanni. Her reputation could only take so many knocks.

"Four passes," Rocco promised. "Four passes down that catwalk and you're done. Put it on automatic pilot and go."

She had to. She had to do it, she realized. For Giovanni. For herself.

"Okay." She swiped the tears from her cheeks. "Okay."

Frederic materialized. She stood, legs wobbly, Rocco's arm firm around her waist. The urge to hang on to him and never let go consumed her. He nodded at her, a smile curving his lips. "I'll be right here waiting for you."

Frederic swept her to the front of the line of models, but her cue had just come and went as the music pounded to life and general pandemonium ensued. She gave him a panicked look. "Forget it," he muttered, "go on the next line."

She focused on the long, light-encrusted runway rather than the crowd, sitting dozens of rows deep. The glare of the lights hit her as she walked onto the catwalk. She'd forgotten how hot they were, how long that thirty-six feet seemed when you were like a star in the sky…when all the attention was focused on you. The loud, pulsing beat of the music propelled her forward. Her walk wasn't her trademark cocky swagger, but it was steady and purposeful into the blinding light. She made it to the end of the runway, paused, stuck her hand into her hip and let the camera flashes reign down on her. Showed the dress off to its full advantage. The applause was deafening, but she blocked it out.

Just walking down a runway. That was all she was doing.

The three changes that came after, the brilliant showing that Mondelli and its new designers put in that night, it was all a blur. It wasn't until she did the final walk down the runway with the designers that she realized how weak her knees were. How close to collapsing she was. She shifted her weight, stood back, clapped for the designers and told herself to hold on for sixty more seconds.

After several standing ovations, they led the designers off the stage, Olivia willing herself through the curtain.

* * *

Rocco congratulated the designers as they came off the runway. The auditorium was abuzz, the evening triumphant, returning a resounding yes to the question many had posed as to whether Mondelli could survive without Giovanni. But his attention wasn't on the buzz; his eyes were locked on the curtain for Olivia.

She appeared, the rest of the models spilling through after her. The way her body slumped the minute she was through sent alarm slicing through him. She blinked to adjust to the light after the glare of the catwalk and scanned the wings. Searching for something. *Someone.*

A wave of protectiveness flashed through him. A smile curved his lips, his heart throbbing at her bravery. He was so proud of her, *so damn proud.*

Guillermo Villanueva stepped in front of him. He held his arms out to Olivia, and when she walked toward him, Rocco's heart stopped in his chest. Her name sprang to his lips, but he savagely stuffed it back in. His body tightened as he braced himself to watch Olivia walk into her former lover's arms. Then he realized she wasn't looking at Villanueva, she was looking past him. At *him.* Their gazes collided, the way Olivia's face fell apart as they did destroying something inside of him.

Villanueva turned around, focused on Rocco. A grimace twisted his lips as his arms fell to his sides. Rocco ignored him and moved toward Olivia. Her last shaky steps carried her into his arms. Her delicate floral scent enveloped him as he folded her against his chest.

"Sei stata magnifica," he murmured. "You were magnificent."

She stayed buried in his embrace for a long time. He was partially holding her up, but as the moments passed he felt the strength move back into her. When she finally pushed her palms against his chest and moved back, a tremulous smile curved her lips. "Just a walk down a runway," she whispered. "That's all it was."

He smiled. "That's all it was."

There were interviews to do, a reception to attend. Dinner he'd promised her mother. Olivia did the interviews with remarkable composure, following Savanna's instructions to gloss over any questions about missing her cue and put it down to backstage madness.

The desire not to leave her side, to anchor her, was unlike anything Rocco had ever felt before. It evoked a restless, uncomfortable feeling inside of him. As if for the first time in his life he had no idea what he was doing.

He smothered it, moved it aside. It had no place here. Not now.

Everyone at the reception, it seemed, wanted a piece of the return of Olivia Fitzgerald. And why wouldn't they? She was spectacular in the midnight blue gown that hugged every curve of her body and made her eyes glitter like the ocean on a particularly haunting night. Her hair plunged down her back in a swath of golden silk. But most powerful was the current that ran between them as he played guard dog and spirited Olivia through the necessary rounds. It stretched like a live force between them, cementing something both of them had known for weeks.

There was no escaping this.

They spent some time talking to Tatum Fitzgerald, whom Rocco found to be vain and narcissistic. So unlike Olivia it was almost impossible to believe they came from the same blood, except for their clearly matching outward genetics. He got them out of dinner with a promise to do so in Italy as Olivia's eyes begged for a reprieve. And then they were in the car being whisked through the warm Manhattan night.

CHAPTER TEN

THE APARTMENT WAS SILENT, bathed in the glow of the ever-present light of New York. After the pounding, pulsing rhythm of the night that had preceded it, the utter silence was like slamming on the brakes of his Aventador after he'd put the pedal to the floor. Full stop, jarring awareness. *Of everything.*

He threw his jacket over a chair, stripped his tie off and rolled up his sleeves. "Drink?" he asked Olivia, who was sitting on the sofa unbuckling her shoes.

She nodded.

He poured himself a much-needed tumbler of Scotch along with a glass of wine for her and crossed over to where Olivia stood at the windows.

"She was only twenty-five when she died." Her profile was ridiculously beautiful in the moonlight. "We met at a panty hose shoot when we were nineteen. They were asking us to say these ridiculous lines about how sexy the panty hose made us feel, and we both giggled our way through it. After that, we were best friends."

"You loved her a great deal."

She nodded. "She was the one who kept me sane. When there was too much money, too many people wanting to know us only because of who we were, too much partying and too much drinking. We were young and we had everything."

"But you didn't have everything."

"No." She turned to face him. "We were out of control near the end. I wasn't an alcoholic, but I was close. I always managed to rein myself in, but Petra couldn't. Her new boyfriend liked to do drugs, and it was a dangerous combination. I tried to get her to break up with him, but she was strong willed. One night—" her voice took on a gravelly note "—we were at a party and we split up. She went home with Ben and I stayed. A few hours later, I went to her apartment to check on her. But it was too late." A hot tear escaped the brimming pools of her eyes and slid down her cheek. "She was by herself and she didn't have a pulse."

His insides turned over. He captured her hand in his, wrapping his fingers tight around hers. "That must have been awful."

She looked down at the hand he held. "I was still holding her body when the paramedics told me she was dead. When they told me I had to let go."

"Mi dispiace." His voice was rough. "I am so very sorry, Olivia."

Her brilliant blue gaze clung to his. "If you hadn't been there tonight, I couldn't have done it. I would have destroyed myself."

He shook his head. "You would have walked out of there and you would have found your way."

"Not the right way." She pulled her hand free to swipe the tears from her face. Blinked hard. "I needed to face it. Face the past."

"And you did."

She nodded slowly as if just realizing that now. Her creamy skin was blotchy, her eyes red rimmed, but she was still the most bewitching woman he'd ever seen in his life and, with Olivia, it was not all on the outside. So much of what he hadn't seen in the beginning was inside that stunning exterior.

"Is that when the panic attacks started? When Petra died?"

She shook her head. "Those started when I was a teenager. My mother was emotionally unavailable, my father was gone, and there I was traveling to all these foreign countries under so much pressure." She looked out at the lights. "I went to see a therapist, learned how to try to control them, but they never went away. Sometimes they were worse than others."

"And that night in New York, that's what it was?"

"Yes." Her gaze stayed glued on the cityscape. "It was the end."

"Not the end," he countered softly. "You conquered it tonight."

"With you." She turned back to him, eyes brimming with emotion. "Thank you."

"That isn't necessary."

"Yes, it is. Rocco?"

"Sì?"

She brought her fingers to his lips. "Can we not talk anymore?"

Need roared to life inside of him, so fast and sharp it blinded him for a moment. He was in complete agreement, because to keep talking was rational, and *this* was not rational. He didn't want to think.

He captured her hand and pressed an intimate, openmouthed kiss against it. The way she tensed made his blood fire in his veins. "Do you still love him?"

She frowned. "Guillermo? I told you I never loved him the right way."

"Do you still *lust* after him, then?" He was shocked at how dark and gritty the words came out.

She looked down at the trembling hand he held in his. "What do you think?"

He put his drink down with a jerky movement. Took

hers and set it on the table beside his. Her gaze tracked him as he bent his head and allowed himself a mouthful of her bare, smooth shoulder. She was a silken, golden feast for him to explore, and she shuddered beneath his mouth. His stomach jammed into a tight, hard ball. Five weeks of wanting her had weakened him. Badly.

He blazed a path from her shoulder across the delicate skin of her collarbone to the throbbing pulse at the base of her neck. He was so enthralled with the taste of her, with the salty, sweet essence he had finally secured access to, he didn't hear her speak at first.

"Rocco?"

"Sì?" He lifted his head and focused on her shimmering stare, glistening with the remnants of her tears.

"When did this become real?"

His heart stuttered in his chest, then stopped completely, his tongue unable to form the words.

Her gaze darkened. "I'm not asking for promises. I just need to know that *this*, tonight, whatever it is, it's real and not another of your games."

That he could answer. He lifted her palm and pressed it against the pounding beat of his heart, echoing her words. "What do you think?"

Her pupils dilated until they were dark glowing orbs in a sea of blue. She slid a hand behind his neck, tangled it in his hair and brought his mouth down to hers. He nipped at the lush fullness of her lower lip, teased her with tiny pulls that telegraphed his impatience. She was equally impatient, tugging on his hair and demanding his full attention. He consumed her then, taking her mouth in a series of hot, openmouthed kisses that made up for every last minute of these interminably long past few weeks. He kissed her until he'd explored every centimeter, every angle, of her, learned every mystery of her irresistible heart-shaped mouth. And then he demanded more, because his need for her was insatiable.

They broke apart finally, breathing hard, eyes on each other. Olivia was the first to break the standoff, reaching for the top button of his shirt. His breath caught in his throat as her knuckles brushed against his bare skin. He'd had a lot of women undress him, had had a lot of women period. But he had never held his breath as they'd done so. Had never anticipated a touch so much he'd almost jumped out of his skin by the time she'd freed all the buttons and slid her hands up his bare abdomen.

"You are the most beautiful man I have ever seen in my life," she murmured, tracing the ridges of his abs with her fingers. "And I've seen a few."

"I'd rather not hear about your ex-lovers," he growled. "I had one in my face tonight."

"On shoots," she reprimanded quietly. "Guillermo was my first and only lover."

That burned a searing path through him. If he hadn't hated the Venezuelan before, he did now. He didn't want to think about any man's hands on Olivia. Only his.

He dipped his shoulders as her fingers slid under the collar of his shirt and pushed it off. Thoughts about ex-lovers vanished as Olivia brought her mouth to his pecs and scored her lips and teeth across the width of him. When she had thoroughly tasted his skin, the ridges of his muscles that flexed beneath her touch, she brought her mouth to one of his nipples and teased it to erectness with soft, flicking motions of her tongue. He braced a hand against the window as she sucked it inside her mouth. *Cristo.* Helen of Troy had nothing on her.

She transferred her attention to his other nipple. He closed his eyes and let himself feel. Feel what this woman did to him, because he rarely, if ever, relinquished control in anything he did, but with her it was impossible not to.

"The photo Alessandra took of you," he rasped, a spasm of pleasure shaking him as she drew his nipple deeper inside her mouth. "That better have been me in your head."

She looked up at him, dragging her fingertips over his hard, burning nipples. "You made sure it was... Did you like it?"

"*Like* is an understatement."

He reached down, slid his arm beneath the curve of her hip and swung her up into his arms. She fit perfectly there, as if she was made for him. It intensified the skittery, antsy feeling he'd been experiencing all night. *Dangerous*, his senses told him. But tonight he wasn't listening to his head. Wasn't focusing on anything but slaking his lust until there was none left.

He carried her into the penthouse and into the bedroom, which had become a war zone between them, a symbol of their mutual antagonism. But not tonight. He set her down on the carpet and reached for his watch, his socks. Peeled them off with deliberate intent. Liv moved her hands to the straps of her dress.

"*Nessuno.*" His quiet command brought her head up. He crooked a finger at her. "Come here."

She walked toward him, myriad emotions in her blue eyes. Anticipation, definitely. Uncertainty... *Maybe*. She stopped inches from where he stood, so close he could feel the warmth of her breath on his cheek. He ran the pad of his thumb across the generous sweep of her lower lip. "I haven't forgotten what you started in the restaurant that night, Liv. *Finish it.*"

Her eyes widened. Hot color flamed her cheeks. He watched her mouth form words, but they never came. He wrapped his fingers around hers and brought them down to rest against the straining bulge beneath his trousers. "Sitting at that table that night, all I could picture was you touching me, *cara*." His fingers tightened over hers. "I burned for it. I burn for *you*."

Color infused her neck and chest now, touching every centimeter of her. A muscle worked convulsively in her throat as she brought her other hand down to join the one he'd placed there, her fingers working the leather strap free of his belt. She pulled hard, uncinching it. He sucked in a sharp breath. Then her fingers were undoing the top button of his trousers, pulling his zipper down. The remainder of his breath left his lungs as she slid her hands inside his pants to cup the length of him.

Maledizione. He closed his eyes. "That's it. *Just like that.*"

She moved her fingers up and down him, explored the hard length of his shaft molded by the close-fitting boxers he wore. Her touch goaded him onward, pushed him to an aching, desperate hardness. *"Di più,"* he murmured. *More.*

She slipped him out of his boxers and took him in her palms. He was big, harder than he'd ever been in his life, and her soft gasp made him swell even larger. "That's right, *cara*. You do that to me. Only you."

She ran her fingers up and down the pulsing length of him, taking her time to learn the contours of him, the silky tip of him. When he couldn't take it anymore, he allowed his eyes to slit open.

Her gaze locked with his. The lust he read there almost pushed him over the edge. "In your mouth, sweet Liv. Do it. *Now.*"

The last word came out ragged and hoarse. A plea as much as it was a command. She must have been as lost as he because she gathered him in her hands and did as he said. He tensed, his entire body going stiff. His first slide inside her hot, welcoming mouth almost unmanned him. He tipped his head back and focused on the cloudless, dark sky through the skylight as he pushed himself back from the edge, forced himself to last so he could enjoy the insane pleasure Olivia was lavishing on him with decadent sweeps of her tongue.

When she had taken him as far as he could allow without ending it right there and then, when his sanity was failing him, he buried his fingers in her hair and brought her to her feet. His own essence mixed with her sweetness as he kissed her was the most heady pleasure he'd ever experienced. But he knew it could be better. Much better.

Olivia returned Rocco's devouring kiss, her fingers buried in his hair, consumed with a sexual frustration, a need, the likes of which she'd never felt. He had built her up, played her, with such skill. Used her desire for him to inflame her own. And now she had to have him. *Desperately.*

Rocco lifted his mouth from hers, cupped her scalp in his fingers as his gaze meshed with hers. "You want me to touch you, beautiful Liv? Make you as crazy as you have made me?"

She could do nothing but nod mindlessly. He sat down on the bed and drew her between his legs. Her heart boomed in her chest, slamming against her ribs so hard she feared she might develop a heart condition right there and then. The strongest organ in her body felt as if it was going triple speed, the insistent pulse of it reaching into the base of her throat, making it hard to breathe. Her knees, which had just about had enough tonight, quivered at the carnal expression on Rocco's face as he took her in.

He reached up and slipped the straps of her dress off her shoulders. The lightest touch of his fingers on her skin made her shudder. A smile tipped his lips. "*Sì*, Liv. We either survive this or we go up in flames. But we do it together."

She was afraid it was going to be the latter. She was afraid she wasn't going to survive *him*. He tugged her to him, pushed the dress down over her hips and off. Her eyes followed the dress as it fell in a pool of silk at her feet instead of looking at him, because he was too intense for her to handle.

Rocco slid his fingers under her chin and brought her gaze back up to his. "You look at me. No hiding tonight."

He reached around, released the clasp of her bra and let it drop to the floor with her dress. His gaze moved down over her, lingering on the swell of her breasts, then her last remaining piece of clothing, a tiny navy blue lace thong. "Out," he growled, urging her out of the pool of her dress and bra and kicking them aside. Then he brought her back between his legs.

His gaze held hers as he slid his palm between her thighs. Her panties were damp, betraying her desire for him. She closed her eyes at the satisfaction that glittered in his eyes. His fingers tightened on her thighs. "Open them," he commanded. "Do not close your eyes to me, Olivia."

She did. She was pretty sure she would have done anything he asked right about now, she was that turned on. But it was excruciatingly hard to make herself look at him as his stare burned into hers. As he removed the sliver of damp material and ran his thumb along the wet seam of her most intimate part.

A low moan broke from her throat. *"Oh."*

He filled her with a finger then, his caress aided by just how intensely she wanted him. It was perfect, exactly what she needed when she was on fire for him.

"Like that, *cara*?"

"Yes." She gasped. "Just like that."

He brought his thumb to the center of her and rubbed her slowly, deliberately. She threw her head back and gave herself over to it. He left her alone for long moments while she pushed her hips against his hand and savored his delicious torment. But soon it wasn't enough. Not nearly enough.

"Rocco, *please.*"

He stopped his delectable movements until her gaze was back on his. Then he eased another finger inside of her, filling her even more completely. She gasped as he invaded her tightness, stretched her body.

"I can feel you clenching around me, *mia cara.*" His eyes were a hot, dark brown on hers. "Imagine how I will feel inside of you, filling you completely."

She already had when her hands had been all over him… She closed her eyes and focused on the rhythm he set, because now it really was too much. Concentrated on the release she craved. He slowed it down, drew out her pleasure until she almost screamed. Then he did it all over again. Faster, harder, he played her until heat infused every centimeter of her body and she was out of her head.

She didn't realize the animallike groan had come from her until he pulled his fingers from her, pushed her back on the bed and came down between her splayed thighs. She thought he might take her then, but he pushed her thighs farther apart instead, moved his broad shoulders between them and slid down her body until his warm breath fanned her thigh. *Oh, Lord.* His tongue skated over her hot, aching nub in the briefest of movements. She grabbed the bedspread with her hands and clenched it between her fingers.

His soft laughter filled the air. "Tell me, sweet Liv. I want to hear you say it."

She squeezed her eyes shut, too shy to say it. He slid two fingers inside of her again, penetrating her slow and easy. Driving her to distraction.

"Say it."

"Please."

"Please what?"

Her brain clouded over. "Your tongue," she groaned. "Your tongue… God, Rocco, please, I want it *there.*"

He rewarded her with long, slow laps of his tongue that

built her pleasure to such an excruciatingly good level that it was almost, almost enough. But not quite. She begged him then, husky, broken entreaties that sounded so wanton to her ears she would have stopped if she hadn't been so desperate. But she was, and when he drove his fingers deeper and concentrated the expert flick of his tongue on the throbbing heart of her, she came apart beneath him like Fourth of July fireworks, pleasure radiating through every last centimeter of her skin.

She was incoherent, thanking him with broken sentences when he worked his way back up her body and took her mouth again with his. The intimacy of the kiss after what they had just shared was shattering.

"Sì," he growled thickly as they broke apart to breathe, his eyes blazing into hers. "It is the most perfect thing I have ever encountered. You and me, Olivia. How we taste together. How we fit together."

Her heart exploded in an emotion she had never felt. He was the most raw, sexual lover she could ever have imagined. But *this*, what they shared, was so much more than that. She closed her eyes to hide what she knew was blazing from them. To protect herself from *him*.

The sound of a foil wrapper being ripped open snapped her eyes wide. The way he slid the condom on the pulsing, thick length of him, his movements a sensuous caress, sent a hot wash of desire flaming back through her. She couldn't imagine coming again after what he'd just done to her, but looking at him on his knees like that made her insides quiver.

Rocco read her expression. *"Sì, bella,"* he murmured, hooking a heavy thigh over her and straddling her. "That was only a warm-up. You get more."

Her insides contracted, imagining him there, filling her. He took her mouth in a long, lingering kiss. Ran his palm down her leg to lift her thigh around his waist. "Take me inside you," he prompted in a throaty, raspy voice, his lips against hers. "Show me how much you want me, sweet Liv."

She reached down and wrapped her fingers around him, guiding him to her damp flesh. He eased inside of her with a gentle push, giving her time to accommodate his size and girth. She arched against him, demanding more. He pressed kisses against her mouth, told her how good she felt, giving her more and more of him until he was buried deep inside of her, and her body cried out at the fullness of it.

"*Cristo*. Liv." His gaze clung to hers as he held himself still. "You are so tight."

It was perfect. *He* was perfect. Her eyes told him so as he started to move. Her leg snaked tighter around his waist. The hypnotic quality of his lovemaking demanded her full and complete attention, and she gave it to him, savoring every deep drive of his body into hers.

"Tell me," he insisted, his gaze a hot brand on her face. "Tell me how I make you feel."

"So good," she moaned. "Like nothing I've ever felt before…"

Something passed between them then, deep and irretrievable. She saw it in his eyes, watched him register it before his face went blank; he lifted himself up on his forearms and took her with a fierceness that stole her breath. The show of pure strength sent her lust into overdrive. Her body pulsed back to life as his thick hardness caressed her insides. His eyes glittered as her face telegraphed her pleasure. "Touch yourself," he commanded. "I want to watch you make yourself come."

She squeezed her eyes shut, that particular demand a bit much for her even at this point. But his deep strokes were promising a release that wasn't coming, and she needed it badly. She moved her fingers between her thighs and against the hard nub of her. His low growl of approval reverberated in her ear. "That's it, *bella*. That is so sexy."

She stroked faster, harder, the deep throb of his body sending her close to a release she knew would break her. His breathing turned harsh in her ear, his strokes coming quicker, deeper, his rough encouragement in her ear spurring her on until she teetered on the edge.

"Now, Liv," he ordered hoarsely. "Come with me."

She sent herself over the edge with a desperate slide of her fingers against her throbbing flesh. His hoarse curse as his body swelled inside of her and he came amplified her mind-shatteringly good orgasm to make her whole body shake. He let his body cover hers, carried her through the storm until she stopped shaking and came out the other side.

They stayed like that, their bodies joined, for so long that her eyes drifted shut. The last thing she remembered before passing out from pure exhaustion was Rocco withdrawing from her, leaving the bed, then returning moments later to gather her in his arms and press her against his long, hard body. She felt safe then, safe to let go. So safe she ignored the fact that she had just given her soul away.

Rocco woke with his habitual insomnia at 2:00 a.m. This time, however, he lay with perfection in his arms. Olivia was curved into his side, fast asleep, his arm slung around her waist, her silky hair spilling across his chest.

He captured a lock of her hair in his fingers. Watched the moonlight play across its golden strands. The singularity of what they'd shared last night slammed into his head like the most potent of wake-up calls. His hand froze, tangled in the golden strands. What did he think he was doing? Did he actually even know?

Gingerly, silently, he slid out of bed and found his boxers lying on the floor. He slid them on, took a bottle of water out of the fridge and went out to the living room to settle in his favorite chair. It would be an hour or two before he found sleep again. It had been this way since he'd been a little boy. It had started after his mother had died and his father had gone out to gamble at night, leaving him and Alessandra alone in the house. Rocco had woken in the middle of the night to find his father still gone and paced the house, instinctively playing guard dog over Alessandra. Missing his mother terribly. He would stay up until he could no longer keep his eyes open or his father came home. Whichever happened first. Later when Giovanni had taken them to Villa Mondelli, he continued to wake at night. He would sit on the stone wall of the majestic house on the water and stare out at the silent, dark lake and mountains.

What a huge, dark world, he'd thought. Had his mother's essence been swallowed up by this massive, endless lake? Or was she still there looking over him? He'd ached for her those nights. Ached to have her warm, reassuring voice soothe him to sleep, not a nanny who wasn't the same. He'd dealt with his childish fear of the unknown by making up stories of friendly sea monsters who would come up to shore and take him to play in those dark depths, returning him before dawn.

Now in the middle of a New York night decades later, a full-grown man with the weight of the world on his shoulders, he craved the reprieve Olivia had given him last night.

In helping her to move through the darkness, to move on from the past, he had lost himself in her. He had allowed himself to take what he wanted, to hell with the consequences. And there would be consequences. His insides shifted, rearranging themselves in a foreign pattern he didn't recognize. He wasn't sure there was any going back from last night.

Wasn't sure he wanted to go back.

He tipped the water into his throat, welcoming the cool rush against his overheated senses. But of course he had to. Last night he had allowed himself Olivia because she'd needed him. Because they were in this together, as he'd promised her, and this wasn't just a deal to him anymore. But to allow himself to become more emotionally invested in a woman like Olivia, who needed someone to help her become whole again? Who needed to see her through the dark and the light? *Impossible.*

Even if she had the potential to be *the one*, he was incapable of love. "The one" didn't exist for him. Everyone he'd ever loved had left him in some form or another. His mother and Giovanni through death. His father through extreme neglect. Needing no one was the only way he knew how to cope. And Olivia? Olivia deserved more. *Someone like goddamn Guillermo Villanueva.*

Whose heart she had broken. He winced inwardly as he recalled the look on the other man's face when Olivia had walked into his arms. The guy was torn up. Olivia had that kind of an effect on a man.

He tilted his head back and took in the rough, unstructured skyline of Manhattan. He'd broken his promise to stay away from her. Perhaps that had always been inevitable, given the attraction between them. Given how emotional last night had been. He could tell himself he wouldn't touch her again, but he knew now he couldn't keep that promise. And maybe, he thought grimly, he'd been approaching this all wrong. Maybe he just needed to do like he did with all the other women in his life—allow himself as much as he wanted of Olivia with the knowledge that one morning he'd wake up and have had enough.

Olivia was alone in the bed when she woke, thirsty and disoriented. It came back to her in a rush. She was in New York, she had walked in Fashion Week last night and Rocco had pulled her out of the fire.

They had made love with an intensity she would never, ever be able to get out of her head.

The dark sky told her it was still the middle of the night. She put a hand out to touch the spot where Rocco had lain beside her and found it cool to the touch. He was up again. An insomniac who never seemed to sleep more than five hours a night.

She downed a glass of water, slipped on a T-shirt of Rocco's that was lying on a chair and went in search of him. He was in the living room, reclining in his favorite chair, staring up at the sky through the floor-to-ceiling windows.

"Why don't you sleep?"

He sat up, blinked hard as if he'd been in another world. "I've been this way since I was a boy. It's not a particular skill of mine."

...'d been minding the fort while his father had engaged in all sorts of debauchery. Protecting his sister. Giovanni had told her more than she'd ever admit to Rocco. How he had sheltered Alessandra from all the twists and turns in life and put himself last, always.

She moved closer, feeling braver with the connection they'd shared. Lines of fatigue depressed the skin around his eyes and mouth, his expression remote. His hair was rumpled, his only clothing the tight-fitting pair of boxers he'd worn earlier.

"You don't sleep because you're always on duty. With Mondelli. With your sister." With her. A pang filled her chest. "Alessandra is lucky to have you."

He lifted a shoulder, a naked, stunningly muscled shoulder that made her remember what he did with all that power. "She drew the short end of the stick when it came to a father. I couldn't make up for what Sandro did, but I did what I could."

"You did a lot. She adores you."

"We are...complicated."

Silence stretched between them. She didn't know

whether he wanted her to stay or go, so she remained rooted to the hardwood floor. A question came, unbidden. "Why didn't Giovanni leave you a controlling stake of Mondelli? It makes no sense."

He sat up straighter, his brows drawing together. "How do you know that?"

"I overheard it at Mondelli," she lied.

His expression darkened. "I have no idea what was going on in Giovanni's head when he made that decision."

"You think he didn't trust you."

His gaze narrowed on her, razor-sharp and infinitely dangerous now. "What makes you think that?"

Her teeth pulled at her lower lip. "It's a natural assumption. He didn't leave you a controlling stake. You wonder why. But that's not the case, Rocco. Giovanni thought you were utterly brilliant."

"More things you talked about?" His ebony eyes glittered in the moonlight. "He thought I was a loose cannon. That's why he did it."

She wrapped her arms around herself, a shiver making its way up her spine at the aggression emanating from him. "Everyone has limits. He felt sometimes you didn't recognize yours. No man is an island, Rocco. Although you try very hard to be."

The glitter in his eyes intensified. "Oh, but I am. Don't fool yourself, Olivia."

She recoiled from the sarcasm lacing his tone. It was a clear warning of where the line was. But fool that she was, she'd walked right over it last night, and it was a one-way street.

She might have left then, her skin stinging, but he snaked an arm out, captured her around the waist and dragged her down on his lap.

His gaze fused with hers. "While you're here…"

Held against all that delicious hard muscle, every centimeter of her skin burned with the impact of his on hers. Antagonism blended with want as she absorbed his erection pressing against her bottom. He was angry. She *should* walk away. But her body wasn't in agreement with her head. It was tightening, *remembering*, anticipating him.

Her breath jammed in her throat. Yanking it forcefully into her lungs she tried to resist. "Maybe we should..."

"Do it again." He slid his gray T-shirt up and cupped her breasts. The rasp of his thumbs over her nipples made every inch of her tighten. "I ignored these earlier," he murmured, his gaze hot on her skin. "A travesty. They are so...*fantastici.*"

All thoughts of walking away fled as he rolled her nipples into hot, aching points between his fingers. She wanted him inside her again desperately. Craved the way he'd brought her such intense pleasure.

He lifted her up with the power of those amazing biceps and turned her so she was facing the skyline of Manhattan, her back against his hard, hot body.

"Rocco..." She didn't like that she couldn't see him. That he had complete control...

His hand slid between her thighs, his thumb making electric contact with her still-tender skin. She moistened where he touched, her body readying itself for his possession. "So responsive," he murmured in her ear. "You take me so perfectly, Olivia."

She closed her eyes and gripped the sides of the chair as he used her arousal to moisten her flesh, to slide over her in insistent, deliberate caresses that had her arching against his skillful fingers. He was hard, pulsing beneath her, promising heaven.

He sucked her earlobe into his mouth, the heated pull sending another shock to her core. "Tell me when you're ready for me," he murmured. "It will be deeper, more intense for you this way."

"What way?" Her words were a low croak, wrestled from her throat.

He removed his fingers from her, released himself from his boxers and sank his hands into her waist to lift her above him. She felt the hard pressure of his erection brushing against her.

"This way, *cara.*" He brought his mouth to her ear. "Take what you want."

She wanted all of him. She reached down and guided him into her. He lowered her slowly onto his hot, turgid flesh, his strong arms controlling the penetration. Which was a good thing—she gasped as he filled her—because he had been right. In this position he felt so big; she felt him *everywhere.* Unable to look at him, to experience this with him, all she could do was close her eyes and feel.

Rocco shifted his hands to her buttocks and took the weight of her in his palms. He was buried inside of her now, the sensation so wickedly good she dropped her head back on his shoulder and just breathed. His soft laughter filled her ear. "I told you you would like it."

He pushed her forward gently with a palm to the small of her back so she was angled forward. His hands took the weight of her buttocks again, lifting her up and down on him in a delicious rhythm that stole her breath. Every time she came back down on him, he filled her breathtakingly full, stroking every centimeter of her. And then her hips caught the rhythm. She increased the pace, taking him inside her, retreating, then claiming him again. His thumbs slid over the unbearably sensitive tips of her breasts, pinching and rolling.

She knew then that whatever this man asked of her, she would give him. It was that good between them.

His breath came harder in her ear, *strained.* She wanted to let go for both of them, but she couldn't get the friction she needed, not in this position. Frustration escaped her throat in a low mewl. Rocco brought her back against his chest, one arm wrapping around her waist to hold her secure. He slid his free hand between her legs and found her clitoris. She was crazy for him, arching against him uncontrollably as he rubbed two long fingers over her time and time again. "Come for me, *bella*."

One last press of his wicked fingers and she cried out, her release so intense and centered it was more like a scream. His mouth came down to smother the bulk of it in a long, hot kiss as he drew out the pleasure for her, made her rock against his fingers a second time.

His low groan filled her ear as she regained sanity. "I need a condom."

"I'm on the pill," she managed to get out. "It's fine."

His fingers bit into her hips, then, needing no second urging as he tipped her forward, filled her again and again with hard thrusts that made her release reverberate through her body. He chased his orgasm fast and hard, and it was explosive when it came, his essence filling her with a sweet, hot warmth that seemed to touch every part of her.

She wasn't sure how long it was—five, ten minutes perhaps—before he pulled his T-shirt over her head, cleaned them up and carried her back to bed.

Olivia wrapped herself around his big warm body and willed her complex, hardened lover to sleep. He passed out in her arms minutes later.

The triumphant, warm feeling that filled her at being able to soothe him was matched only by the stark, fairly terrifying knowledge that she was lost, totally irrevocably lost, to him. And he would likely never, ever return those feelings.

CHAPTER ELEVEN

ROCCO WAS CONSIDERING going in search of his fiancée with a Milan Fashion Week kickoff party on the agenda when Gabriella returned from an errand she'd been running for him and stuck her head in his office, a horrified look on her face.

"Did you forget your meeting with Renzo Rialto?"

His stomach plummeted. *Dio del cielo.* He had. He'd been fixing a last-minute seating glitch with the wedding planner.

"His PA just sent me a message to reschedule." Gabriella's gaze searched his face as if to say he'd been off lately and was he okay?

No, he wasn't, he decided, raking a hand through his already rumpled hair. In the week and a half since he and Olivia had been back from New York, his attempts to drown himself in his soon-to-be wife's charms and get her out of his system had failed miserably. If anything, he was falling harder.

He was distracted and antagonized, and it was a problem he couldn't seem to fix.

"I clear forgot," he said to Gabriella. "What did you tell Renzo's PA?"

"That you were detained in another meeting, were ever so sorry and would reschedule."

"Bene." He flashed her a smile, grateful for his PA's tact. But inside, his guts were churning. He and Renzo had

been meeting to discuss North American business strategy, a key priority for Mondelli in the coming year. His fingers tightened around the pen he was holding. Renzo would drag him over the coals for this. Ask him where his priorities were...

"Could you reschedule for next week, same time?"

Gabriella nodded and disappeared.

He threw down his pen, furious with himself. The damn wedding was turning into a beast he couldn't control. So was Olivia's stress. He'd watched her push her way through her fears to walk in London Fashion Week. Watched her brave press speculation she wasn't the model she had once been with rumors running rife about what had happened backstage in New York.

"She doesn't have her usual swagger," one commentator had pronounced. Panic Attacks Wreak Havoc on Top Model's Career blared another tabloid that had apparently been able to find someone backstage that night in New York who would talk.

Olivia had transgressed it all with a determined focus on the end goal that said she'd let it kill her before she gave up. She wanted her line. She wanted her dream. But the stress was clearly taking its toll. She was looking gaunt, she wasn't sleeping much and the tabloid viciousness was eating away at her like a slow-moving disease.

He stared vacantly at the original Monet on the wall opposite him, its magnificent colors and lighting a favorite of his. The light in *Olivia* was fading daily. And nothing he did seemed to help.

He ran his palms over his stinging eyes. It should make him happy his fiancée was keeping it together, because *his* future was just as intertwined with Olivia's success as hers was. The board was thrilled with the rise in Mondelli's stock price, business was booming with the brand's newfound cool factor and Olivia was the hottest name in the industry.

It seemed the more miserable Liv was, the more speculation surrounding her, the more the brand skyrocketed. His chest tightened with that interminable, inescapable guilt he had been feeling for weeks. It was like a two-edged sword he was constantly being impaled on.

The only time Olivia *was* happy was when she was in the studio with Mario creating. And in bed with him. And since that was also a source of confusion between them, because it could never be more than sex for him, and he could see from her eyes when they were together that it was more for her, he felt like the biggest bastard alive.

The late-afternoon sun spilled into the room, blinding him momentarily. He dropped his gaze to the pile of research he'd intended to take to his meeting with Renzo this afternoon, ironclad evidence Mondelli was on an upswing in the American market. He had never, ever forgotten a meeting in his career. Certainly nothing of this magnitude.

Where was his head?

A glittering jewel he couldn't resist... That was how Giovanni had described Tatum. And her daughter was that for him. His weakness.

It was what Renzo had been warning him about. About allowing his concentration to slip when he needed it most.

His mind took him back to that bottle of Scotch he and Giovanni had shared one summer evening at the villa as the sun set over the mountains. It had started out as a celebration of his new job as CEO, then devolved into a long, meandering discussion of life, one in which his grandfather had opened up like never before.

"Your father," he had stated baldly, "had much of you in him. Same razor-sharp brain, same instinct for business... But he has a weak streak a mile wide, and he allowed himself to be ruled by it."

Giovanni had turned his dark, wise gaze on Rocco, the younger man still shaking in his shoes at the responsibility he now carried. "He was my biggest shame, my biggest disappointment."

And that had been the last Giovanni had ever spoken of his son's failures. Rocco had gone on to be what his father hadn't, but always with the latent fear buried deep inside of him he might carry his father's flawed gene.

The antagonism that gripped him now was stark, clutched at his insides with insistent, grasping hands. Showing weakness like he did toward Olivia was a slippery slope down the path his father had traveled. Not only did she get to him like no other woman had, but her instability had the power to take him down with her.

He returned his gaze to the vibrant Monet. Somehow, some way, he had to stabilize the situation. Help Olivia help herself. And take back control with her while he was at it.

He picked up the tickets to the Fashion Week gala and headed for the studios. There would be more press there tonight. More opportunities for Olivia to go sideways. And frankly, he couldn't put her through it. Couldn't put himself through it watching her.

He found her in the studios with Mario and a group of young women seated around one of the large design tables. Ten sets of eyes planted on him in unison. *The mentoring program.* Olivia had mentioned to him on the drive in this morning it was starting today.

She caught his gaze and held up five fingers. He nodded and melted into the background, watching her from the sidelines. Her cheeks were flushed with an excitement he hadn't seen in weeks. Her joie de vivre, that brilliant smile of hers when she was in her element like this, made his breath constrict in his throat.

This was what she should be doing. Not walking a runway or posing for a camera, although she was amazing at that, too. She should be waking up with that smile on her face every morning instead of dreading the day.

He turned away and walked to the window facing the courtyard. That kind of thinking was ludicrous. He couldn't give Olivia what she needed on any level. Her name was turning Mondelli into a hot commodity, making the industry focus on her, and not the loss of Giovanni.

It was out of his control.

Olivia smiled and waved as the last of the women left the room, delaying the confrontation with her fiancé as long as she could. Brooding and unapproachable, he appeared to be in a filthy mood. *Wonderful*, since they had to spend the evening together making small talk.

Mario wandered off to talk to another designer. Rocco handed him something on the way out. Olivia studied his stormy gaze. "I can be dressed in five minutes. Where's your tux?"

"We aren't going."

"Really?" She tried to temper the excitement in her voice.

"Sì."

"Why?"

"Because neither of us are up to it, and you need some sleep."

"I can do it," she protested. "I'm fine. Did something happen today?"

"Niente. I just think you need some rest. All anyone cares about is seeing you walk for Mondelli in Italy for the first time anyway, which will happen tomorrow. It's not necessary."

The familiar noose around her neck tightened. Never mind that her appearance in London had been flawless.

The press were out for blood… How long could she keep running before she cracked?

She swallowed her nerves back. "You aren't going to pepper me with wedding stuff, are you? The gala might be preferable." They were marrying in three and a half weeks after Paris Fashion Week, the last event of the season. Half the world was attending, and ever-in-control Rocco had it all under his thumb along with that efficient wedding planner of his.

Rocco gave her an even look. "Have you worked out your dress with Mario?"

"Yes." It was exquisite. The very dress she would have picked if she'd been marrying him for love. Which she was. But he didn't love her and it wasn't a real marriage, so more the fool for her for wasting her dream dress on a sham wedding.

"He's got Alessandra's dress under control, too." She'd asked Alessandra to be her maid of honor, as they'd gotten close these past few weeks, and somehow it just felt right with Petra gone.

His mouth twisted in a half smile. "Then you're free and clear. If you can put up with me for an evening."

Her whole body lit up like a Christmas tree at the thought of spending a real evening with him. Which was insane, really. She'd been latching on to that look she'd seen in his eyes that night in New York, the look she saw every now and again when they were making love. He cared. She wanted to turn it into love. She was a fool.

They ate fresh perch and baby potatoes, accompanied by a light pinot grigio, on the patio overlooking Lake Como. Olivia felt herself falling more in love with her fiancé with every minute that passed. When he was like this, when he was relaxed and not obsessed with business, he was that man she'd met in Navigli. Utterly, overwhelmingly gorgeous and charismatic.

Her stomach in knots, she gave up trying to eat and put her fork down.

"Finished?"

Rocco had pushed his plate away and was looking at her expectantly. She nodded. He stood up and held out his hand. "Bring your wine. I want to show you something."

They walked down the stone steps that descended from the twelfth-century villa into the waters of Lake Como. Flanked by two exquisite marble statues, they were formal steps, meant for receiving company by boat. Rocco sat down on them with his wine and tugged Olivia down beside him. The view as the sun set on the lake and sheer mountain face on the unseasonably warm evening was so utterly exquisite neither of them spoke for a long while.

"I used to come here at night," Rocco finally said. "When I couldn't sleep. We scattered my mother's ashes in this lake."

Her heart turned over in her chest.

"Everything seemed so big and vast at seven without two parents. I was trying to make sense of something that didn't *make sense* in my father's defection and my mother's death. To control the chaos around me. So I made up sea creatures, sea friends, to keep me company. My nanny found me asleep down here one morning. They were all panicked looking for me."

An ache in her throat joined the one in her chest. "You were doing your best to cope."

"*Sì.*"

She swallowed. "I bet they were pretty amazing sea creatures. What did they look like?"

His mouth twisted. "Big, green scary-looking things with scales and long tails. But they had great smiles. That used to make them okay."

She slid her hand into his free one, feeling its warmth

engulf her, soothe her as it always did. "You're telling me this because you want me to slay my dragons."

He turned his head, his dark gaze sinking into hers. "You've already slayed half of them, Olivia. Now slay the rest."

She thought about that long and hard, because she was doing her best. She had been for weeks. She wasn't as strong as him. He was a rock, and she was not.

"I'll try."

He stood up and insisted she go to bed.

Standing there, in her mere wisp of a nightie in their bedroom with its magnificent view of the glistening lake, she thought he might leave her then to go to work.

His gaze fused with hers in that electric connection they shared, the one he couldn't control even though he wanted to. He reached for her, tugging the wisp of silk over her head and bringing the heat of their bodies together.

He desired her, wanted her desperately; she could feel it in the intensity of his lovemaking as he deposited her on the bed and staked claim to every inch of her. But there was more. She saw that naked emotion on his face again now when he took her, their bodies fitting together perfectly.

Her heart stopped in her chest as she waited for him to say it. *Willed* him to say it. But then he turned his head away from her and buried his lips in her throat. Switched it off like he always did when she got too close.

Her heart stuttered back to life. Went back to where it should have been. If he hadn't said it now, that he loved her, he never would. It was time for her to start accepting that. Protecting herself against the inevitable. Because it was coming. The day he shut her out completely.

CHAPTER TWELVE

MILAN'S PIAZZA DUOMO, the city's central square, and home to the massive, silver-spired, Gothic Duomo Di Milano cathedral, was the site of Mondelli's opening night Fashion Week show. Lit with eclectic green-and-blue lighting that cast an otherworldly glow over the square, the buzz in the crowd was palpable as Rocco negotiated the crowds, heading for the tent that housed the models and his fiancée, who would open the show. The cobblestones reverberated beneath his feet, the air around him sizzling with an electric energy as Italy's revered fashion brand made its triumphant return to Fashion Week with its fall/winter Vivo collection.

Renzo Rialto waved him over, his wife by his side in the front row. Beautiful even in her sixties and perfectly coiffured, Veronique Rialto was the epitome of elegance with her short-cropped silver hair and black cocktail dress. Rocco bent and kissed her on each cheek, wondering what it was like to spend your life in a loveless marriage. He'd always thought if he did marry, it would be just that. But for some reason lately, he thought he'd be better off on his own when Olivia left.

Did Veronique know Rialto didn't love her? he wondered. That she had been used for her status… Did she care?

Veronique gave his arm a warm squeeze as she pulled back. "You are a magician, Rocco. Mondelli is all anyone can talk about these days. But then again—" she teased with a smile "—your lovely fiancée is doing all the work, it seems. I can't wait to see her wearing Mario tonight."

The guilt that had been eating away at him took another large bite of his insides. He needed to find Olivia and make sure she was okay. She'd been her usual mess this morning with the show looming.

He nodded to the couple. "Will you excuse me? I was just on my way to find her."

He wound his way around the rows of seats back to the tent that held the models and designers. It was filled with the usual preshow frenzied activity, bodies scurrying in all directions.

"Have you seen Olivia?" he asked one of the models.

"Bathroom," she said, stretching an elegant, slim arm toward the portable toilets. He strode toward them only to walk straight into his fiancée, who was so chalk white in the face his heart rate quadrupled. *"Va tutto bene?"* he asked her in Italian. *Are you all right?*

She nodded and started to walk past him. "I'm fine. The show's about to start."

"Olivia," he growled, catching her arm. "What's wrong?"

"I just puked my guts out," she rasped, shaking off his hand. "That's what's wrong."

The pounding music increased in volume. She started walking. "I need to go."

He watched her join the floor director at the front of the tent, her shoulders set back. Savanna stopped beside him. "I didn't know the reporter from *Fashion Report* had been given a backstage pass. She was all over Olivia before I got to them."

Great. He felt his internal temperature grow to dangerous proportions. "We need to watch these things more carefully."

Savanna nodded. "I know. I'm sorry, Rocco. The publicist should have warned me."

He took his seat for the show. Fury at that damn reporter who'd been hounding Olivia every waking minute burned through him. Fury at himself for not stopping it all. He might command a multibillion-dollar fashion empire, but he had never felt so helpless in his entire life.

A spotlight bathed the stage in Mondelli blue. Olivia posed motionless beneath it. Camera flashes popped from every direction, adding to her otherworldly appearance. Resplendent in a lime-green evening gown that left her entire back bare, her incredible hair cascading down her back in a curtain of gold, her eyes glittering like blue fire, she almost didn't seem real. Every curve of her beautiful body he coveted, every dip he ached to possess—but every night he had her, his desire for her only got worse. Because he could not have her truly—not when he was breaking her soul.

He could see it in her eyes as she got closer and trained her gaze on him. The fire in her was a message for him. She was done.

The end of the show came; the interviews happened. When the party started, he didn't even ask if they were attending, just bundled Olivia in the car and drove to the apartment.

Olivia headed straight for the heated gardens—her place of peace. He followed and found her sitting, staring into the rock pools. "What happened?"

She turned to face him. "*Fashion Report* is going to run a feature on me next week. They plan to interview several other models who have suffered from anxiety disorders to round the piece out, since I won't talk."

He brought his back teeth together. "I'll get an injunction. I won't let them run it."

A resigned expression twisted her face. "You were the

one who told me I can't keep running. Let it go, Rocco. It needs to happen. Then maybe they'll stop."

She was right; he knew it. He sat down beside her and rested his elbows on his knees.

"You of all people know the positive effect the dirt on me is having on Mondelli." Her tone was resolute. "People can't get enough. The only thing that can stop this for me is you releasing me from my contract. And since I know you won't do that, there's no point in having this discussion."

Frustration seared through him. "It's not a question of what I want—I *can't* do it, Olivia. You know that as well as I do. You were brilliant tonight. Why can't you just focus? Do exactly what you did tonight and, after Paris next week, this will all be over."

Her mouth twisted. "And then there's the spring/summer shows. It will never stop until I'm out."

"You agreed to do this," he pointed out harshly. "You know you have to wrestle these demons of yours. Me pulling you from this campaign, making *me* the bad guy, won't help you do that. It will only make you feel like a failure. And that will hurt you more than those reporters ever could."

Her eyes flashed that blue fire they'd spit at him onstage. "*I* am not *you*. I am not some impenetrable force that can cut off my emotions at will, who puts work above everything else."

He rocked back on his heels, her accusations hitting him like a blow to the chest. "I do *not* put business above everything else. I have been by your side every minute these past few weeks when you needed me, Olivia. I have been there for my family *my entire life*. So do not say I don't care."

Her gaze drilled into him. "You are making me your wife for the sake of your company, Rocco. How much more evidence do you need that you are married to Mondelli?"

"I do not feel," he bit out, "that sacrificing a year of my

life is too much to do for the company I've built into an international powerhouse. A symbol beloved and revered by all Italians."

She nodded. "Exactly my point. It isn't a problem because you will never allow yourself to feel. You won't even talk to your father because you're afraid he'll be the kryptonite that fells you."

His gaze narrowed. "Are we talking about something other than our deal? Because the way I remember it, you were right there with me. You agreed to marry me because you don't believe in the concept of love."

Her shoulders slumped. "That was before I met you, Rocco. Before I let myself get to know the part of you that you don't bury ten miles deep."

His chest seized. "Olivia…"

"No." She cut him off with a wave of her hand. "You don't get to hide on this one. You know I'm in love with you. I've been in love with you since that night in New York when you pulled your pumpkin carriage up to the Lincoln Center and saved my soul like the fairy-tale hero you are. Actually—" she pursed her mouth "—maybe it was before that, maybe it was that night in Navigli when you rocked up to my table, sat down and blew my mind apart with your intellect and charm." She held his gaze, regret in her blue eyes. "But none of that really matters, does it? I've gone and done the unforgivable. I've fallen in love with a Mondelli, and that only ever ends in heartbreak for the Fitzgerald women."

He took a step toward her. She moved back with a shake of her head. "You don't get to solve this one with sex, Rocco. You don't get to sweep me off my feet and use that superior skill of yours on me, because we both know you can do it. We both know you *will* do it if I let you." She held her hands up. "This is me saying I'm done. Walking away from my addiction."

"*Maledizione*. Olivia." His hands dropped to his sides. "What do you want me to say? Do you want me to say I care about you, because you know I do?"

Her eyes dimmed. "If you cared about me, you would set me free. You would allow yourself to tell me how you really feel. Because only a fool would spend the rest of her life pining away for a man who's always going to put her second to his real marriage."

He worked his jaw. "You are asking for the impossible."

A sad smile curved her lips. "Funny, Giovanni always told me to reach for the impossible. I'm surprised he didn't teach you the same."

She stood up. "I will do Paris next week and then I'm reevaluating. *Everything.*"

The hair on the back of his neck rose, his stomach hardening to stone. "We are marrying in front of five hundred people in three weeks, Olivia."

She lifted her chin. "That was included in the everything."

"*Olivia.*" He growled the warning at her.

She nodded. "I know. You will make me rue the day I put pen to paper." Her bleak gaze held his. "The thing is, I'm terrified if I follow through with this. If I make myself last this year, there will be nothing left of me at the end. And then what does it really matter?"

She turned and walked away. He let her go. Because she *was* asking for the impossible, and he couldn't give it to her no matter how much he wanted to. He'd been over it in his head a million times, and he'd still come up with the same answer. Taking Olivia out of the ten-million-dollar Vivo campaign would be brand suicide. It would destabilize Mondelli when it was still rocking from the loss of Giovanni.

His fingers bit into his thighs, his knuckles gleaming white. His feelings didn't matter in this. Duty over his freedom. It was the way it had always been. He could only hope that his fiancée carried out hers. Because this wedding was a machine that couldn't be stopped. It was a multimillion-dollar affair with implications way beyond the two of them. It would determine his future. The future of Mondelli.

CHAPTER THIRTEEN

OLIVIA SPENT THE days leading up to Paris Fashion Week at the apartment in Milan, avoiding her fiancé, who reluctantly agreed to give her space. She kept herself busy working with Mario on her designs while mentally preparing herself for one last walk down a runway. After that she truly didn't know what she was going to do. There was also that walk down an aisle with a man who didn't love her looming—and her head to get in order.

The *Fashion Report* segment aired the night before Paris. She watched the in-depth exposé on the pressures models faced in a world that valued perfection above all else in her hotel room alone, having insisted Rocco stay home. In some ways, the airing of her most private fears, the knowledge that she wasn't alone, helped a great deal. On another level, the fact that the whole world was now intimate with her private terror made Paris fifty times more intimidating.

She made it through the show with sheer willpower and the knowledge that if she chose to end things now she'd never have to walk a runway again. And yes, because she loved her fiancée and she didn't want to let him down. Then she did as she'd promised and took the time she needed. Instead of following Rocco's summons to board the Mondelli jet at Charles de Gaulle the morning after the show, she caught a flight bound for New York.

It was the last place she wanted to be. But if slaying her demons was her goal, it had to be done.

Her mother, busy packing for her wedding and a two-week vacation, took one look at her and opened a bottle of wine. "Please tell me you're not having second thoughts," she murmured, settling herself in the sofa across from Olivia in the Chelsea apartment she'd bought with her daughter's money.

Olivia took a sip of her wine. "Why? Because you can't bear for the gravy train to end?"

Her mother, whose poise was usually ironclad, flushed a deep red. "I deserve that, I know it. I let things get out of hand." She gave her an imploring look. "I didn't know. I swear I didn't know how dire things were or I never would have…"

"It doesn't matter." Olivia cut her off with a wave of her hand. And it really didn't anymore. "I forgive you for the money. What I can't forgive you for is never being there for me. For pushing me when you knew I was on the edge."

Her mother's gaze fell away from hers, making an elaborate study of the ruby-red liquid in her glass. "It was wrong. But I thought you were like me, Livvie. I thought you thrived on the excitement."

"I was having panic attacks at fifteen." Olivia threw the words at her in disbelief. "How did that make you think I was coping well?"

Her mother was silent at her outburst. Then she nodded. "You're right. I've been self-involved my entire life. It was the only way I knew how to be."

"Including Giovanni," Olivia challenged.

Her mother's surgically enhanced mouth tightened. "Including Giovanni."

Olivia tucked her legs underneath her and took a sip of her wine. "Tell me about what happened with him."

Her mother shrugged a slim shoulder. "I was in love with him."

"Mother." Olivia pressed her hands to her temples and massaged her throbbing head. "I did not fly thousands of miles for you to feed me the same lines you always do. You tore my life apart over him. I don't have a father because of him. Give me *something*."

Her mother's lips pressed into a straight line. "He was everything I ever wanted and everything I couldn't have. I knew it, I told myself not to do it, and when he left I wanted to curl up in a ball and die."

It was the most emotion she'd witnessed in her mother in a decade, and it knocked her back against the sofa for a moment. "What about his wife? Did you ever think of her? How she must have felt?"

Her mother's long lashes settled down over her blue eyes, identical to hers. "It wasn't that kind of love, Olivia. It was the once-in-a-lifetime kind. Giovanni and I were both starstruck. There wasn't any rationality to it."

Like her and Rocco.

She chewed on her lip. "I still don't understand what you were thinking. He was a married man." *Unobtainable.* "Why put yourself through that?"

Her mother shook her head. "I thought he'd choose me. I was *convinced* he would choose me. There was no other alternative."

And yet he hadn't. Giovanni had walked out of her mother's life without a backward glance and crushed her. Her mother had married her father and broken his heart, unrequited love at its most bittersweet.

It was why she'd walked away from Rocco. The fear that what she saw in his eyes might never translate into what she felt.

She stared at her mother. At the fragility she'd never seen in her eyes. And finally she understood why she was the way she was. To lose that kind of love did that to a person.

"If you could go back," she asked, "would you do it differently?"

Her mother shook her head. "This isn't me we're talking about, Olivia. Giovanni and I made our decisions. It's you and your inability to let yourself be vulnerable that is at issue here. And yes, I realize much of the blame for that stems from me. I wasn't there for you and I abused your trust. But," she said, "I can tell you one thing. I saw how you looked at Guillermo when you were with him and I see how you look at Rocco, and there is no comparison. You *love* him. And he is marrying you. So what's the problem?"

It wasn't a real marriage; that was the problem. But even as she said it she knew that wasn't true on so many levels. Everything on the surface between her and Rocco had ostensibly been about their deal, but none of it ever had, really. The raw emotion and passion between them was *real*. The naked emotion on his face when she'd boarded that jet for Paris had been real. The walls that had come down in New York that night had been real.

It is the most perfect thing I have ever encountered. You and me, Olivia. How we taste together. How we fit together.

Her stomach contracted in a long, insistent pull. He loved her. She knew he did. He just didn't know how to say it. He was too busy slaying her dragons, slaying everyone else's dragons, to figure it out.

Maybe he just needed an adult version of his yellow-eyed sea creature to come and rescue him. Maybe the unanswered calls on her cell phone from him weren't about him tracking down an asset, but him needing her as much as she needed him.

Hot liquid burned the backs of her eyes, blurring her

vision. She needed to talk to him. To see him. But there was one more thing she needed to do first.

She looked at her mother. "Will you take a drive with me?"

Her mother blinked. "You're getting married in two days, Olivia."

"I know."

Rocco stood on the runway in the blazing Milanese sunshine, a bouquet of calla lilies in his hand. He knew they were Olivia's favorite from what little input she'd given on her wedding bouquet. What he didn't know exactly was what he was doing here with them in his hands.

His eyes picked up the blue-and-white Mondelli jet banking its way through the clouds, his heartbeat increasing in anticipation along with it. Why he'd ever let Olivia go to Paris alone he didn't know. He'd watched that *Fashion Report* piece sitting in the den at the villa while Olivia prepared to walk in Paris and he'd physically hated himself in that moment. He had glossed over her anxiety, told her to be tougher when he could have shut her down completely in his zealousness to see Mondelli fly.

What did that say about him? That Olivia was right? That he put business above everything else in his life? That he was a machine programmed to do only one thing?

He rubbed a hand over his face as the jet turned and made its final approach, a fatigue it seemed he'd had his whole life making his limbs feel heavy and sluggish. The past few weeks had been hell. He had buried himself in work, told himself it was better this way with distance between him and Olivia, when all he'd really wanted to do was bury himself in *her*. And not just in a sexual way. She brightened everything about his life every minute she was in it, and he'd been numb without her. Witness the morning he'd just spent in board meetings going over insanely good financials that should have left him pumped and victorious, but instead had made his eyes glaze over. What did any of it matter if he didn't have anyone to share it with? And not just any woman, but the woman who had come to mean everything to him.

He *had* made work his entire life. It had been necessary to ensure his family business thrived. He'd sacrificed his own happiness willingly because, he could admit now, he had been too frightened to admit he had needs. That he had the ability to love like everyone else. Because doing so would have made him have to face his choices. Would have made him vulnerable. And it was the one emotion he could not tolerate.

The jet's nose pointed down as it swooped toward the asphalt. His stomach went right along with it. He'd told himself giving Olivia space would allow her perspective. *Perspective about what?* About the words he couldn't say? About the lies he'd been telling himself again and again?

His shame sank deeper. He had branded Olivia a coward when *she* had been the one courageous enough to tell him how she felt. Because he did love her. The only reason he'd agreed to this marriage was because, deep down, he did want to marry her. He wanted to have her. Protect her. Be that heroic figure she needed.

The jet touched down on the tarmac and taxied to the terminal. He waited at the bottom of the steps while the crew secured the plane and opened the doors. The two Mondelli designers who'd accompanied Olivia to Paris disembarked. He greeted them, then rested his elbow on the railing of the steps as he waited for Olivia to emerge. The designers gave him a funny look as they walked toward the terminal. Chris, his pilot, appeared in the doorway, gave the flowers in his hand a glance and came down a couple of steps. "I, um…" He raked a hand through his hair. "Did Olivia not tell you she was taking another flight?"

"Mi scusi?"

The pilot's face reddened. "She's not with us, Rocco. She said she was taking a break before heading home. I thought you knew."

His heart went into free fall. He'd thought she'd already had a break. That she was coming home to talk this over...

He had given her too much time. He had given himself too much time.

He narrowed his gaze on his pilot. "Tell me exactly what she said."

Chris handed him an envelope. "She asked me to give this to you."

His heart pounded as he tore open the envelope. It took no time to read the short message in Olivia's handwriting because it was only three sentences.

I have some things I need to do in New York. I need time to think, Rocco. Give it to me.

Disbelief blanketed him. They were marrying in front of five hundred people in two days, and she was in *New York*? Was she even coming back?

He left, shoving the bouquet of lilies at a bewildered terminal attendant as he exited the building. He hadn't known much about what he was going to say to Olivia, but he had known he was going to be honest about his feelings. And he was going to release her from her contract. Set her free.

Poor, unsuspecting Adamo was the first person to see him upon his return to the Mondelli offices. *"What?"* Rocco bit out, dropping his briefcase on the floor.

Adamo set an envelope on his desk. "The prenuptial agreement is finalized."

Perfetto. The bitter irony of it hit him like a block to the head. The bride was missing and a document that was now not worth the paper it was printed on was ready. He picked it up and tossed it in the shredding bin. If he was marrying Olivia, there would be none of that between them, only her and him.

Adamo gave him a long look. "I also have something else for you."

Rocco's gaze swung to him. "I would suggest later is a better time."

Adamo laid a smaller envelope on his desk. It had an ornate *G* inscribed on the upper right-hand corner. *Giovanni's personal stationery.* Rocco stared at it. Now he was haunting him from the dead...

He lifted his gaze to the lawyer. "Where did that come from?"

"Giovanni told me to give it to you before your wedding day."

Maybe he should give it back given that wasn't likely to happen.

He gave Adamo a curt thanks and waved him out of his office. The envelope beckoned from the desk. It was sealed. He wasn't actually sure he could take its contents right now, but his curiosity overcame him and he sliced it open.

My dearest grandson Rocco,
When you receive this letter I will have passed from this world to the other side. You of all people will know that this is actually a blessing for me, because I get to be with my Rosa again. There has been an ache in my heart ever since she left me, and now I will be whole again.

By this time you will also have discovered the story of Tatum and myself through Olivia. It was never my intention to disrespect the love of my life. I know you will find this a particularly difficult pill to swallow, Rocco, as honor is the code you live your life by. However, I hope you will get to experience what it feels like to love like this someday and come to understand my actions. I never thought I could love two people with the depth that I have. None of my actions were taken easily, and I hope in resolving this as I did, any heartbreak I caused was minimized.

I know you will be questioning why I did not leave you control of Mondelli, and it was not, as I suspect you will think, because I do not trust you. You have more strength than your father and me combined— you always have. I wanted to give you the time to explore yourself. To learn that to love is not a weakness, but a strength. You have it in your heart, *nipote*, I have no doubt. We Mondellis love big and whole-heartedly. And you will, too.

Be kind to Olivia, who needs to be loved unconditionally after what she has been through. I know you have this in you, too, which is why I entrusted her to you.

Finally, walk lightly, Rocco, and remember the power of your actions. You carry a heavier stick than even you know.

Giovanni xx

Something frayed and weakened inside of Rocco tore open. He sat there for a long moment, heat burning the backs of his eyes. The questions he'd been asking for weeks had found answers, the niggling uncertainties that had made it even more difficult to sleep at night eased. He couldn't say he approved of all of his grandfather's decisions; Giovanni had been right on that. But his thoughts on where he was at the moment, his feelings for Olivia, rang uncannily true.

The fact that he had found his capacity to feel with Olivia was a potential his grandfather had foreseen. The fact that he had messed it up so badly was his to own and his alone.

He sat staring at the letter. Every bone in his body told him to go find Olivia and fix them. He had been fixing things his entire life. But she had said she needed time, and he risked losing her forever if he went after her. So all he could hope was that she showed up for this bloody circus of a wedding of theirs so he could say the words he needed to say.

If he'd thought he'd felt helpless before, that had nothing on this.

CHAPTER FOURTEEN

THE WEDDING DAY of Rocco Mondelli and Olivia Fitzgerald dawned crisp and clear on the shores of Lake Como in the shadow of the Alps. Referred to by the ancient poet Virgil as "our greatest lake," Lake Como was Europe's deepest at over thirteen hundred feet in depth, its deep blue waters stretching for a majestic thirty miles in length.

A perfect setting for the wedding that was capturing headlines around the world, Rocco thought, standing on the front steps of Villa Mondelli, the historic former Cistercian nunnery dedicated to the Holy Virgin. Except with four hours to go before the nuptials began, the palatial villa and grounds a hive of frenzied activity, one key component was missing. His bride.

He took in the two priceless carved statues of the Holy Virgin flanking the pillars of the front stairs and wondered if *she* was the problem. Maybe the wedding was on the rocks because no Mondelli had ever dared get married here given the villa's sacrosanct past. Maybe the nuns were protesting…

He rubbed a hand over his jaw and swept aside the dark humor. Because really nothing was humorous about being stood up at the altar. About suffering the ultimate public humiliation in front of five hundred guests from every corner of the world.

Stefan Bianco, Christian Markos and Zayed Al Afzal, resplendent in designer tuxedos and mauve bow ties to match the maid of honor's dress, stood beside him, all with identical expressions on their faces. Christian would call it the "what the hell do we do now?" look. Stefan, however, would have added a slightly more vicious edge to it, he knew. "I said she was trouble," he'd muttered last night when they'd arrived at the villa to find Olivia Fitzgerald was nowhere to be found twenty-four hours before the wedding. Zayed, the future king, had looked shocked. Which had now faded into his "ready for anything" expression, fitting for a man whose nation might soon be at war.

Three warriors who had conquered global markets and more than their fair share of hearts—and there was nothing they could do to make this right.

Christian frowned. "What next?"

Rocco shrugged, far more casually than the turmoil racking him inside. "If she loves me, she'll come."

"A good point," Zayed agreed.

"Goddamn her," Stefan exploded, turning on the future king. "This is not okay, *fratelli*. I want to find her and strangle her with my bare hands."

"That would not help the situation," Zayed countered. "Clear thinking is what is called for."

"And what," Stefan bit out, "would your *clear-thinking* head suggest? Five hundred people are on their way here *right now. The Pope*, a personal friend of the Mondelli family, is coming. And we are minus a bride."

"I'm going to drive into Milan and check the apartment." Rocco voiced the only solution he had left. "She loves the gardens there. It's a possibility."

"It's also a possibility she might use her phone," Stefan exploded, throwing his hands in the air.

Rocco gave him a look. He knew Olivia was on Italian soil. Her flight had landed early this morning in Milan. What she was doing now was another question. He intended to find out.

"Stay here with Zayed and keep things running," he instructed his hotheaded friend. "Make sure what needs to happen happens. You," he said, tossing his car keys at Christian, "drive."

He didn't trust himself to. Not now. When he'd decided to give Olivia her time to think, he hadn't meant *this*. He had things to say to her, important things to say to her, before they walked down that aisle. *If* they walked down that aisle. And he needed to be articulate about it.

He and Christian walked through the preceremony madness to the far driveway. The lead singer of Olivia's favorite rock group ambled across the lawn, a cigarette hanging out of his mouth. Chairs were arranged in endless rows of white against the sweep of green facing the lake. The ceremony would take place on its shore.

He steadfastly ignored it all, sliding into the passenger seat of the Aventador beside Christian. Just over an hour later they walked into the Milanese apartment. The housekeeper gave him a scandalized look and asked what he was doing there, then relayed the information that no, Olivia was not there. She hadn't seen her in a week.

Rocco mopped his brow. They were on their way out when his cell phone rang. He fished it out of his pocket, heart pounding, only to see it was Stefan.

"I thought you might like to know your fiancée is in the building. Well, actually," he drawled, "not anymore. Alessandra and the wedding planner have whisked her off to wherever she's supposed to be. That is, if you still want to marry her, because I can pass on a message. I would be *thrilled* to."

Rocco's pounding heart stopped in his chest. When it started again, he pressed the phone tighter to his ear. "Do not say *one word* to her. We're on our way."

As if anything else could go wrong, the main highway to Como was blocked by an accident on their return. They took the alternate, smaller highway, and this time Rocco commanded the wheel of the Aventador, pushed the pedal to the floor and prayed for time.

"They're on their way back."

Olivia peeled her gaze from the clear blue waters of Lake Como and nodded at Alessandra. After she'd spent the night with her mother in New York, they had driven to Brooklyn to banish Olivia's final demon. She hadn't been able to make herself visit Petra's grave because to do so would be admitting she was gone. But she'd realized now, it was preventing her from moving on. And if she was to face this day with what was truly in her heart, she'd had to let her go.

It had been painful and tougher than she'd expected. But she'd left New York with the feeling the city would no longer haunt her. That she could come back to visit. And maybe it had been the first step in repairing her relationship with her mother.

They had arrived in Italy early this morning. Even though her heart had known what it had wanted, her head had been engaged in a final desperate effort to protect itself. Rocco might hurt her. But was that worth a lifetime of wondering if she'd let the love of her life slip away?

She'd finally made up her mind and arrived here hours ago, only to find Rocco and Christian engaged in a wild-goose chase to find her. Guilt had set in. Then panic as Alessandra and the wedding planner had rushed her off to the neighbor's villa to get dressed prior to her arrival at the ceremony by boat. She hadn't intended to leave it this late. She needed to talk to Rocco. *And no one was listening to her.*

"Please," she said one more time to the wedding planner ninety minutes later as the flustered-looking blonde announced the men were back. "I need five minutes with Rocco."

"Not doable," the planner replied. "There are dignitaries who have to leave as soon as the ceremony is over, the fireworks are scheduled and we're already almost half an hour late." Her mouth compressed. "I told this to the men's camp, too. You have the rest of your lives to talk once this is done, so please, *focus*."

Rocco wanted to talk to her, too? Olivia started to argue, but the planner cut her off with a tersely delivered request to get her shoes on. She slid them on, pulled in a breath as Alessandra slipped her veil into place and straightened her shoulders. She *was* going to marry Rocco. She'd spent her entire life thinking she couldn't rely on anyone but herself, refusing to allow herself to love. But now she was going to take a leap of faith, because she knew with Rocco by her side she could do anything.

If he didn't kill her first for doing this.

The spray of the water split to the left and the right of the covered speedboat they rode in as Olivia and Alessandra were spirited toward Villa Mondelli. The sight of hundreds of wedding guests seated in chairs on the lawn, many of them foreign dignitaries she had never met, had her heart slamming against her chest as they neared the ornate front steps of the villa where Rocco's sea creatures had visited.

Her first priority as they docked was ensuring she had enough oxygen in her lungs to get through this without passing out. Second was getting out of the boat without tripping and falling flat on her face in the exquisite dress with the long flowing train Mario had made her.

Third was the man standing a hundred feet in front of her as she stepped out of the boat with the help of the waiting attendant. Flanked by the priest, Christian Markos,

Zayed Al Afzal and Stefan Bianco, Rocco was so ridiculously handsome in his tux it stole what little breath she
had left. Her gaze locked on his but he was too far away
for her to read the emotion in his eyes. Her knees wavered.
What if he didn't love her?

The quartet started playing Pachelbel's "Canon." The
tears she'd been holding back threatened. She blinked them
away furiously, her hands clutching her bouquet of lilies.
Alessandra started down the aisle, stunning in Mario's
silk lavender creation, followed by their three flower girls
in matching lavender dresses. Olivia's heartbeat acceler-
ated in tandem with the further weakening of her knees.
Her decision to give herself away seemed ill-advised now
as her legs shook. She wished desperately she had something to hang on to. The aisle seemed a mile long and she
couldn't read his eyes.

The cue for her to move came and went. And suddenly
she knew she had to know what he was feeling, *see him*,
before she took another step.

The panic that plummeted through Rocco at the sight of
Olivia frozen at the end of the red-carpeted aisle was of
the all-consuming fashion.

A sheen of perspiration broke out on his brow. His feet
felt heavy, weighted down, as he willed her to start moving. His heart didn't seem to know how to beat. It hung
in suspended animation for a long moment, then thudded heavily against his chest. *Nothing.* He kept his gaze
on her as the music played on, ignoring the murmurs that
swept the crowd. She looked so beautiful in the sleek gown
Mario had designed for her. It was the one detail he hadn't
planned. The one surprise from today, other than the fact
that she almost hadn't shown up.

Done in off white, the sheer gossamer fabric clung to
every curve, setting off Olivia's honeyed skin to perfec-

tion. It fell to the ground in a tulip-shaped hem, her long beautiful hair left loose, floating around her shoulders.

She looked like a mermaid come to life. His mermaid emerging from the steps he'd sat on as a boy, a living, breathing piece of perfection who had come to save the man.

Stefan's low curse pierced his haze. *She wasn't moving.*

"Now might be a good time to do something," Christian murmured. But Rocco was already moving, striding down the aisle toward Olivia. The murmurs came to a crashing halt, all eyes on him.

He kept his gaze on Olivia as he stopped in front of her and took her hands in his. They were ice-cold despite the warmth of the day. Her gaze fastened onto his, blue eyes wide and brilliant.

"You came," he murmured.

"I did," she said softly, her fingers tightening around his until she had a death grip on him. "I'm sorry to be so late. You look so very handsome."

"And you," he returned huskily, emotion overcoming him, "look like my very own mermaid come to life. Tell me you're staying."

She looked down at her dress with a tentative smile. "I don't have any scales, and green wasn't appropriate, but I do love you, Rocco. I'd like to help you slay your dragons if you'll let me."

He felt the world sway beneath his feet as everything became right with those few simple words from her. He absorbed them for a moment, savored them for the precious things they were, then blinked to clear his head and brought her hand to his mouth. "I didn't think I was going to get a chance to tell you how I feel," he murmured against her knuckles.

Her eyes remained glued to his. "Tell me. I need to hear it."

He lowered their hands and brought his mouth to her

ear. "Olivia Fitzgerald, I have been desperately in love with you since the night you walked off that stage in New York and into my arms. And if you'd walked into Guillermo Villanueva's, I would have taken him apart. No one is supposed to have you but me."

She melted into him. He kept talking, because he needed to get it out. "You were right. I have always put work first because I was afraid of turning into my father. Of being weak. Of getting hurt. But then you came into my life and I had no choice. You got to me in every way."

"Rocco…"

He leaned back and put a finger to her mouth. "I'm releasing you from the contract. Whether you decide to marry me or not. Focus on your work with Mario, bring your and Giovanni's line to market and make me proud. That's all I care about. All I care about is you."

Her eyes glistened. "The thing is, I've been thinking that I want to do it. For you. I went to see her grave, Rocco, Petra's, and I've let her go now. I think I needed to do that before I could move on."

He shook his head. "All I've done is push you. I won't lose you, Olivia."

A tremulous smile curved her lips. "You won't lose me. *I'm* the only person who can lose me. And it won't happen if I have you."

He rested his forehead against hers as the music drew to a close. "Do you think we could argue about this later? That is, if you are going to marry me today, because I think we should do that now."

That brilliant smile he loved lit her face, and in that moment he knew everything he'd ever wanted was within his grasp. She nodded and kept her forehead pressed to his. "Just you and me walking down an aisle, right? Nothing to it."

He smiled against her lips. "Nothing to it."

His heart ached with an almost unbearable pressure as he changed his grip on Olivia's hand so she was standing by his side. He nodded at the wedding planner, who looked as if she was on the verge of passing out. The music intended for their walk the other way played, and it didn't matter. Nothing mattered as the rather stunned-looking priest began the ceremony. Rocco held Olivia's hand throughout it, afraid to let her go.

He restrained himself, just, as they exchanged rings and the priest pronounced them husband and wife. The opportunity to kiss her had been too long coming, and he made the most of it. Christian made a joke about them getting a room. Rocco let Olivia go reluctantly. Later he would have her, and this time it would be with nothing but the truth between them.

Applause broke out as they walked back down the aisle as husband and wife. Perhaps unusual for such an elegant affair, but on a day like this, anything could happen.

Olivia didn't recall much of what occurred after Rocco told her he loved her. There was the receiving line full of his relatives, her parents, friends, dignitaries, celebrities and the *Pope*. There were canapés and champagne while they took photographs and a six-course dinner served in the ballroom as the night chill set in.

She and Rocco sat at a table with Stefan, Zayed, Christian, Alessandra, Violetta and Sophia. Olivia was grateful for her girlfriends' presence when Stefan was seated beside her. He had been glowering at her since the reception started, and had murmured in her ear she was damn lucky she made his friend so happy. She was more than relieved to turn Mr. Glower over to stunning-looking Violetta and Sophia in beautiful gowns, who charmed the pants off him and Zayed. Christian and Alessandra remained much more low-key, a surprisingly quiet corner of the table.

Her mother, assigned to keep Sandro Mondelli in line at the table next to them, was doing a fabulous job in her duties while multitasking by flirting with a widowed Saudi prince. Her father and his wife, on the other hand, looked a bit awkward sitting at their table with some of Rocco's relatives, but as the night went on seemed to loosen up and enjoy themselves.

When Rocco drew her to her feet for their first dance, Olivia's eyes nearly popped out of her head as Darius Montagne, the aging rock star she had been infatuated with since she was a teenager, took the stage solo with a guitar.

"Oh, my God. You did not."

"I did." He captured her hand and led her to the middle of the dance floor, where the spotlight picked them up. "And if you give him one sideways look I'll send him packing."

She moved into his arms, finding that funny given how mad she was about the man she had just married. "Oh, Rocco," she murmured, lacing her fingers through his and swaying into his embrace. "I think you underestimate how badly I have it for you."

He pulled her closer to his powerful body as Darius Montagne began singing a ballad. "Forgive me for acting a bit possessive," he growled, "because up until a couple of hours ago, I wasn't sure on that point."

"I told you I loved you on the balcony that night."

"That was a lifetime ago."

"I'm sorry." She burrowed closer to him. "One could look at it as suitable payback for that night in Navigli if one were so inclined."

"One could," he returned softly, his mouth at her ear. "One could expect retribution for that, too. Very *pleasurable* retribution."

A shiver snaked through her at his silky promise. She shut her mouth then because she wanted to enjoy the private serenade Darius Montagne was giving them in his raspy, husky tone.

Her gaze fell on Christian and Alessandra, who had joined them on the dance floor. Alessandra liked him, she knew, maybe more than liked the very stunning blond-haired investment genius. Yet they weren't looking at each other at all and Alessandra looked *miserable*.

She pushed back from Rocco, jerking her chin subtly in their direction. "Do you have any idea what's going on there?"

Rocco looked over at his sister. "She's been heartbroken without Giovanni. They were very close."

And maybe you are a blind, blind man. But Olivia wasn't about to stick her nose where it didn't belong. She'd caused enough waves today.

Rocco passed her to her father after that for a dance. What should have been extremely awkward given the little communication they'd had with each other over the past years was instead another kind of closure.

"You look happy with Ella," she said. "I'm glad."

"As do you with Rocco," he replied. "Liv, I…"

She shook her head. "It's okay, Dad. I understand. I do."

His eyes grew watery. "Sometimes you looked so much like her, it just…hurt to see you."

A fresh wave of tears pooled at the back of her eyes. She blinked them resolutely away. Sometimes life was heartbreaking. She saw that now. And sometimes you just had to forgive and move on.

"It's okay," she whispered, her hand tightening around her father's. "I'm glad you're here."

When she had made the requisite rounds of the dance floor with the rest of the Columbia Four, her husband stole her back for another dance. He, too, had taken some first baby steps with his father, the two of them having had a long talk while she'd been gone. It hadn't been perfect, but it was a start.

Rocco's warm, familiar scent wrapped itself around her as she tucked herself into his big warm body. She let most of the song go by before she drew back and looked up at him. "Rocco?"

His dark eyes, almost ebony tonight against the black tux, held hers. *"Sì?"*

"I'm not so interested in dancing. Do you mind if we skip it?"

He didn't bother to answer, just wrapped his hand around hers and pulled her through the dancers and up the two flights of stairs to their suite.

The windows were open as he worked the buttons on the back of her dress free. Darius Montagne's sexy rasp floated on the air up to them. Rocco's curse as his fingers fumbled over the tiny buttons made her smile.

"Mario again."

He continued doggedly, until he had most of them undone, then pushed the dress off her shoulders to fall in a pool of silk in the moonlight. She disposed of his jacket, shirt and tie as fast as her hands could move. Impatient with her lack of speed, even at the rate she was going, Rocco undid his belt and pushed the rest of his clothes off until there was only his magnificent, olive-skinned body to ogle.

He didn't give her much of a chance to do so, swinging her up into his arms and depositing her on the rose petal–covered bed. He took his time, lavishing every centimeter of her body with sensuous kisses until she was arching up against him, begging for his possession. His name a soft cry on her lips, he slid his hand between her thighs, prepared her for him and brought the tip of his impressive erection exactly where she needed him.

"Ti amo," he murmured as he possessed her body and

soul. He said it over and over again, as if he couldn't say it enough, until his kiss captured her scream and forever with him was all she could see.

I love you, too, my dragon slayer. She wound her arms around his neck and laid her face against his chest. Because sometimes you needed to fight your own battles, and sometimes you needed a warrior to help you along your way.

* * * * *

SECURING THE
GREEK'S LEGACY

JULIA JAMES

For Franny, my dearest friend, in her brave fight against cancer – a fight shared by so many.

CHAPTER ONE

ANATOLE TELONIDIS STARED bleakly across the large, expensively furnished lounge of the penthouse apartment in the most fashionable part of Athens. It was still as untidy as it had been when his young cousin Marcos Petranakos had last walked out of it a few short nightmare weeks ago, straight to his death.

When their mutual grandfather, Timon Petranakos, had phoned his older grandson he had been distraught. *'Anatole, he's dead! Marcos, my beloved Marcos—he's dead!'* the old man had cried out.

Smashed to pieces at twenty-five, driving far too fast in the lethal supercar that had been Timon's own present to Marcos, given in the wake of their grandfather's recent diagnosis with cancer.

The death of his favourite grandson, whom he had spoiled lavishly since Marcos had lost his parents as a teenager, had been a devastating blow. Timon had since refused all treatment for his cancer, longing now only for his own death.

Anatole could understand his grandfather's devastation, his mind-numbing grief. But the fallout from Marcos's tragic death would affect more lives than their own family's. With no direct heir now to the vast Petranakos Corporation, the company would pass to an obscure Petranakos relative whose business inexperience would surely, in these parlous economic times, lead inevitably to the company's collapse and the loss of thousands of jobs, adding to the country's sky-high unemployment levels.

Though Anatole had his own late father's business empire to run—which he did with tireless efficiency and a pressing sense of responsibility—he knew that, had Marcos lived, he could have instilled a similar sense of responsibility into his hedonistic young cousin, guiding him effectively. But the new heir—middle-aged, self-important and conceited—was resistant to any such guidance.

Frustration with the fate awaiting the Petranakos Corporation—and its hapless workforce—Anatole started on the grim process of sorting out his young cousin's possessions. Bleakly, he began his sombre task.

Paperwork was the first essential. As he located Marcos's desk and set about methodically sorting out its jumbled contents a familiar ripple of irritation went through him. Marcos had been the least organised person he'd known—receipts, bills and personal correspondence were all muddled up, demonstrating just how uninterested Marcos had been in anything other than having a good time. Fast cars, high living and an endless procession of highly temporary females had been his favoured lifestyle. Unlike Anatole himself. Running the Telonidis businesses kept him too occupied for anything more than occasional relationships, usually with busy, high-powered businesswomen he worked with in the world of finance.

Frustration bit at Anatole.

If only Marcos had married! Then there might have been a son to inherit from Timon! I'd have kept the Petranakos Corporation safe for him until the child grew up!

But to the fun-seeking Marcos marriage would have been anathema! Girls had been for casual relationships only. There'd be time later for getting married, he'd always said.

But there was to be no later...

Grim-faced, his honed features starkly etched, Anatole went on sorting through the papers in his cousin's desk. Official in one pile, personal in another. The latter pile was not large—not in this age of texting and the internet—but one drawer revealed a batch of three or four envelopes addressed to Marcos in cursive Roman script with a London postmark and UK stamps. Only one had been opened.

Anatole frowned. The lilac-coloured envelopes and the large, looping script suggested a female writer. Though Marcos's dramatic death had been splashed across the Greek tabloids, a British girlfriend might not have heard of it. It might be necessary, Anatole thought reluctantly, for him to let her know of Marcos's fate. That said, he realised as he glanced at the envelopes' postmarks, none of these was dated more recently than nine months ago. Whoever she was, the affair—or whatever it had been—was clearly long over.

With a swift impatience to be done with the whole grim business of sorting through Marcos's personal effects Anatole took the folded single piece of paper from the one envelope that was open. He flicked open the note and started to read the English writing.

And as he did he froze completely...

Lyn made her way out of the lecture hall and sighed. It was no good, she would far rather be studying history! But accountancy would enable her to earn a decent living in the future and that was essential—especially if she were to persuade the authorities that she was capable of raising a child on her own: her beloved Georgy. But for now, while she was still waiting so anxiously to learn if she could adopt him, she was only allowed to be his foster carer. She knew the welfare authorities would prefer for him to be adopted by one of the many childless couples anxious to adopt a healthy baby, but Lyn was determined that no one would take Georgy from her! *No one!*

It didn't matter how much of a struggle it was to keep at her studies while looking after a baby as well, especially with money so short—she would manage somehow! A familiar regret swept over her: if only she'd gone to college sooner and already had her qualifications. But she hadn't been able to go straight from school because she'd had to stay home and look after Lindy. She hadn't been able to leave her young teenage sister to the indifference and neglect which was all her mother had offered. But when Lindy had left school herself and gone to London, to live with a girlfriend and get a job, her mother had been taken ill, her lungs and liver finally giving in after decades of abuse from smoking and alcohol, and there had been no one else to look after her except Lyn.

And now there was Georgy...

'Lyn Brandon?'

It was one of the university's admin staff.

'Someone's asking to see you,' the woman said briskly, and pointed to one of the offices across the corridor.

Frowning, Lyn walked inside.

And stopped dead.

Standing by the window, silhouetted by the fading light, was an imposing, dark-suited figure. Tall, wearing a black cashmere overcoat with a black cashmere scarf hooked around the strong column of his neck, the man had a natural Mediterranean tan that, along with his raven-dark hair, instantly told Lyn that he was not English. Just as the planes and features of his face told her that he was jaw-droppingly good-looking.

It was a face, though, that was staring at her with a mouth set in a tight line—as though he were seeing someone he had not expected. A frown creased his brow.

'Miss Brandon?' He said her name, his voice accented, as if he did not quite believe it.

Dark eyes flicked over her and Lyn felt two spots of colour mount in her cheeks. Immediately she became conscious of the way her hair was caught back in a stringy ponytail. She had not a scrap of make-up on, and her clothes were serviceable rather than fashionable.

Then suddenly, overriding that painful consciousness, there came a jolt of realisation as to just who this clearly foreign man must be—could only be...

The Mediterranean looks, the expensive clothes, the sleekly groomed looks, the whole aura of wealth about him... She felt her stomach constrict, filling with instinctive fear.

Across the narrow room Anatole caught the flash of alarm and wondered at it, but not nearly as much as he was wondering whether he had, after all, really tracked down the woman he'd been so urgently seeking ever since reading that letter in Marcos's apartment—the woman who, so his investigators had discovered, had most definitely given birth to a baby boy...

Is he Marcos's son? The question was burning in hope. Because if Marcos had had a son then it changed everything. *Everything!*

If, by a miracle, Marcos had a son, then Anatole had to find him and bring him home to Greece, so that Timon, who was fading with every passing day, could find instead a last blessing from the cruel fate that had taken so much from him.

And it was not just for his grandfather that a son of Marcos's would be a blessing, either, Anatole knew. This would persuade Timon to change his will, to acknowledge that his beloved Marcos had had a son to whom he could now leave the Petranakos Corporation. Infant though he was, Anatole would guard the child's inheritance, keep it safe and prosperous for him—and save the livelihoods of all its employees.

Tracking down the author of the letters had led him first to a council house in the south of the country and then, through information given to his detectives by neighbours, to this northern college, where he'd been told the young woman he was so urgently seeking—Linda Brandon—had recently moved.

But as his eyes rested now on the woman he was addressing he felt doubt fill him. *This* was the woman he'd trekked to this grim, rainswept northern town to find in a race against time for his stricken grandfather? Marcos wouldn't even have looked twice at her—let alone taken her to his bed!

'*Are* you Miss Brandon?' he asked, his voice sharper now.

He saw her swallow and nod jerkily. Saw, too, that her entire body had tensed.

'I am Anatole Telonidis,' he announced. His voice sounded clipped, but his mission was a painful one—and an urgent one. 'I am here on behalf of my cousin, Marcos Petranakos, with whom I believe you are...' he sought the right phrase '...acquainted.'

Even as he said it his eyes flicked over her again doubtfully. Even putting aside her unprepossessing appearance, Marcos's taste had been for curvy blondes—not thin brunettes. But her reaction told him that she must indeed be the person he was looking for so urgently—she had instantly recognised Marcos's name.

And not favourably...

Her expression had changed. Hardened. 'So he couldn't even be bothered to come himself!' she retorted scornfully.

If she'd sought to hit home with her accusation she'd failed. The man who'd declared himself Marcos Petranakos's cousin stilled. In the dark eyes a flash of deep emotion showed and Lyn saw his face stiffen.

'The situation is not as you suppose,' he said.

It was as if, she realised, he was picking his words carefully.

He paused a moment, as if steeling himself to speak, then said, 'I must talk to you. But the matter is…difficult.'

Lyn shook her head violently. She could feel the adrenaline running through her body. 'No, it's not difficult at all!' she retorted. 'Whatever message you've been sent to deliver by your cousin, you needn't bother! Georgy—his *son*!—is fine without him. Absolutely fine!'

She saw emotion flash in his dark eyes again, saw the shadow behind it. Out of nowhere a chill went through her.

'There is something I must tell you,' Anatole Telonidis was saying. His voice was grim, and bleak, as if he were forcing the words out.

Lyn's hands clenched. 'There is nothing you can say that I care about—!' she began.

But his deep, sombre voice cut right through hers. 'My cousin is dead.'

There was silence. Complete silence. Wordlessly, Anatole cursed himself for his blunt outburst. But it had been impossible to hear her hostility, her scorn, when Marcos lay dead in his grave…

'Dead?' Lyn's voice was hollow with shock.

'I'm sorry. I should not have told you so brutally,' Anatole said stiffly.

She was still staring at him. 'Marcos Petranakos is *dead*?' Her voice was thin—disbelieving.

'It was a car crash. Two months ago. It has taken time to track you down…' His words were staccato, sombre.

Lyn swayed as if she might pass out. Instantly Anatole was there, catching her arm, staying her. She stepped back, steadying herself, and he released her. Absently she noticed with complete irrelevance how strong his grasp had been. How overpowering his momentary closeness.

'He's dead?' she said again, her voice hollow. Emotion twisted in her throat. Georgy's father was dead...

'Please,' Anatole Telonidis was saying, 'you need to sit down. I am sorry this is such a shock to you. I know,' he went on, picking his words carefully again, she could tell, his expression guarded, 'just how...deep...you felt the relationship was between yourself and him, but—'

A noise came from her. He stopped. She was staring at him, but the expression in her face was different now, Anatole registered. It wasn't shock at hearing about Marcos's tragic death. It wasn't even anger—the understandable anger, painful though it was for him to face it—that she'd expressed about the man who had got her pregnant and then totally ignored her ever since.

'Between him and *me*?' she echoed. She shook her head a moment, as if clearing it.

'Yes,' Anatole pursued. 'I know from your letters—which, forgive me, I have read—that you felt a strong... attachment to my cousin. That you were expressing your longing to...' He hesitated, recalling vividly the hopelessly optimistic expectations with which she had surrounded her announcement that she was carrying Marcos's baby. 'Your longing to make a family together, but—'

He got no further.

'I'm not Georgy's mother,' Lyn announced.

And in her bleak voice were a thousand unshed tears.

For a moment Anatole thought he had not heard correctly. Or had misunderstood what she had said in English. Then his eyes levelled on hers and he realised he had understood her exactly.

'*What?*' His exclamation was like a bullet. A blackening frown sliced down over his face. 'You said you were Linda Brandon!' he threw at her accusingly.

His thoughts were in turmoil. What the hell was going on? He could make no sense of it! He could see her shaking her head—a jerky gesture. Then she spoke, her voice strained.

'I'm...I'm Lynette Brandon,' Anatole heard her say.

He saw her take a rasping breath, making herself speak. Her face was still white with shock with what he'd told her about Marcos.

'Lindy...Linda—' she gave her sister's full name before stopping abruptly, her voice cutting off. Then she blinked.

Anatole could see the shimmer of tears clearly now.

'Linda was my sister,' she finished, her voice no more than a husk.

He heard the past tense—felt the slow, heavy pulse of dark realisation go through him. Heard her thin, shaky voice continuing, telling him what was so unbearably painful for her to say.

Her face was breaking up.

'She died,' she whispered. 'My sister Linda. Georgy's mother. She died giving birth. Eclampsia. It's not supposed to happen any more. But it did...*it did*...'

Her voice was broken.

She lifted her eyes to Anatole across a divide that was like a yawning chasm—a chasm that had claimed two young lives.

Her mind reeled as she took in the enormity of the truth they had both revealed to each other. The unbearable tragedy of it.

Both Georgy's parents were dead!

She had thrown at Anatole Telonidis the fact that his uncaring, irresponsible cousin wasn't wanted or needed by his son, but to hear that he had suffered the same dreadful fate as her sister was unbearable. As unbearable as losing her sister had been. Tears stung in her eyes and his voice came from very far away.

'You should sit down,' said Anatole Telonidis.

He guided her to a chair and she sat on it nervelessly. His own mind was still reeling, still trying to come to grips with what he had just learnt. The double tragedy surrounding Marcos's baby son.

Where was he? Where was Marcos's son?

That was the question he had to have answered now! A cold fear went through him. Newborn babies were in high demand for adoption by childless couples, and a fatherless baby whose mother had died in childbirth might have been just such a child...

Had he been adopted already? The question seared in Anatole's head. If so, then he would have a nightmare of a search to track him down—even if he were allowed to by the authorities. And if he had already been adopted then would his adoptive parents be likely to let him go? Would the authorities be likely to let him demand—*plead*!—that they accede to his need for Timon to know that he had an heir after all?

He stood looking down at the sister of the woman who had borne his cousin a child and died in the process. He swallowed.

'Where is my cousin's son?' he asked. He tried not to sound brusque, demanding, but he had to know. *He had to know!*

Her chin lifted, her eyes flashing to his.

'He's with *me*!' came the answer. Vehement, passionate.

Abstractedly Anatole found himself registering that when this drab dab of a female spoke passionately her nondescript features suddenly sharpened into life, giving her a vividness that was not drab at all. Then the sense of her words hit him.

'With *you*?'

She took a ragged breath, her fingers clutching the side

of the chair. 'Yes! With me! And he's staying with me! That's all you need to know!'

She leapt to her feet, fear and panic impelling her. Too much had happened—shock after shock—and she couldn't cope with it, couldn't take it in.

Anatole stepped towards her, urgency in his voice. 'Miss Brandon, we have to talk—discuss—'

'No! There's nothing to discuss! *Nothing!*'

And then, before his frustrated gaze, she rushed from the room.

Lyn fled. Her mind was in turmoil. Though she managed to make her way into her next lecture she was incapable of concentrating. Only one single emotion was uppermost.

Georgy is mine! Mine, mine, mine!

Lindy had given the baby to her with her dying breath and she would *never*, never betray that! *Never!*

Grief clutched at Lyn again.

'Look after Georgy—'

They had been Lindy's final words before the darkness had closed over her fevered, stricken brain and she had ebbed from life.

And I will! I will look after him all my life—all his life—and I will never let any harm come to him, never abandon him or give up him!

'Just you and me, Georgy!' she whispered later as, morning lectures finally over, she collected him from the college crèche and made her way to the bus stop and back home for the afternoon.

But as she clambered on board the bus, stashing the folding buggy one-handed as she held Georgy in the other, she completely failed to see an anonymous black car pull out into the road behind the bus. Following it.

Two hours later Anatole stood in front of the block of flats his investigator had informed him was Lynette Brandon's place of accommodation and stared bleakly at it. It was not an attractive building, being of ugly sixties design, with stained concrete and peeling paint. The whole area was just as dreary—no place for Timon Petranakos's great-grandson to be brought up!

Resolve steeling, he rang the doorbell.

CHAPTER TWO

LYN HAD SAT down at the rickety table in the corner of the living room and got out her study books. Georgy had been fed and changed, and had settled for his afternoon nap in his secondhand cot, tucked in beside her bed in the single bedroom the flat possessed. She was grateful for Georgy's afternoon sleep, even though if he slept too much he didn't sleep well at night, for it gave her an hour or two of solid homework time. But today her concentration was shot to pieces—still reeling with what had happened that morning.

Hopefully she had made her position clear and the man who had lobbed a bombshell into her life would take himself off again, back to Greece, and leave her alone. Anxiety rippled through her again. The adoption authorities believed that there was no contact with Georgy's father or any of his paternal family. But since this morning that wasn't true any more...

No, she mustn't think about that! She must put it behind her. Put behind her all the dark, disturbing images of the man whose incredible good looks were such a source of disturbance to her. For a moment his image formed in her mind, overpowering in its masculine impact. She thrust it impatiently aside and started reading her textbook.

Two minutes later she was interrupted. The doorbell had sounded. Imperative. Demanding.

Her head shot up. Who on earth...? No one called on her here.

The bell rang again. Warily, heart thumping suddenly, she went to the door, lifting up the entryphone.

'Who is it?' she asked sharply.

'Miss Brandon—we need to continue our conversation.' It was Anatole Telonidis.

For a moment Lyn remained motionless. *Don't let him in!* The childish, fearful words sounded in her head, but she knew she could not obey them. She had to get this conversation over and done with. Then she could send him away and never see him again—never be troubled again by the existence of Georgy's father's family. Nervelessly she pressed the entry buzzer, and a few moments later opened her front door.

He was just as tall and formidable as she remembered. Taller, it seemed, in her poky flat. But it was not just his size and demeanour that pressed on her senses. His physical presence was dominating more than just the space he stood in. It was making her horribly aware all over again of his dark, devastating looks.

Desperately she tried to crush down her awareness of them. It was the last thing she should be paying any attention to right now!

Besides, a vicious little voice in her head was reminding her to think about what *he* was seeing! He was seeing a plain-faced nobody who was wearing ancient baggy jeans and a thick frumpy jumper, with her hair tied back and not a scrap of make-up. A man like him wouldn't even look once, let alone twice!

Oh, for God's sake, what are you even thinking of? Focus—just focus! This is about Georgy and what this man wants—or doesn't want.

And how quickly she could get rid of him...

She stared at him. He seemed to be looking about him,

then past her into the small living room, with its shabby furniture, worn carpet and hideously patterned curtains. Her chin went up. Yes, the place was uninviting, but it was cheap, and it came furnished, and she wasn't going to be choosy. She couldn't afford to be—not until she was earning a decent salary. Till then Georgy didn't care that he wasn't anywhere nice. And neither did she.

This man who had dropped a bombshell into her life, however, looked as if he cared—and he didn't like what he was seeing.

'I hope,' he said evenly, 'that you have now had a chance to come to terms with what I told you this morning, and that you understand,' he continued, 'how imperative it is that we discuss my cousin's son's future.'

'There's nothing to discuss,' she replied tightly.

Anatole's mouth tightened. So she was still taking that line. Well, he would have to disabuse her of it—that was all. In the meantime there was something that was even more imperative. He wanted to see Marcos's son—see him with his own eyes. He looked around the room.

'Where is the baby?' he asked. He hadn't meant it to sound like a demand, only a question, but it seemed to make the girl flinch. Seeing her now, like this, had not improved her looks, he noted absently. She was still abysmally dressed, without any attention to her appearance.

'He's asleep,' she answered stiffly.

The dark eyes rested on her. 'I would like to see him.'

It was not a request. It was a statement of intent. His eyes went past her to the half-open bedroom door and he stepped towards it. Inside was a cot beside a bed, and in the cot the small figure of a baby nestled in a fleecy blanket. In the dim light from the drawn curtains Anatole could not make out the baby's features.

Are you Marcos's son? Are you the child I've come to find? The questions burned in his head. Instinctively he moved to step into the room. Immediately a low-voiced hiss sounded behind him.

'Please don't wake him!'

He could hear a note in her voice that was not just a command but a plea. Abruptly, he nodded, reversing out of the cramped room, causing her to back away into the equally small living room.

Once again she felt his presence dominate the poky space.

'You had better sit down, Miss Brandon,' he said, indicating the sofa as though he, not her, was the host.

Stiffly, she did so. Somehow she had to find a way to make him go away—leave her and Georgy alone. Then it came to her just why he might be here. What he might be after.

'If you want me to sign papers saying I forfeit any claim to his father's estate, I will do so straight away,' she blurted out. 'I don't want any money, or maintenance, or anything like that. Georgy and I are fine as we are—we're all sorted!' She swallowed again, altering her tone of voice. Her eyes shadowed suddenly. 'I'm sorry to hear that your cousin is…is dead…but—' her eyes met his unflinchingly '—but it doesn't change the fact that he was not in the slightest bit interested in Georgy's existence, so—'

Anatole Telonidis held up a hand. It was a simple gesture, but it carried with it an expectation that she would cease talking.

Which she did.

'My cousin is…*was*,' he corrected himself painfully, 'the only Petranakos grandson of our mutual grandfather, Timon. Marcos's parents died when he was only a teenager and consequently…' Anatole paused. 'He was very precious to our grandfather. His death has devastated him.' He took another heavy breath. 'Marcos's death came as a viciously cruel blow—he was killed driving the car that our grandfather had given him for his birthday. It was a birthday Timon knew would likely be the last he would see, because…' Anatole paused again, then finished the bleak saga. 'Because Timon had himself just been diagnosed with advanced incurable cancer.'

He fell silent, letting the information sink in. Lynette Brandon was sitting there, looking ashen.

'You will understand, I know,' he went on quietly, 'how much it will mean to Timon to know that, although he has lost his grandson, a great-grandson exists.' He read her expression. It was blank, rejecting. He *had* to convince her of the argument he was making. 'There is very little time,' he pressed. 'The cancer was very advanced at the point of diagnosis, and since my cousin's death my grandfather has refused all treatment—even though treatment could keep him alive for a little while longer. He is waiting to die—for with the loss of his grandson he has no reason to live at all. Not even for one single day.' Then he finished what he had come to say. 'Your sister's baby—my cousin's son—gives him that reason.'

He stood looking down at her. Her face was still ashen, her hands twisting in her lap. He spoke again, his voice grave. He had to convince her of the urgency of what had to happen.

'I need to take Georgy to Greece with me. I need to take him as soon as possible. My dying grandfather needs to know that his great-grandson will grow up in the country of his father—'

'*No!* No, I won't let you!' The words burst from her and she leapt to her feet.

Anatole pressed his lips together in frustration. 'You are overwrought,' he repeated. 'It is understandable—this has come as a shock to you. I wish that matters were not as urgent as they are. But with Timon's state of health I have to press you on this! The very last thing I want,' he said heavily, 'is to turn this into any kind of battle between us.

I need—I *want*—your co-operation! You do not need me to tell you,' he added, and his eyes were dark now, 'that once DNA testing has proved Marcos's paternity, then—'

'There isn't going to *be* any DNA testing!' Lyn shot back at him.

Anatole stopped. There was something in her voice—something in her face—that alerted him. There was more than obduracy in it—more than anger, even.

There was fear.

His antennae went into overdrive. *Thee mou*, might the child not be Marcos's after all? Everything about those plaintive, pitiful letters he'd read indicated that the baby's mother had been no promiscuous party girl, that she had fallen in love with his cousin, however unwisely. No, the child she had been carrying *was* his. He was certain of it. Timon, he knew, would require proof before he designated the baby his heir, but that would surely be a formality?

His thoughts raced back to the moment in hand. The expression on Lynette Brandon's face made no sense. She was the one objecting to any idea of taking Marcos's son back to Greece—if the baby were not Marcos's after all surely she would positively *want* DNA testing done!

He frowned. There was something else that didn't make sense, either. Something odd about her name. Its similarity to her sister's. Abruptly he spoke. 'Why is your sister's name so like yours?' he asked shortly. He frowned. 'It is unusual—confusing, as I have found—for sisters to have such similar names. Lynette and Linda.'

'So what?' she countered belligerently. 'What does it matter now?'

Anatole fixed his gaze on her. His antennae were now registering that same flash of emotion in her as he'd seen when he had mentioned DNA testing, but he had no time to consider it further. Lynette Brandon was launching into him again. Her voice was vehement, passionate.

'Have I finally got you to understand, Mr Telonidis, that your journey here has been wasted? I'm sorry— sorry about your cousin, sorry about your grandfather— but Georgy is staying here with me! He is *not* going to be brought up in Greece. He is *mine*!'

'Is he?'

His brief, blunt question cut right across her. Silencing her.

In her eyes, her face, flared that same emotion he had seen a moment ago—fear.

What is going on here?

The question flared in his head and stayed there, even though her voice broke that moment of silence with a single hissing word.

'*Yes!*' she grated fiercely.

Anatole levelled his gaze at her. Behind his impassive expression his mind was working fast. Since learning that morning about the double tragedy that had hit this infant, overturning his assumption that Marcos's son was with his birth mother, he had set his lawyers to ascertain exactly what the legal situation was with regard to custody of the orphaned boy—and what might be the outcome of any proposition that the baby be raised in Greece by his paternal family. He had no answers yet, but the baby's aunt had constantly—and vehemently!—expressed the fact that *she* had full legal charge in her sister's place.

But *did* she?

'And that is official, is it? Your custody of Georgy?' His voice was incisive, demanding she answer.

Again there was that same revealing emotion in her eyes, which was then instantly blanked.

'*Yes!*' she repeated, just as fiercely.

He frowned. 'So you have adopted him?'

A line of white showed on her cheekbones. 'It's going through,' she said quickly. 'These things take time. There's a lot of paperwork. Bureaucracy and everything. But of *course* I'm adopting him! I'm the obvious person to adopt him!'

His expression did not change, but he could see that for the British authorities she would be the natural person to adopt her late sister's son if she were set on doing so. Which she evidently was! Anatole felt a ripple of respect for her determination to go through with it. Her life could not be easy, juggling studying with childcare and living in penny-pinching circumstances.

But for all that, he still had to find a way to convince her that Marcos's son just could *not* be raised by her in such penurious circumstances. It was unthinkable. Once Timon knew of his existence, he would insist with all his last strength that his beloved grandson's son be brought home to Greece, to be reunited with his father's family.

Just how, precisely, Marcos's son was to be raised—how a small baby, then a toddler and a schoolboy was to grow up—was something that could be worked out later. For now, just getting the baby to Greece, for his grandfather to see him—make him his heir—before the cancer claimed Timon was his only priority.

And to do that he had to get this totally impossible intransigent aunt to stop blocking him at every turn!

But how?

A heavy, unappetising thought forced its way forward. His mouth tightened. There was, of course, one very obvious method of attempting to stop any objections to what he was urging. A way that worked, as he knew well from his own business experience, to win compliance and consensus and agreement.

A way he did not want to use here, now, for this—but if he had to...if it worked...?

He must. If nothing else he must attempt it. He owed it to Timon, to Marcos—to all the thousands employed by the Petranakos Corporation whose livelihoods were threatened.

Reluctantly, for what he was about to say went against the grain, he spoke. His tone of voice was measured, impassive. 'I know full well that Timon will insist on thanking you for your care and concern for his great-grandson—that he will fully appreciate the accommodation you make towards granting his fervent wish for Marcos's son to grow up with his paternal family—and that he will wish to settle a sum on you in respect of his gratitude and appreciation such that your financial security would be handsomely assured for the future.'

There—he had said it. He had said outright that if she stopped stonewalling him her life of poverty would be over for good. He let the words sink in, not taking his eyes from her.

Her expression was blank, however. Had she not heard what he'd said?

Then she answered him. 'You want to *buy* Georgy from me?' Her voice was as blank as her eyes.

A frown immediately shaped Anatole's face. 'Of course not!' he repudiated.

'You're offering me money to hand him over to you,' the same blank voice intoned.

Anatole shook his head. Did she have to put it in such unpalatable terms? 'What I am saying,' he spelt out, 'is that—'

'Is that your grandfather will pay me if I let him have Georgy to bring him up in Greece.' Her voice was flat.

'No! It is not like that—' Anatole's voice was sharp.

Suddenly the blank look in her eyes vanished utterly. She launched herself to her feet, anger blazing in her eyes.

'It is *exactly* like that!' she cried. 'How *dare* you? How dare you sit there and tell me you'll *buy* Georgy from me? How *dare* you do such a thing?' Her voice had risen; her heart was thumping furiously. 'How *dare* you come here and offer me *money* to hand my dead sister's son over to you? How dare you?'

He was on his feet as well. He filled the room, intimidating and overpowering. But she would not be intimidated! Would not be overpowered! Would not be paid to part with Georgy!

She took a heaving breath, words pouring from her.

'I swore to my sister on her *deathbed* that I would never, never abandon her baby! That I would never hand him over to *anyone*! That I would always, *always* look after him and love him. Because she was not going to be able to do it! Because she was dying, and she knew she was dying, and she was never going to see her baby grow up, never going to see him become a boy, a man—never, never, *never...*'

Her voice was hoarse, the words torn from her, from the very depths of her being. Her hands were clenched into fists at her sides, as if she could—and would—and *must*—fight off the whole world to keep Georgy with her!

For a second there was silence. Absolute silence between them. Then into the silence came a high, solitary wail.

With a cry of consternation Lyn wheeled about. Oh, no—now she had gone and woken Georgy! With all this awful arguing about what was never going to happen—because she was never giving Georgy up! *Never!*

The wail came again. She rounded on Anatole. 'Please go!' she said. 'Please—just go!'

She rushed from the room into the bedroom, where Georgy was wide awake, his little face screwed up. She scooped him up with a hushing noise, soothing and rocking him in her arms until he had quietened.

The feel of his strong, solid little body, so familiar, so precious, calmed her too. She took long slow breaths, hugging him tightly, and felt his warmth and weight in her arms like a blessing, a benediction.

How could anyone think to ask her to give him up? She loved this little child more than anyone in the whole world! He was everything to her—and she was everything to him.

Love flowed from her, enveloping and protective, as she cradled him against her, her eyes smarting, her throat tight. Slowly the heaving emotions in her breast, her heart, eased. Georgy was safe. He was in her arms. He was with her. She would never let him go, never abandon him. Her hectic pulse slowed. Cradling him, her hand curved protectively around his back, she crooned soothingly at him, wordless sounds murmuring, familiar and comforting. The rest of the world seemed very far away...

'May I see him?'

The voice behind her made her spin round. Anatole was standing in the doorway of the bedroom.

But there was something different about him. Something quite different. She'd seen him only as dark and tall and formidable—telling her things she did not want to hear, his very presence a terrifying threat to everything that she held most dear.

Now, as she gazed at him, her expression stricken, across the dimly lit curtained room, he did not seem formidable at all. Or threatening. He seemed merely—tense. As if every muscle in his body were pulled taut. In the dim light the bone structure of his face was stark.

She felt Georgy lift his head from her shoulder, twist his neck so that he could see where the voice had come from. He gazed at the figure in the doorway with eyes just as dark as those which were fixed on him.

For a moment the tableau held all of them immobile. Then, with a gurgling sound, Georgy lurched on her shoulder, his little arms reaching forward towards the man standing in the doorway. The man with eyes like his own.

The man who was kin to the father he had never known. Never would know now....

As if in slow motion, Anatole found his hand reaching inside his jacket pocket, drawing out something he had brought with him from Greece. It was a silver photo frame from his grandfather's opulent drawing room, displaying one individual alone. Slowly he shifted his gaze down to the photo he held in his hand, then back to the baby cradled so closely in his young aunt's arms.

'He is Marcos's son.' Anatole's voice was flat. But there was emotion in it. Powerful emotion. His gaze cut suddenly to Lyn. 'Look,' he instructed, holding up the photo.

It was an old one, pre-digital, an informal shot and unposed, but the likeness to the baby in it was unmistakable. The same wide brown-eyed gaze. The same-shaped mouth and head. The same expression.

How was it, Anatole found himself thinking, emotion rising in his chest, that the genes Marcos had carried could be so clearly visible even at this tender age? What was it about the human face that revealed its origins, its kinship? Yet so it was—this scrap of humanity, less than a year old, stared back at him in the baby he himself could just dimly remember from his own boyhood.

'I couldn't be sure,' he heard himself saying. 'Knew that I must get DNA testing. Knew there would be doubts that necessitated such measures.' He paused. 'But I have no doubts—not now.' His voice changed, and so did his expression. 'This is my cousin's son—his *only* son! The only trace left of him in this life! He *must* be part of his father's family.' He held up a hand as if to pre-empt what he knew would be her response to that unarguable statement. 'But we must find a way...there must be one—' He broke off, taking a sharp breath, his focus now on Lyn.

'I am sorry—sorry that I said what I did just now. It

was offensive, and you have every right to be angry.' He paused. 'Will you accept my apology?'

His eyes met hers, seeking a way past the stormy expression in them. Slowly, painfully, Lyn swallowed. There was a large stone in her throat, but it was not only from her anger at his vile offer. It was because of the way he'd stared at Georgy...the emotion in his eyes...his voice.

He was seeing his dead cousin in the baby she was holding in her arms...

Just as I see Lindy in him.

She felt her throat close—felt something change, somehow, deep within her. Slowly she nodded, taking a ragged breath.

'Thank you,' he said in a low voice.

His eyes went from her face back to Georgy. That expression returned to them, making her breath catch as the same emotion was aroused in herself.

Warily Lyn made her way past him into the living room, heading for the sofa onto which she sank down on shaky legs, her heart rate still ragged. But something had changed. She could feel it—sense it as clearly as if the wind had changed its quarter, as if the tide had turned in the depths of the sea. It was in his voice, his stance, his face, as he sat down at the far end of the sofa.

And it was in her, too, that change. Was it because she was finally accepting that Georgy was more than her dead sister's son? That he had a family on his father's side too, to whom he was precious—as precious as he was to her?

She did not want to accept that truth—had tried to fight it—but she had to. Must.

For a moment—just a moment—as Anatole Telonidis lowered his tall frame on to the sofa, he seemed far too physically close to her. She wanted to leap to her feet—away from the intensely physical presence of the man. But even as she fought the impulse she could feel Georgy using his not inconsiderable strength to lean forward, towards this interesting addition to his world. And as he did so, he gave another crowing gurgle, his little arms stretching forward towards his father's cousin.

And then Lyn saw something quite extraordinary happen.

Before her eyes she saw this tall, dark, forbidding man who had walked uninvited into her world, catalysing her deepest fears with his demands, his assumptions, all the power of his wealth and family, transform. Greek words sounded from his mouth and then slowly, as if he were moving through thick, murky water, she watched him reach a hand out towards the infant. Immediately a little starfish fist closed around the long, tanned finger and tugged it hopefully, if ineffectually, in the direction of his mouth.

'Hello, Georgy,' said Anatole. His voice sounded strained, as if his throat weren't working properly. 'Hello, little fellow.'

There was, Lyn could see as plain as day, extraordinary though it was, a look of stunned wonder on his dark, formidable face.

She felt emotion stab at her but did not know what it was. Only that it was powerful. *Very* powerful…

Her eyes could not leave his face, could not stop staring at the transformation in the man. But Anatole had no eyes for her stunned scrutiny of him. He had eyes only for one thing—the baby in her arms who had brought him here. His dead cousin's child.

Lyn heard him murmur something in Greek. Something that sounded soft and caressing. Something that felt like a warm touch on her skin even though it was not directed at her. It drew a response from her, all the same, and she felt a strange, potent flickering of her senses.

Then Georgy was wriggling impatiently in her arms, tugging on the finger he was clutching. She loosened her hold automatically, so that he could gain his objective, but now he had seen something more enticing to clutch, and he dropped the finger he'd been gripping. Instead he made a lunge at the dark silk tie dangling so tantalisingly close to him as its wearer leant forward. To his own considerable pleasure he made contact, grasped it greedily, and pulled the end into his mouth, sucking vigorously.

A burst of laughter broke from Lyn. She couldn't help it. 'Oh, Georgy, you monkey!' she exclaimed ruefully.

She lifted a hand to disengage the tie, conscious as she did so that the gesture brought her disquietingly closer to the man wearing it. Deprived of his tasty morsel, Georgy gave a howl of outrage. Lyn took his tiny hands and busied herself in remonstrations that enabled her to straighten up, increasing the distance between herself and this most disturbing of men.

'No, you can't have it! You little monster, you! Yes, you are! A little monster!' She nuzzled his nose with an Eskimo kiss and set him laughing. She glanced across at Anatole at what was doubtless a hideously expensive tie now somewhat soggy at the end. 'I'm sorry about that. I hope it's not damaged too much.' Her voice was apologetic, constrained with an embarrassment that was not just due to Georgy's misdemeanours but also to the awkward self-consciousness of sharing a sofa with Anatole Telonidis.

Anatole surveyed the soggy item. 'It is of no consequence,' he remarked.

Then, before Lyn realised what he was doing, he was unfastening his gold watch and offering it to Georgy. Eyes widening in disbelieving delight, Georgy snatched up the shiny treasure and clutched it to his chest, gazing wide-eyed at the giver of such largesse.

'You're mad!' exclaimed Lyn, throwing a shocked glance at Anatole. 'He'll try and eat it!'

But Anatole merely looked at the baby. 'Georgy. No eating. A gentleman does not eat his watch. Understood?'

Georgy stared, his eyes wide in wonder. This stern, deep voice had clearly made a deep impression on him. Dutifully, he made no attempt to ingest the Rolex, contenting himself with continuing to clutch it while staring riveted at this oracle of good advice.

Anatole cast a long-lashed sardonic look at Lyn—a strangely intimate glance that sent a quiver through her. Then the next second his moment of triumph evaporated. With a jerky movement Georgy slammed the watch to his mouth.

'Georgy—no!' Both adults moved fast but, alas, Anatole's belated attempt to remove his watch incited outrage in the infant, whose little face screwed up into angry tears.

Hastily Lyn fumbled in the plastic toy bucket beside the sofa to fetch out Georgy's favourite—a set of plastic keys—and managed to swap them, with some difficulty, for the precious gold watch. Charily, she handed the latter back to its owner, avoiding eye contact this time, and then busied herself settling Georgy in her lap as he chewed contentedly on his keys. She felt unbearably awkward, and yet she knew that something had changed. Thawed.

Imperceptibly, she felt a tiny amount of the tension racking her easing. Then, into the brief silence, a deep voice spoke.

'So, what are we to do?'

CHAPTER THREE

LYN'S EYES FLEW upwards. Anatole Telonidis was looking at her, and as he did so she knew for sure that something had definitely changed between them. She was still wary, yes—wariness was prickling through her every vein—but that wash of rage and outrage against him had gone. His tone of voice was different too. It was more—open. As if he were no longer simply dictating to her what must happen. As if he were truly asking a question of her.

A question she could give no answer to other than the one she had hurled at his head five minutes ago. She could not—*would* not—ever give Georgy up!

She gave an awkward shrug, dropping her eyes again. She didn't want to look at him. Her self-consciousness had soared suddenly, and whereas before she might have found refuge in animosity and resentment and rage against him and his autocratic demands, now she felt raw and exposed.

Anatole watched her sitting there, with the baby on her lap, her attention all on the infant who was busily chewing on his keys and chuntering away to himself. Emotion poured through him, powerful and overwhelming. Even without the formality of DNA testing his heart already knew that this was Marcos's son. And already he felt a powerful urge to protect and cherish him.

Which is what she feels too! That is what is driving her!
Her obduracy, her angry outburst, were both fuelled

by the deepest of emotions—emotions that he understood and recognised.

Love and grief.

She could not give up the child. Not now. Not like this. It was impossible for her to conceive of such a thing. Impossible for her to do anything other than what she had done—rage at the very notion of it! A flicker of a different emotion went through him—one he had not envisaged feeling. One that came again now as he let his eyes rest on her while her attention was on the baby in her lap.

There was something very moving about seeing her attend so tenderly to the tiny scrap of humanity she was engaged with. Her face seemed softer somehow, without that pinched, drained, defensive look that he'd seen in it. The contours of her profile, animated by her smiles of affection for the infant, were gentler now.

He found an irrelevant thought fleeting through his head. *If she had her hair done decently, took some trouble over her appearance, she would look quite different—*

He reproached himself. What time or funds did she have to pay any attention to her appearance? She was studying full-time and looking after a baby, on what was clearly a very tight budget. And it was obvious, too, from the circles under her eyes, that she wasn't getting enough sleep.

A sudden impulse went through him.

I could lighten her burden—the load she is carrying single-handed.

But not by taking from her the baby she was so devoted to.

He heard himself speaking. 'There must be a way we can reach agreement.'

Her eyes flew to his. Back in them, he could see, was the wariness and alarm that he was so familiar with.

'You're not taking Georgy from me!' Fear and the hostility raked through her voice, flashed in her eyes.

He held up a hand. His voice changed, grew husky. 'I can see how much Marcos's son means to you. But *because* he means so much to you I ask you to understand how much he means to his father's family as well.' He paused, his eyes holding hers, willing the wariness and resistance to dissolve. 'I need you to trust me,' he said to her. 'I need you to believe me when I say that there has to be a way we can resolve this *impasse*.'

She heard his words. Heard them reach her—strong, fluent, persuasive. Felt the power of that dark, expressive gaze on her, and the power, too, of the magnetism of the man, the power of his presence, the impact it had on her. She felt her senses stir and fought them back. But she could not fight back the intensity of his regard—the way those incredible eyes were holding hers, willing her to accept what he was saying to her.

He pressed on. 'I do not wish,' he said, making his words as clear as he could, 'for there to be animosity or conflict between us. A way can be found. I am sure of it. If...' He paused, and now his eyes were more intense than ever. 'If there is goodwill between us and, most importantly, trust.'

She felt her emotions sway, her resistance weaken.

As if he sensed it, saw it, he went on. 'Will you bring Georgy to Greece?' he asked. 'For a visit—I ask nothing more than that for now,' he emphasized. 'Simply so that his great-grandfather can see him.'

His eyes searched her face. Alarm flared again in her eyes.

Lyn's hand smoothed Georgy's head shakily. 'He hasn't got a passport,' she replied.

'That can be arranged,' Anatole responded promptly. 'I will see to it.'

Her expression was still troubled. 'I...I may not be allowed to take him out of the country—?' she began, then stopped.

Anatole frowned. 'You are his aunt—why should he not travel with you?'

For a second—just a second—he saw in her eyes again that same emotion he had seen when he had challenged her as to whether she had adopted Georgy or not.

'You said that the process of adoption is not yet finalised,' he said. 'Does that affect whether you can take him out of the country?'

She swallowed. 'Officially I am still only his foster carer,' she replied. There was constraint in her voice, evasiveness in the way her gaze dropped from his. 'I...I don't know what the rules are about taking foster children abroad...'

'Well, I shall have enquiries made,' said Anatole. 'These things can be sorted.' He did not want her hiding behind official rules and regulations. He wanted her to consent to what he so urgently needed—to bringing Marcos's son to Greece.

But he would press her no longer. Not for now. Finally she was listening to him. He had put his request to her— now he would let her get used to the idea.

He got to his feet, looking down at her. 'It has been,' he said, and his voice was not unsympathetic now, 'a tumultous day for you—and for myself as well.' His eyes went to the baby on her lap, who had twisted round to gaze at him. Once again Anatole felt his heart give a strange convulsion, felt the pulse of emotion go through him.

There was so much of Marcos in the tiny infant!

Almost automatically his eyes slipped to the face of the young woman holding his infant cousin. He could see the baby's father in his little face, but what of the tragic mother who had lost *her* life in giving *him* life? His eyes searched the aunt's features, looking for an echo of similarity. But in the clear grey eyes that were ringed with fatigue, in the cheekbones over which the skin was stretched so tightly, in the rigid contours of her jaw, there was no resemblance that he could see.

As his gaze studied her he saw colour suffuse her cheeks and immediately dropped his gaze. He was making her self-conscious, and he did not want to add to her discomfort. Yet as he dropped his gaze he was aware of how the colour in her cheeks gave her a glow, making her less pallid—less plain. More appealing.

She could be something...

The idle thought flicked across his mind and he dismissed it. He was not here to assess whether the aunt of the baby he'd been so desperately seeking possessed those feminine attributes which drew his male eye.

'Forgive me,' he said, his voice contrite. 'I can see my cousin so clearly in his son—I was looking to see what he has inherited from his mother's side.'

He had thought his words might reassure her that he had not been gazing at her with the intention of embarrassing her, but her reaction to his words seemed to have the opposite effect. He saw the colour drain from her face—saw, yet again, that emotion flash briefly in her eyes.

Fear.

He frowned. There was a reason for that reaction—but what was it? He set it aside. For now it was not important. What was important was that he took his leave of her with the lines of communication finally open between them, so that from now on they could discuss what must be discussed—how they were to proceed. How he was to achieve his goal without taking from her the baby nephew she clearly loved so devotedly.

He wanted his last words to her now to be reassuring.

'I will leave you for now,' he said. 'I will visit you again tomorrow—what time would be good for you?'

She swallowed. She had to make some answer. 'I have lectures in the morning, but that's all,' she said hesitantly.

'Good,' he said. 'Then I will come here in the afternoon. We can talk more then. Make more plans.' He paused, looking into her pinched face. 'Plans that we will *both* agree to. Because I know now that you will not give up Georgy—you love him too much. And *you* must surely know that since he cannot be taken from you without your consent, for you are his mother's sister and so the best person to adopt him, that you have nothing to fear from me. Whatever arrangements we make for Georgy's future it will be with your consent and your agreement. You have nothing to fear—nothing at all.'

Surely, he thought, *that* must give her the reassurance that would finally get her to make long-term plans for the infant's upbringing?

But her expression was still withdrawn. Anatole felt determination steal through him. Whatever it took— *whatever*!—he would ensure that his Georgy was reunited with his father's family.

Whatever it took.

He took a breath, looking down at the baby and at the aunt who held him.

'I will see myself out,' he told her. 'Do not disturb yourself.'

Then he was gone.

In the silence that followed his departure the only sound was Georgy contentedly chewing on his plastic keys. Lyn's arms tightened unconsciously around him. She felt weak and shaky and devastated. As if a tsunami had swept over her, drowning her. Her expression was stark.

An overwhelming impulse was coursing through her, imperative in its compulsive force.

The impulse to run. Run far and fast and right away! Run until she had hidden herself from the danger that threatened her—threatened her beloved Georgy! The danger that was in the very person of the tall, dark figure of Anatole Telonidis.

Fear knifed through her.

Anatole threw himself into the back of his car and instructed his driver to head back to the hotel. As the car moved off he got out his mobile. It was time—most definitely time—to phone Timon and tell him what he had discovered.

Who he had discovered.

He had kept everything from Timon until now, loath to raise hopes he could not fulfil. But now—with or without DNA testing—every bone in his body was telling him that he had found Marcos's son.

The son that changed everything.

As his call was put through to his grandfather, and Timon's strained, stricken voice greeted him, Anatole began to speak.

The effect was everything he'd prayed for! Within minutes Timon had become a changed man—a man who had suddenly, miraculously, been given a reason to live. A man who now had only one overriding goal in his life.

'Bring him to me! Bring me Marcos's boy! Do anything and everything you need to get him here!'

Hope had surged in his grandfather's voice. Hope and absolute determination.

'I will,' Anatole replied. 'I will do everything I have to do.'

But as he finished the call his expression changed. Just what 'everything' would need to be he did not fully know. He knew only that, whatever it was, it would all depend on getting Lyn Brandon to agree to it.

As the boy's closest living relative—sister of his mother—his current caregiver and foster mother, with the strongest claim to become Georgy's adoptive mother, it was she who held all the aces.

What would it take to persuade her to let Marcos's son be raised in Greece?

Whatever it was—he had to discover it.

As his mind started to work relentlessly through all the implications and arguments and possibilities a notion started to take shape within his head.

A notion so radical, so drastic, so...*outrageous* that it stopped him in his tracks.

CHAPTER FOUR

'ARE YOU SURE he is not cold?' Anatole frowned as he looked down at the infant sitting up in his buggy.

Lyn shook her head. 'No, honestly, he isn't. He's got lots of layers over him.'

She glanced at the tall figure sitting beside her on the park bench they had walked to. It was a drier day than previously, but spring was still stubbornly far off and she could see why someone used to warmer climes would think it very cold. But it was Anatole Telonidis who had suggested that they take the baby outdoors. Probably, Lyn thought tightly, because a man like him was not used to being in a place as shabby as her flat. Not that this scrappy urban park was a great deal better, but it had a little children's play area where Georgy liked to watch other children playing—as he was doing now.

Even though they had the bench to themselves, it seemed too small to Lyn. She was as punishingly conscious today of Anatole Telonidis's physicality as she had been the day before.

How can he be so devastatingly good-looking?

It was a rhetorical question, and one that every covert glance at him confirmed was unnecessary. It took an effort of will to remind herself brusquely that it was completely irrelevant that she was so punishingly conscious of just how amazing-looking he was.

All that matters is that he wants Georgy to go to Greece...

That was all she had to hold in her mind. Not how strange it felt to be sitting beside him on a chilly park bench, with Georgy's buggy pulled up beside them. A flicker went through her. Others would see a man and a woman in a children's park with a baby in a buggy.

As if they were a family.

A strange little ripple went through her—a little husk of yearning. She was being the best mother she could to Georgy, her beloved sister's son, but however much she tried to substitute for Lindy there was no one to do the same for Georgy's father.

She pushed the thought away. He had *her*, and that was what was important. Essential. Vital. Whatever Anatole wanted to say to her this afternoon, nothing on earth would change that!

'Have you given any more thought to what we spoke of yesterday?' he opened. 'Bringing Georgy out to Greece to meet his grandfather?' He paused minutely. 'I spoke to Timon yesterday.' Anatole's voice changed in a moment, and Lyn could hear the emotion in it. 'I cannot tell you how overjoyed he is to learn of Georgy's existence!'

Lyn's hands twisted in her lap. 'I don't know,' she said. 'I just don't know.' Her eyes went to the man sitting beside her, looking at him with a troubled expression. 'You talk about it being just a visit. But that isn't what you said initially! You said you wanted Georgy to be brought up in Greece! What if you simply don't let Georgy come back here with me? What if you try and keep him in Greece?'

He could hear, once again, the fear spiking in her voice. Resolve formed in him. 'I need you to trust me,' he said.

'How *can* I?' she cried wildly.

Anatole looked at her. Was it going to be like this the whole time? With her doubting everything, distrusting him, fearing him—fighting him? Because he didn't have

time for it—and nor did Timon. Timon had undertaken
to talk to his oncologist, to find out whether he was too
weak to try the strong drugs that he would have to take if
he wanted to keep death at bay, even for a little while. For
long enough to see his great-grandson and make him his
heir, as Anatole so fervently wanted him to do.

He took a deep, scissoring breath that went right down
into his lungs. He had promised he would do whatever it
took to get Marcos's son out to Greece, to ensure his future
was there. But with the baby's aunt resisting him every
step of the way, so it seemed, was it not time to take the
radical, drastic action that would dispose of all her arguments? All her objections?

It would surely disarm her totally. Yet he was balking at
it, he knew. The idea that had sparked in his mind the afternoon before was still alight—but it was so drastic that he
still could hardly credit that it had occurred to him at all!

But what else would it take to get her to stop fighting
him all the time on what had to happen?

'I understand your fears,' he said now, keeping his voice
as reassuring as he could. 'But they are not necessary. I
told you—there must be a way to resolve this *impasse* that
does not entail conflict.'

Her eyes were wide and troubled. 'I don't see *how*!' she
exclaimed. 'You want Georgy to be brought up in Greece,
with his father's family. I want to keep him here with me.
How can those two possibly be resolved?'

Anatole chose his words with care. 'What if you came
with Georgy?' he asked.

She stared at him blankly. 'Brought him out to visit
your grandfather?'

He gave a quick shake of his head. 'Not just to visit—
to live.'

'To *live* in Greece?' she echoed, as if she had not heard
properly. 'Georgy and me?'

'Why not?' Anatole's eyes were studying her reaction.

'But I'm British!' she replied blankly, because right now it was the only thing that occurred to her.

The corner of his mouth curved, and irrelevantly Lyn thought how it lightened his expression—and sent a pulse of blood around her veins. Then he was replying.

'Many British people live very happily in Greece,' he said dryly. 'They find the climate a great deal warmer!' he said pointedly, glancing around at the bleak, wintry landscape.

'But I haven't got any accountancy qualifications yet, and even when I do I probably wouldn't be able to practise out there. And besides, I don't speak any Greek! How could I make a living?'

Anatole's eyebrows rose. Had she *really* just asked that question?

'It goes without saying,' he said, and his voice was even drier, 'that there would be no necessity for you to do so.'

His reply was a flash of her grey eyes that gave animation to her thin face.

'I'm *not* living on charity!' she objected.

Anatole shook his head. 'It would not be a question of charity!' he retorted. His tone of voice changed. 'Timon would insist that you have an allowance.'

Her mouth pressed together. 'So I'd be Georgy's paid nursemaid? Is that what you're saying?'

'No!' She was taking this entirely the wrong way, he could see. He tried to recover. 'How could you be a nursemaid when you are going to be Georgy's adoptive mother?'

He had thought his words would be reassuring to her, yet for a second there was again that flash of fearful emotion he had seen before in her eyes. His gaze narrowed infinitesimally. 'Tell me,' he heard himself saying, 'is there some problem with your application to adopt Georgy?'

It was a shot fired with a calculated aim to expose any

weaknesses in her claim. Weaknesses, he knew with grim resolve, he would have to exploit if she reverted to being as obdurate and uncooperative as she had been yesterday. But surely that would not be so—not now that they had finally reached the stage where they could at least discuss Georgy's future without her flying into an emotional storm!

He watched her face, saw her expression close. His shot had hit home, he could see.

'What is it?' he asked bluntly.

Lyn's hands twisted in her lap. Unease and fear writhed in her. But she had to reply—that much was obvious.

'From the moment Lindy died,' she said, her voice low and strained, 'the authorities wanted Georgy taken into care and put up for adoption. Adoption not by me but by a childless couple. There are so many desperate for a baby!'

A cold spear went through Anatole. It was just as he had feared the moment Lyn Brandon had said that she was not Georgy's birth mother!

'Even now,' she said tightly, 'if I dropped my application they would hand him over straight away to a married couple!'

'But you are his maternal aunt. That surely gives you a priority claim to him!'

The fear darted in her eyes again. 'They say I'm too young, that I'm a student still, that I'd be a single mother—' Her voice broke.

For a moment Anatole was silent.

'But I'm not giving in!' Lyn's voice was vehement now. 'I'll *never* give in—no matter what they say or how much they drag their heels! I'll never give up Georgy! *Never!*'

Her hands spasmed in her lap, anguish knifing inside her. Then suddenly her hands were being covered by a large, warm, strong hand, stilling their convulsion.

'There is a way.' Anatole heard himself speaking but

did not quite believe he was doing so. 'There is a way that could solve the entire dilemma.'

Lyn's eyes flew to his. He felt their impact—read the fear in them.

'You say that two of the arguments being used against your adopting Georgy are that you are still a student— unwaged and unmarried,' he said. Part of his brain was still wondering whether he would truly say what he was about to hear himself saying. 'What if neither of those things were true any more? What if you became a stay-at-home mother who could devote her days to Georgy—who had a husband to provide for you both and be the father figure that Georgy needs?'

She was looking blank. Totally blank.

'I don't understand,' she said.

Anatole's hand pressed hers. 'What if,' he said, 'that husband—that father figure—were me?'

For a timeless moment she simply stared at him with huge, blank eyes. Then, with a jolt, she moved away, pulling her hands free from his. They felt cold without his covering clasp, but that didn't matter. All that mattered was that she say what was searing through her head.

'That's insane!'

Anatole gave a quick shake of his head. He had expected that reaction. It was, after all, exactly the reaction he'd had himself when the notion had first inserted itself into his brain yesterday, as he sought for ways to sort out the infernally complicated situation he was in.

'Not insane—logical.' He held up a hand. 'Listen to me—hear me out.' He took a breath, his eyes going absently to Georgy, who was still, he was glad to see, totally absorbed with chewing on his beloved set of keys while avidly watching the toddlers tottering about on the park's play equipment.

JULIA JAMES

'This is what I propose,' he said, turning his gaze back to Lyn.

She had gone white as a sheet, with the same stark expression in her face he had seen yesterday. It did not flatter her, he found himself thinking. But he brushed that aside. Her looks were not important right now. What was important was getting her to see the world his way—as fast as he possibly could.

'If we were to marry, it would solve all our problems in one stroke. For the authorities here it would dispose of their objection to you being a single mother, as yet unable to support a child financially. Moreover, in addition to your being Georgy's maternal aunt, the fact that you would be marrying someone who's the closest thing to Georgy's uncle as can be has to be compelling! And finally—' his voice was dry now '—there would be absolutely no question about my ability to support a family financially!'

She was still staring at him as if he were mad. 'But you're a complete stranger! I only met you yesterday!'

And you are about as far removed from anyone I am likely to marry as it is possible to be!

That was the consciousness that was burning in her most fiercely, making her feel hot and cold at the same time, overriding all that he had been saying about the logic behind his insane idea!

Anatole gave a shrug. 'All married couples were strangers once,' he pointed out. There was still a sense of disbelief within him. Was he *really* saying this to the girl sitting beside him? Seriously talking about *marrying* her?

Yet the logic was irrefutable! It was *the* most effective way of achieving what had to be achieved—getting Marcos's son out to Greece, to be raised as Timon's heir.

'Think about it,' he urged. 'I'll give you time—obviously! —but I beg you to give it serious consideration.'

As he looked at her he thought, privately, that right now

she couldn't give serious consideration to anything short of a tornado heading for her—she was still staring at him totally blankly.

'I can't *possibly* marry you! It's…it's just the most absurd thing I've ever heard!' Her voice was high-pitched with shock.

'It isn't absurd—' he began.

'Yes, it is! It's completely absurd—and…and…'

She couldn't go on, was bereft of speech, and he took ruthless advantage of her floundering.

'The purpose of our marriage would be solely to ensure Georgy's future,' he said. 'Once that has been achieved, then…' he took a breath, never taking his eyes from her '…then there will be no need for it to exist.'

She blinked. 'I don't understand.'

'This is what I envisage,' Anatole explained. 'Marriage between us will surely secure Georgy's adoption—we are the closest living relatives he has—but once he has been adopted then there will be no compelling reason why we have to stay married. We can get divorced.' His expression changed. 'Provided Georgy continues to be raised in Greece.'

'Why is that so important?' she asked.

'Timon will insist,' he answered. He paused a moment. 'Timon will make Georgy his heir. He will inherit the Petranakos Corporation when Timon dies—just as Marcos would have done, had he lived.'

Lyn frowned. 'But *you* are his grandson too,' she said. 'Why won't you inherit?'

Anatole gave a quick negating shake of his head. 'I am Timon's *daughter's* son—I am not a Petranakos. I have my own inheritance from my late father and I do *not*,' he emphasised, 'seek Georgy's. What I *do* seek—' he took a scissoring breath '—are the powers required to run Petranakos until Georgy's majority.' His eyes rested on Lyn.

'I do not need to tell you how very grave the economic situation is in Greece at the moment. Unemployment is rife and causing considerable distress. The situation at Petranakos is…difficult. And it has become more so since Timon's illness. Worse, when Marcos was killed Timon decided to make a distant Petranakos cousin his heir—a man who, quite frankly, couldn't run a bath, let alone a multi-million-euro business in a highly precarious economy! If he inherits,' Anatole said flatly, 'he'll run it in to the ground and thousands will lose their jobs! I will *not* stand by and watch that happen!'

He took another breath and kept his eyes on Lyn, willing her to understand what was driving him. 'I know exactly what I need to do to get it on track again and safeguard all the jobs it provides. But for that to happen Timon will insist that Georgy grows up in Greece.'

She heard the steel in his voice, the determination. Yet that did not change her reaction to what had to be the most absurd, insane suggestion she'd ever heard in her life! Even if he was wishing they could divorce later…

She opened her mouth to say so, but he was still speaking.

'You can see just why a marriage between us makes sense! Not only does it keep the adoption authorities happy, but it keeps Timon happy too! He will know that Marcos's son will be raised in Greece, under my guardianship, once his days are gone.'

And that, Anatole knew, would be exactly what Timon would want. He would expect Anatole to take care of Marcos's son, raise him as his own.

That is what I want, too!

The realisation hit him as his eyes went once again to the diminutive figure in the buggy. Emotion welled through Anatole. Of *course* he would look after Marcos's son—there was no question that he would not! He had known of his existence such a short time, known the tiny bundle for even less, but already that tiny bundle had seized upon his heart. He would never abandon him—*never*. That was an indelible certainty now.

Whatever it took to make certain of it!

Whatever...

'It's still impossible! Completely impossible!'

Her voice, still high-pitched and strained, made him twist his head back round to her. She saw his expression change. Something about it sent a shaft of fear spearing through her.

He spoke quietly, but there was a quality to that quietness that made her tense—something about the way his veiled eyes were resting on her. 'Please understand that if we cannot agree on this, then…' he paused a moment, then said what he knew he must say to her, to make it clear that he was set on this course. 'Then I will put in an application to adopt Georgy myself, as his closest, most suitable relative on his father's side.'

He had said it. And it had on her the impact he'd known it must. She paled again, her skin taut and white over her cheekbones.

He pressed on relentlessly. 'Do you really want to take the risk that my claim to Georgy may supersede yours, despite my only being his second cousin, not his mother's sister, as you are?'

She seemed to shrink away from him, and the flash of fear in her eyes was the strongest yet. He could see her face working, her hands clenching and unclenching in her lap.

He covered them again with his own. Set his gaze on her. 'It doesn't have to be like that—truly it does not. I do not want confrontation or conflict. I want you to trust me—trust me that what I am suggesting, that we solve this situation by agreeing to marry, is the best way forward.'

She was still shrinking away from him, her expression still fearful.

'I need you to trust me,' he said again.

She could feel his gaze pouring into her, willing her to accept what he was saying. But how could she? How could she possibly accept it?

He'll try and adopt Georgy himself! He'll use the pots of money he's got—that Georgy's great-grandfather's got—and throw it at lawyers and judges and just go on and on and on...

And it was not just his money that would give him the power to take Georgy from her...

Fear coursed through her again—so familiar—so terrifying.

She gave a little cry, jumping to her feet, pulling free of the clasp that was so warm and strong on her hand.

'I don't want this! I don't want any of this! I just want to go back to the way it was!'

He got to his feet too. A sigh escaped him. He understood her reaction.

'I, too, wish we could go back,' he said quietly, but now the quietness was different. It was threaded with sombre emotion. 'I wish I could go back to before Timon was diagnosed with terminal cancer, to before he gave that lethal car to Marcos, to before Marcos smashed himself to pieces in it. But I can't go back. And neither can you. All we *can* do...' his eyes sought to convey the ineluctable truth '...is go forward as best we can.'

His eyes went to Georgy. Softened. Then back to Lyn, standing there trembling in every line of her body.

'And the best that we want is for Georgy.'

Right on cue Marcos's baby son seemed to hear himself addressed and turned his head enquiringly. Anatole went over and hunkered down to pay him attention. Lyn stood, looking down at them both. Emotion was churning in her over and over, like a washing machine inside her.

Anatole glanced up at her. He could see how over-wrought she was. It was time to lighten the atmosphere.

'Come,' he said, holding out a hand towards her. 'We have had enough heavy stuff for the moment. Let's take a break from it. Tell me,' he asked, glancing towards the swings and slides, 'can Georgy go on any of those yet?'

She nodded, swallowing. 'He likes the slide, but you have to hold him—don't let him go!' she said.

'Great,' said Anatole.

He unfastened the safety belt of the buggy and drew Georgy out. Georgy gave a crow of excitement. Lyn stood watching them interact—Anatole talking to him in what she realised must be Greek. A little pang went through her. Georgy was as much Greek as he was English. Could she truly deny him all that his father's family could offer him?

He will be the heir to a fortune.

She might not care, but wouldn't Georgy want that inheritance when he grew up? Wouldn't he want to be part of his Greek heritage as well?

Yet what Anatole Telonidis had just proposed was absurd—no one could say otherwise, no one at all!

A chill crept through her. Except if she did *not* agree to that absurdity then he had made it very clear—ruth-lessly clear—that he would seek to adopt Georgy himself.

Fear knifed her. *I can't lose Georgy—I can't!*

The cry—so familiar, so desperate—sounded in her head, her heart.

She watched Anatole carry Georgy over to the slide, hold him on the slippery surface halfway up and then whoosh him down to the end, to Georgy's patent delight. He repeated the whole process over and over again, and she heard his words resonate in her head. She could not go back to the way it had been when it was just Georgy and her. That was over now—*over*. All she could do was go forward. Forward into a future that seemed frighteningly uncertain. Full of risks of losing Georgy for ever.

I have to do whatever I can to prevent that—whatever I can to safeguard him, keep him with me. I have to do whatever it takes.

And if that meant taking the most insane, most absurd decision of her life then she would have to do it…

'If…' Lyn began slowly. 'If we…go ahead…with what you said…then…' She tried to make herself stop talking so hesitantly, but couldn't. 'How long do you think—um—before we could—well—divorce?'

'It depends,' said Anatole. He'd lifted Georgy off the slide and returned to sit next to Lyn, keeping hold of Georgy. It felt good to have the weight of his solid little body perched on his knees. He'd presented Georgy with his favourite plastic keys, and the little hands shot them straight to his mouth to start chewing on them enthusiastically.

He felt his heart clutch, thinking of the tragedy that had befallen his wayward, headstrong young cousin, who had not deserved to die so young, so brutally. Leaving his helpless child behind.

But his son has me now—me to care for him—to guard his interests, ensure his future.

'On what?'

Lyn's thin voice dispersed his memory, his vehement thoughts. He took a breath, focusing on what she'd said, this woman he'd met only the day before whom he was now telling he wanted to marry.

And then divorce again as soon as possible.

'Well, I guess whatever is the minimum time needed, really. I'm not sure what the law is—or if it's different in Greece from here. Obviously the adoption has to go through first, since that's the whole reason for getting married.'

Lyn frowned. 'I think there are laws about not getting married…well, *artificially*. You know—the law says it has to be a genuine marriage.' She swallowed uneasily.

Anatole did not seem fazed. 'Well, it will be, won't it? We will genuinely get married in order to provide security for our orphaned relative. I don't see any problem with that.'

The problem, thought Lyn wildly, was in the very idea of her marrying Anatole Telonidis at all! She swallowed again. 'When…when would it actually happen? The—um—wedding?'

'Ah…' he answered. 'Well, again, I believe there are legal timescales—and, again, I don't know what the law is here on how soon a couple can marry.' His eyes moved to her and held hers. 'The thing is, we will need to marry in Greece. Timon,' he said, 'is not well enough to travel.'

'Greece…' echoed Lyn, her voice hollow.

Anatole's mouth quirked, and Lyn felt that little pulse go through her, as it had when she had first seen humour lighten his face.

'You speak of my country as though it were the far side of the moon,' he said wryly.

'I—I've never been there,' she answered.

'Then you are in for a pleasant surprise. My grandfather lives outside Athens, within commuting distance, on the coast. His villa is at the shoreline, with its own beach, where Marcos and I used to play as children when we visited our grandfather. What I suggest is that you and I make our base not in the main villa—which is massive and very old-fashioned—but in the beach house, which is much more manageable and also goes straight out onto the sand beyond the terrace. It will be ideal for Georgy.'

His voice had warmed and Lyn tried to sound appreciative. 'That would be nice...' she said.

Nice—the word echoed in Anatole's head. Yes, Timon's palatial villa with its luxuriously appointed beach house set in extensive private gardens would indeed be 'nice' for someone whose current accommodation was a cramped, dingy furnished flat in a hideous sixties concrete block...

'Does that reassure you?' he asked.

No! she wanted to shout. *No. Absolutely nothing about this insane idea reassures me!*

But what was the point of saying that? Of course the idea was insane and absurd and outrageous—but Anatole Telonidis was taking it seriously. Talking about it as if it were really going to happen.

Am I really going to go through with this? Go through with marriage to a man I never knew existed forty-eight hours ago?

A man she was a million miles removed from—a man who lived in the distant stratosphere of the rich, while she was an impecunious student struggling along the breadline.

It wasn't as if she were like Lindy, she thought bitterly. Lindy with her lovely blonde hair, her blue eyes and curvaceous figure. No wonder she'd drawn the philandering eye of Marcos Petranakos when she'd lived in London. If Lyn had possessed Lindy's looks she wouldn't feel so abysmally awkward, sitting here talking about something as intimate as marriage to a man like Anatole Telonidis.

But it won't be 'intimate' will it? she castigated herself roundly. *If it's absurd and insane to think of marrying him, it's beyond either to think of anything at all beyond the merest formality. It will be a marriage in name only, solely and simply for the purpose of safeguarding Georgy.*

She and Anatole would be presenting a united front to convince the adoption authorities that they were the best possible parents for him. And if they didn't present a united front...if Anatole applied for Georgy entirely on his own...

Fear stabbed at her. If that happened then he would inevitably discover what she must not let him find out...

Must not!

'Lyn?'

His deep, accented voice interrupted her troubled emotions. She jerked her head up and felt the impact of his gaze, felt the flurry in her veins that came as his eyes rested on her, his look enquiring.

'Are we agreed?' he asked. 'Have I convinced you that this is the very best possible step for us to take?'

She bit her lip. She wanted time—time to think, to focus! But how would that help? The longer she delayed, prevaricated, the more likely it was that Anatole Telonidis would get impatient and set his lawyers to the task of making a formal application to adopt Georgy himself.

She took a breath, ragged and uneven. 'OK,' she said. 'OK, I'll do it.'

CHAPTER FIVE

Lyn gazed around her. The room Anatole Telonidis had ushered her into, Georgy clutched in her arms, was huge. Pale pristine carpet stretched in front of her, upon which was set cream-upholstered sofas and armchairs. Vast picture windows took up one entire wall, looking out over one of London's West End parks. It couldn't have been more different from her cramped little flat. Yet it was where she was going to stay until she went to Athens.

To marry Anatole Telonidis.

She felt the familiar eddy of shock go through her as she faced up to what she had agreed to. But it was too late now—the decision had been made. She had quit her college course, moved out of her flat, travelled down to London with Anatole in his chauffeur-driven car, and her personal belongings had been conveyed by carrier.

He had taken charge of everything, sweeping her along with him so that she hardly knew what was happening any more—except that it was an overturning of everything familiar. Now he turned to look at her as she stared at the luxury apartment he'd rented.

'Come and choose which bedroom you want for you and Georgy,' he said, and led the way back out in to the spacious hallway, off which several bedrooms opened. She knew which one she would choose—whichever was furthest away from the master bedroom, where Anatole would be.

A flush went through her. How on earth was she to live in such close quarters with a man who was a complete stranger to her? And, worse than that, a man who was, when it came to physical attributes, a million miles away from her nondescript appearance.

What on earth does that matter? she robustly admonished herself as she inspected the bedrooms. As she kept reminding herself, hoping to be reassured, theirs was to be a marriage in name only, solely for the purpose of adopting Georgy, placating the authorities.

Anatole was speaking again, and she made herself listen.

'There is a gym and a swimming pool for residents in the basement. The park is accessible directly from the apartment block, which will be convenient for taking Georgy out. The apartment is fully serviced, so all meals can be delivered as in a hotel. Plus, of course, groceries and anything else you want can be delivered too. Obviously there's a maid service, so you won't have any housework to do.' He took a breath and then went on. 'Order whatever you want for Georgy by way of equipment, toys and clothes. Everything can be taken out to Greece when we go. A credit card will be delivered to you shortly, and I am arranging for a new bank account for you, into which I will pay sufficient funds for you to draw on.'

He paused, and looked at her. She seemed to be taking it in, but it was hard to tell. She had scarcely opened her mouth. Well, she was still in a state of shock, he conceded. Her life had been turned upside down, and she was trying to come to terms with it. Just as he was....

For a treacherous moment he heard his inner voice remonstrating with him, telling him that it was insane to do what he was doing, but he silenced it. There was no

backing out now. Not for him—or her. They just had to
get on with it.

He made his voice soften. 'It's strange for you, I know,'
he said, taking a step towards her. 'But you will get used to
things soon enough. I am sorry I have to leave you straight
away, but it is necessary. I have to see my grandfather and
talk to his doctors about what treatment he might be able
to have. I have to tell him our plans and urge him to make
Georgy his heir, put me in charge of the Petranakos Corporation as soon as possible. Then I have to attend to some
urgent business affairs of my own, which have been neglected since I flew to England. In the meantime,' he finished, 'my lawyers are liaising with your social services
on an application for Georgy's passport and permission
to take him out of the country, as well as everything to do
with our forthcoming marriage and how it can accelerate
the adoption process. I'll only be in Athens a couple of
days. Then I will come right back here.'

He smiled at her in a way he hoped was reassuring. 'I'm
sure that you will be feeling more settled by then. You
have my personal mobile number, so of course do phone
whenever you want if there is anything that worries you.'

A little burst of hysteria bubbled through Lyn. *You mean
like anything other than the fact I'm actually going to go
ahead and marry you?*

But there was no point saying that. No point doing anything other than nod and clutch Georgy more tightly to her.

'Good,' said Anatole briskly, and lifted his hand to
take Georgy's outstretched fingers. This tiny bundle of
humanity was what was bringing him and this alien female
together. His expression softened. He murmured some in-
fantile nonsense to the baby in Greek, then shifted his gaze
to the woman holding him.

'It will be all right,' he said. 'Trust me—please.'

He flickered a brief smile at her, and a warmer one at

Georgy, who was trying to get at his tie again. 'Uh-uh,' he said reprovingly, and chucked him under the chin. 'Be good, young man, and look after your aunt for me,' he instructed.

Georgy gazed at him wide-eyed. Lyn gave an awkward smile.

'See you at the weekend,' said Anatole, and headed for the door.

Behind him, Lyn slowly sank down on to one of the pristine sofas.

She felt completely numb.

Over the next two days she gradually started to feel less numb—less in shock. And gradually, too, she became used to her new surroundings. Although she was worried Georgy might make a mess of the pristine decor, she could not help but find the luxury, warmth and comfort of the apartment very easy to appreciate after the privations of her dingy flat. The milder air of the capital drew her out to the park, with Georgy enthroned in a brand-new, top-of-the-range buggy delivered from a top London store.

She was just returning from such an outing on her third day in the apartment, wheeling Georgy into the spacious hallway, when she realised she was not alone.

Anatole strolled out of the living room.

Immediately Georgy crowed with delight and recognition, holding out his chubby arms. Lyn's senses reeled as she took in Anatole's tall, elegant figure and dark good-looks. He was wearing a suit but had discarded the jacket, loosened his shirt collar and cuffs. The effect of the slight informality of his appearance made her stomach tighten. He looked lean and powerful and devastatingly masculine.

He glanced a smile of greeting at her, and hunkered down to extract Georgy. Hefting him out, he held him up and swung him high in both hands. He greeted him in Greek, then did likewise, in English, to Lyn.

'Hi,' she murmured awkwardly, and busied herself folding up the buggy and putting it away in the hall cupboard.

She let Anatole keep Georgy and, taking off her baggy jacket and hanging it up beside the buggy, followed them into the living room. It was no longer quite as pristine as it had once been. One sofa had been covered by a fleecy throw—more to protect its pale covers than to protect Georgy—on the thick carpet another throw was spread out, arrayed with a good selection of Georgy's toys.

She watched Anatole carefully lower the baby down on to the floor, where Georgy gleefully seized upon one of his soft toys.

Anatole stood back, watching him. His mood was resolute. The time he'd spent in Greece had seen to that. His grandfather was a changed man, summoning all his doctors and demanding the very latest drugs, determined to live now for as long as he could. Determined, too, to see his great-grandson restored to his family. Even if it required Anatole to resort to this drastic strategy to make that happen.

Timon had seemed to take a moment or two to absorb Anatole's announcement, his face blanking as if in shock, but then he had simply waved an impatient hand. 'If it keeps all the damn officials happy and speeds everything up, it's worth it,' Timon had said. Then he'd cast a sly look at his grandson. 'I take it she's got other charms than just being the boy's aunt?'

Anatole's eyes rested on the figure stiffly sitting herself down on sofa, busying herself playing with Georgy. No, the charms that Timon had been implying she might have were conspicuously absent. She still looked just as she had when he'd first set eyes on her, with her dark hair pulled back apart from some straggly bits pushed behind her ears, no make-up, and wearing a shapeless jumper and jeans that bagged at the knees. Yet as he studied her, watched her playing with Georgy, his eyes went to her face and his blighting assessment wavered.

If he dragged his gaze away from her dire hair and worse clothes he could see that her pale skin was clear and unblemished, and her grey eyes were well set beneath defined brows, sparkling now with animation as she laughed with Georgy. The shape of her face was oval, he noted, with a delicate bone structure, and there was something about the line of her mouth that held his glance...

He watched her a moment longer, resolve forming within him. She could not possibly turn up in Greece as his fiancée looking the way she did now, so badly dressed and unkempt.

Well, that could be sorted, but right now he was hungry. He hadn't eaten on the flight, and it was lunchtime. First he needed a shower, a change of clothes and to check his e-mails, and then he would take Lyn and Georgy for lunch.

And after lunch, he resolved, he would take them shopping. Toys for Georgy—new clothes for Lyn.

Everyone would be happy. Including him.

An hour later they were ready to set off. Lyn was not enthusiastic about the expedition, Anatole could tell, but she had acquiesced docilely enough. She'd changed her clothes, though the brown skirt and pale cream blouse were not a great improvement, to his mind. The skirt was overlong and the blouse too baggy. But that didn't matter—after lunch she would be getting a whole new wardrobe.

Over lunch, his sense of resolve strengthened. He would start getting to know her. There must be no awkwardness between them. Georgy united them, and that meant they could not remain strangers. Little by little he had to win her over, get her to relax in his company.

Get her to trust him.

But she was clearly feeling awkward and totally un-relaxed—that much was obvious to him as they made their way into the restaurant he'd selected. A few diners cast disapproving glances at Georgy in his carrier as they took their seats, but since he was looking both angelic and deeply slumberous no one said anything.

Lyn sat down on the plush banquette, feeling acutely uncomfortable. Her dull, chainstore clothes were com-pletely out of place in such an expensive locale, but there was nothing she could do about it. Since she didn't look like the kind of woman a man like Anatole Telonidis would socialise with, there was no point making an idiot of her-self by trying to and failing.

Anatole took charge, ordering drinks and food. Lyn stared around her uneasily, unused to such expensive sur-roundings. She jumped as the wine waiter reappeared and opened a bottle of champagne with a soft pop.

The effervescent liquid was poured out, and as the waiter departed with a bow Anatole lifted his glass. 'Let us drink to Georgy's future,' he said.

He was trying to be encouraging, she could see. Gin-gerly, Lyn raised her glass and took a nervous sip. It tasted very dry, and the bubbles burst on her tongue with a slightly acerbic texture. She set the glass down.

'You don't care for it?' Anatole's voice sounded sur-prised. It was an excellent vintage.

'Sorry, the only fizzy wine I've ever had before has been very sweet,' Lyn apologised.

'This is not "fizzy wine",' said Anatole severely. 'This is champagne.'

Lyn flushed. 'I'm sorry,' she mumbled again.

'There is absolutely no need for apology,' he said promptly.

He started on an explanation of what constituted cham-pagne, and Lyn found herself listening attentively. It wasn't a subject that had ever crossed her path before. As she listened she took some more little sips of the crisp, sparkling liquid, and as she sipped she started to feel that taut wire of tension running down her spine lessening almost imperceptibly.

Their first course arrived—little *rondelles* of salmon pâté lightened with a lemon *jus*—and Lyn found them delicious.

From champagne, Anatole broadened out into discussing wine in general. It seemed a pretty safe topic, in the circumstances.

'Even here in the UK you are starting to produce some very acceptable white wines,' he commented.

'It was the Romans, I think, who first planted vines in Britain,' Lyn ventured. She had to make some kind of effort with conversation. She owed it to Anatole to make this intensely awkward meal less awkward. 'The climate was warmer then—the Roman Warm Period that ended around 400 AD.'

Anatole's expression registered surprise. 'That's very detailed historical knowledge for someone studying accountancy,' he said.

'I really wanted to study history,' Lyn explained diffidently. 'But it's not the best subject for post-graduate employment—especially not since I already count as a mature student, being in my mid-twenties now. Accountancy's far more likely to earn me a good enough living to raise Georgy—' She broke off, conscious that Georgy's financial future was very different now.

'Well, Greece has more history than anywhere else in Europe,' Anatole said. 'And a great deal of it is in Athens.' He spoke lightly, steering the conversation towards classical Greek history. The champagne, he could tell, was starting to help her relax, become more talkative.

'How did you find the service dining in the apartment while I was in Greece?' he enquired as they ate.

She looked up. 'Oh, I haven't used it. It's bound to be very expensive. I've found a small grocery store locally, down a side street, so I've been cooking for myself and Georgy.'

'You really do not have to stint yourself when it comes to the facilities of the apartment,' Anatole said dryly. 'Tell me, have you taken Georgy swimming in the pool?'

She shook her head. 'Not yet,' she said.

'We shall buy him some pool toys this afternoon,' Anatole said. 'All sorts of toys,' he added expansively while he was at it.

Lyn brightened. 'Oh, yes, please—that would be wonderful! He really needs some that are more advanced for the next stage of his development.' She smiled. 'He's very nearly ready to crawl, and when that happens he's going to take off like a rocket!'

The conversation moved on to Georgy, the subject of their mutual interest and the reason for their marriage. As if hearing his name mentioned, Georgy decided to surface from his slumber. Enlivened by his sleep, he made it clear he wanted out of his carrier and into Lyn's arms. Settling him on her lap, she busied herself feeding him from a pot of baby yoghurt she'd thought to bring with her in between taking sips of coffee to finish her meal.

Then, replete and ready for the off, they left—Georgy borne happily aloft as they exited the restaurant, his little arms waving cheerily at what he fondly took to be his admiring fellow diners. Settled into the waiting chauffeured car, they set off for the shops.

The department store they went to was, Lyn resigned herself to accept, one of London's most expensive and luxurious. Since the buggy and baby carrier had been delivered from there, she was not surprised that Anatole seemed to regard it as the obvious place to shop. Certainly the toy department was lavish beyond anything—and so, she very shortly realised, was Anatole's determination to purchase a substantial amount from the infant section of it, much of it way too advanced for Georgy.

'He can't possibly do a fifty-piece jigsaw!' Lyn exclaimed. 'He needs toys that say nine to twelve months— that's all.'

Anatole frowned. 'He is a very intelligent child,' he observed.

'Nine to twelve months,' Lyn repeated firmly. 'Look— that thing there is ideal!'

She pointed to a large moulded plastic construction, a colourful house and farmyard, with big doors and windows and a roof that all came to bits and slotted together again. Around the perimeter was a railway track with a train and truck, containing people and animals for the house and farmyard. A large, baby-operable lever set the train whizzing around the house, ringing a bell as it did so. Lyn demonstrated its mode of operation on the display model and instantly caught Georgy's attention.

Anatole promptly lifted down a boxed unit. 'What else?' he said, looking around him.

Lyn found herself guiding him through the selection process. It felt awkward, initially, having to be so proactive, but she soon realised that she knew a lot more about what was suitable than Anatole did. He deferred to her without demur, and gradually she found that it was getting easier to be in his company like this. It was even, she realised, enjoyable. And Georgy took such enthusiastic interest in this Aladdin's cave of toys, as well as clearly relishing the presence of lots of other babies and infants, that she found her eyes meeting Anatole's as they shared Georgy's enjoyment.

But that sense of communication ended abruptly as they left the toy department.

'While we are here, Lyn, I would like to look in at the women's fashion floor,' Anatole said.

She halted. 'What for?'

He looked down at her face. She had tensed immediately and her expression was wary. Carefully, he sought the right way to say what he wanted.

'I appreciate that your circumstances till now have been straitened financially,' he began, keeping his tone neutral, 'and of course you have had a great deal to cope with, looking after Georgy while pursuing your studies. I can understand those have been your priorities. Now, however, things are different.' He took a breath. 'New clothes for your new life—'

'I don't need any new clothes!'

'Lyn, you need a whole new wardrobe,' he said.

'No, I don't! It's fine as it is! *Really!*'

He could hear the intensity in her voice and found himself wondering at it. Didn't she want something better to wear than what she had to put up with?

'Please,' she went on, with the same intensity in her voice, 'I don't want you spending money on me!'

His mouth pressed tightly. 'Lyn, you are going to be my wife—of *course* I will spend money on you! I have quite a lot to spend,' he reminded her. 'I don't mean to sound extravagant, and I know you have had to be very careful with money—I have a great deal of respect for you for that—but now things are different.' He paused. 'Don't you *want* to have a new wardrobe? I thought new clothes were something all women wanted!' He put a note of humour into his voice, as if to lighten the tension.

It didn't work. She was staring at him, and her expression remained fraught. Did he really think lashing out on expensive clothes would actually do anything for her? Of

course it wouldn't! She would just feel awkward and embarrassed and horrible!

'I'm fine with what I've got,' she managed to get out.

Dark flashes glinted in Anatole's eyes, but he veiled
them. She might be fine with what she had, but he was
not—it was absurd for her to be dressed the way she was.
But he took a silent breath. For now he would not pressure her.

'OK,' he said, holding up his hand. 'If that's truly what
you prefer.'

'It is,' she said gratefully. Then, casting about to change
the subject, she said hurriedly, 'But what I *do* need, however, is some more clothes for Georgy—he's growing rapidly.' She hesitated. 'I'm sure the baby clothes here will
be very expensive—I can get them much cheaper else-
where, so—'

'Here is fine, Lyn,' Anatole interrupted her firmly, and
set off towards babywear, next to the toy department.

Lyn hurried after him, pushing the buggy. She felt weak
at the narrow escape she'd had. It would have been unen-
durable to go down to the fashion department and have
some snooty vendeuse look pityingly at her while she tried
on designer fashions to try and conceal her nondescript
looks. She would have writhed with embarrassment and
self-consciousness!

Instead, all she had to do now was try not to blanch
when she looked at the price tags on the baby clothes that
Anatole was holding up for her inspection. If he was going
to spend his money at least it would be on Georgy, not her,
so she made little objection. Nor did she object when, purchases made, Anatole had them taken down to his chauffeured car. Then, turning to Lyn, he suggested they find
the store's tea lounge.

As she sat herself down on a soft banquette, tea ordered

from the waitress and Anatole amusing Georgy with one of his smaller new toys, she found herself observing them.

Emotion moved within her. He was so good with Georgy—naturally attentive and responsive, clearly enjoying interacting with him—and Georgy, too, was clearly enjoying being with Anatole.

That's why I'm doing this, she reminded herself fiercely. *For Georgy's sake!*

Yet even as she said the words in her head she knew, somewhere deep inside her, a little ache had started up, as she gazed at the man holding her beloved Georgy. What if there were no Georgy and Anatole Telonidis, with his amazing looks, his dark, expressive eyes, his lean strength and honed physique, were going to marry her not because of an orphaned baby but for herself alone?

Even as the thought formed she squashed it flat.

Without Georgy Anatole Telonidis would never even have looked her way…

That was what she had to remember. Only that—however crushing the knowledge.

With a silent little sigh, she got on with drinking her tea.

CHAPTER SIX

OVER THE WEEKEND she slowly got used to Anatole being in such close quarters with her. She took Georgy out into the park a lot, now the weather was more clement, leaving Anatole to work, as he told her he must, for he had a lot to catch up with. The apartment had an office, and Anatole disappeared in there, focusing on his laptop and phone. The plan was, he told her, to go to Athens as soon as Georgy had his passport issued and was cleared to leave the country with his foster carer.

'Hopefully,' Anatole had said over dinner that first night, 'my legal team will be able to put sufficient pressure on the authorities to expedite matters. As for Timon—he's now starting treatment, and we must hope that it takes effect. He'll stay in hospital for the time being, since these drugs have side effects he may find it difficult to tolerate and he is an old man in his eighties. But soon—within a few weeks, I very much hope—he will be discharged and able to come home again. And once he's home...' he smiled at Lyn '...we can get on with getting married.'

He paused, looking at her. Her expression was tense again.

'Lyn,' he said, with deliberate lightness, 'this is your *wedding* we're planning—'

'It's not a real one,' she said, and then wished she hadn't. She hadn't wanted to imply that she wanted a *real* wedding to Anatole Telondis! It would be excruciatingly embarrassing if he thought that!

But all he said was, 'Well, it's going to be a happy occasion, anyway. It will secure Georgy's future, and that is what we want.' He took a breath, his expression changing somewhat. 'That said, it can't be a large wedding, as I'm sure you'll understand. That would be…inappropriate, given how recently Marcos died.'

'Of course,' Lyn said immediately, and knew she was grateful not to have to face some huge society bash. That would be as embarrassing as Anatole thinking she wanted her marriage to him to be a real one.

This is all about Georgy—only about Georgy! That's all I have to remember!

Even so, until they were able to divorce she would have to go through with being in such close quarters with Anatole as she was now. It was becoming easier, she'd discovered gratefully. He was obviously making a real effort to try and get her to feel more comfortable, to draw her out and get to know her. It felt awkward for her, but she did her best to co-operate.

'Tell me,' he went on now, moving on from the subject of their wedding, 'why did you not go to college straight after school?'

'Well, it wasn't really possible,' Lyn answered. 'Lindy was only fourteen, and I couldn't leave her.'

Anatole looked mildly surprised. 'You were so devoted to her?'

Lyn swallowed. 'She needed someone to look after her. My mother—well, she wasn't very good at doing that. She'd ended up single, despite marrying twice, because both her husbands abandoned her. After that she spent most of her time in the pub, if I'm honest about it, and I didn't want Lindy to be a latchkey kid, so I stayed at home and did the housekeeping, cooking and so on. By the time Lindy left school Mum was ill. All the years of heavy smoking and drinking too much caught up with her finally, so I stayed to nurse her until the end. Lindy took a job in a wine bar and then, just after Mum died, took off with a girlfriend to London and lived in a flat share, worked in a flash West End wine bar. That's where she met your cousin.' She took a breath. 'When she realised she was pregnant she came back home, just as I was finally about to set off to university as a mature student. Of course I couldn't abandon her then...'

Anatole was silent a moment. A strange sense of recognition went through him. She had shouldered responsibilities not of her making—and he, too, was shouldering responsibilities he could have walked away from. Responsibilities that had brought him to this point: about to embark on a marriage to a woman he would never have known existed had it not been for the baby he'd set out to find...

But it was because of that baby—the baby who had stolen his heart already—that he was doing what he was doing now. The baby was all that was left of his young cousin, all the hope left to his ailing grandfather.

And I will see him right, whatever that takes!

His eyes went to the woman across the table from him. She'd opened up to him just now, more than she had yet done, so he knew he was making progress in gradually getting her to relax, getting her to feel less tense. Getting her to trust him.

He worked away at his goal assiduously, little by little making her feel more comfortable in his company.

Dinner on his second night back in London was a little easier than the preceding one. The main topic of conversation was Georgy, and Anatole could see that when Lyn talked about her nephew her eyes lit up, her face lost its pallor, and the animation in her expression made her seem noticeably more attractive. He found his curiosity as to what grooming and decent clothes might do for her intensifying. He found it curious that she seemed to be so reluctant to be made over. Most women, as he knew perfectly well, would have adored the prospect!

He'd backed off from pressing her the day before, when they'd been in the department store, but that evening he did no such thing.

'How did your swim go this afternoon?' he enquired at dinner, having spent the day working via his laptop. 'You said at breakfast you would take Georgy down to the pool. Did he enjoy the new pool toys we bought him?' he asked encouragingly.

Her reply confounded him.

'Um…the man at the desk said…' Lyn's voice tailed off. What the man at the desk had said still made her squirm.

'Sorry, love. Pool's for residents only. Nannies don't count—even if they have their charges with them.'

'Yes? The man at he desk said…?' Anatole prompted.

'Well, I think he thought I was Georgy's nanny,' she explained reluctantly.

An explosive noise came from Anatole and his expression darkened.

Immediately Lyn tried to mitigate the situation. 'It's very understandable,' she said. 'I know I don't look like I'm a resident here, so—'

'So *nothing*, Lyn!' Anatole's voice was firm. 'I trust you told the man who you were?'

She coloured. 'Um…no. It was a bit…a bit embarrassing. And I didn't want to make a fuss. He was only doing his job.'

He gave an exasperated sigh. 'Lyn, you must surely see that this cannot continue! Tomorrow I am taking you shopping for clothes and that is that!'

She nodded numbly. Clearly Anatole's patience was at an end. Well, she thought resolutely, not all rich women were beautiful, but they still wore expensive clothes. Now so would she.

'Good,' he said. He smiled at her encouragingly. 'Most women, Lyn, adore clothes-shopping!'

She gave a constrained smile in return, saying nothing. Thankfully, he let the topic go, and suggested they take their coffee into the lounge.

She set the coffee tray on a low table between the sofas and took a seat on the sofa opposite Anatole. He was wearing casual grey trousers and a beautiful soft cashmere jumper, the sleeves of which he now pushed back, revealing strong, tanned forearms. Immediately, Lyn made herself look away.

'Would you like any music?' she asked, for Anatole had not turned the TV on.

'Some Mozart, perhaps?' Anatole suggested, stretching out his arms along the back of the sofa and hooking one long leg casually over his thigh as he relaxed back.

The soft sweater stretched, moulding his torso. Punishingly conscious of his intense masculinity, she crossed to the music deck and made a suitable selection.

The scintillating tones of the *Linz Symphony* started to resonate through the room and she came back and resumed her place, curling her legs up under her and prudently removing several of Georgy's discarded toys from under various cushions, where he'd stuffed them earlier.

She leant forward to pour out the coffee. Black and unsweetened for Anatole. She knew that now. For herself, weak and milky. She proffered the cup to him and he reached a long arm forward to scoop it up.

As he did so his fingers touched hers. Jerking, she nearly dropped the saucer, but managed to avoid it, recoiling into her seat swiftly. She knew two spots of colour were in her cheeks. Covertly, she flicked her eyes across to

the man opposite her. Large table lamps stood either side
of the sofa, throwing a pool of soft light over him.

He is just so gorgeous-looking.

It dominated her consciousness, that constant awareness of his physical magnetism. A magnetism he seemed
to be unconscious of himself. Or he just took it for granted,
probably, she realised. If you grew up with looks like that
you *did* take them for granted.

No wonder he wants me to look better than I do!

She bit her lip. Surely once she had got some smart
clothes, done her hair, that sort of thing, she would look
better than she did now? Not much, she knew dispiritedly,
and certainly not enough to put her anywhere near Anatole's league, but surely better?

It was a hope that had to sustain her when, the next
morning, back once again in the very swish department
store in the West End they'd been to previously, Anatole
went with her to the instore beauty salon.

'Hair and all the treatments first,' he told her decisively,
'then clothes and accessories. And while you're doing
that...' he smiled reassuringly '...I'll take Georgy back to
the Aladdin's Cave of the toy department.'

'He'll love that,' said Lyn, trying to hide her nervous-
ness as the receptionist hovered, ready to usher her into
the inner sanctum and the treatment rooms.

'When you're all done we'll go for lunch,' Anatole said,
and then, with a final reassuring smile, he wheeled Georgy
off.

'This way, madam,' said the receptionist, and Lyn was
led away to her fate.

Anatole was enjoying himself. So was Georgy, nestled in
the protective crook of Anatole's arm and gazing in openmouthed delight at the miniature trains hurtling around
the elaborate track layout of the vast display centrepiece

of the store's toy department. Anatole was giving an explanation of the finer points of rail transport to him, which would probably have drawn indulgent amusement from the other shoppers present, being way too technical for a baby of Georgy's age, had it not been conducted in Greek.

Following Georgy's butterfly attention span, Anatole diverted towards the array of soft toys nearby, drawing the buggy along single-handed. A brief, if one-sided discussion with Georgy as to which soft toy he liked best of all resulted in Georgy becoming the highly satisfied owner of a floppy-limbed teddy bear almost as large as he was, and they set off for yet another circuit of the huge toy department. From time to time Anatole glanced at his watch, but he knew Lyn would not be ready yet.

What would she look like when she emerged? he wondered. He found it hard to envisage. He'd had little glimpses, sometimes, of what she *might* look like—when she wasn't looking tense and reserved and awkward.

But he wanted more than glimpses.

He glanced at his watch again impatiently.

'What about this one?' The stylist's voice was encouraging. 'It will turn heads,' she said enthusiastically, holding up a dress in fuchsia silk jersey.

Lyn stared uneasily.

Sensing it was too bright for her diffident client, the stylist immediately swapped the vivid dress for the same model in a soft coral instead.

'Or this one?' she asked.

'Um…OK,' said Lyn, nodding gratefully. Turning heads was not what she wanted to do—that was far too scary a thought.

But then this whole experience had been scary. For the last two hours she'd been subjected to one beauty treatment after another, and now—finally—with hair, nails and make-up all done, it was time to choose new clothes. The beautifully made dress slipped easily over her and the stylist got to work smoothing it and fastening it, then standing back to view her efforts. Lyn stood meekly, reluctant to look at herself in the mirror. A lot of effort had gone into improving her, and she was not at all sure about the results...

'Now—shoes,' said the stylist, and went to consult the trolley full of shoeboxes that had accompanied the dress rack. She pulled out a pair and held them momentarily against the fabric of the dress, then nodded. 'Yes, these are the ones.'

She helped Lyn into them, even though her client was looking at them, alarmed.

They had a high heel and a very narrow fitting. Yet they felt surprisingly comfortable on—presumably a sign of how scarily expensive they were. But it wasn't her place to object to any of this vast expenditure, so she said nothing. Nor did she say anything when she was presented with a matching clutch and, as a final touch, a piece of costume jewellery consisting of a couple of linked chunks of a copper-coloured stones was draped around her throat.

The stylist stepped back. 'There!' she exclaimed. 'Ready to roll.'

Even as she spoke another member of staff put her head around the door behind her. 'Mr Telonidis is at Reception,' she said.

'Just in time.' The stylist smiled at Lyn.

Stiltedly, Lyn smiled back. 'Um...thank you very much for everything,' she said.

'My pleasure,' said the woman.

Her voice was warm, and Lyn knew she was trying to be encouraging.

'I do hope you're pleased with the results.'

'The clothes and accessories are beautiful,' Lyn assured her, feeling awkward. Then she turned away from the window she'd been standing next to, doggedly staring out over the London skyline beyond, ready to go out and face the man she was going to marry and hope—just hope—that all the money he'd spent on her had not been completely wasted!

As she turned a woman came into view and Lyn halted. Where had *she* come from? She hadn't heard the door open again. She must be the stylist's next client. Curiously, she seemed to be wearing a very similar dress to the one the woman had put on her. Maybe it was a favourite of the stylist's, she thought, confused. It certainly looked wonderful on the other woman, with the soft neckline draping over her bust and the dress lightly skimming her slim hips. The total image was one of effortless chic, from her beautifully cut hair to the elegant high heels and soft clutch handbag.

She gave herself a mental shake. She couldn't stand here gawping. The other woman obviously wanted her to vacate the room, as she was still standing there expectantly. Lyn took a step forward, wavering slightly on the high heels she wasn't used to, and saw the woman step towards her as well.

As if her brain cells were ungluing painfully, the truth dawned on her.

Oh, my God, it's me!

She stopped dead, frozen and motionless. Just staring. Her reflection—because of course, as her brain cells had belatedly worked out, that was what it was—stared back.

The stylist was by the door, holding it open for her, and numbly Lyn walked through and went out into the reception area.

Anatole was there, leaning over Georgy in his buggy, but he straightened as she emerged.

Then, in front of her eyes, he too froze. And stared.

'Lyn?' The disbelief in his voice was evident—he

couldn't hide it—but it was impossible to believe what his eyes were telling him. That the woman walking up to him had once been the drab, badly dressed female he'd handed over earlier. That woman was gone. Totally gone.

And she is never coming back!

The thought seared unbidden through his brain. Unbidden, but undeletable. That old version of Lyn was gone for ever! But this one—oh, *this* one could stay as long as she liked!

From deep inside him came an ancient, powerful emotion. Whatever it was that was calling it from him—the lissom lines of a figure he'd never had the faintest idea was underneath her old shapeless clothes, or the silky swing of freshly styled hair that had been released from its customary straggly knot and now skimmed her slender shoulders—his eyes narrowed infinitesimally as his masculine assessment moved to her face. Quite extraordinarily, the skilfully applied make-up now finally revealed her features—no longer muted but defined, enhanced...

Her eyes! Clear, wide-set, luminous. With delicately arched brows and their sockets softly deepened, the lashes richly lush. And her mouth—yet again Anatole felt all his male hormones kicking in powerfully—her mouth was as tender and inviting as a budding rose.

He murmured something in Greek. He didn't even know what it was, but it was repeating itself in his head as he finally gelled into movement. He stepped towards her and reached for her hand—the one that wasn't clutching a soft leather handbag as if it were a life-preserver—drew her towards him.

'You look fantastic!' he breathed.

His eyes worked over her. And over her again. Disbelief was still not quite dissipated. He took a step back again, and looked again still keeping her hand in his, try-

ing to take in what exactly had been done to her. It was…
everything! That was all he could think. Just…everything.

And yet it must have been there all along…

That was the most remarkable aspect of all. That underneath that wouldn't-look-once-let-alone-twice image there had been *this* waiting to be revealed.

He went on staring—oblivious, for now, of the fact that the expression on her face had reverted to the kind of stiff, self-conscious, tense awkward one she had had right at the beginning, when she hadn't been able to relax in his company even an iota.

Then, breaking into his studied scrutiny, he heard Georgy demanding attention.

Dropping Anatole's hand, Lyn jerked forward. Thank God for Georgy! Thank God for her being able to escape that jet-powered, laser-intense gaze focused on her like that…

She hunkered down beside Georgy and started to make a fuss of him. Behind her Anatole finally surfaced and, with a start, stepped towards the counter to settle up. As he handed over his credit card it came to him that never had his money been better spent. He turned back to Lyn and another wash of disbelief hit him—followed by a very strong male response.

'Time for lunch, I think,' he said as he took the buggy handles and executed a neat turn of the wheels. His voice was warm with satisfaction.

They lunched at the same swish restaurant they had before. Anatole reckoned that Lyn would probably prefer a familiar place. Though this time she looked like a totally different woman! His feeling of satisfaction intensified. Yes, he had done the right thing—absolutely the right thing—in insisting on her having a makeover. To think that this elegant, soigné woman he could not take his eyes off had been there all along! He still found it hard to credit. What he did *not* find hard, however, was having her sitting opposite him like this. It meant he could study her in detail, take in every last dramatic improvement.

The only problem, to his mind, was that she seemed so ill at ease. He wondered why, and asked her right out.

She stared at him as if he had asked a really stupid question. Which, to her mind, he had. Of *course* she was feeling awkward and self-conscious! She'd felt that way when she'd looked awful—badly dressed and shabby—and now she felt that way when she looked the exact opposite! For exactly the same reason.

Because he makes me feel excruciatingly self-conscious all the time! Because I'm just so punishingly and constantly aware of how devastating he is! Because I just want to gaze and gaze at him, but I can't, because that would be the most embarrassing thing in all the world!

The stark truth blazed through her: Anatole Telonidis the man—not the millionaire, nor the man who was Georgy's father's cousin, nor the man she was marrying so she could keep the baby she adored—who sat there, effortlessly devastating from the top of his sable-haired head right down through the long, lean length of his body, was a man who could have an effect on her senses no other man had ever had.

That was why she could only sit there, quivering in every limb, unable to make eye contact, feeling so totally and utterly aware of him on every female frequency any woman could possess!

His sloe-dark expressive eyes were resting on her, expecting some kind of answer to his question. She had to say something. Anything.

'Um…' she managed, fiddling with her cutlery with fingers whose tips were now beautifully shaped with varnished nails. 'I guess I'm just getting used to being all dressed up like this.'

And to being stared at. Not just by you, but by everyone as I walked in here. And not just because we've got Georgy with us. This time they are staring at me, too, and I'm not used to it. It's never happened to me in my life before and I feel so, so conspicuous!

'You are not used to being beautiful,' Anatole answered, his expression softening. 'Don't poker up again. I said beautiful,' he told her, 'and I meant it.'

And he did, too. Her beauty, so newly revealed, was not flashy or flaunting. No, it was subtle and graceful. He wanted to gaze at it, study it.

Enjoy it.

But it was clear she was finding that difficult. Goodness knew why, but she was.

Ever mindful of her sensitivities, he made an effort to stop gazing at her, but it was almost impossible. Thoughts rippled through his head as he made that realisation, eddying and swirling out of the depths of his consciousness. Something was changing, something about the way he was thinking about her—but he couldn't give time to it. Not right now. He would think about it later. Right now he wanted her to feel comfortable. To enjoy lunch with him.

He gave her a smile. The kind he was used to giving her. Kindly and encouraging.

'What do you think you'd like to eat today?' he asked.

He started to go through the menu with her, and the exercise gave them both some time to regroup mentally. So did Georgy's requirements. He'd already had his lunch, in the children's café in the store's toy department. He'd relished it with enthusiasm—if rather more messily than Anatole had been prepared for. But he'd mopped up Georgy—and himself and the tabletop—manfully, and then purchased another top for him to wear, which he was now sporting colourfully. Spotting it, Lyn remarked upon it, and their conversation moved on to an account of Georgy's entertainment that morning.

'Sounds like you coped really well,' said Lyn. It was her turn to be encouraging. Having sole care of an infant could be quite a challenge, but Anatole was not shy of undertaking it.

'It's a delight to be with him,' Anatole said frankly.

He smiled, catching Lyn's eyes in mutual agreement, and a little rush went through her. Oh, Anatole might look like a Greek god, and be a high-powered millionaire business tycoon from a filthy-rich top-shelf Greek dynasty, but his loving fondness for his baby second cousin shone through! It was the one indisputable shared bond between them.

'A delight,' he repeated. 'But definitely full-on!'

'Oh, yes,' said Lyn meaningfully, glancing down at Georgy in his carrier, snoozing peacefully after all the excitement of the morning.

Anatole closed the leather-bound menu with a snap. 'After lunch,' he announced, 'we shall attend to the rest of your new wardrobe. There is a great deal to buy.'

She looked startled. Anatole reached across the table to take her hand. The delicately varnished nails glowed softly, and her skin was soft and warm. It felt good to hold her hand...

'Do not look so alarmed,' he said. 'It will be fine. I promise you. Trust me.'

She gazed at him. She was trusting him with so much already. Trusting him to ensure she could keep Georgy. Trusting him to sort out all the legalities. Trusting him to know the best way to ensure Georgy would never be wrenched from her.

With a little catch in her throat, she nodded. 'I will,' she said.

For a moment their eyes met, gazes held.

Then, with an answering nod, Anatole released her hand.

'Good,' he said. 'That's exactly what I want to hear.'

CHAPTER SEVEN

'IT'S A BEAUTIFUL day. Since we can't leave for Greece yet, let's go for a drive in the country,' Anatole announced.

His mood was good—very good. It had been good ever since Lyn had walked out of the beauty salon looking so totally unlike the way she had looked before that he had scarcely been able to credit the transformation.

Now, as he smiled at her across the breakfast bar in the kitchen of the apartment, he still could hardly credit it. She was wearing one of the outfits they'd purchased the previous afternoon after their leisurely lunch, and it emphasised her amazing new look.

His eyes rested on her warmly. Georgy, securely fastened in his throne-like highchair, was waving a spoon around and blowing bubbles. But for once Anatole's primary concern was not Georgy. It was wondering just how Lyn had got away with looking so drab for so long when she could have looked the way she did this morning.

Her hair was clasped back into a loose ponytail, but the new style with its flattering colour tint made all the difference. So did the subtle, understated make-up she was wearing—little more than mascara and lipgloss, but all that was needed to turn her face from a collection of blank features into a face that had contours and depths. As for the sweater she was wearing—well, it was a million years away from the baggy items she'd used to hide herself in.

The soft lambswool jumper she had on, a light caramel, shaped her beautifully.

His eyes slid to her breasts. Before her makeover he'd never even noticed she had any.

But she does—she has beautiful rounded breasts. Slight, but well shaped...

Unbidden, the thought slid between his synapses.

What would she look like bare? Her slender body revealed to me? The sweet mounds of her breasts beneath my touch?

Joltingly he grabbed at his coffee. It was inappropriate to think in those terms.

Up till now he never had. But since her makeover those thoughts, questions, speculations had made themselves conscious in his head.

He pushed them aside.

'So, what do you think?' he said. 'Shall we get out of London today? Take Georgy out for the day?'

Lyn busied herself getting Georgy out of his highchair. The way Anatole was looking at her was making her colour.

I didn't know that was going to happen—I didn't think!

It was confusing—disturbing—to have his sloe-dark eyes resting on her like that. As if he was seeing her for the first time—for the first time as a woman...

Confusing—disturbing—making her blood pulse in her veins...

She forced her mind to focus on what he'd said—not on the effect his gaze was having on her, making her so self-conscious, making her body feel alive, somehow, in a way it never had been. Making her breasts feel fuller, rounder.

'That would be lovely!' she said brightly. 'Whereabouts do you want to go?'

'Heading south sounds good,' said Anatole.

And so it proved. Once across the girdle of the M25,

the North Downs behind them, the Weald stretched before them. With Georgy safely secured in his car seat, Lyn was seated in the passenger seat next to Anatole. She could feel her eyes drawn to the way his strong hands were shaping the wheel, his eyes focused on the road ahead. She wanted to gaze at him, drink him in.

Instead, she made herself tell him what she knew about this part of the country.

'It's called the Weald—from the Saxon word for forest— like the German *Wald*,' she said. 'It's completely rural now, but it was actually the industrial heartland of England for centuries.'

'How so?' Anatole asked, glancing at her. He wanted to go on looking, because in profile she was well worth looking at, but he had to keep his eyes on the road—which he was finding a nuisance.

'The wood was used for charcoal, and that was used for iron smelting,' she explained. 'And many of the trees were cut down for shipbuilding as well.'

She went on to talk about some of the more notable events in English history that had taken place in this part of the country.

'Including the Battle of Hastings?' Anatole said knowledgeably.

'Yes.' She sighed. 'The end of Anglo-Saxon England. The Norman Yoke was harsh to begin with, imposed on a conquered people.'

'Ah…' said Anatole, commiserating. 'Well, we Greeks know about being conquered. We spent nearly four hundred years being ruled by the Ottoman Empire.'

The conversation moved to the subject of Greece's history as the powerful car ate up the miles. From the back seat Georgy gazed contentedly out of the car window, but when they pulled over at a pleasant-looking pub for lunch he was ready to get out. The weather had warmed signif-

icantly, and they decided to risk eating in the garden—
helped in their decision by the presence of a children's
play area complete with sandpit.

'Don't let him eat the sand!' Lyn warned as Anatole
lowered him onto its fine, dry golden surface.

'Georgy, a sensible boy never eats sand!' Anatole admonished him, as the baby rashly prepared to break this
wise edict.

Memory stabbed at Lyn. In her head she heard Anatole
similarly admonishing Georgy not to eat his watch, that
first time he'd been with him.

How totally and irrevocably her life had changed since
then!

*I had no idea then that I would do what I have—that I
would be here, now, like this, with him!*

How far she had come since those first excruciatingly
painful and awkward days as her life changed beyond recognition. Her eyes rested on Anatole now, hunkered down
by the sandpit, engaging with his infant second cousin.
Emotion went through her—and not just because of the
sight of him and Georgy playing so happily, so naturally
together. So much at ease.

She was at ease with him too now. Finding his company not fraught or awkward. Well, not in the same way,
at any rate, she amended. Having her makeover had set
off that intense awkwardness again, but she was getting
used to her new look now. Finding it easier to cope with.

Enjoying it…

Because it was good to know she looked good! The nov-
elty of it had lost its terror for her, leaving only pleasure.
She'd caught sight of herself in the mirror in the ladies'
here and a little ripple of pleasure had quivered through
her. The designer jeans hugged her hips and thighs, the
ankle boots, soft and comfortable, lengthened her legs, and
the caramel lambswool jumper warmed and flattered her.

One of the young male servers came out and took their drinks order. His eyes, as he smiled down at Lyn, told her that she looked good to him too. That little ripple of pleasure came again.

From where he sat, Anatole watched Lyn interacting with the young man. It was good to see her being chilled about the effect she was having on the male population.

If she gets used to it from other men, she will get used to it from me too....

The words slid into his head and he busied himself with Georgy again, who was taking another lunge at the enticingly crunchy sand.

Lunch passed enjoyably, and afterwards they resumed their drive, finally reaching the South Downs. An airy walk on the high chalk expanse, with Georgy hoisted high on Anatole's shoulders, his little fists impaling his hair, laughing heartily, gave them some exercise. They paused at a viewpoint to look out and down over the blue glittering Channel beyond. Lyn tried to make out the coastal geography, hazarding some guesses as to what they were seeing.

'Do you know this part of England?' Anatole asked her.

'It has special memories for me,' she admitted.

Her gaze went out to the coast, and he saw a faraway look in her face—a look that was taking her back down the years.

'We came here on holiday once,' she told him. 'It was just about the only happy holiday I can remember. We stayed on a caravan park, right on the seashore, and Lindy and I were set loose to head down onto the beach every day. It was wonderful! We were so happy, I remember—so carefree! There were some beautiful houses at the far end of the bay, where the gardens opened right out onto the beach, and Lindy and I used to walk past them all and discuss which one we'd live in when we were grown up and had pots of money and no worries and cares.'

Anatole glanced at her. 'That sounds like you had a need for escapism,' he ventured, hoping she might say more.

It was good that she was starting to open up to him—to talk about her own life, herself, and Georgy's mother, too. He wanted to go on drawing her out. It was a sign that she was really starting to trust him, and he needed her to do that. The changes to her life he was imposing on her were so fundamental he did not want her shying away from them, panicking about what she was agreeing to do—bringing Georgy out to Greece and settling him there. So the more she confided in him, the more that trust would grow.

Lyn gave a little sigh. 'Yes, I suppose it *was* escapism, really. I remember that sometimes after that holiday, when things were particularly grim at home, I used to let myself fantasise that Lindy and I had run away to live in one of those lovely seaside houses on the beach—far away from the stress and strain of coping with Mum and all that went with her...'

'Was it *so* difficult when you were growing up?' he asked, his voice sympathetic.

She made a face. 'Well, I know many children have it loads, loads worse! But even so...for Lindy and me it was—well, difficult. That word you used fits the description.' She took a breath. 'Looking back, I can see that Mum probably suffered from depression. But whether it came from inside her, or whether it was because she couldn't really make a relationship last, I don't know. She'd have downers and take off for the pub, drown her sorrows. It's why I ended up more or less bringing up Lindy myself.' Her voice changed. Softened. 'Not that it wasn't a joy to do so. Lindy was always so sweet, so loving! And she had an infectious sense of humour—she could always set me laughing to cheer me up.'

Anatole saw a reminiscent smile cross her expression.

'What is it?' he probed. He let his gaze dwell on how, when she smiled, it lifted her features, lighting up her clear eyes and curving her tender mouth to show pearl-like teeth.

How could I ever have thought her unremarkable? If her sister had half her appeal Marcos must have been lost!

But, much as he might want to indulge himself in gazing at how her lovely smile enhanced the beauty that her makeover had revealed to him, he focused on her answer.

'The caravan park we stayed at was in a place called the Witterings,' Lyn explained. 'It's a pair of villages— East Wittering and West Wittering—and Lindy found the names hilarious! She only had to say them out loud and she fell into fits of giggles—and set me laughing too.'

There was fondness in her voice, and her expression had softened even more, but Anatole could see that faraway look in her eyes again—a shadow of the sadness that haunted her, at knowing her sister had barely made it into adulthood.

Let alone lived long enough to raise the child *they* were now caring for...

'We can go and visit there some time,' he said. 'If you would like?'

Lyn lifted her face to his. 'Can we? Oh, that would be lovely! I would love Georgy to know the place where his mother was happy as a child!'

He felt a spear of emotion go through him. As she gazed at him, her face alight, something moved inside him. He, too, longed for Georgy to know the beach by his grandfather's house, where he and Marcos had played as boys.

'We shall definitely do it,' he said decisively. 'Too far, alas, to include it in today's excursion, but we'll find an opportunity another day.'

He started walking again, and Lyn fell into stride beside him.

She must not let herself be endlessly sad for Lindy, she

knew that—knew that her beloved sister would not want it. Would want, instead, for Lyn to do everything within her power to ensure the son she hadn't been able to look after herself had the very best future possible!

Her eyes went to the man walking beside her. A stranger he might be, but with each day he was becoming less so—and, like her, he wanted only one thing: that Georgy should be kept safe, safe with them, not given to others to raise. And if that meant carrying out this extraordinary and un-likely plan of making a marriage between them, then she would see it through!

Marrying Anatole is the way I can keep Georgy safe with me—that's all I have to focus on!

Yet even as she repeated her mantra to herself she stole a glance sideways and felt her breath give a little catch that was nothing to do with the exertion of walking along these high, windswept downs and everything to do with the way she wanted to gaze and gaze at the compelling profile of the man beside her. At the way the wind was ruffling his sable hair, the way the sweep of his long lashes framed those sloe-dark eyes of his…and the way his long, strong legs strode effortlessly across the close-cropped turf, his hands curled around the chubby legs of Georgy, borne aloft on his wide shoulders.

He is just so incredible-looking!

The words burned in her consciousness and so too did the realisation that today—just as yesterday—she was fi-nally looking like the kind of female a man like him would be seen with. Her style of looks might be quite different from Lindy's blonde prettiness, but she would have been lying if she had not accepted that with her new hairstyle, her new make-up and her beautiful new clothes she drew his approbation.

The transformation he had wrought in her appearance was just one more of the good things he was doing for her!

A sense of wellbeing infused in her and she heard scraps of poetry floating through her head as they walked the iconic landscape. The chalk Downs that ran along the southern coast of England plunged into the sea further east at Dover, and the peerless White Cliffs that defined the country. It was a landscape that had been celebrated a hundred years ago by one of England's most patriotic poets, Rudyard Kipling.

"'The Weald is good, the Downs are best—I'll give you the run of 'em, East to West,'" she exclaimed.

Anatole threw her an enquiring look and then his glance went down to her upturned face. Colour was flagged in her cheeks as the breeze crept up the steep scarp slope from the glittering Channel beyond. It lifted her hair from her face, and her eyes were shining as clear as the air they breathed. She seemed more alive than he had ever seen her. Vivid and vital.

And so very lovely.

A thought slid into his head. A thought that had been building for some time now. Ever since she'd walked out of the beauty salon and blown him away with the transformation in her looks. A thought that, once there, he could not banish. Found he did not want to banish. Wanted, instead, to savour...

Because why not? Why *not* do what he suddenly realised he very, very much wanted to do?

Why not, indeed?

He strode onward. Life seemed very good.

'What would you like to order for dinner?' Anatole enquired solicitously, strolling into the kitchen where Lyn was warming Georgy's bedtime milk.

'To be honest,' she said, 'I'd prefer something light. That cream tea we tucked into was very filling!'

They'd found an olde-worlde teashop in an olde-worlde

Sussex village to round off the day before setting off back to London, and Anatole found himself remembering the way she'd licked a tiny smear of cream from her lip with the tip of her tongue. He'd found it very engaging.

She was speaking again, and he made himself focus.

'If you want,' she ventured, her tone tentative, 'I could just knock up something simple for us both. Pasta or an omelette—something like that.'

His eyes smiled. 'Pasta sounds good. But I don't want to put you to any trouble.'

'No trouble,' she assured him.

'In exchange, I'll get Georgy off to sleep,' he volunteered.

'Thank you.' She smiled too.

He took the bottle from her and headed off.

She watched him go. It was so…contradictory. That was the only word she could find. On the one hand she felt so much easier now in his company. So much more relaxed. Yet on the other hand, since her makeover, 'relaxed' was the last thing she felt!

She felt as if a current of electricity were buzzing through her all the time—a current that soared whenever she saw him or he came near to her.

She took a breath. Well, hopefully, once they'd both got used to her new look it would dissipate—just as her initial stiltedness had.

It had better…

She gave her head a little shake and determinedly yanked open the door of the huge double fridge that occupied a sizeable space in the palatial kitchen. There were several bags of fresh pasta, as well as cream, eggs, butter and smoked salmon. A pot of fresh basil graced the windowsill by the sink, and she busied herself snipping at the fragrant leaves. By the time she had measured out the pasta, whisked some eggs, beaten cream in and chopped up the salmon, Anatole strolled back into the kitchen.

'Out like a light,' he said cheerfully. 'We clearly exhausted him today!' He crossed over to stand beside Lyn. 'Mmm...' he inspected her handiwork. 'Looking good.' He wandered across to the temperature controlled wine cabinet and extracted a bottle. 'I think this should wash it down nicely,' he said.

His mood was good. Very good. They'd had a good day out, Georgy had had fun, and he'd repaid their efforts by falling swiftly and soundly asleep. That left the evening to him and Lyn.

Yes, definitely a good day.

'You OK with eating in here?' he enquired.

'Yes, of course,' she assured him.

The breakfast bar was huge—plenty of room to dine at it. She heard him open the wine and got on with boiling a kettle of water to cook the pasta. Outside, the night sky was dark, but in the kitchen it felt cosy and companionable, warm and friendly.

Happiness filled her.

I didn't realise how lonely I've been since Lindy died...

But she was not lonely now. She had Anatole to be with.

Yet even as she thought that she felt a pang go through her. How long would they be together? This time next year it might very well all be over. His grandfather might have succumbed to his cancer, Georgy's adoption might be finally approved, and she and Anatole might have their mutually agreed divorce underway.

Somehow the thought chilled her.

'Why so sad?' Anatole's voice was kindly. 'Are you thinking of your sister?'

'Yes,' she lied. She poured boiling water into the pasta pan and fed in the spaghetti as it came back to the boil.

She did not want to look at Anatole. Did not want to let her eyes feast on him.

He isn't mine—he never will be. That's what I have to remember. The only thing I must remember.

Not the way her eyes followed him wherever he went. Not the way her breath caught when he smiled at her. Not the way she felt her pulse quicken when he came near her.

Not the way his face was imprinted on her mind, day and night…

'Then let us drink to her—and to my cousin, too.'

He slipped onto one of the high stools that flanked the kitchen bar. One of the ceiling spotlights caught the glint of pale gold in his glass as he lifted it, proffering the other one to Lyn as she took her place opposite him. They toasted their lost ones silently, each thinking their own thoughts about those they had loved who had died so tragically young.

'He wasn't all bad, you know—Marcos,' Anatole found himself saying. 'I know he treated your sister badly, but—well, I've come up with an explanation. It won't make you forgive him, but maybe you'll think of him a little less harshly.'

He looked across at Lyn.

'I think the reason he ignored your sister when she wrote to him is that he thought Timon would insist on him marrying her once he knew your sister was carrying his great-grandchild. Marcos was only twenty-five—and a young twenty-five at that. He wanted fun and no responsibilities. Timon encouraged him in that. He'd spent ten years trying to compensate Marcos for losing his parents at sixteen. A bad age to lose them. I think that learning that your sister was pregnant scared Marcos. Made him hide from it—hope it would all just go away.'

He looked at Lyn.

'I think that, had he not been killed, he would have

faced up to his responsibilities. He'd have come to me and told me first, I'm sure, and I would have helped him deal with it. Got him to make contact with Lindy. I believe,' he finished slowly, 'had your sister not died, he would have asked her to marry him. Made a family with her and Georgy just as she dreamed he would.' He paused again. 'He was a decent kid inside.'

Lyn heard him speak, felt her sympathy rising.

'It's all so sad,' she said. She was feeling choked. 'Just *so* sad.'

She felt her hand being taken, gently squeezed. 'Yes, it is. Sad and tragic and dreadful, and a hideous waste of young lives, their future stolen from them.'

She felt tears spring in her eyes. Felt Anatole's finger graze across her cheekbone, brushing them away. Felt his sympathy towards her.

'I hope they're happy together now, somehow. In that mysterious realm beyond mortal life. I hope,' he said, 'they're looking down at us and knowing their child is safe, his future assured.'

She nodded, blinking away her tears. He patted her hand and then, glancing at the stove, got up to drain the cooked pasta. She got to her feet as well, and busied herself stirring in the creamy concoction she'd prepared. She heaped it into wide pasta bowls and placed them on the bar. Her tears were gone now. Lindy was at peace and so, she hoped, was the man she'd fallen in love with. Who might one day, had they lived, have come to love her back.

Who knew? Who knew the mysteries of the heart? Who knew what life and fate and circumstance could do?

As she took her place opposite Anatole, letting her eyes savour him as they always did, she felt her heart swell.

Not with hope, for that would be impossible, but with a yearning that she could not still.

Anatole broke the moment and got to his feet. 'You

forgot the parmesan,' he said, and went to fetch it from the fridge.

It was such a simple meal, Lyn knew, but it was the most enjoyable she'd yet shared with Anatole. Despite her assurance that she was not very hungry she put away a good portion of pasta, and when Anatole extracted a tub of American ice cream from the freezer she did not disdain that either.

'Let's go next door,' he said, and led the way with the ice cream, leaving her to bring through the coffee tray.

She felt more relaxed than she had ever felt with him. The wine she'd drunk had helped, and it seemed to be giving her a very pleasant buzz in her veins. Carefully she set down the coffee tray and lowered herself onto the sofa beside Anatole as he indicated she should, taking one of the two long spoons he was holding out. He'd wrapped the ice cream carton in a teatowel, to make it easier to hold.

Sharing ice cream, Lyn swiftly discovered, meant getting a lot more up close and personal with Anatole than she'd initially realised. Digging into frozen ice cream was also, she discovered, enormously good fun when done in the right spirit.

'That lump of cookie dough is definitely mine!' Anatole informed her with mock severity. 'You had the last one!'

A giggle escaped her, and she made herself busy to focus on a hunk of chocolate in the icy mix.

'What would make this even more decadent,' Anatole observed, 'would be to pour a liqueur over it.'

'Or golden syrup,' contributed Lyn. 'Lindy and I used to do that as kids. The syrup goes really hard—it's great!' She stabbed at another bit of embedded cookie dough.

Finally, when they'd both OD'd on ice cream, they abandoned the carton and Lyn poured out the coffee. As she leant back, curling her legs underneath her into her usual posture, after handing Anatole's cup to him, she realised that his arm was stretched out along the back of the sofa. She could feel the warmth of his sleeve at the nape of her neck.

I ought to move further away from him, she thought. But she didn't. She just went on sitting there, feeling the heavy warmth of his arm behind her, sipping at her milky coffee.

'What's on TV?' Anatole asked.

Lyn clicked it on with the remote. The channel opened on one of her favourites—an old-fashioned, retro detective series, set back in the 1950s, just starting up.

She felt the arm behind her neck drape lower around her shoulders. He didn't seem to notice what he'd done, and for the life of her Lyn could not alter her position. She felt herself relax, so that her shoulder was almost nestled against him.

It felt good. It felt good to be almost snuggled up against him like this on the sofa, warm and well-fed, relaxed and rested.

Very good.

Another programme came on—this time a history show about the classical world. They watched with interest, Anatole contributing a little and Lyn listening avidly. He read out the Greek inscriptions on the monuments on show and translated them.

'Do you think you could face learning Greek?' he asked Lyn.

'I'll give it a go,' she said. 'The different alphabet will be a challenge, though.'

'It will come to you, I'm sure,' he said. 'I'll arrange lessons for you when we get there. Speaking of which,' he continued, 'it could be sooner than we think. The latest from the lawyers is that there's no objection to Georgy coming abroad with us, so his passport can be issued. We'll fly out as soon as we've got it.'

For a moment Lyn's eyes were veiled, her expression

troubled and unsure. The reality of taking Georgy to Greece was hitting her. It would be soon now—very soon.

Anatole saw her doubts—saw the flicker of unease in her expression. He knew she was remembering her old fears about letting Georgy out of the UK to visit his father's family.

'It will be all right,' he said. 'I promise you. Trust me.'

She gazed into his dark eyes. He was right. She had to trust him. He had done everything he had promised her he would and she must do what she had undertaken. Go out to Greece with Georgy, trusting the man who had taken the responsibility of his care upon his own shoulders.

'I do trust you,' she whispered.

He smiled. 'Good,' he said.

Then, with a casual gesture, he moved her closer. She nestled against him, his hand still cupping her shoulder, as if it were the most natural thing in the world. She found herself getting drowsy, the warmth of the room, the effect of a couple of glasses of wine and the filling food all contributing. Her head sank back against his shoulder, her eyes fluttering as she tried to keep them open.

'You're falling asleep,' Anatole murmured, glancing sideways at her. He flicked off the TV programme.

She smiled drowsily. 'I'd better get Georgy's midnight bottle going. He'll surface for it soon.'

'I'll get it,' said Anatole. 'You head for bed. I'll bring the bottle in when it's warm.'

She uncurled herself and padded off. Five minutes later she was propped up on the pillows, wearing her nightdress, when Anatole entered with Georgy's milk.

'He's just waking up,' she said as he started to stir and kick at his quilt. 'Up you come, then.' She lowered the side of the cot and scooped him up.

'May I feed him?' Anatole requested, looking at Lyn.

'Yes, of course,' she said, slightly confused.

He moved to sit down beside her on the bed and she shuffled sideways against the edge of the cot, hastily putting a couple of pillows behind his back. He leant back, taking Georgy from her and settling him with the bottle. Lyn felt she should get up, but she was between Anatole and the cot. So she went on sitting there. Propped up. Shoulder to shoulder with Anatole. With only the low nightlight for illumination, the physical closeness between them felt very intimate.

Georgy sucked greedily and then, replete, let Lyn wind him gently before consenting to resume his slumbers in his cot. As she raised the side again, to lock it in place, she was burningly aware that Anatole was still beside her. She turned to make some kind of anodyne remark but the words died on her lips.

Anatole was looking at her with dark, deep, long-lashed eyes, his face half in shadow but the expression on it as clear as day. She felt her heart stop, her breathing stop. Everything stop.

Everything in the entire universe stopped except for one thing.

The slow dip of his head to hers. And then the slow, soft brush of his lips on hers. The slow rush of sensation it aroused.

'My lovely Lyn,' he murmured.

Then his kiss deepened.

His hand closed around her shoulder, covered only in the thin material of her nightdress. His hand felt warm and strong, kneading at her flesh as he turned her into his embrace. His mouth opened hers effortlessly, skilfully, and sensation exploded within her. Wonder and disbelief swept over her like a rushing wave.

Was this happening? Was this really, truly happening? Was Anatole kissing her? How could it be?

But it was—oh, it was. It *was*! His mouth was exploring

hers and his free hand was around the nape of her neck, moulding her to him. He was murmuring something in Greek that sounded honeyed and seductive. Warm fire lit within her, her senses flared...soared...and then suddenly he was sliding off the bed, taking her with him. Sweeping her up, striding out of the room with her in his arms, kissing her still.

She could say nothing, do nothing, only let him take her, carry her into his own bedroom, lower her down upon the bed's wide surface. She wanted to speak, to say something—anything—but it was beyond her. Totally beyond her.

He came down beside her, indenting the mattress with his long, lean length. His hands cupped her face as she gazed up at him.

'My lovely Lyn,' he said again. And his mouth came down on hers.

Helplessly, willingly, she gave herself to him, letting him ease her nightdress from her, letting his eyes, so deep and dark, feast on her form, letting his hands shape her breasts, glide along the lines of her flanks, slip under her back at her waist and half lift her to him with effortless strength. And all the while his lips worked their magic on hers, deepening the passion and the intensity.

She was in a state of bliss. Unable to think, to reason, to understand—able only to wonder, only to give herself to the sensations of her body, her yielding, arching body, which yearned and sought and found what she had never dreamed possible: the wonder of being embraced and caressed by this man.

Never had she thought it possible! Never had she dreamt of it in her wildest dreams! Yet now it was real—true. He was sweeping her to a place she had never imagined.

For how could imagination possibly have revealed to her what it would be like for Anatole to make love to her like this? Drawing from her, arousing in her, such incredible feelings that she could hardly keep her senses—so overwhelmed by his touch, his caresses, his sensuous, intimate kisses that sought and found her, every exquisitely sensitive place until her body was a living flame.

A flame that seared into the incandescence of quivering arousal as, stripping his clothes from his heated body, he came over her, his strongly muscled thighs pressing on her limbs, parting them. His hands closed around hers on either side of her head as his body—naked, glorious—arched over her, his questing mouth taking the honeyed sweetness of hers.

His eyes were hazed with desire, molten with urgency, as he lifted his head from her. She arched her hips towards his, yearning for the hot, crushing strength of his body. For one endless moment he held back, and then, with a triumphant surge, he filled her, fusing his body with hers, melding them,

She cried out—a high, unearthly sound—as sensation exploded through her. She heard his voice, hoarse and full-throated, felt the tips of her fingers indenting deeply, so deeply, into his sculpted back. Every muscle strained. Her hips arched against his.

It was like nothing she had ever experienced! It flooded through her, the whitest flame of ultimate consummation, further and further, reaching every cell in her body, flooding every synapse. She cried out again and the cry became a sob, emotion racking through her at the wonder of it, the beauty of it…

And then he was pulsing within her, and she was drawing him in, deeper and deeper, with more and more intensity of sensation, more wonderful yet, flowing and filling her like a molten tide. She clasped him to her, tightly and possessively, holding his body to her as, reaching its golden glowing limit, the tide began to ebb, drawing back through her body, releasing her from its wondrous thrall.

They lay together, their heated bodies limp now, sated, a tangle of limbs half wrapped around each other.

He cradled her to him, murmuring in his own language words she could not tell. But his hand was warm, splayed around the back of her head, holding her. Her breathing slowed and she felt an echoing slowing in him as well—a slackening of his embrace. Wonder washed like the sweetest wine through her fading consciousness as sleep finally overcame her, and she lay cradled and encircled within the embrace of his arms.

CHAPTER EIGHT

IT WAS THE distant, distressed crying of an infant that awoke her from heavy sleep. Fully waking, she heard Georgy's wailing. Instantly she was up, fumbling for her long-discarded nightdress and stumbling from the room towards her own. Stricken, she lifted his squalling body and clutched him tight. She never let him cry—*never*! Guilt smote her and she hugged him, swaying, soothing his little back until he eased, comforted and reassured finally that she was there and all was well. Slowly, very slowly, she eased him back into his cot, stroking his head.

A sound in the doorway made her turn. Anatole was there, naked but for a towel twisted around his hips, a questioning look on his face in the early light of the dawn.

'Is he all right?' he asked.

His voice was throaty, the timbre of it resonant.

She nodded dumbly as memory swept over her, hot and vivid. Dear God, had it really happened? Had she been swept off into Anatole's arms, his bed? Could it be real? True?

Then he was walking up to her, enfolding her in his arms.

'Come back to bed,' he said.

The voice was huskier than before. Its message clear.

Desire was in his eyes.

He kissed her. Soft, then not so soft. Slipped his hand into hers, leading her away…

Much, much later they surfaced.

This time they did not sleep. This time pale daylight edged past the folds of the curtains, proclaiming the day. She lay in the crook of Anatole's arm, half propped on soft pillows, drowsy. Fulfilled.

Hazed still with disbelief.

'Georgy will be waking,' she said. 'He'll be hungry.'

Anatole reached to the bedside table to glance at his watch. 'The day awaits,' he said. He turned back to kiss her softly. His eyes gazed down at her.

'My lovely Lyn,' he said. His eyes caressed her. 'So very lovely.'

Then, with a decisive movement, he threw back the coverings and got to his feet. His nudity was overwhelming, sending her senses into overdrive. Ruffling his hair, as if to wake himself further, he disappeared into the bathroom. Lyn hurried to her bedroom, swiftly showering before Georgy awoke.

In the shower, her body seemed fuller somehow—more rounded. She was still in a daze, yet it had happened. Her body felt it in every stretched and extended muscle, felt it in the warm, deep glow within her. Her breasts were crested, and she could see with amazed wonder the soft marks of his caressing.

As warm water sluiced over her, the shower gel gliding sensuously over her skin, she felt again the echo of the heat that had consumed her.

She dressed hurriedly, pulling on a pair of leggings and shouldering her way into a long, dark blue jersey wool top, loose and comfortable. She dried and brushed her hair out rapidly, not troubling to tie it back, and it tumbled around her shoulders—wavy, wanton. For a moment she caught sight of herself in one of the long wall mirrors in the room, and her reflection stayed her.

Her eyes glowed with sensual memory. Her breasts strained against the soft fabric of her top. She felt desire stir.

Then, with a rattle of cot bars, Georgy was pulling himself up to a sitting position and holding out his arms to her. With a smile, she scooped him up and out, and bore him off to the kitchen for his breakfast.

Anatole was there already, wearing a bathrobe, his hair still damp, fetching cereal and milk, and a baby yoghurt for Georgy. A sudden overpowering sense of shyness swept over Lyn. But he came towards her, bestowing a kiss on her cheek.

'Your tea is brewing,' he told her, smiling, and settled himself on a stool at the kitchen bar. He nodded at Georgy, still held in her arms. 'How is our infant prodigy today?' he enquired humorously.

Georgy responded to his attention by gurgling, and evincing a desire for his yoghurt, which he'd just spotted. Lyn took her seat, Georgy on her lap, and poured milk into her cup of tea, taking a first sip before reaching for the yoghurt. Somehow her shyness was gone.

'So,' said Anatole expansively, 'what shall we do today?'

He knew what he wanted to do. What he had wanted to do, he acknowledged, since the moment she'd walked out of the beauty salon, transformed and revealed. What had been building since then, hour by hour, until last night it had seemed the obvious, the only thing to do. Follow his awakened instincts to their natural fulfilling conclusion.

He was not about to question it, analyse it, challenge it. It was, after all, incredibly simple. Desire—simple and straightforward. And overwhelming.

Quite, quite overwhelming.

He had not expected it. He knew that. Had not thought that it would happen—*could* happen. But it had and he was glad of it! Totally, incredibly glad! It made sense on every level.

He let his gaze rest on her now. Georgy was snuggled on her lap as she spooned yoghurt into his gaping mouth, hungrily gulping it down, ready for more. Her features were soft, tender, as she smiled fondly at her charge.

Well-being filled him.

'How about,' he suggested, 'we take Georgy swimming this morning?'

It proved an excellent idea. Excellent not just because it was so enjoyable to see the fun that Georgy had—his little body safely held in the water with water wings, bobbing merrily as he chuckled gleefully at all the splashing, fully enthusiastic about the exciting inflatable pool toys acquired especially for him—but also because it afforded Anatole the considerable pleasure of seeing Lyn in one of the several new bathing costumes he'd insisted on her buying. True, it was a one-piece, but it was quite sufficiently revealing for him to feel desire stir all over again.

A desire that, when Georgy finally conceded defeat after lunch and succumbed to his nap, Anatole had no reason to defer any longer, and he swept Lyn off to bed.

'We have to take ruthless advantage of Georgy's sleep patterns,' he justified, overcoming Lyn's slight sense of shock at such diurnal amorousness.

But as she journeyed with him to that wondrous place of union she could only agree.

Anything that Anatole wanted was wonderful! Anything at all! She was ardent, adoring, her eyes lit with wonder and pleasure.

I can't think beyond this! It's impossible—impossible! All I can do is go with what is happening.

She was in a haze—a daze of happiness. And beyond each day, each night, she would not think.

Anatole walked out of his office to see Lyn sprawled on the floor with Georgy, who was on all fours, lurching forward in his newly developing crawl.

'The lawyers have just phoned me,' Anatole announced. He took a breath. 'Georgy's passport is being delivered by courier this morning. We fly to Athens tomorrow.'

He came to Lyn, whose eyes had flown up to his, and hunkered down beside her. Her expression was mixed.

'I know you are nervous,' he said, taking her hand and pressing it reassuringly, 'but once we are there you will find it less alarming, I promise you.'

His eyes met hers, but even as they did so they slid past, down to Georgy, intently progressing towards the teddy bear that Lyn had deliberately left out of his reach, to encourage him to try and crawl towards it. Thoughts swirled opaquely in his head. Thoughts he did not want to put into words. Thoughts he banished with the words he always used to reassure her.

'Trust me,' he said. He leant forward and brushed her mouth with his lightly. 'This is the right thing to do,' he said, his voice low, intense. 'It is the best way forward for Georgy—that is all you have to hold on to.'

Yet doubt, unease, still flickered in her face. He kissed her again, more deeply, and felt her shimmer with response. When he took his mouth away the doubt had gone from her eyes, replaced by the glow that was always in them when he kissed her, made love to her...

'That's better.' He smiled a warm, intimate smile and got to his feet. 'Now, do not worry about packing,' he instructed her. 'The maid service here will do that—both for you and for Georgy. We'll enjoy our last day here. Then, tomorrow, we'll be off!'

He headed from the room.

'I'm going to phone Timon—tell him we'll be there tomorrow and get an update from his doctors. They tell me the drugs are kicking in and starting to work, which is just the news I want.'

Lyn watched him go, and as he went from view she felt again that jittery feeling of unease return. It was such a big, frightening step—to leave the UK, to go to a foreign country and put herself entirely into the hands of a man who, such a short time ago, had been a stranger to her.

But Anatole was no longer a stranger! He was the man she had committed herself to with all her body, all her desire. He had swept her away on a wonderful, magical tide of passion and forged an intimacy between them that made a nonsense of her fears, her doubts.

Thanks to Anatole, everything would be for the best now.

Everything will be all right! I know it will! There is nothing to be afraid of—nothing! I must do what he keeps telling me to do—trust him!

And how could she fail to do so? How could she fail to trust him now that he had transformed her life? In his arms, his embrace, she had found a bliss that overwhelmed her with its wonder! There was no more awkwardness with him, no more shyness or diffidence.

Now everything between them was different! Magically, wonderfully different! Since Anatole had swept her into his arms, into his bed, her head had been in a constant daze. It was still so unbelievable, what had happened between them! So unbelievable that she could not make sense of it—could do nothing but simply go with it…with every wondrous, shining moment of it! She would allow herself no doubts, no questions.

The flight to Athens proved straightforward. Georgy took a keen interest in the proceedings, especially all the admiring fuss that was made of him by the cabin staff, and apart from being affected by the change in cabin pressure on take-off and landing had a smooth journey. At Athens airport they were whisked through deplaning and into the chauffeured car waiting for them. Lyn barely had time to take in her new surroundings before the car was leaving the airport, heading for the coast.

'It should take less than an hour, depending on traffic,' Anatole assured her. 'We'll have plenty of time to settle into the beach house this afternoon. As you know,' he went on, 'we have the whole place to ourselves—and I think that will be good. Give you a chance to get used to everything. With Timon still in hospital for the moment, under medical supervision, we can have more time together. That said—' he made a face '—I can't deny that I'm going to have to spend a great deal of time working. Both at my own affairs, which I've neglected, and even more importantly on Timon's business affairs.'

His expression tightened.

'My priority is persuading Timon to relinquish control of the Petranakos Corporation to me. I'm limited at the moment as to what I can and can't do, and I can see that a great deal needs to be done. A lot of the workforce at too many of the sites and premises are very jumpy—they know Timon is old and very ill, they know Marcos is dead, and they don't know what is going to happen. Bankers and investors are restless too, as well as suppliers and customers. None of that is good. I need to take charge—make it clear that I'm going to run the company on behalf of the new heir. And I most urgently want Timon to designate Georgy.' He took a breath. 'Whatever it takes, I *have* to get Timon to hand over the reins of power to me.'

Whatever it takes...

The words echoed in Anatole's head. He had used them so often in these past weeks since Marcos's fatal car crash.

His eyes went to the woman and child seated beside him and he felt them echo again.

Whatever it takes...

Emotion swirled within him. Whatever it took to safeguard Marcos's son and safeguard the jobs of the thousands of people employed by Timon. That was what he must cling to.

His mind refocusing, he started to point out to Lyn the various landmarks they were passing, giving her a sense of the geography of the region.

'We are heading for Glyfada,' he told her. 'It's on the shore of the Saronic Gulf—where, as I'm sure you already know, the famous battle of Salamis was fought in the fifth century BC to defeat the invading Persians. My grandfather's villa is beyond the resort, on a quiet peninsula, well away from all the glitz of Glyfada and its neighbours, like Voula.'

'I see the roadsigns are in the Latin alphabet, as well as Greek,' Lyn remarked.

'That's pretty common in Greece now,' Anatole reassured her.

She frowned. 'It's the hardest part of learning Greek, I think,' she said. 'Having to learn to read a different script.'

'It isn't so bad,' he said encouragingly. 'Lots of the symbols are the same. One or two can be confusing, though— like the Latin capital P, for example, which is our R: *rho*.' He smiled. 'But don't worry. You'll get the hang of it. I'll get a teacher organised, and you can start lessons as soon as you like.'

'Thank you,' she said gratefully. Her heart warmed. He was taking so much trouble to make her feel easier, more comfortable about moving here to Greece.

Yet even so, as the car turned off the main highway, and started to head down smaller roads, threading between what were clearly private and expensive residences all around them then pausing to go through electronically controlled gates to curl around a driveway that led to the huge white villa at the far end, Lyn felt her heart quail again.

But yet again Anatole sought to assuage her fears as she stared, daunted, at the massive ornate mansion.

'Timon likes to live in style,' Anatole commented dryly. 'But the beach house is a lot less grandiose.'

The car took a fork off to the right that went around the main house and down through extensive manicured grounds that led towards the sea, and drew up outside a much more modest-looking building.

'This will be far more suitable for us,' said Anatole.

Lyn could not help but agree.

It was a single-storey, low-level building, with shutters and a terrace to the front, which overlooked the far end of a private beach that fronted the shoreline of the main villa, from which it was separated by formal gardens set with tall cypress trees and a lot of cultivated greenery.

'I've had the beach house opened up, but no one's been here for a while, so it might be a bit musty,' Anatole apologized.

Lyn only smiled. 'It looks lovely,' she said. She definitely felt relieved that she wouldn't have to cope with the huge imposing-looking villa that was Timon Petranokos's residence.

They made their way indoors, leaving the driver to bring in their luggage. Indoors, Lyn immediately felt even more reassured. Although it was clearly a luxury residence the house was small-scale, and simply furnished, but she liked it that way.

'The staff from the main house will do the housekeeping here,' Anatole explained, 'and the kitchen there will always be on call. Tonight,' he went on, 'we'll definitely make use of my grandfather's chef!'

Lyn was grateful, and by the time she had sorted out her unpacking and got Georgy settled in his new nursery in the bedroom next to hers, she was glad to sit down to a dinner that someone else had prepared.

She still felt strange, but knew she must simply get on with settling in. This was to be her life now.

But for how long?

The thought arrowed through her head and she wished it had not. She didn't want to think about the future right now.

All she wanted to do was be with Georgy—and Anatole...

With Anatole's arms around her, his lips kissing her, his hands caressing her, his words murmuring in her ear as he took her to a place that made everything else in the universe disappear...

She wouldn't think about anything else. Just what she had now.

Take each day...each night...and do what he asks you to do. Trust him.

It was all she needed to do.

The following morning they drove to the specialist cancer hospital outside Athens where Timon Petranakos was being treated.

'I hope you do not mind, Lyn,' Anatole said, 'but for this first meeting I want to take Georgy to see Timon on his own.'

Lyn was understanding. 'Of course,' she agreed readily.

It was understandable that he should want that. This would be a very emotional encounter for a man, old and dying, who, still raw with terrible grief, had lost his beloved grandson but who now was to receive a blessing he had never hoped for: his grandson's baby son. She did not wish to intrude on such a special moment.

Anatole was tense, she could see. So much was resting on this encounter, and she did not want to add to that tension. She leant across to give Georgy, already hoisted up in Anatole's arms, a quick final mop of the face, ready to be presented to his great-grandfather, then she stood back, watching Anatole walk out of the visitors' lounge at the swish private clinic. As the door closed behind them, taking Georgy from her sight, a little bubble of anxiety formed inside her. She deflated it swiftly.

What did she imagine was going to happen? That a frail, sick man like Timon was somehow going to whisk Georgy away, never to be seen by her again? Of course he wasn't! She must stop fretting like this. Just as Anatole kept reiterating, everything would be all right...

She sat back on the chair and reached for a magazine to while away the time until Anatole emerged again. She could do little but glance at the pictures, and it strengthened her determination to get to grips with the Greek language without delay. This might only be the first day after their arrival, but the sooner she could cope with the language the better.

It was a determination she found she had ample time to put into practice in the days that followed. Anatole had warned her that once in Greece he would have to focus primarily on work so, like it or not, she had to wave goodbye to him in the mornings as he headed into Athens, leaving her to her own devices during the day. Not that she had any housework to do—maids from the main house appeared and duly disappeared after taking care of all the chores, and food shopping was also taken care of by Timon Petranakos's staff. They all made a huge fuss over Georgy, who clearly revelled in the admiration, and those who spoke English told her, with visible emotion, how like his poor tragic father he was. She herself was treated with great deference as well, as the fiancée of Timon's other grandson, which she found a little awkward. It brought home to her the very different worlds she and Anatole came from.

But it doesn't matter—we are united in Georgy. He bridges any gap between us.

Not that there *was* any gap. She might not see anything of Anatole during the day, but when he came home in the evening he was everything she could desire.

She'd made a point of cooking dinner herself some evenings, for she was reluctant to rely totally on Timon's house staff to do so for her, but she knew her meagre repertoire would soon pall for someone like Anatole, used to gourmet cuisine all his life, so she restricted herself to easy dishes like pasta, leaving anything more complex to the chef from the main house. Baby food, though, she attended to herself, and soon discovered that shopping for fresh fruit and vegetables with Georgy in the nearby little coastal town—to which she was delivered and collected by Timon's chauffeur—made for a pleasurable excursion every day or two. The Greeks, she swiftly realised, were a lot more volubly enthusiastic about infants than the reserved British, and everyone from passing old ladies to shopkeepers made a huge fuss of him whenever she wheeled him along in his buggy, much to his evident enjoyment.

Having bought herself some teach-yourself and tourist phrasebooks for Greek, Lyn steadily tried to put her first stumbling efforts with the language into use as she shopped. They were aided when the teacher Anatole had promised he would organise arrived at the beach house. He was an earnest young man—the graduate son of the brother of Anatole's PA—and with his assiduous help Lyn started to feel less intimated by the Greek script, started to make definite progress with grammar and vocabulary.

While she had her daily lesson one of the housemaids

would look after Georgy. She spoke to him in Greek, as did Anatole quite a lot, and Lyn knew that it was essential that he grow up to be bilingual from the start—a tangible sign of his dual heritage.

But she also knew she didn't want him growing up unaware or under-exposed to his mother's heritage too. It was something that caused her some anxiety now that she was actually here in Greece. It might not matter while Georgy was little, but as he grew to boyhood Lyn knew she would want him to be as much English as Greek. She owed it to Lindy...

She said as much one evening to Anatole over dinner. She felt a little awkward raising the subject, but steeled herself to slip it into the conversation at an opportune moment. He had made some remark about their day out to the South Downs while they'd been in England, and Lyn seized her chance.

'We *will* be able to go back to England some time?' she asked. 'I know we'll have to go back after the wedding at some point, to be present at the adoption hearing, but once that is done do we come back here for good?'

For a moment he stilled completely, and she realised he might have misunderstood her question.

His eyes rested on her. 'Are you not happy here?' he asked.

There was a concerned note in his voice and immediately Lyn replied. 'No, it's not because of that at all—I promise you! I'm settling in, just as you promised me I would! Please, *please* don't worry about that! You've got enough to deal with as it is—with Timon's state of health and all the work you've got to do! I suppose it's simply dawning on me that once Georgy starts talking he's going to have Greek as his predominant language and culture— and I don't want him to lose touch with his English side completely. It would be reassuring to know that he can spend time in England, still—for holidays...that sort of thing! Touch base with that side of his cultural heritage.' She finished hastily. 'But that's all for the future, I know.'

'Yes, it is,' said Anatole. 'But of course I can see why you think about it.' He took a breath. 'We can work something out, I am sure,' he said.

There was reassurance in his voice, but suddenly Lyn saw a veil come down over his expression, as if he were thinking of something he was not telling her about.

She frowned inwardly, and a thread of anxiety plucked at her. It dissipated almost immediately, however, as Anatole's expression cleared.

'I'm going to try and take the day off tomorrow,' he said. 'What's that expression in English? Playing hockey?'

Lyn laughed. 'It's playing *hookey*—but I have no idea what hookey is, or why you play it when you skive off work!'

Anatole gave a quirking smile. *'Skive?'* he queried.

'It's slang for bunking off—which is also slang for going AWOL, I guess...taking a day off work when really you're not supposed to.'

'Well, I think I deserve it,' Anatole said firmly. 'I've been flat out since we got here, and the pressure is only going to get worse when I'm running Petranakos fully. For the moment I'm going to take a long weekend for once.' He looked at Lyn. 'How about if I take you into Athens and show you the sights? I feel bad that you've been stuck away here and haven't seen anything yet.'

Lyn's face lit. 'Oh, that would be wonderful! Thank you! But please, *please* don't feel I've been "stuck" here—this is such a lovely house, with the beach right in front, and the weather is so lovely and warm.'

Anatole looked at her. 'Are you sure you're happy here, Lyn?' he asked.

She could hear the concern in his voice again, and immediately wanted to reassure him. 'Yes, truly I am! It's getting less strange every day. And so is the language.'

'Good,' said Anatole, and relief was clear in his eyes. 'The other good news is that Timon's oncologist tells me he's continuing to do well. The cancer is responding to the drugs and he is coping better with the side effects. He's talking about letting him come home next week, maybe.' His eyes warmed. 'And then, Lyn, we can really get going on our wedding.'

His gaze caressed her, and she felt herself melt as she always did.

'Not that we need to wait for the wedding…' he murmured, and his message was clear—and potent.

Lyn felt a little shimmer as her blood warmed. No, they did not need the formality of a wedding to unite them. It might be needed to expedite the adoption process, which was still progressing back in the UK, but she and Anatole needed no marriage lines to release the passion between them!

Happiness welled through her.

She had everything she could ever dream of here with Anatole, in his arms, in the life he had made for her here with her beloved Georgy!

And if there was a shadow over her happiness, over the future that was yet to come—well, she would not think about that now. Would not let herself be haunted by it.

She would give herself only to the present—this wonderful, magical present that Anatole had created for her!

'There's something else the oncologist was saying, Lyn.'

Anatole's voice penetrated her haze of happiness. She brought her mind back smartly.

'He thinks that Timon is now sufficiently strong to receive visitors—I mean beyond just me and Georgy. I know you've been very understanding that Timon has really not felt up to coping with meeting you yet, and you know how brief I've had to keep my own visits to him, but of course he is keen to meet you. So...' He took a breath. 'How about if on our way into Athens tomorrow we go via the clinic? How would that be?'

His expression was encouraging, and Lyn knew she must acquiesce. She might have her own apprehension about finally meeting Georgy's formidable great-grandfather, the patriarch of the family, but it was something that had to be faced some time. And tomorrow, after all, was as good a day as any.

She dressed the next morning with particular care, and was conscious of a feeling of tension as they arrived at the clinic—conscious, too, of Anatole's warm, strong hand holding hers as they went indoors, dissipating her tension. Georgy was in her arms, and was already a clear favourite with the reception staff, and with the nurse who escorted them to Timon's room.

Anatole went in first, just to check his grandfather was ready for the encounter, and a moment later emerged to escort Lyn inside. He took Georgy from her, hefting him easily into his strong arms, and guided Lyn forward.

'Lyn—come and meet my grandfather,' he said.

She stepped towards the bed, her eyes going to the occupant. So this, she thought, was Timon Petranakos.

A lion of a man, she realised, but one on whom old age, grief and extreme illness had taken a heavy toll. Yet his eyes, as dark as Anatole's, held her with a penetrating regard. For a moment he said nothing, simply looked at her as if taking her measure. Then he nodded.

'It is good to meet you,' he said. His voice was somewhat rasping, and his accent in English strong.

'How do you do?' she said politely.

He gave a short, rasping laugh. 'Not well, but better than I might.' His dark eyes turned to Georgy, who was blowing bubbles at him from Anatole's arms. 'And all the better for seeing *you*!'

He switched to Greek, bestowing what Lyn took to be words of warm affection for Georgy and holding out his gnarled hands for Anatole to place him on his lap. She watched them interact—the old, sick man who had lost both son and grandson before their time and the infant who represented to him all the hope he had for the future. Anatole joined in, speaking Greek as well, and making a fuss of Georgy, who clearly loved being the centre of attention.

Lyn stood at the foot of the bed, feeling suddenly awkward.

Excluded.

Then, abruptly, Timon's head lifted. 'Tell me about his mother,' he commanded.

And it definitely *was* a command, she realised. But she made allowances. A man of his generation, his wealth, the head of a powerful Greek family, would be used to giving commands to all around him.

She swallowed, wondering what to say, where to begin. 'Lindy was…the sweetest person you could know,' she said. 'Loving and gentle.'

It hurt to talk about her, and yet she was glad that Timon Petranakos was asking.

'Beautiful?' he probed.

She nodded. 'Blonde and blue eyed,' she answered.

The short, rasping laugh came again. 'No wonder my Marcos wanted her! He had good taste, that grandson of mine!' There was an obvious note of indulgence in his voice as he talked about Georgy's father. Then the dark eyes went to his other grandson, seated beside him. 'As does this grandson too,' he added.

His gaze slid back to Lyn, and she felt herself flushing slightly. She dropped her eyes, feeling awkward.

'So,' Timon went on, 'you have the wedding all prepared, the two of you?'

Was there something different about his voice as he threw that at them? Lyn wondered uneasily. But perhaps it was just the thickness of his accent.

Anatole was answering him. 'We want you to be out of here first. Back at home.'

Timon nodded. 'Well, the wretches who are my doctors tell me that another week should make that possible.' His eyes went back to Lyn. For a moment there was that measuring expression in them again, and then his face creased into a smile.

'We are going into the city after we have left you,' said Anatole. 'Lyn wants to see the sights.'

Timon's eyes lit. 'Athens is the cradle of civilisation,' he told Lyn. 'No city in the world can compare to it!' His eyes went to his great-grandson. 'It would be unthinkable for Marcos's son to grow up anywhere else. *Unthinkable!*'

'Well,' said Anatole, 'that is what we are making possible.'

He nodded at his grandfather and said something to him in Greek that she did not understand. It was probably, she thought, something to do with the legal issues surrounding Georgy's adoption, because Timon answered in an impatient tone, to which Anatole gave a reply that seemed to have a warning note to it. Lyn could understand how Antole's grandfather might feel irked by the ponderous and exhaustive bureaucracy of the adoption process.

Then Timon's dark, sunken eyes were turned on her again, and once more Lyn felt herself being measured—assessed. She made herself hold the penetrating gaze, though, returning it with a clear, transparent expression. Abruptly Timon's lined face broke into a smile and he nodded.

'Good, good,' he said, in his strong accent. Then he

lifted a hand. 'Go—go, the pair of you.' He turned to-wards Anatole. 'Take her into the city. Buy her things she likes,' he instructed.

A nurse came bustling in, telling them that Kyrios Pe-tranakos needed to rest now and take his medication. Ana-tole got to his feet, scooping up Georgy with him. He spoke affectionately to his grandfather in Greek, then came to Lyn as they made their farewells. Lyn was conscious of a feeling of slight relief as they left. Timon Petranakos might be old and ill, but there was an aura of power about him that meant it was more comfortable being out of his pres-ence, however kindly he had been towards her.

As they settled back into the car and set off for the city centre Anatole looked across at Lyn.

'Not too bad, was it?' he asked, cocking an eyebrow at her. But his eyes had a sympathetic glint in them.

'He is quite formidable,' she allowed.

Anatole nodded in agreement. 'He is of his genera-tion,' he said. 'As he demonstrates,' he added dryly, 'by his belief that the way to win a woman over is to "buy her things she likes…"'

Lyn couldn't help but smile. 'You don't have to buy me anything!' she said. Her expression changed as she gazed at him. 'And you've won me over anyway, already—totally and completely!'

His eyes caught hers. 'Have I?' he said softly

'You know you have…' she breathed, her eyes and face alight with everything she felt for him.

He reached across Georgy's infant seat and lightly, so lightly, brushed Lyn's mouth.

'Good,' he said. Then he sat back.

Just for a moment Lyn thought she could see in his air and attitude the same aura of satisfaction she'd seen in Timon's smile.

Well, why not? Anatole is his grandson—of course there will be physical similarities!

Then Georgy was patting at her arm, wanting her attention. She gave it instantly and fully, as she always did, for never, *ever* would she dream of neglecting him—not even for Anatole.

The day they spent in Athens was magical for Lyn. Timon Petranakos had spoken the truth—the city *was*, indeed, the cradle of civilisation, the birthplace of democracy. As they made their way up to the Parthenon Anatole regaled her with millennia of history.

'How extraordinary,' Lyn said as they stood and gazed at the peerless ancient monument that had withstood all the centuries had thrown at it, 'to think that in this very place your ancestors came to worship! Two and half *thousand* years ago!'

Anatole gave his wry smile. 'We take it for granted sometimes and forget how much history we have compared with many other nations.'

She hooked her hand into his arm. 'You'd never run out of history here if you were a student,' she said.

He glanced across at her. 'Tell me,' he asked, 'if I could track down a suitable course of historical study would you be interested in taking it?'

She looked at him doubtfully. 'In Greek?' she asked. 'I don't think I'm anywhere near being able to cope with that.'

Anatole shook his head. 'I'm sure there must be courses in English. The British School at Athens, for example, runs English language summer courses in archaeology, I seem to remember. There are probably other opportunities as well—I'm sure we could find something that would suit you. After all, history was what you originally wanted to study before you had to divert to accountancy.'

'It would be wonderful if I could have a go at history

again!' she enthused. Then she frowned slightly. 'But I don't think it's practical now I'm looking after Georgy.'

Anatole looked at her with his familiar amused expression. 'Lyn—it's one of the many perks of wealth that childcare can easily be sorted! Speaking of which…' His tone of voice changed again, and Lyn looked at him. 'Timon was telling me that he wants to provide us with a nanny for Georgy.'

She looked startled. 'What for?' she said blankly.

He made a slight face. 'Like I said, he is of his generation. To him it is natural for children to be looked after by nursemaids and nannies.'

'I don't *want* to hand Georgy over to nursemaids and nannies!' Lyn exclaimed.

Anatole kissed her forehead. 'Don't worry about it, Lyn.' His tone of voice changed again. 'Now, do you feel up to visiting the temple of Nike as well? Or shall we take a coffee break first?'

They continued with their excursion, and Anatole regaled Lyn with everything he knew about all the monuments they were seeing. By the time they were finished Lyn was glad to set off back home again.

She looked at Anatole as they settled back into the car. 'It will most definitely take more than one visit to see everything in Athens!' she said with a smile.

'In the summer it will get too hot for sightseeing,' he replied, 'so it's best to see as much as possible now, while it's still relatively cool.' He smiled. 'We can drive in again tomorrow, if you like, or if you prefer we could drive out and see more of Attica itself—the whole region that Athens is set in.'

'Oh, that would be lovely!' enthused Lyn.

So they took off the next morning, with Anatole driving this time, touring through the Greek landscape, eating lunch at a little vine-shaded *taverna*, then heading for the majestic temple of Poseidon at Sounion, which stood in breathtaking splendour on the edge of the sea.

The following day they took a launch across the Saronic Gulf to the holiday island of Aegina, and spent a relaxed day there.

It was bliss, Lyn thought happily, to have Anatole all to herself—to spend the day with him, enjoying Georgy between them. Happiness ran like a warm current through her—a contentment such as she had never known. Walking, chatting comfortably, eating ice cream, Georgy aloft on Anatole's shoulders as they strolled along the seafront— it seemed to her so natural, so right.

We're like a real family...

That was what it felt like. She knew it did! And if there were to come a time when they would no longer be united like this for Georgy's sake then it was something she did not want to think about. Not now—not yet.

For now all she wanted to do was give herself to what she had, what there was between them—which was so, *so* much! For now this was enough. This happiness that bathed her in a glow as warm as the sunshine...

CHAPTER NINE

TIMON ARRIVED HOME from hospital at the end of the follow-ing week in a private ambulance and with his own large personal nursing team. Anatole had escorted him from the clinic, and when he was safely installed in his master bedroom, with all the medical equipment around him, Lyn brought Georgy in to visit him.

This second visit was less intimidating, and although Timon was polite and courteous to her most of his atten-tion was, understandably, focused on his great-grandson. Now that he was back in his palatial mansion she would wheel Georgy up through the gardens to visit him every day, Lyn resolved.

The following day Anatole arrived back from Athens earlier in the evening than usual.

'We've been summoned,' he told Lyn wryly, kissing her in greeting. 'Timon wants us to dine with him.'

Lyn frowned slightly. 'What about Georgy? He'll be in bed by then.'

'One of the maids can babysit,' answered Anatole, head-ing for the shower room. 'Oh, and Lyn...' His voice had changed. 'I'm afraid Timon has gone ahead with hiring a nanny for us.'

She stared after him in some consternation.

Immediately he continued, 'Please don't be anxious— she will be based up at the villa, not here, and she will only be for our convenience. Nothing else. Such as for evenings like this.'

Lyn bit her tongue. It wasn't an outrageous thing for Timon to have done, but it was unsettling all the same. And she would have preferred to have had some say in just who the nanny would be. Timon's ideas were likely to run to the kind of old-fashioned, starchy, uniformed nanny who liked to have sole charge of her infant and keep parents— adoptive or otherwise—well at bay.

But she put her disquiet aside. She would deal with it after their wedding—which was approaching fast now that Timon was out of hospital. This time next week she and Anatole would be husband and wife. A little thrill went through her—a bubble of emotion that warmed her veins. But with it came, yet again, that sense of plucking at her heartstrings that always came when she let herself think beyond the present.

This time next week we'll be married—and this time next year we might be already divorced...

She felt her heart squeeze, her throat constrict.

Don't think about this time next year—don't think about anything but what you have now! Which is so much more than you ever dreamed possible!

With a little shake she went to get ready herself for going up to the big house and dining in what she was pretty sure would be a much more formal style than she and Anatole adopted here in the little beach villa.

And so it proved.

Timon might still be an invalid, and in a wheelchair, but he commanded the head of the table in the huge, opulently appointed dining room as he must surely have done all his life. The meal was as opulent as the decor, with multiple courses and an array of staff hovering to place plates and refill glasses. Though she did her best, Lyn could not but help feeling if not intimidated, then definitely ill-at-ease.

It didn't help matters that Timon focused most of his conversational energies on Anatole, and that the main subject under discussion appeared to be a situation that was developing at one of the Petranakos factories in Thessaloniki, in the north of Greece.

Anatole elaborated a little to her, in English, as the meal progressed. 'The workers there are on short time already,' he said to her, 'and now the manager is issuing redundancies. It's not proving popular, as you can imagine.'

'Redundancies are unavoidable!' snapped Timon, interjecting brusquely.

Anatole turned back to him. 'It's been badly handled,' he said bluntly. 'Without any consultation, discussion or explanation. The manager there should be replaced.'

'He's *my* appointment,' growled Timon.

Anatole's mouth set, but he said nothing.

Timon's dark eyes flashed as they rested on his grandson. 'You're not in charge of Petranakos yet!' he exclaimed. 'And I don't *have* to put you in charge, I'll have you remember—'

He changed to Greek, speaking rapidly, with little emotion, and then broke off as a coughing fit overcame him. Lyn sat awkwardly, aware of the strong currents flowing between grandfather and grandson. Anatole looked tense, and she longed to smooth away his worries.

She got her chance when they got back to the beach house finally. After checking on Georgy, thanking the maid who'd babysat and sending her off back to the big house, she went into the kitchen to make Anatole his customary late-night coffee. When she took it into the bedroom he was already in bed, sitting back against the pillows, his laptop open on his knees. He glanced at Lyn, gratefully taking the coffee.

'I ought to be glad that Timon is—very clearly!—feeling better, but I have to say,' he went on darkly, 'it's making him reluctant to relinquish his chairman's role to me.' He made a wry face. 'The trouble is his management style is not suited to the current dire economic conditions. It's out of touch, too authoritarian, and that's far too inflammatory right now!' He took a mouthful of coffee. 'I need to get him to resign from chairing the executive board and put me in his place, so I can sort things out properly, in a more conciliatory fashion, without having all the employees up in arms! But Timon's proving stubborn about it!'

Lyn knelt beside him and started working at the knots in his shoulders.

Anatole rolled his head appreciatively. He caught her hand. 'I'm sorry this is erupting now,' he told her, 'so close to the wedding. But if things don't calm down in Thessaloniki soon I may have to go there. And,' he finished, his mouth tightening, 'I am going to have to do whatever it takes to persuade Timon to hand over the reins of power to me irrevocably! Too much is at stake! He says he wants to wait until Georgy's adoption is confirmed—but I can't wait till then now that all this has flared up. If the workers in Thessaloniki come out on strike it will cost the company millions in the end! I have to stop it getting that far, and to do that I need to have free rein to take what action is necessary!' He took a breath. 'I'm going to tackle Timon tomorrow. Get him to agree to the handover finally!'

He set down his coffee cup, turned off his laptop, and wrapped an arm around Lyn.

'The next few days are going to be tough,' he warned her apologetically. 'It's going to be a race against time to get everything sorted out before the wedding.' He gave a heavy sigh. 'I'll have to be up early tomorrow, just to tell you in advance, and you won't see much of me for the rest of the week, I'm afraid. It makes sense for me to stay in my apartment in Athens until the weekend. There's even a chance that the situation in Thessaloniki will require me

to fly up there myself now. I hope not, but I'd better warn
you about the possibility all the same.'

Lyn felt a little stab of dismay at the thought of being
without Anatole, but knew she must not add to the heavy
pressure on him already by showing it. Instead she put on
a sympathetic smile and kissed his cheek.

'Poor you,' she said. 'I hope it turns out all right.'

'Me too,' he agreed.

His eyes started to close, and Lyn reached to put out the
light. Tonight, sleep was clearly on the agenda.

But in just over a week we'll be on our honeymoon! she
reminded herself.

That little thrill of emotion came again as she settled
herself down, nestling against the already sleeping Anatole. She wrapped an arm around him, holding him close.

Very close…

'Right, then, Georgy my lad—no use us sitting here mop-
ing!' Lyn instructed her nephew and herself roundly as
she carried him through into the bathroom to get dressed
and ready for the day.

She'd woken to discover that Anatole had, as he had
warned her, taken himself off at the crack of dawn to get
to his desk, and she had immediately felt her spirits flat-
ten at the dispiriting prospect of his absence for several
days to come. Sternly, she'd admonished herself for her
craven wish that Anatole were not so diligent in the execution of his responsibilities towards Timon's affairs. She
had dramatic testimony that it was those very qualities
that she had so much reason to be grateful for. It was, she
knew, totally *because* Anatole had such a strong sense of
responsibility that he had undertaken so drastic a course
of action in safeguarding Georgy's future.

*Marrying me! Bringing me here to live with him, with
Georgy! Making a home for us here!*

Automatically she felt her cheeks glow. He'd done so much more than that!

He's transformed me—transformed my life! Given me a wondrous happiness that I never knew existed! In his arms I have found a bliss that takes my breath away!

Her eyes lit with the light that was always in them when she thought of Anatole and how wonderful he was—how wonderful it was to be here with him.

To think I once feared that he would take Georgy from me! To think that I wished he had never discovered his existence—never come into my life!

Because it was impossible to think that now! Utterly impossible! With every passing day, every hour spent with him, her gratitude and her happiness increased beyond measure! He was doing everything to make her feel comfortable here in Greece, to make her feel at home...valued and cherished.

His concern for her, his solicitude, his thoughtfulness, were all so precious to her!

With deft swiftness she got Georgy ready, then followed suit for herself. It was another warm sunny day, and even if she wished that she could look forward to Anatole coming home, however late he might be, she would not let her spirits sink. She had another Greek lesson in the afternoon, and she was making steady progress in the language—both speaking and reading it. She thought ahead. In the evening she would busy herself reading some of the hefty history books about Greece that Anatole had provided her with in English. She was determined to be as informed as possible when she applied to the history studies course Anatole had suggested she take after the summer.

A little glow filled her again. He was so thoughtful! Despite being rushed off his feet at work he had still found time to think about what she might like to do after they were married, getting her brain engaged again and not neglecting her love of history.

To think that, were it not for him, I'd be stuck studying accountancy and facing making a living endlessly totting up rows and rows of dull figures! I can study at my leisure, study the subject I love most, and it's all thanks to Anatole!

She headed downstairs with Georgy, telling him just how wonderful his big second cousin was—information that her nephew received with equanimity and a familiar chortle. When they reached the kitchen he wriggled in her arms to be set down, but then, as she was about to settle him into his highchair, ready for breakfast, something caught his eye.

It caught Lyn's too.

It was a package on the kitchen table, set in the place she usually sat. It was wrapped in gold coloured wrapping paper and bound up with a huge silver bow. Puzzled, she went round the table to look at it. Georgy immediately lunged for the enticing bow, and she had to busy herself getting him secure in his chair and then hastily unfastening the bow and presenting it to him. He did what he always liked doing best, which was to cram it straight in his mouth to sample. She let him do so absent-mindedly as she undid the rest of the wrapping.

Inside the gold paper was a document case—a tooled leather one—and on the top of it was a card. She lifted it and turned it over. Anatole's familiar handwriting leapt at her.

Timon instructed me to buy you things you like—I hope this fits the bill.

Curious, emotions running, she opened the document case and withdrew its contents.

She gasped.

Attached to some thick, headed paper was a photograph of a house.

An obviously English house in mellow brick, with roses round the door, set in a lovely English garden. In the foreground was a white picket fence, into which a little wicket gate had been set. The photo, she suddenly realised, had been taken from the wide strip of sand onto which the wicket gate opened.

Memory shot through her.

And a spear of emotion with it!

She knew exactly where this house was—exactly where the photo must have been taken! In her head she heard herself telling Anatole about when she had first seen houses like this one.

'Lindy and I used to walk past them all and discuss which one we'd live in...'

She picked up the photo and stared at it. This was certainly one of the prettiest she and Lindy must have seen!

Her eyes dropped to the rest of the contents of the document case and then widened in disbelief. With a catch in her throat she lifted them up.

It was a set of title deeds—deeds to the house whose photo she was gazing at.

Deeds made out to *her*...

Incredulously she let go of the papers, her hands flying to her face, not believing what she was seeing. Yet it was there—all there in black and white. The formal headings and the language was telling her that *she* was the owner of the house in the photo...

She gave a little cry and her eyes lit upon a note clipped to the corner of the deeds. It was in Anatole's handwriting. She picked it up and stared at it, emotion lighting within her.

'So you can always have a place you love in England for yourself.'

'Oh—*Anatole*!' she exclaimed. Incredulity went through her and through her—along with wonder and a wash of gratitude. She could not believe it—for him to have done such a thing for *her*!

She rushed to find her mobile and with fumbling fingers texted him straight away.

It's the most wonderful surprise—and you are the most wonderful man in the world! Thank you, thank you, thank you!

Moments later a reply arrived.

Glad you like it—in haste, A

For the rest of the day she was in a daze of wonder and happiness. If she had thought it a sign of his solicitude and care for her that he wanted her not to neglect her studies, *this* incredible act of generosity and concern overwhelmed her!

That Anatole had taken to heart her concerns that Georgy should not lose all his English heritage—and even more, that he had remembered her telling him about her seaside holiday with Lindy, a precious little island of carefree happiness in a difficult childhood—was a shining testimony to just how wonderful he was!

How am I going to bear divorcing him?

The thought sprang into her head unbidden—unwelcome and unwanted—and she felt it stab at her. She had got used to trying to keep it at bay, for with every passing day spent in her new and wonderful life she knew she was finding the prospect of just how temporary their forthcoming marriage was supposed to be increasingly unwelcome. How simple it had sounded when she had first let herself be drawn into this drastic solution to safeguard Georgy!

But things are now completely and totally different from then! Never in a million years did I imagine just how my relationship with Anatole would be transformed by him! Now the last thing I want to do is for us to part...

The cold wash of knowing that at some point in the future Anatole would extract himself from their marriage, conclude what had never been intended to be anything more than a temporary arrangement solely to enable them to adopt Georgy and settle him out here in Greece, chilled her to the bone.

Words, thoughts, sprang hectically in her brain.

I don't want us to part! I don't want us to go our separate ways, make separate lives for ourselves! I don't. I don't!

She gazed at Georgy, anguish in her eyes.

I want to go on as we are, being together, bringing up Georgy together, making our lives together...

Her face worked.

Maybe Anatole does too! That's what I have to hope—that he is finding the life we are making here as good as I do! That he is happy, and does not want us to change anything, for us to divorce and go our separate ways...

She could feel hope squeezing at her heart—hope and longing.

Let it be so—oh, please, please let it be so!

Didn't that incredible gift of his—the fantastic gift to her of a house of her own, where she could take Georgy sometimes to walk in the footsteps of his mother—show all his generosity, all his thoughtfulness? Wasn't that tangible proof of how much he felt for her?

And how easy it was to spend time with him—how comfortably they chatted and talked! That was good, wasn't it? It must be, surely? And the way they could laugh together, too, and smile at Georgy's antics...

And Georgy—oh, Georgy was beloved by them both. How doting they were to him, how dedicated!

A quiver of fire ran down her veins as she thought of the passion they exchanged night after night, the incredible desire she had for him, that he too must feel for her. Surely that most of all must tell her that what they had between them was not something unreal, temporary, that could be turned off like a tap?

Oh, please, let me mean as much to Anatole as he does to me... Please let it be so!

Anatole rubbed at his eyes as he sat at Timon's huge desk at Petranakos headquarters. God, he could do with some sleep! He was used to working hard, but this was punishing. Non-stop, just about, for the last four days on end. And nights. Nights spent here in Athens, at his apartment. He didn't like to leave Lyn and Georgy at the beach house, but there had been no option. Now that he'd finally got the chairmanship of the whole Petranakos Corporation, with full executive powers, there was a huge amount to do, on far too many fronts, at the huge, complex organisation that would one day be Georgy's.

The deteriorating situation in Thessaloniki was the most pressing, but by no means the only one. For with Timon having been hospitalised until so recently, daily management had become lax in many quarters. Even so, the threatened strike was requiring the bulk of his attention. So much so that he knew he was going to be hard-pressed to find the time to do something even more vital.

Get out of Athens tonight and back to Lyn—to talk to her.

Talk to her as quickly and as urgently as possible. The day of their wedding was approaching fast, and he could hear the clock ticking. He was running out of time.

Tonight—tonight I'll sit her down and tell her.

Tell her what he *must* tell her without any further delay

He glanced at the document lying in its folder at the side of his desk. It had been delivered to him by courier only an hour before. It seemed to lie there like a heavy weight on the mahogany surface of Timon Petranakos's desk.

For a moment Anatole's face blanked. Had he done the right thing?

Yes! I didn't have a choice. I had to do it! It's the reason I undertook this whole business—right from the very moment of reading those sad, pleading letters to Marcos...

The phone rang on his desk, cutting dead his thoughts, and he snatched it up. Now what?

A moment later he knew—and his expression said it all. Face black, he pushed back Timon's huge leather chair, packed away his laptop in his briefcase and strode out of the office. Timon's PA looked up expectantly.

'Put the jet on standby. I'm flying up to Thessaloniki,' he barked.

Then he was gone.

Lyn was both pleased and surprised to receive a call from Anatole in the middle of the day. But she quickly realised that the call was serious rather than tender. He told her that he was calling from his car on the way to the airport, just to let her know what was happening.

'I'll keep this brief,' he went on crisply. 'I'm going to have to fly up to Thessaloniki right away. A strike has just been declared, there's a mass walk-out, and protests are building outside the factory gates. The riot police have been marshalled by the manager—just what I don't need!' He took a heavy breath. 'But at least—finally!—I've got the power to sort it out myself.' He paused. 'I don't know when I'm going to be able to get back, Lyn.' His voice changed suddenly. 'And I have to talk to you urgently the moment I do.'

'What is it?' Alarm filled her throat.

She heard him give a rasp of frustration at the other end of their connection. 'I need to explain to you face-to-face. But, listen, please—I hope you'll understand—'

He broke off. Lyn heard a staccato burst of conversation in Greek, then Anatole was audible again.

'I'm sorry! I have to go. I'm flying up with the chief finance director and he's just heard on his own phone that there's been a clash with police outside the factory—and that TV crews are arriving to film it! I've got to speak to the officer in charge and get the police to back off for the moment. This can't escalate any further!'

The connection went dead.

Dismay filled Lyn. Not just at the fracas that Anatole was going to have to deal with, but because of what he'd just said to her—that he needed to talk to her urgently.

He had sounded so sombre...

What's wrong?

The question burned in her head but she could find no answer. It went on burning even as she crossed to the TV and turned to the Greek news channel. Even without understanding much Greek she could see that the angry dispute at the Petranakos facility in Thessaloniki was making the headlines.

If you want to help Anatole let him get on with sorting it out without making any demands on him yourself! she told herself sternly.

She'd done her best to do that for the past few days. Yet the beach house felt lonely without him. Their bed empty...

Worse, when she set off for the main house later, with Georgy in his buggy, for his daily visit to his great-grandfather, she was intercepted by a uniformed woman who informed her that she was Georgy's new nanny.

'I will take Baby to Kyrios Petranakos,' she announced in accented English.

Lyn hesitated. She didn't want this to happen, but this was not the moment to make a fuss, she knew. Reluctantly, she let the nanny take Georgy from her.

'I will bring him home later,' the nanny said punctiliously, with a smile that Lyn made herself *not* think of as condescending.

She shook her head. 'No, that's all right. I'll wait.'

She went out into the gardens and settled herself on a little bench in the sunshine. Despite the warmth, she felt chilled. Clearly Timon, now that he was back home again, wanted to make his presence felt—and to arrange things the way he liked them.

Well, she would wait until after the wedding—when Anatole was not having to deal with a strike on his hands— to take issue over the nanny and agree just what her role and function would be, if any. For now she would be accommodating. Bothering Anatole with something so trivial when he was up to his eyes in trying to sort out a costly and disruptive strike was the last thing she wanted to do!

She clung to that resolve now, knowing that he had flown up to Thessaloniki to deal with the problem there first-hand. But another concern was plucking at her. Would Anatole even be back in time for the wedding? And, even if he were, would they be able to get away on honeymoon at all?

Well, like the nanny situation, there was nothing she could do about it right now. Their wedding was going to be small and private anyway, and only a civil one since both parties knew it was going to end in divorce at some point, so there would be no guests to unarrange. On top of that, because Timon and Anatole were still in mourning for Marcos, it would have been inappropriate to have a large wedding anyway. So, Lyn made herself reason, if the wedding had to be postponed for the time being, and the honeymoon too—well, that was that. Anatole would sort out the strike, find a resolution that kept everyone happy, then come back home again. Then they would marry, and everything would be all right.

While their marriage lasted...

That chill formed again around her heart. She didn't want to think about the terms of their marriage—didn't want to think how it was supposed to end once Timon was no more. Didn't want to think about how, at some point, Anatole would divorce her and they would make suitable, civilised arrangements to share custody of Georgy...

Suitable. Civilised.

Such cold-blooded words—nothing like the passion that flared between her and Anatole! Nothing like the emotion that swept through her as he swept her into his arms...

She closed her eyes a moment, swaying slightly.

If only...

Words formed in her head—tantalising, yearning.

If only this marriage were not just for Georgy's sake...

She made herself breathe out sharply. She must not think such thoughts! This marriage *was* for Georgy's sake— that was the truth of it. And anything else—anything that had happened between her and Anatole—could not last any longer than their marriage...

It could not.

However much she yearned for it to do so...

CHAPTER TEN

SHE WOKE THE next day in low spirits to the sound of Georgy grizzling in his cot. His grumpy mood seemed to echo her own lowness, and nothing could divert him. She got through most of the morning somehow, restricting her urge to phone Anatole and merely sending him an upbeat e-mail, assuring him that everything was fine on her end and refraining from expressing her own down mood or mentioning Georgy's tetchiness. By early afternoon she was glad to be able to set off with Georgy to the big house, for at least it gave him something to think about other than his grouchiness. Maybe he was starting to teethe, she thought. Whatever it was, he was not a happy bunny—and nor was she.

She eked out their expedition to the big house, first wheeling Georgy along the shoreline and pointing out things that might cheer him up, and then, giving up on that, heading into the gardens towards the house. She took a meandering route, not caring if she were running late.

When she duly presented herself the new nanny did not come forward to remove Georgy from his buggy. Instead she gave Lyn a tight smile and informed her that she would take Baby for a stroll in the gardens.

'Kyrios Petranakos wishes to see you without Baby,' she announced loftily, and took the buggy handles from Lyn.

'Oh,' said Lyn, feeling mildly surprised and mildly apprehensive.

What could Timon Petranakos want? she thought. She reasoned it must be something to do with the forthcoming wedding.

Oh, please don't say it's going to have to be postponed because of all that's going on in Thessaloniki!

She took a breath. Well, if it had to be postponed, so be it. Anatole was under quite enough pressure as it was.

She let the nanny wheel Georgy away, warning her that he was a bit grouchy today and getting a condescending smile in return, and then set off after the manservant who was conducting her to Timon's quarters. When she was shown in he was in his day room, next door to his bedchamber—a huge room with the same ornate, opulent decor as the dining room that Lyn found a tad oppressive and overdone, but she appreciated it was a bygone style suitable for a man of his age and position in society.

When she was shown in his wheelchair was in front of his desk and he was clearly studying the documents laid out on it. He wheeled the motorised chair around to face her as the manservant backed out of the room, leaving Lyn facing Georgy's great-grandfather.

There was something different about him. At first she thought it was something to do with his state of health, but then she realised it was his expression.

Especially his eyes.

They were resting on her, but the brief, penetrating glance she'd got used to was now a more focused stare. She stood still, letting him look her over. Somewhere deep inside her, unease was forming.

What was going on?

With a hideous plunging of her heart, she heard her voice blurting out, 'Has something happened to Anatole?'

Dear God, was *that* what this was about? Had something happened to him? Something to do with the protest, violent clashes?

Please don't let him be injured! Or worse...

Fear pooled like acid in her stomach.

'Yes—something has happened to Anatole.'

She heard Timon's words and faintness drummed through her. Then, at his next words, her head cleared.

Brutally.

As brutally as the harsh words came from Timon Petranakos in his hoarse voice.

'Anatole is free—finally free. Of *you*!'

She stared. 'What do you mean?' she said, a confused expression filling her face.

A rasp came from him, and she could see his clawed hand clench the arm of his wheelchair.

'I mean what I say!' he ground out. 'My grandson is free of *you*!' His expression changed, his eyes hardening like flint. '*Hah!* You stare at me as if you cannot believe me! Well, believe me!' The dark eyes pinioned her. 'Did you really think,' he ground out, his accent becoming stronger with the emotion that was so clearly visible in his lined face, 'that I would permit him to be trapped by *you*?'

Lyn's face worked, her senses reeling.

'I...I...don't understand,' she said again. It sounded limp, but it was all she could think right now. What was happening? Dear God, what was *happening*? It was like being hit by a tsunami—a wall of denunciation that she had never expected! Never thought to receive! Her mind recoiled and she clutched at flying words and thoughts to try desperately, urgently, to make some kind of sense of them! Find some kind of reason for what was going on here.

Timon's jaw set. The flint in his eyes, sunken as they were with age and illness, hardened.

'Then understand *this*, if you please! Your dreams of being Kyria Telonidis are over! *Over!*'

A little cry came from her throat, tearing it like a raw wound. She wanted to speak, shout, yell, but she couldn't—not a single word. She was silenced. Helpless to make sense of any of this—anything at all!

Timon was speaking again, his voice harsh and accusing. His words cut at her, slashing into her.

'You thought to trap him. You took one look at him and thought you had it made. Thought you could use *my* grandson's boy to trap my other grandson! To land yourself a life of ease and luxury that you have *no* right to! None! You saw your opportunity to make a wealthy marriage and a lucrative divorce and you took it!'

The bitter eyes flashed like knives, stabbing into her.

Shock spiked her riposte. 'Anatole *offered* to marry me—it was *his* idea, not mine! He said it would make it easier to adopt Georgy—I agreed for Georgy's sake!' Lyn tried to fight back, tried to stand her ground in the face of this onslaught.

Timon's face twisted in anger. 'For your *own* sake!'

'No!' she cried out desperately. 'It isn't like that! It's for Georgy! It's all for Georgy!'

The lined face hardened. 'Then you will be overjoyed to realise that you have achieved that! Marcos's boy is here now—in the country where he belongs—and whatever those infernal, interfering, officious bureaucrats in England say, no court in Greece will hand him back. No court in Greece will take *my great-grandson* from me! And as for you—know that for all your scheming you have been well served in turn!' His expression twisted. 'Did you truly think that because Anatole took you to his bed he would actually go through with *marrying* you? He did it to keep you sweet—and it achieved his purpose—to get Marcos's boy here the quickest way!'

'No! I don't believe it! *No!*' She covered her ears with

her hands, as if she could blot out the hateful, hideous words.

'Well, believe it!' Timon snarled at her. 'Believe it to be justice served upon you—justice for your scheming, for your lies!'

She froze, her hands falling inert to her sides. Her face paled. 'What do you mean—lies?'

His dark eyes glittered with venom. 'Ah—*now* she is caught! Yes—*lies*! The lies you've told Anatole...'

Her face paled. 'I...I don't understand...' Her voice faltered.

A claw-like hand lifted a piece of paper from his desk and held it up. Gimlet eyes bored into her. 'Did you think I would not have you investigated? The woman who stood between me and my great-grandson? Of course I did!' His voice changed, became chilled. 'And how very right I was to do so.'

As if weights were pulling at them her eyes dropped to the paper in his hand. She could read the letterhead, read the name of an investigative firm, read the brief opening paragraph with her name in it...

She felt sick, her stomach clenching.

'You don't understand...' she said. But her voice was like a thread.

'I understand *completely*!' Timon Petranakos threw back at her, dropping the paper to the desk.

Lyn's hands were clenching and unclenching. She forced herself to shift her gaze to the dark, unforgiving eyes upon her. The claws in her stomach worked.

'Have...have you told Anatole?'

It was the one question burning in her veins.

A rasp came from Timon. 'What do *you* think?' he exclaimed, and she could hear the bitterness in his voice, the anger.

'I can explain—' she started, but he cut her off with
another harsh rasp of his voice.

'To what purpose? You lied to Anatole and now you are
caught out! It is justice upon your head—nothing more
than justice that all your schemes were always going to be
in vain! That you were never going to achieve your ambition to marry my grandson, enrich yourself for life! And
use *my* great-grandson to do it! Well...' He threw his head
back, eyes raking her like talons. 'Your schemes are over
now!' The claw-like hand reached for another paper on his
desk, and thrust it at her. 'Look—*look!* And see how all
your schemes have come to nothing!'

She felt her arm reach out, her fingers close nervelessly
on the thick document that Timon was thrusting at her. It
was typed in Greek, with a printed heading, and the unfamiliar characters blurred and resolved. It looked formal—
legal—and she could not read a word of it. But at the base
was a date—two days ago—and, above it a signature.

Anatole Telonidis.

Timon was speaking again. 'Here is a translation,' he
said. 'I had it drawn up for you. For just this moment.' He
lifted another piece of paper. The layout was exactly the
same as the Greek document, but this was in English. Only
the signature at its base was absent. With trembling hands
she took the paper, held it up. Again the words blurred,
would not resolve themselves.

'Keep it,' said Timon Petranokos. 'Keep them both. This
document gives Anatole everything he wants—everything
he's been asking for! He has taken over as chairman. Total
control. Full executive power. I've given it to him. And all
he had to do to get what he wanted,' he went on, the dark,
sunken eyes glittering with animosity, 'was undertake not
to marry you.' He paused. 'He signed it without hesitation,'
he finished harshly, his mouth twisting.

He took another rasping, difficult breath, as if so much speaking had drained him of his scarce reserves of energy.

She should pity him, Lyn thought, but she could not.

She could only fear him.

But fear was no use to her now. It hadn't been when Lindy had died. It hadn't been when the social workers had sought to take Georgy for adoption. It hadn't been when Anatole Telonidis had turned up, dropping his bombshell into her life about Georgy's dead father and the vast fortune he would inherit one day from his dying great-grandfather—the fortune Anatole was now safeguarding for Georgy by agreeing to what his grandfather demanded: shedding the bride-to-be he did not want...

Had never wanted.

It was like a spear in her side, hearing those words in her head—a spear that pierced her to her very core! Her vision flickered and she felt her heart slamming in her chest, her lungs bereft of oxygen. She gasped to breathe.

Timon was speaking again, vituperation in his voice. 'So you see there is nothing here for you now. *Nothing!* All there is for you to do is pack your bags and go! Take yourself off!' His dark eyes were filled with loathing. 'Your lies have come to nothing! And nothing is all that you deserve! To get rid of you as fast as I can do so I will hand you this, to speed you on your way!'

He thrust yet one more piece of paper at her—a small one this time—the size of a cheque.

'Take it!' he rasped.

Lyn stared at it blindly, frozen. She couldn't think, couldn't function—could only feel. Feel blow after blow landing upon her. Hammering her with pain. But she must not feel pain. Must not allow herself to do so. Later she would feel it, but not now. Now, at this moment, pain was unimportant. Only her next words were important.

To buy time.

Time to *think*, to work out what she must do—whatever it took—to keep Georgy safe with her.

She took a breath, tortured and ragged, forced her features to become uncontorted. Forced herself to think, to do something—anything other than just stand there while she reeled with what was happening.

She lifted her head. Stared straight at Timon. She should pity him—old and dying as he was, with his beloved grandson Marcos dead and buried so short a time ago. But she could not—not now. All she could do was what she was forcing herself to do now. To reach her hand out jerkily, as if it were being forced by an alien power, and take the cheque he offered.

She was at the beach house, staring at her mobile on which sat an unread text from Anatole, which had arrived while she was out having her life smashed to pieces. Beside the laptop on the dining room table were the documents Timon had thrust upon her and her Greek dictionary open beside them. Her frail and desperate hope that the translation he had given her was a lie had died. As she had slowly, painfully forced herself to read the original version, with Anatole's signature on it, word by damning word her last hope had withered to nothing

Anatole had done exactly what Timon had told her he had done. He had taken control of the Petranakos Corporation with full powers, just as he had always aimed to do.

Lyn's insides hollowed with pain. And he had done what he had always intended to do with her too. *Always*—right from the start! It was obvious now—hideously, crucifyingly obvious!

Not marry me—

A choking breathlessness filled her. The air was sucked from her lungs, suffocating her with horror.

He was never going to marry me! Never! It was a lie—all along!

And now he did not need to lie any more. There was no need for it. No need for any more pretence, any more charade.

As she sat there staring at the damning evidence the phone rang. For a moment, with a jolt, she thought it was her mobile, then she realised it was the landline. Almost she ignored it, but it went on and on, so with nerveless fingers she picked it up.

It was not Anatole. It was a voice speaking to her in Greek and immediately changing to English when the speaker heard her halting reply. It was an official from the town hall, confirming that the wedding due to take place in four days' time was indeed, as requested by Kyrios Telonidis via e-mail the previous day, cancelled.

She set down the phone. There was no emotion left within her. None at all. She could not allow any—must not—dared not. She stared back at her mobile, at the unread text from Anatole. She pressed her finger down to open it. To read her fate. She stared as the words entered her brain.

Lyn, I'm cancelling the wedding. I need to talk to you. Urgently. Be there when I phone tonight. A

She went on staring. Numbness filled her the way it had filled her when she'd sat beside Lindy's dead body, all the life gone out of it. All hope gone. Then slowly she got to her feet, picking up the damning documents, looking around her at the place she had thought so *stupidly* was going to be her home…

The home she'd share with Anatole.

The man who had just cancelled their wedding.

Not just postponed—but cancelled…

There was a tapping at the French windows leading out

to the garden. She looked round. The nanny was there, smiling politely, with Georgy in his buggy. The nanny, Lyn now realised bleakly, Timon had hired to take her place.

How she got rid of her Lyn didn't know, but she did somehow. Somehow, too, she made herself go upstairs, walk into the bedroom she'd shared with Anatole and gaze down blindly at the bed where he'd taken her into his arms so often. She found her vision blurring, her throat burning.

She made herself look away, go to the closet, pick out the largest handbag she possessed. She put into it all the changes of clothes that she could cram in and, far more importantly, her passport, credit card and what little money she possessed. Then she went into Georgy's room and packed his bag with nappies and two changes of outfit, his favourite toys. Then, still with her vision blurred and her throat burning, she made herself go downstairs again, scoop him up and hug him tight, tight, *tight*...

With the shawl she had brought downstairs with her she made a makeshift sling and fitted him in the crook of her shoulder, awkwardly hefting the two bags onto her other shoulder. Her shoes were stout walking shoes and she needed them, for when she went outdoors she headed to the boundary of Timon Petranakos's property, scrambling over the rocky outcrop there precariously with her precious burden and then, on the other side, gaining the track that led up from the seashore to the main road, running east to west about a quarter of a kilometre inland. There, she knew, was a bus stop. From there she could take the bus to the nearby seaside town and then pick up a tram. The tram would take her where she so desperately, urgently needed to get to.

Piraeus, the port of Athens. Her gateway to escape...

It was crowded when she got there—crowded, busy and confusing. But she made herself decipher the notices, found the ferry she wanted—the one that was the safest—and bought a ticket with her precious store of euros. She would not risk a credit card. That could be traced…

She hurried aboard the ferry, head down, Georgy in her arms, trying not to look anxious lest she draw attention to herself. The ferry was bound for Crete. If she could lie low there for a while, and then somehow—anyhow!—get a flight back from Crete to the UK she could lie low again, consult a family lawyer…do something that might stop her losing Georgy.

Will I have any chance now even to be his foster-carer? What will happen now that Anatole isn't marrying me after all? What happens to the adoption application?

Questions, questions, questions—multiple and terrifying! Timon would make a move to claim Georgy, and surely Anatole would too? She had to get to a lawyer, find out what chance she had herself.

But, however puny her hopes, one thing was for sure—if she stayed here in Greece then the long, powerful arm of the Petranakos dynasty would easily overpower her! Georgy would be ripped from her and she would stand no chance—no chance at all—against what Timon and Anatole could throw at her, with all their wealth and influence behind them.

I have to get back to the UK! At least there I stand a chance, however frail…

Her mind raced on, churning and tumultuous, trying to think, think, *think*, trying to keep her terror at bay.

Trying to keep at bay something that was even worse than the terror.

It stabbed at her like a knife plunging deep into her.

Pain. Pain such as she had never known before. Pain that savaged her like a wolf with a lamb in its tearing jaws. That made her want to hunch over and rock with the agony of it.

She stumbled forward, gaining the seating area in the bow of the ferry, collapsing on one of the benches in the middle section, settling Georgy on her lap. He was staring about delightedly, fascinated by this new environment. She stared blindly out over the busy, crowded harbour, feeling a jolt as the ferry disengaged from the dock and started its journey. She willed it on faster, though she knew it would take until morning to reach Heraklion in Crete. She tried to think ahead, plan in detail what she would do once she arrived there, but her mind would not focus. The wind picked up as they reached the open sea, buffeting her where she sat exposed, feeling the savage jaws of pain tearing at her.

Anatole's name on the paper Timon had so triumphantly thrust at her.

Anatole's name betraying her.

His message to her confirming his betrayal.

His breaking of all the stupid trust she had put in him!

Her mind cried silently in anguish. *I trusted him! I trusted everything he said—everything he promised me!*

But it had meant nothing, that promise. Only one thing had mattered to him—getting Georgy to his grandfather and thereby getting control of the Petranakos Corporation.

And if that promise had meant nothing to him… Her eyes stared blindly, haunted, pained. Nor had anything else…

The stabbing pain came again. *Nothing about me mattered to him! Nothing!*

Like a film playing at high speed in her head all the time she had spent with Anatole flashed past her inner vision. Their time together with Georgy…

I thought we were making a family together! I thought he was happy to be with Georgy and me, happy for us to be together.

Being with her when Georgy slept…

Anatole's arms around her, his mouth seeking hers, his strong, passionate body covering hers, taking her to a paradise she had never known existed! Murmuring words to her, cradling her, caressing her...

But it had meant nothing at all—only as a means to lull her, to deceive her as to his true intentions. She heard his voice tolling in her head. Over and over again he'd said those words to her.

'Trust me—I need you to trust me...'

Bitter gall rose in her. Yes, he'd needed her to trust him! Needed her to gaze at him adoringly and put her trust in him, her faith in him.

Like a fool...

She heard his words again, mocking her from the depths of her being. She had meant nothing to him. Nothing more than a means to an end—to get Georgy out here the quickest and easiest way.

To get him here and keep him here.

Keep him here without her.

He lied to me...

But he had not been the only one to lie.

Like a crushing weight the accusation swung into her, forcing her to face it. She did not want to—she rebelled against it, resisted it—but it was impossible to deny, impossible to keep out of her head. It forced its way in, levering its way into her consciousness.

The brutal accusation cut at her. *You lied to him too—you lied to him and you knew that you were lying to him.*

And it was true—she *had* lied...lied right from the start...

Sickness filled her as she heard Timon's scathing denunciation of her—heard him telling her that she had got nothing but her just deserts...

A ragged breath razored through her as she stared out to

sea, the wind buffeting her face, whipping away her tears even as she shed them. But even as the wind sheared her tears away they fell faster yet. Unstoppable.

CHAPTER ELEVEN

ANATOLE RAISED A weary hand—a gesture of acknowledgement of what the union rep had just said. He was exhausted. His whole body was tired. He'd gone without sleep all night, going over and over figures and facts with the management team at the Thessaloniki plant, trying to find a viable alternative to the redundancies. Then he'd gone straight into meetings with the union representatives, trying to hammer out something that would preserve jobs.

At least he was making some kind of impact on the union. They were listening to him, even if they were still disputing with him. His approach was not that of the former manager, or his autocratic grandfather, issuing to the employees lofty diktats that had resulted in an instant demonstration outside the plant and ballots for full strike action. Instead he had disclosed the true finances of the division, pulled no punches, inviting them to try and find a way forward with him.

He sat back, weariness etched into his face. There was still muted discussion around the table. He wanted to close his eyes and sleep, but sleep could wait. It would have to. Would the deal he was offering swing it? He hoped so. Strike action would be costly and crippling, benefitting no one. Worse, in the terrifyingly volatile Greek economy it was likely to spread like wildfire through the rest of the

Petranakos organisation, possibly even beyond, to other companies as well, with disastrous consequences.

To his intense relief the union reps were looking thoughtful, and a couple of them were nodding. Had he swung it? He hoped to God he had—then maybe he could get some sleep finally.

But not before speaking to Lyn. It was imperative he do so! He'd managed to find the time to text her about the cancellation of the wedding, but that brief text was utterly inadequate. He had to see her, talk to her, explain to her...

Frustration knifed through him. He had to sleep, or he'd pass out, but he had to talk to her too. Had to get back to her...

'Kyrios Telonidis—'

The voice at the door of the meeting room was apologetic, but the note of urgency in it reached him. He looked enquiringly at the secretary who had intruded.

'It is Kyrios Petranakos...' she said.

He was on his feet immediately. 'Gentlemen—my apologies. My grandfather...' He left the sentence unfinished as he strode from the room. It was common knowledge how very gravely ill Timon was. In the outer office he seized the phone the secretary indicated. As he heard his grandfather's distinctive voice his tension diminished. He had feared the worst. But then, as he heard what his grandfather was saying, he froze.

'She's gone! She's gone—taken the boy! She's taken the boy!' It was all his grandfather could say, over and over again. Totally distraught.

'What did you say to her? Tell me what you said to her!'

Anatole's voice was harsh, but he needed to know what it was that had sent Lyn into a panic, making her flee as she had. Taking Georgy with her...

Since the call had come through to him in Thessaloniki life had turned into a nightmare. He had flown straight back to Athens, raced to Timon's villa, stormed into Timon's room.

His grandfather's face was ravaged.

'I told her what you'd done!'

Anatole's eyes flashed with fury. 'I told you to let *me* tell her! That I would find the right way to say it! I knew I needed to—urgently—but with that damn strike threatening I had to tell her to wait for me to talk to her! Why the hell did you go and do it?'

He wasn't being kind, he knew that, but it was Timon's fault! Timon's fault that Lyn had bolted. *Bolted with Georgy!* He felt fear clutch at him. Where were they? Where had Lyn gone? Where had she taken Georgy? They could be anywhere! Anywhere at all! She'd taken her passport, and Georgy's, but even with his instant alerting of the police at the airport there had been no reports of them. His face tightened. Athens Airport was not the only way out of Greece—there were a hundred ways she could have gone…a hundred ways she could have left Greece!

'Why?' Timon's rasping voice was as harsh as his. *'This* is why!' He seized a piece of paper from his desk, thrust it at Anatole.

Anatole snatched it, forcing his eyes to focus, to take in what he was reading. It was Latin script, in English.

As he read it he could feel ice congeal in his veins. He let the paper fall back on the desk, staring down at it with sightless eyes.

Beside him he could hear his grandfather's voice speaking. Coming from very far away.

'She lied to you—she lied to you and used you. Right from the start! So I told her—I told her exactly what you'd done.'

Lyn was pushing Georgy around a park. The buggy was not the swish, luxury item Anatole had bought. This one was third-hand from a jumble sale, with a wonky wheel, a stained cover and a folding mechanism that threatened to break every time she used it. But it was all she could afford now. She was living off her savings. Getting any kind of work was impossible, because it would never be enough to cover childcare.

She'd found a bedsit—the cheapest she could get—a single room with a kitchenette in a corner and a shared bathroom on the landing, so cramped and run down it made the flat she'd lived in while at college seem like a luxury penthouse! Whenever she stared round it, taking in every unlovely detail, a memory flashed into her head.

The beautiful colour photo from the estate agent that had come with the title deeds to the seaside house in the Witterings in Sussex…

Her expression darkened. She had thought in her criminal stupidity that it was a gesture of Anatole's generous sensitivity to her plea that Georgy should not lose his English heritage…

She knew now what it really was—had known from the moment Timon had destroyed all her stupid dreams.

It was my payoff.

Well, she wouldn't touch it! Wouldn't take it! Would take nothing at all from him! She'd left all her expensive new clothes in the wardrobe in Timon's beach house, leaving Greece in her own, original clothes. Clothes that were far more suited to the place she lived now.

Yet even taking the cheapest bedsit she'd been able to find was eating into her funds badly. She could not continue like this indefinitely. She knew with a grim, bleak inevitability that a time of reckoning was approaching— heading towards her like a steam train. The knowledge was like a boot kicking into her head. She could not go on like this…

And not just because she would eventually run out of money.

But because she'd run off with Georgy.

Run from the man who was trying to take him from her! The man she had trusted never to do that.

Pain knifed her. Pain that was so familiar now, so agonising, that she should surely be used to it? But it was still like a stab every time she felt it—every time she thought of Anatole. Every time she remembered him.

Being with him—being in his arms! Being with him by day and by night! All the time we spent together—all the weeks—all that precious, precious time...

She closed her eyes, pushing the buggy blindly around the little park that was not too far away from the shabby bedsit she'd taken here in Bristol, which had been the destination of the first flight out of Heraklion. As she walked, forcing one foot in front of the other, memories rushed into her head, tearing at her with talons of sharpest steel. Memories of Anatole walking beside her in another city park like this, in the cold north country spring, sitting down by the children's play area. She heard his voice speaking in her head.

'There is a way,' he'd said. 'There is a way that could solve the entire dilemma...'

Her hands spasmed over the buggy's push bar. Yes, there had been a way to solve it! A way that he'd had all worked out—in absolute detail. Totally foolproof detail...

He had known—dear God—a man like him must have known from the off that she would be putty in his hands! That he could persuade her, convince her into doing what he wanted her to do!

'I need you to trust me...'

The words that she had heard him say so often to her burned like fire in her head.

And what better way to win her trust, keep her doting and docile, than by the most foolproof method of all…?

He took me to bed to get me to trust him. Just to keep me sweet.

Until he did not need to any more.

Her heart convulsed and she gave a little cry, pausing in her pushing and hunkering down beside Georgy. He turned to look at her and patted her face, gazing at her. She felt her heart turn over and over.

I love you so much! I love you so much, my darling, darling Georgy!

Yet as she straightened again, went on pushing forward, she felt as if a stone inside was dragging at her. She could not go on like this.

The harsh, brutal truth was that, though she had panicked when Timon had smashed her life to pieces, had followed every primal instinct in her body and fled as fast and as far as she could with Georgy in her arms, she was now on the run.

Hiding not just from Anatole and Timon but from the authorities in whose ultimate charge her sister's son still was…

It could not go on. She knew it—feared it—must face it.

Face, too, against the resistance that had cost her so much to overcome, that she was also hiding from the truth. The truth of what *she'd* done…

I used him too.

That was what she had to face—what Timon had thrown at her. Her own lie—her own deceit to get from Anatole what she wanted so desperately.

But it had all fallen apart—everything—and now she was reduced to this. Fleeing with Georgy—on the run—with no future, no hope.

It could not go on. There was only one way forward now. Only one future for Georgy.

If you love him, you must do it. For his sake!

In her head she heard the words she had cried out so often.

I can't do it! I can't—I can't! Lindy gave him to me with her dying words...Georgy is mine—mine!

But as she plodded on through the scruffy urban park that was a million miles away from the Petranakos mansion, with its huge private grounds and pristine private beach, her eyes staring wildly ahead of her, her face stark, she could feel the thoughts forcing their way into her tormented mind as desperately as she tried to keep them out.

They would not be kept out.

You must not think of yourself—your own pain, your own feelings! What you must think of is Georgy! If you love him, then do what is best for him!

He could not go on living like this, in some run down bedsit, hand to mouth. Hiding and on the run. Being fought over like a bone between two dogs in a cruel, punishing tug-of-love.

Slowly, as if she had no strength left in her, she wheeled the buggy around and headed back out of the park.

She had a letter to write.

Anatole walked into the air-conditioned building that housed the London offices of his lawyers. It hardly needed air-conditioning, because the London summer was a lot cooler than the Greek summer, but the temperature was the last thing he was thinking of. He had only one thought in his mind—only one imperative. He gave his name at the desk and was shown in immediately.

'Is she here?' was his instant demand to the partner who handled his affairs as he greeted him in his office.

The man nodded. 'She's waiting for you in one of our meeting rooms,' he said.

'And the boy?'

'Yes.'

The single word was all Anatole needed to hear. Relief flooded through him. It flushed away the other emotion that was possessing him—the one he was trying to exorcise with all his powers, which had possessed him ever since that fateful call from Timon.

'Do you wish me to be present at the meeting?' his lawyer enquired tactfully.

Anatole gave a curt shake of his head. 'I'll call you when I need you. You've outlined my legal position clearly enough, so I know where I stand.' He paused, not quite meeting the man's eyes. 'Did she say anything to you?'

The lawyer shook his head.

Anatole felt another stab of emotion go through him. He tensed his shoulders. 'OK, show me in.'

He blanked his mind. Anything else right now was far too dangerous. He must focus on only one goal—Georgy.

Nothing else.

No one else.

Lyn was sitting in one of the leather tub chairs that were grouped around a low table on which were spread several of the day's broadsheet newspapers, a copy of a business magazine and a law magazine. Georgy was on her lap, and she was nuzzling him with a soft toy. It was one of the ones that she and Anatole had bought for him in London, at the very expensive department store and with Aladdin's Cave of a toy department. It seemed they had bought it a lifetime ago—in a different universe.

She wondered what she was feeling right now and realised it was nothing. Realised that it had to be nothing—because if it were anything else she could not go on sitting there.

Waiting for Anatole to walk in, as she knew he would at any moment now.

There was a clock on the wall and she glanced at it. Time was ticking by. In a few minutes she would see him again, and then she would say to him what she must say.

But she must not think about that. Must only go on sitting here, absently playing with Georgy, while the minutes between her and her endless empty future ticked past.

The door opened. Her head jerked up and he was there. Anatole.

Anatole.

Here—now—in the flesh. Real. Live.

Anatole.

As overwhelming and as overpowering to her senses as he always had been, right from the very first...

The nothing she had been feeling shattered into a million fragments...

Like a tidal wave emotion roared into her, the blood in her veins gushing like a hot fountain released from a cave of ice. Her sight dimmed and her eyes clung to him as he walked in.

On her lap, Georgy saw him too—saw him, recognised him, and held out his chubby arms to him with a gurgle of delight.

In two strides Anatole was there, scooping him up, wheeling him into the air, folding him to him and hugging him, a torrent of Greek coming from his lips. Then, as he nestled Georgy into his shoulder, he turned to Lyn.

For a moment—just a moment—there was a flash of emotion in his eyes. It seemed to sear her to the quick. Then it was gone.

He stood stock-still, Georgy clutched to him, his face like stone. But she could feel his anger coming off him. Feel it spearing her.

'So you brought him. I did not think you would.' His voice had no expression in it.

She made herself answer. 'I said in my letter I would.' Her voice was halting. As expressionless as his. It was the only way she could make herself speak. Say the words she had to say.

He frowned a moment, his eyes narrowing. 'So why did you? Why did you bring him here? What are you after, Lyn?'

She heard the leashed anger and knew that *she* had caused it. But his anger didn't matter. She gave a faint, frail shrug. 'What else could I do? I ran, Anatole, because I panicked. It was instinct—blind, raw instinct—but once I was back here I realised there had been no point in running. No point in fleeing.' She looked at him. Made herself look at him. Made herself silence the scream inside her head against what she was doing. What she was saying. What she was feeling...

What you feel doesn't matter. Seeing Anatole again doesn't matter. It doesn't matter because you never mattered to him—you were just an impediment, in his way, a stepping stone towards his goal. It wasn't real, what happened between you. You were nothing to him but a means to an end. An end he has now achieved.

She looked at him holding Georgy, the baby sitting content in Anatole's arms. She had seen them like that a hundred times—a thousand. She felt her heart crash.

You were nothing to him—Georgy is everything!

And that was what she must cling to now. That and that alone. It was the only way to survive what was happening. What was going to happen.

'I thought,' he bit out, 'you might have gone to the house.'

She frowned. 'House? What house?'

A strange look flitted across his face. 'The house by the sea—the house I gave you.'

She stared. 'Why would I have gone there?' Her voice was blank.

'Because it's yours,' he riposted flatly. But the flatness was the flatness of the blade of a knife...

'Of course it isn't mine! Nothing's mine, Anatole. Not even—' She closed her eyes, because the truth was too agonising to face, then forced them open again. 'Not even Georgy.'

There—she had said it. Said what she had to say. What she should have said right from the start.

If I had just admitted it—admitted the truth—then I would have been spared all this now! Spared the agony of standing here, seeing Anatole, knowing what he came to mean to me!

Dear God, how much heartache she would have saved herself!

She took another breath that cut at her lungs, her throat, like the edge of a razorblade.

'I'll sign whatever paperwork needs to be signed,' she said. 'I can do it now or later—whatever you want. I'll have an address at some point. Though I don't know where yet.'

As she spoke she made herself stand up. Forced her legs to straighten. She felt faint, dizzy, but she had to speak—had to say what she had come to say.

She took a breath. Forced herself to speak.

'I've brought his things—Georgy's. There isn't much. I didn't take much with me. And I've only bought a little more here in the UK. It's all in those bags.' She indicated the meagre collection on the floor by the chair. 'The buggy isn't very good—it's from a jumble sale—but it's just about useable until you get a new one. Unless you brought his old one with you... Be careful when you unfold it, it catches—' She pointed to where it was propped up against the wall.

She fumbled in her bag. Her fingers weren't working properly. Nothing about her was working properly.

'Here is his passport,' she said, and placed it on the little table. There was the slightest tremble in her voice, but she fought it down. She must not break—she *must* not... 'I hope—' she said. 'I hope you can take him back to Greece as quickly as possible. I am sure...' She swallowed. 'I'm sure Timon must want to see him again as soon as he can.'

Her voice trailed off. She picked up her bag, blinked a moment.

'I think that's everything,' she said.

She started to walk to the door. She must not look at Anatole. Must not look at Georgy. Must do absolutely nothing except keep walking to the door. Reach it, start to open it...

'What the *hell* are you doing?'

The demand was like a blow on the back of her neck. She turned. Swallowed. It was hard to swallow because there was a rock the size of Gibraltar in her throat. She blinked again.

'I'm going,' she said. 'What did you think I would do?'

He said something. Something she did not catch because she was looking at his face. Looking at his face for the very last time. Knowing that it was the very last time was like plunging her hand into boiling water. But even as she looked his expression changed.

'So he was right.' The words came low, with a lash that was like a whip across her skin. 'Timon was right all along.'

Slowly he set Georgy down on the thickly carpeted floor, pulling off his tie to keep him happy. Lyn found her eyes going to the strong column of his neck as he unfastened the top button of his shirt now that he was tieless. Felt the ripple in her stomach that was oh, so familiar— and now so eviscerating.

'Timon was right,' he said again. His voice was Arctic. 'He said you only wanted money out of all of this! I didn't believe him. I said you'd turned down cash from me to hand over Georgy. But he read you right all along!' His voice twisted. 'No wonder he set his private investigators on to you—and no wonder you took his money to clear out!'

She didn't answer. Only picked up Georgy's passport. Thrust it at him.

'Open it,' she said. Her voice was tight. As tight as the steel band around her throat, garrotting her.

She watched him do as she had demanded. Watched his expression change as he saw Timon's uncashed cheque within, torn into pieces.

'I took it from him to give me time to make my escape. Because I could think of nothing else to do.' She took a ragged shredded breath. 'I never wanted money, Anatole,' she told him. 'I never wanted anything except one thing— the one thing that was the most precious in my life.'

Her eyes dropped to Georgy, happily chewing on Anatole's silk tie.

She was lying, she knew. Lying because she'd come to want more than Georgy—to want something even more precious to her.

You! You, Anatole—I wanted you so much! And a family— you, and Georgy and me—I wanted that so much! So much!

That had been the dream that had taken shape in Greece—that had made her heart catch with yearning! Anatole and Georgy and her—a family together...

She lifted her eyes to Anatole again. To his blank, expressionless face.

'I kept telling you Georgy was mine,' she said. 'I said it over and over and over again. As if by saying it I might make it true.' She stopped. Took a razoring breath that cut at the soft tissue of her lungs. Then said what she had to say. *Had* to say.

'But he isn't mine. He never was.'

She looked at Anatole—looked straight at him. Met his hard, masked gaze unflinchingly as she made her damning confession.

'Not a drop of my blood runs in his veins.'

CHAPTER TWELVE

ANATOLE'S FACE WAS stark. Hearing Lyn say what he now knew...

'I know that now,' he said. His voice was strange, but he kept on speaking all the same. 'I know that Lindy wasn't your sister. She wasn't even your half-sister. She was nothing more than your stepsister. Timon showed me what his investigators found. She was the daughter of your mother's second husband, who left her with your mother and you when he abandoned the marriage—*and* his daughter.'

He shook his head as if he were shaking his thoughts into place—a new place they were unaccustomed to.

'When he told me it made such sense. Why Georgy doesn't look like you. Why your name is so similar to Lindy's—no parent would have done that deliberately—and why I sometimes caught that look of fear in your eyes. Like when you didn't want a DNA test done.' He paused. 'Why didn't you tell me, Lyn? You must have known I would find out at some point?'

She gave a laugh. A bitter, biting laugh.

'Because I wanted to be married to you before you did!' she cried. 'I was scheming to get your ring on my finger—the ring you never intended to put there!'

His expression changed. He opened his mouth to speak but she ploughed on. 'Timon told me! He told me that the whole damn thing had been nothing more than a ruse! All that stuff about getting married to strengthen our joint claim to adopt Georgy between us! All that was a fairy tale! You never meant a word of it!'

'What?' The word broke from him explosively.

She put her hands to her ears. 'Anatole—don't! Please— don't! Don't lie to me now—we're done with lies! We're done with them!' That brief, bitter laugh came again. It had no humour in it, only an ocean of pain, and she let her hands fall to her sides. 'Timon threw it at me that I deserved everything I was ending up with because I'd lied to you by not telling you that Lindy was only my stepsister. I knew perfectly well that your claim to Georgy would be stronger than mine ever could be! Because you were a blood relative and I wasn't! I was trying to trap you into a marriage you never needed to make!'

She threw her head back.

'When he tried to give me money to leave, told me he knew I only wanted to marry you because you were rich, I was angry! I've never wanted your money—*never*! I only wanted Georgy!'

She took a shuddering breath, shaking her head as if the knowledge of what she had done was too heavy a weight to carry. 'But none of it matters now. It's over. I know that— I've accepted it. I've accepted everything. And I've accepted most of all that I have to do what I am doing now.'

Her eyes went to Georgy again, so absolutely and utterly unaware of the agonising drama above his head.

'I called him mine,' she whispered. The words would hardly come, forced through a throat that was constricted with grief. 'But he never was. He was never mine. Only my stepsister's baby. Your cousin's son. Which is why...'

She lifted her eyes again, made them go to Anatole, who was standing like a statue, frozen. She felt her heart turn over. Turn over uselessly in her heart.

'Which is why,' she said again, and her voice was dead

now, 'I'm leaving him. He isn't a bone to be fought over, or a prize, or a bequest, or anything at all except himself. He needs a home, a family—*his* family. *Your* family. You'll look after him. I know you will. And you love him—I know you love him. And I know that Timon loves him too, in his own way.' She took a heavy razoring breath that cut into her lungs. 'I should have seen that from the start—that I had no claim to him. Not once you had found him. He's yours, Anatole—yours and Timon's. It's taken till now for me to accept that. To accept that I should never have put you through what I have. I see that now.'

She picked up her bag. It seemed as heavy as lead. As heavy as the millstone grinding her heart to chaff.

'I won't say goodbye to Georgy. He's happy with you. That's all that counts.' Her voice was odd, she noticed with a stray, inconsequential part of her brain.

She turned away, pulling open the door. Not looking back.

An iron band closed around her arm, halting her in her tracks. Anatole was there, pulling her back, slamming the door shut, holding her with both hands now, clamped around her upper arms.

'Are you insane?' he said. 'Are you completely insane? You cannot seriously imagine you are just going to walk out like that?'

She strained away from him, but it was like straining against steel bonds. He was too close. Far, far too close. It meant she could see everything about him. The strong wall of his chest, the breadth of his shoulders sheathed in the expensive material of his handmade suit, the line of his jaw, darkening already, see the sculpted mouth that could skim her body and reduce her to soft, helpless cries of passion.

She could see the eyes that burned with dark gold fire.

Catch the scent of his body.

See the black silk of his lashes.

She felt faint with it.

She shut her eyes to block the vision. Stop the memories. The memories that cut her like knives on softest flesh.

'What else is there to do?' she said. Her voice was low and strained. 'You don't want to marry me—you've never wanted to marry me—and Timon doesn't want you to marry me. He made that clear enough! And now you're not marrying me I can do what Timon told me to do—clear off and leave you alone. Leave Georgy alone, too. Because he doesn't need me. He's got you, he's got Timon, he's got everything he needs. The nanny will look after him while you're at work. She's very good, I'm sure. He doesn't need me and he won't remember me—he won't miss me.'

'And Georgy is the only person you're concerned about? Is that it?' There was still something odd about Anatole's voice, but she wouldn't think about that. Wouldn't think about anything. Wouldn't *feel* anything.

Dared not.

She opened her eyes again, made herself look at him. 'No,' she said. She stepped back and this time he let her go. She took another step, increasing the distance between them. The distance was more than physical—far, far more. 'There's you, too,' she said.

She made herself speak. 'I'm sorry I put you through so much anxiety—running away from Greece as I did— but at the time I was still…still in denial. Still thinking I had a right to Georgy. And that made me so…so angry with you.' She picked the word *angry* because it was the only safe one to use. Any of the other words—*anguished, agonised, distraught*—were all impossible to use. Quite impossible! 'Because I trusted you—just like you kept telling me to trust you—when you said you would make it all work out. That if we married we'd have a much better chance of adopting Georgy.'

She took another heaving breath, and now the words broke from her.

'But all along you were just telling me that in order to get me to agree to bring Georgy out to Greece. Because with me as his foster-carer it was the quickest way to get him there—me taking him—rather than going through the courts for permission on your own behalf. You knew I was fearful of bringing Georgy to Greece, so you spun me all that stuff about marrying and then divorcing. And to keep me sweet—'

She heard her voice choke but forced herself to speak, forced herself to say it all to voice every last agony.

'To keep me sweet you...you... Well, you did the obvious thing. And it worked—it worked totally. I actually believed you really were going to marry me—and I desperately wanted that to happen, because marrying you gave *me* my best chance to adopt Georgy!'

The words were pouring from her now, unstoppable.

'It's because I'm not a blood relation that that the authorities have always wanted him to be adopted by someone else! But then there was you—a close relation to his father—and being your wife would have been *my* best chance as well! That's why I did it, Anatole—that's why I agreed to marry you. And I've been well served. I have no claim to him and that's what I've finally accepted. Georgy isn't mine and never was—never will be!'

As her gaze clung to the man standing there—the man she had given herself to, the man who meant so much to her, who had caused her such anguish—she heard her mind whisper the words that burned within her head.

And nor are you mine! You aren't mine and never were—never will be! I'll never see you again after today— never! And my heart is breaking—breaking for Georgy... Breaking for you.

It *was* breaking. She knew it—could feel it—could feel

the fractures tearing it apart, tearing *her* apart as she spoke, as she looked upon him for the very last time in her life... The man she had fallen in love with so incredibly stupidly! So rashly and foolishly! She had fallen in love with him when to him she was only a means to an end—a way to get hold of the child he'd so desperately sought with the least fuss and the most speed!

She took another harrowing breath. 'So I can finally do what I know I have to do—walk away and leave Georgy to you. Because you love him and you will care for him all his life. He won't need me—I can see that clearly now... quite, quite clearly.'

'Can you?' Again he seemed only to echo her words.

She nodded. Her eyes were wide and anguished, but she made herself say the words she had to say. Say them to Anatole. The man who would be Georgy's father—she would never, *never* be his mother!

'Like I said, I accept now that he doesn't need me. He has you, Anatole, and that is enough. You'll be a wonderful father! You love him to pieces, and he adores you. *And* your silk ties,' she added.

But she mustn't attempt humour—not even as a safety valve. Emotion of any kind now was far too dangerous. Being here in this room, with Anatole and Georgy, was far too dangerous. She had to go now, while she still could...

'You can't see straight at *all*! You can't even see what's right in front of you!'

Anatole's harsh voice cut across her. Then it changed.

'But I can understand why.' He took a ragged breath. 'I can understand everything now.'

He reached forward, took her wrist. Drew her away from the door towards the group of chairs. He sat her down in one, and himself in the other. She went without resistance. Her limbs were not her own suddenly.

Georgy, still on the carpet, seeing her close by, started

to crawl towards her, a happy grin on his face. He reached her leg and clung to it with chubby arms. Her face worked.

'Pick him up, Lyn,' said Anatole.

She shook her head.

'I can't,' she said. 'I mustn't—he isn't mine.'

Her throat was aching, as if every tendon was stretched beyond bearing.

Anatole leant down, scooped up Georgy, put him on Lyn's lap.

'Hold him,' he told her.

There was something wrong with his voice again. It was harsh and hoarse.

'Hold him and look at me. Tell me again what you've just said. That you are going to walk out on Georgy. Abandon him.'

A vice closed over her heart, crushing it. 'I'm…I'm not abandoning him. I'm…I'm doing what is right. What has to be done. What I should have done from the moment you first found him. He isn't mine. He never was mine….'

Her throat closed again but she made herself go on, made herself lift her stricken gaze to the dark eyes that were boring into her like drills…

'I should have given him to you straight away—when you first came to me! Then you would never have had to go through that charade, that farce—the one your grandfather called time on. The one…' She swallowed. 'The one that you were just about to end yourself away.' She looked at him, her gaze heavy as lead. 'I got a phone call from the town hall after Timon had spoken to me—a phone call confirming that the wedding had been cancelled. And then…' She swallowed again. 'Then I got your text, telling me the same thing.'

'In that text I told you I would *explain everything* when I spoke to you later!'

Anatole's voice seared her.

'Timon had already made everything clear to me—and when I tried not to believe him he set me straight too. He showed me the document you'd signed—the one giving you the chairmanship of the Petranakos Corporation, the one affirming that you would not be marrying me. So what would have been the point, Anatole, in you telling me that yourself when I had it in writing already?'

Greek words spat from him.

Lyn's gaze slid away, down to the baby sitting on her lap, placidly chewing on Anatole's tie, content just to be on her knees. She wanted to put her arms around him but she must not. Not any more.

Anatole was speaking again and she made herself listen—though what could he say that she could want to hear?

'The *point*, Lyn,' he bit out, and each word was cut like a diamond from the air, 'was that *I* would have told you the truth!'

'I knew the truth,' she answered. 'Timon told me.'

'Timon,' said Anatole carefully—very carefully, 'lied.'

Lyn's eyes went to his. There was still that dull blankness in them. Why was he saying this? What for?

'I saw the document you signed,' she said. 'I saw it in the English translation and I saw the original—the one in Greek with your signature on it. I translated it myself. It said what Timon told me it said. You are the new chairman and you won't be marrying me.'

'And did it tell you *why*?'

There was still that strangeness in his voice. She heard it, but knew she must not...

'Timon told me why. Because you never intended to marry me. It was all a ruse, to get me to agree to bring Georgy out to Greece.'

'Well,' he said, speaking in the same clear, careful voice, as if she were hard of learning, 'in that case why

didn't I just put you on the first flight back to London once
Georgy was in Athens?'

She gave a shrug. 'I don't know. It doesn't matter.'

It didn't matter. Not now. Not now that everything she
had hoped and dreamed was smashed to pieces. Not now
when her heart was breaking—breaking twice over. For
Georgy and for Anatole.

Georgy was looking up at her and absently she stroked
his hair. It felt like silk beneath her fingers.

*I'll never hold him again on my lap. Never hug him or
kiss him. Never see him grow up...*

Her eyes went to Anatole, standing there—so very dear
to her, so very precious.

And she had never mattered to him at all...

Pain curdled around her heart. She wished he would
stop talking to her, stop asking her things—things that
did not matter that could not matter ever again. But he
was talking again. Still talking at her—like some nightmare *post mortem*...

'Yes, Lyn—it *does* matter. Why would I want you to
stay on in Greece, live with me in the beach house, sleep
with me, if I'd already got what I wanted from you?'

Her brow furrowed. He was going on at her and there
wasn't any point—*there wasn't any point!*

'Well, maybe it was because I might still have come
in useful for some reason or other! You might have found
it helpful to have me on side when you applied to adopt
Georgy. I'd be kept sweet and not contest you.' Her voice
changed. 'Only that wouldn't have been necessary, would
it? Once you knew I was only Lindy's stepsister, it meant I
wouldn't stand a chance of fighting you for Georgy. Then
you could have—*would* have—done exactly what your
grandfather did. Sent me packing!'

He looked at her. 'Do you know why he sent you packing, Lyn?'

It was clear to him now—crystal clear. But she couldn't see it yet. He had to show it to her.

She shook her head dully. Anatole's eyes—his dark sloe eyes that could melt her with a single glance—rested on her.

'He was frightened, Lyn. Once he knew that Lindy was only your stepsister he was frightened that you were using me—using me to strengthen your own claim to Georgy. By marrying me you'd become his adoptive mother if our claim went through, whether you were his aunt or only his step-aunt. It would have been too late then. He was scared, Lyn—scared you'd take Georgy back to England, divorce me there, go for custody. Hold Georgy to ransom.' He paused. 'It was fear, Lyn, that made him say what he said to you.'

She shut her eyes. Why was he saying these things? It was a torment to her! 'And did he fake your signature on that document?' she demanded, her eyes flying open again. '*Did* he?'

Anatole shook his head. 'No—I signed it.' He paused. 'I had to. He gave me no choice.' His voice was steady. Controlled. *Very* controlled. 'I need you to listen to me, Lyn. I need you to hear what I am telling you. I would have told you in Greece, had you not run away.'

He took a heavy breath, keeping his relentless gaze on her. She was as white as a sheet, as tense as stretched wire.

'I signed that document,' he said, 'because Timon was refusing to hand over the chairmanship unless I did. And you know what the situation was in Thessaloniki. But I did not want to sign it.' He took another breath. 'I understand now, as I did not then, that the reason he insisted on my signing it was because he already knew about you and Lindy! He already had that report from his investigators—an investigation I knew nothing about. That is what scared him—and that is why he used the only leverage he had: threatening not to give me the power I needed so urgently, that very day, so that I could end that disastrous strike, unless I undertook not to marry you. I only found out about you being Lindy's stepsister when I rushed back to him from Thessaloniki—*after* you'd fled with Georgy! He told me then—told me and denounced you for taking the cheque he offered you. And *that* is why I've doubted you—*that* is why I was angry when I came here!'

'You had a right to be angry, Anatole—knowing I'd hidden from you how weak my claim to Georgy was compared to yours.' Her voice was the same—dull, self-accusing.

He stared at her. 'You think I am angry at you for *that*?'

'Just as I was angry,' she countered. 'Angry that you said we would marry but you never meant it. That document was proof of that!'

His expression changed. 'I would *never*,' he bit out, his eyes flashing darkly, 'have signed such a document of my own free will! But,' he said, 'I signed it in the end because I didn't think it mattered. Not in the long term. I didn't have time to argue with my grandfather. I didn't have time to debate the issue—question why he was insisting on that condition. I had to focus on what was going on in Thessaloniki! Afterwards I would sort it out! I'd have had to postpone the wedding anyway—because of the strike threatening—and if you'd given me a chance, Lyn, when I got back I would have explained what my grandfather had made me do, why I agreed to it! I would have explained *everything* to you.' He took a razoring breath. 'If you'd trusted me enough not to run away back to England...' His face worked. 'If you'd only trusted me, Lyn.'

'Trust me—I need you to trust me...'

The words he had said so often to her. And he was saying them again!

Emotion speared within her—emotion she could not name. Dared not name.

'Trusted me as I need you to trust me now.'

His voice came through the teeming confusion in her head.

'As I trust *you*, Lyn—as I trust you.'

He stepped towards her and she could only gaze at him—gaze into his face, his eyes, which seemed to be pouring into hers.

He levered himself down beside her, hunkering on his haunches. 'You have proved to me that I can have trust in you now, in the most absolute way possible! There is no greater proof possible! *None!*'

He reached a hand forward. But not to her. To Georgy, who was contentedly sucking at his fingers now, clearly getting sleepy. Anatole stroked his head and cupped his cheek, smoothed his hand down his back. His face softened. Then his gaze went back to Lyn. Clear and unflinching.

'I trust you, Lyn—absolutely and unconditionally. I trust you to do the one thing that shines from you, that has shone from you like a beacon of purest light from the very first!' His expression changed. 'Your love for Georgy, Lyn. *That* is what I trust—and it is why I trust you. Why I will *always* trust you!'

There was a wealth of emotion in his voice, pouring from his eyes, from his whole being. She felt herself sway with the force of it.

'What does it matter, Lyn, whether Lindy was your sister—?' he began.

But she cut across him, her voice a cry. Anguished and trembling with emotion. 'She *was*! She *was* my sister! My sister in *everything*! I loved her as just as much! And when she died a piece of me died as well. But she gave me—' her voice broke '—she gave me her son, for me to look after, to love the way I'd loved her. And that's why... that's why...' She couldn't go on. But she had to—she *had* to. 'That's why I have to give him to you now, Anatole—because it's for *him*.'

Now it was Anatole who cut across her. 'And *that* is why I know how much you love him! *Because* you are willing to give him up!' His voice changed, grew husky. 'And there is only one kind of love that does that, Lyn—only one kind.' He looked at her. 'A mother's love.' He took a shaking breath and swallowed. '*You* are Georgy's mother! *You!* And it doesn't matter a single iota whether your blood runs in his veins! Your sister knew that—knew that when she entrusted Georgy to you! She knew you loved her and she knew you would love Georgy all his life, Lyn—*all his life!* With the love he needs to have—a mother's love... *your* love!'

He reached forward again, and now he was taking her hands with his, so warm and so strong, and he was placing her hands around Georgy's sturdy little body, pressing them around him, his own covering hers.

'And I love him too, Lyn,' he said. 'I love him with the love that Marcos was not able to love him with. I will always love him—all his life.' He paused and took another ragged breath. 'Just as I love you, Lyn.'

There was a sudden stillness. An absolute stillness. An immobility of all the world. All the universe.

She could not move. Could not move a muscle.

But she could feel Anatole lifting her hands—lifting them away from Georgy, who slumped his slumberous body back against her, his eyelids closing. Anatole lifted her hands to his lips, kissing first one and then the other. The softest, sweetest kisses...

'How could you think I didn't?' he whispered. His voice was cracking—cracking and husky. 'How could you possibly think I didn't love you? How did you think I could hold you in my arms night after night, be with you, at your side day after day, and not come to love you as I do?'

Her eyes clung to his. Was this true? Oh, was this true? These words he was telling her? Those sweet kisses he had blessed her hands with? Was it true? Her heart swelled with hope—with yearning that it might be so—that she was really hearing him say those wonderful words she had so longed to hear and had thought could never be said by him.

But she *was* hearing them—hearing him say them—and feeling the blissful brush of his lips on hers, the glowing warmth of his gaze, his fingers winding into hers...

He was speaking still, saying what was bliss for her to hear. 'And I know—I *know*—you love me too! I can see it now—in your face, your eyes, your tears, Lyn, which are pouring down your face. You love Georgy and you love me—and I love Georgy and I love you. And that's all we need, my darling, darling Lyn—all that we will ever need!'

He reached with his mouth for hers and found it, kissed it, tasting the salt of her tears.

'All we'll ever need,' he said again, drawing away. He looked at her. 'You must never, never doubt me again. *Never!* To think that you thought so ill of me that you fled back here—that you felt you had to give up Georgy to me. To think that is like a sword in my side!' He kissed her again—fiercely, possessively. 'We are *family*, Lyn! Family. You and me and Georgy—and we always will be! *Always!*'

She swallowed, fighting back the longing to believe everything he was telling her. 'Our plan was to marry and then divorce,' she said. Her voice sounded wonky to her, the words coming out weirdly. It must be because there wasn't any room for them, she thought. There was only room for the tidal wave of emotion coursing through her—filling her being.

'That,' he answered her roundly, 'was the stupidest plan in the universe! What we are going to do is just marry. And stay married! For *ever*!'

'That document you signed...'

'Timon will tear it up—or I will do it for him!' He gave a ragged laugh. 'Timon will only have to take one look at us to know his fears are groundless—pointless.' His expression changed, and so did his voice, becoming sombre, worried. 'Can you forgive him, Lyn? For lying to you and saying that I never intended to marry you so that he could drive you away? It was fear that made him do what he did. I can see that now. The fear of losing Georgy.'

Her eyes shadowed. She knew what fear was. Knew it in her bones—knew the fear of losing Georgy…knew just what that fear could make one do…

She took a breath, looked at Anatole straight. 'I lied to you because I was so frightened I might lose Georgy,' she said, swallowing. 'I understand why Timon lied to me for the same reason.'

His hands tightened on hers. 'Thank you,' he said. His eyes were expressive. 'And I can tell you with absolute certainty that when he knows that we are to be a real family now he will be overjoyed!'

A little choke escaped her. 'Oh, God, Anatole—is it true? Is *any* of this true? I walked in here and my heart was breaking—breaking in two. Breaking at giving up Georgy, breaking because I love you so much and I thought you'd only used me and thrown me away! I can't believe this now—I can't believe this happiness I'm feeling! I can't *believe* it!'

Did she dare? Did she *dare* believe what Anatole was saying to her? Did she dare believe in the love pouring from his eyes…?

Believe in the love pouring from her heart…

There was only one answer he could give her. Only one answer, and she heard him say the words she had heard him speak so often.

'Lyn, I need you to trust me on this!' He took a ragged

breath. 'I need you to trust that I will love you for the rest of my days! Just—I *beg* you!—trust me!'

As he spoke, with his love for her pouring from his eyes, she felt the dam of her fears break—and all those hideous, nightmare fears that had convulsed and crucified her flowed away, emptying out of her, never to return.

And in their place blossomed the sweet and glorious flower of her love for Anatole—love given and received, each to the other.

Anatole! *Her* Anatole. And she was his—*his*! And she always would be. She would trust him now—for ever, in everything!

He kissed her again, sealing that love in tenderness and passion, with Georgy cradled in her lap, their arms around him. It was an endless kiss…interrupted by the sound of someone clearing his throat from the doorway. She and Anatole sprang apart.

'Oh,' said a surprised voice. 'Ah…' It fell silent.

Lyn bit her lip, looking down at Georgy, unable to look anywhere else. But Anatole got to his feet, slipping Lyn's hand from his but standing beside her, his hand resting on her shoulder warmly. Possessively.

The room was bathed in sunlight—which was odd. Because outside he could see that it was mizzling with the doleful rain of an English summer. Yet the air inside the room seemed golden with the sun…as golden as the happiness flooding through him.

He looked across at his lawyer. 'I think,' he said, 'we've just reached an out of court settlement.' His voice was very dry.

His lawyer's was even dryer. 'Well, I'll just leave you, then, to…ah…hammer out the details, shall I?'

'That,' said Anatole, and his hand pressed down on Lyn's shoulder, 'might take some time.'

He glanced at Lyn and his gaze was as warm as the love he felt for her. Her answering gaze was just as warm.

'It might take a lifetime,' he said.

EPILOGUE

LYN SETTLED BACK into the padded beach chair beneath a striped parasol. Beside her Timon, resplendent in a very grand wheelchair, sat smiling benevolently. A little way in front of both of them, on the beach in front of Timon's villa, was Anatole, in shorts and T-shirt in the late summer heat, sprawled on the sand with Georgy, showing him how to use a bucket and spade. Georgy, recklessly waving his own plastic spade in a manner likely to engage hard with Anatole's tousled head, was happily thumping at his upturned plastic bucket with enthusiastic dedication and muscular vigour.

'I thought you were supposed to be building a sand-castle,' Lyn called out, laughing.

It was good to see Anatole relaxing, having more time to do so. His dedicated attentions to the Petranokos empire had been successful, and it was on a much surer footing now, with all the employees' jobs secure, which allowed him to ease back significantly on his work schedule. Giving him far more time with his family.

With his adored Georgy.

And his adored bride.

They had married as soon as they had returned to Greece. Timon, enthroned in his wheelchair, had proved a benign and approving host for a wedding followed by a luxurious and leisurely honeymoon—with Georgy!—on a tour of the Aegean in the Petranakos yacht.

The honeymoon had been followed by a journey back to England to take possession of the seaside house in Sussex that Anatole had bought for Lyn. It would be their UK base for future visits and holidays. And they had attended, hand in in hand, their closeness and unity and their devotion to Georgy visible to the family court judge, the hearing of their application to adopt the baby they both loved as much as they loved each other. Their application had been approved, and now Georgy was theirs for ever.

Every day Lyn spent a considerable amount of time with Georgy and his great-grandfather—a lot of it here, on the beach that Georgy loved, with Timon's wheelchair shaded by an awning.

'We'll start on the sandcastle any minute now,' Anatole riposted. 'Once Georgy's got bored with hitting things!'

A low rumble of laughter came from Timon. Lyn glanced at him. He was looking healthy, considering… He was still doing well on the drugs, and it was buying him some time. The precious time he so desperately wanted.

As if he could sense her looking at him, Timon reached to take Lyn's hand and pat it affectionately with his own gnarled one. He turned his head to smile at her.

Though she had had some trepidation, they had made their peace.

'I wronged you,' he had told her. 'And from the bottom of my heart I apologise to you. It was fear that made me harsh—fear that you would take Marcos's son from us. But I know now that you would never do such a thing. For you love him as much as we do.' His voice had softened. 'And you love my grandson too. You will both, I know, be the parents that Marcos and your sister could not be. I know now,' he'd said, 'that Marcos's son is safe with you and always will be.'

It had been all she'd needed to hear. Just as now all she needed in the world was to be here, with her husband and their son, a family united in love. Tragedy had reached its dark shadows across them all, but now sunlight was strong and bright and warm in their lives.

Timon turned back to look at his grandson and Georgy.

'The years pass so swiftly,' he said. 'How short a time it seems since it was Anatole and Marcos playing on the beach. But I am blessed—so very blessed—to have been granted this, now.'

She squeezed his hand comfortingly. 'We are all blessed,' she said.

Unconsciously she slid a hand across her still-flat stomach. Timon caught the gesture. They had told him as soon as they had known themselves of Lyn's pregnancy. Timon needed all the reasons they could find to keep on fighting for his life. Another great-grandchild could only help that.

'A brother for Georgy,' he said approvingly.

'It might be a sister,' Lyn pointed out.

Timon shook his head decisively. 'He needs a younger brother,' he said. 'Someone he can look out for, just as Anatole looked out for Marcos. Someone to encourage him to be sensible and wise.'

She smiled peaceably—she was not about to argue. Whether girl or boy, the new baby would be adored, just as Georgy was, and that was all that mattered.

As if sensing he was being discussed, and in complimentary terms, Georgy ceased his thumping and grinned at all of them.

'Right, then, Georgy,' said Anatole briskly, '*this* is how we build a sandcastle.'

Georgy turned his eyes to his new father, gazed at him with grave attention and considerable respect—then hit him smartly on the head with his plastic spade, chortling gleefully as he did so.

'Oh, Georgy!' exclaimed Lyn ruefully. 'You little monster!'

* * * * *

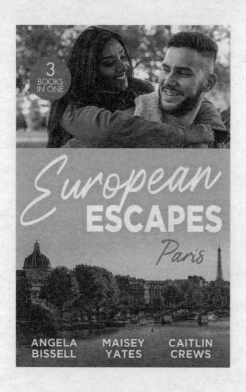